#MILLER4

GONE TOO FAR

STEVEN SUTTIE

GONE TOO FAR

Copyright © Steven Suttie 2017

Published by Steven Suttie 2017

Steven Suttie has asserted his rights under the Copyright, Designs and Patents Act 1988 to be identified as the author of this work.

This novel is a work of fiction. Names and characters are the product of the author's imagination and any resemblance to any persons, living or dead, is entirely coincidental.

This book is sold subject to the condition that it shall not, by way of trade or otherwise, be lent, resold, hired out or otherwise circulated without the publishers prior consent in any form of binding or cover other than that in which it is published and without a similar condition including this condition being imposed on the subsequent purchaser.

Cover design by Steven Suttie

Font type Book Antiqua

P/B 1st Edition – published 28th April 2017
Kindle 1st Edition – published 28th April 2017

Prologue

Kathy Hopkirk, The UK's most notorious super-bitch media commentator had been un-reachable for three days. Her manager, Sally King had been trying to resist this moment. But now, she felt that there was no other option. She was going to have to report the most hated celebrity in Britain, missing.

Sally wasn't rushing into this. The successful media agent had been on the phone none-stop for most of the weekend. Sally had contacted all of Kathy's family and colleagues, as well as her small circle of friends. Sally was now confident that all of Kathy's contacts had been contacted. All had been asked one simple question; had any of them seen or heard from Kathy in the last few days?

Not a single contact had provided a positive reply. One or two of them had however mischievously spoken to the press, alerting them to the fact that Kathy Hopkirk's manager did not know where her star performer was, sure that there was possibly a very juicy story waiting to be picked up on, for a fee of course.

Sally was now completely out of ideas, and most worryingly, had run out of people to ask. Kathy was supposed to have been on that morning's "Sunday View Point" show, discussing her opinions on immigration.

When ITV had phoned Sally to ask where her client, the "star" of the show was, just minutes before the broadcast was due to air, Sally knew that this wasn't just another stupid attention seeking stunt. Sally knew in her heart that something wasn't right. Kathy wouldn't miss a live TV show which attracted over two-million viewers. Two-million people to wind-up and infuriate. After all, it was all Kathy lived for. Sally lifted the phone to speak to the Metropolitan Police, and to report the country's most detested, most widely reviled living woman, missing.

Chapter 1

"Ey, bloody hell fire, Andy, come and look at this!" Manchester's best known detective, DCI Andy Miller was standing at his kitchen sink, peeling some spuds for the Sunday roast. His wife Clare was in the garden with the couple's twins, three-year-olds, Leo and Molly.

"Andy, quick. Come here!"

"What's up?" he asked as he reached the patio doors. The twins were giggling and shrieking at one another as they played on their see-saw and Clare was sitting back in her chair, enjoying the sunshine, holding out her phone. Andy looked at the screen, and saw that it was a news app.

"Kathy Reported Missing" said the headline. Kathy Hopkirk was so famous, she was one of an extremely small group of British celebrities that could be identified just by their first name. Cliff, Ant, Dec, Adele and Jedward were the others. Kathy was so famous, there was no need to mention her surname to identify which Kathy this was about.

Clare laughed when she realised that Andy had no idea what the headline meant. She pulled the phone away and mocked her husband. "You don't even know who Kathy is do you? No wonder nobody invites you onto their quiz teams Andy!" She laughed at him playfully, but returned her attention to the phone screen.

"Go on then, who *is* Kathy?"

"You *do* know her Andy, she's the woman off the telly who always has an outrageous point-of-view about everything! She'll say anything to get in the news." Clare was reading the phone.

"Oh, right, I think I know who you mean. She started off by saying that obese people should be locked away in disused trains and fed lettuce until they were an acceptable weight, didn't she?"

"Yes, that's her! Well, I mean, she says something like that at least once a week."

"Why disused trains though? I never understood that."

"Oh, there was a reason. I think it was because they already have toilets on them or something. She always says bonkers stuff like that to guarantee that people will talk about her. Don't you remember when she said that women who breast-feed are mental?"

"What?"

"Oh, Google her Andy, she is an absolute gobshite." Clare looked quite annoyed, it was amazing how quickly the thoughts and opinions of Kathy Hopkirk could wind people up.

"So, she's gone missing?" Andy's face suddenly changed from vague amusement to professional concern.

"Yes, she was supposed to be on telly this morning, and hasn't turned up. This report says that certain people in the media have known that she's been unaccounted for all weekend – but now its all official, its been reported to the police."

"She isn't very well liked, is she?" asked Andy.

Clare looked up and smiled sarcastically. "Andy, I know you don't really bother with the news or anything, but Kathy is the most hated woman in the country. Nobody likes her, and I really mean nobody. There was a poll that put Margaret Thatcher above Kathy in the popularity stakes!"

Andy screwed up his face, he looked as though he'd just heard that his car had been found in a river. "Well, God bless the poor bastards that have to investigate this. That's going to be a nightmare job."

"Ah, well that's the thing, Andy."

"What?""It says here that the last time anybody has seen or heard from her was on Thursday night, when she left the Midland Hotel in Manchester city centre."

Chapter 2

"Welcome to the ITV Weekend News, I'm Ranvir Chaudhary. Our major story this evening is the disappearance of one of Britain's most famous, and most divisive characters." The TV news presenter looked very serious and intense as she spoke to the millions of viewers on the other side of the lens. "Kathy Hopkirk, the columnist and presenter, famed for hundreds of inflammatory remarks and insensitive opinions, has today been reported as a missing person. Our show-business editor Pamela McNulty is outside the star's home in London, where she sent us this report."

The ITV studio image on the screen switched to a very solemn looking woman who was standing amongst dozens of other broadcasters and crews on a noisy residential street in Hammersmith, West London.

"Thank you Ranvir. This shocking story was released by the Metropolitan Police's press office this morning. The statement confirms that a Missing Person Inquiry has been launched following the complete disappearance of Kathy, who has not been seen, nor heard from since Thursday evening, when she was seen leaving her hotel in Manchester. Kathy's manager has been trying to make contact with her client since Friday morning, when Kathy failed to arrive at a book-signing event at Manchester's Waterstones bookstore. A statement from Sally King, who manages Kathy, and dozens of other high-ranking celebrities was released this afternoon," the screen switched from the correspondent, to a picture of the press-release. Pamela McNulty began reading the statement;

"After doing all we can to make contact with Kathy since Friday morning, and contacting all of her friends, colleagues and family members, we can confirm that nobody has heard from, nor seen Kathy since Thursday evening. This matter is now in the hands of the police. We can only say that we are all hoping, and praying that no harm has come to our bright, confident, and exceptionally talented friend and colleague. We sincerely hope that she turns up safe and sound. We are all desperate to hear what has happened, preferably from Kathy, so that we get her uniquely entertaining viewpoint regarding this extraordinary situation."

*****

"Good God Donna! Have you heard the news?" shouted Paul Cresswell, a former driver of Kathy's, as he slammed shut his front-door and walked quickly into the lounge. His wife, Donna was standing in the middle of the room, watching the news, she nodded sombrely at Paul, her husband of thirty-four years.

"I told you! I bloody told you didn't I love?" Paul had a mysterious look on his face. Donna couldn't quite work out if he was in shock, or if he was excited by this news. "Told you about three years ago that this would happen! You can't go about pissing everyone off, and think you'll get away with it! I bet she's been chucked off the fucking Vauxhall Bridge, I bet she's got a pair of those concrete wellies fitted as well!"

"I'm really worried about it Paul. Do you think this was why Sally phoned yesterday?"

"Yeah, without a doubt! I told her, I said, why would I have heard from Kathy when I told you I never want to drive her anywhere ever again?"

"What did she say to that?"

"She said she was phoning everyone she could think of. So I asked her what was going on and she just told me it was nothing. Well it obviously wasn't nothing, was it? She's been bumped off mate! Told ya, didn't I? I promised you this was going to happen, and that's why I refused to drive her anymore. I thought I'd be getting bumped off with the slag! Didn't I?"

Andy Miller was sprawling out on the sofa whilst Clare was upstairs bathing the twins. Andy was smiling, he was full up and satisfied from the roast beef dinner, feeling grateful for an enjoyable, relaxing day with his family. He had almost mustered enough motivation to stand up and get started on the washing-up, when he felt a text-message vibrate against his leg. He grabbed the phone out of his pocket.

"Oh my days! Have you seen the news?" The text message was from Andy's number-two at the Serious Crimes Investigation Unit, Detective Inspector Keith Saunders. Andy rolled his eyes and deleted the message. It was Sunday, and he had practically managed to get through the entire day without thinking about work. Typically, it seemed that Saunders was getting excited about the potential of having even more work to do.

"You're a one-off you Keith," muttered Andy as he made a loud groaning noise whilst pushing himself up off the sofa. "Right, let's get these dishes sorted out, and then I can relax properly." Andy popped his head around the door and shouted up the stairs. "Do you want a brew love, or a glass of wine?"

"Ooh, tough question Andy! What do you guys think mummy should choose? WINE," she said with her eyes wide open and a great big smile on her face. "Or a brew?"

"Wine mummy!" shouted Leo as he splashed his hands in the water, making Clare roar with laughter. Molly was splashing around and giggling at Leo's quick-decision.

"You're a bad influence on those kids Clare!" shouted Andy as he headed off into the kitchen and began scraping the leftover contents of the plates into a carrier bag.

Fifteen minutes later, the pots were all washed,

and Clare's glass was filled with a generous portion of Merlot.

"Okay, over to you mate. They're washed, dressed and in bed waiting for Daddy's funny story. Don't rush… I want to see the news about Kathy's disappearance." Clare kissed Andy's cheek as she took the wine glass off the side, and sensed that he wasn't as excited about this major news story as she was.

*****

It had been half-an-hour. DI Keith Saunders was checking his phone to see if his boss, DCI Andy Miller had bothered to text him back. He was disappointed when he saw that he had not received any new messages. "Ignoring text messages isn't going to make this go away Sir," muttered Saunders under his breath, even though he knew exactly what Miller's absent reply meant. It meant "not-now-for-fucks-sake-Keith."

Saunders was flicking between the TV news channels, trying to find out if any new angles or fresh reports had been received since the story had been brought to his attention a couple of hours earlier. There was nothing new being reported, just the same basic facts and timeline being repeated over and over. Basically, all the news stations were saying was that Kathy had been reported missing, and that her management company had released a statement confirming this to be the case.

Saunders looked at the time, it was almost 8pm. The story had broken at around lunchtime and he had imagined that it would have climaxed by now, with an embarrassed, sheepish looking Kathy crawling out from whatever rock she'd been hiding under all weekend. But, as that hadn't happened yet, the young DI's head began churning with thoughts and ideas. How could one of Britain's most famous, and most hated people simply disappear like this? And even though it had been on the news all day, no further information had come to light? Was it possible that she was responsible for this disappearance herself? Wondered Saunders. After all, it was well known that Kathy was prepared to do almost anything to hit the headlines. Kathy *was* a professional attention seeker, there wasn't very much more to her act. There was an extremely good chance that she could have faked her own disappearance, that she might have engineered all of this to grab the national headlines on a slow news Sunday. She really did seem that needy and bonkers, considered the DI.

Despite it being Sunday night, and Saunders' day off, he was still concerned that this situation could very possibly dominate the department's work-load the following morning. He began to take some notes, deciding that he wanted to be as sharp as possible in the morning, when this was inevitably going to be the first item on the SCIU's agenda. If it wasn't, and it was all done and finished with by then, well Saunders figured that there was no harm in learning his stuff. It was that, or obsess about another one of the department's cases again. He relished the opportunity to think about something else for a change.

"Forewarned is forearmed," said Keith in a rather exaggerated attempt at his old Headmaster's voice. He Googled the famous "presenter" as her website described her. Thinking about it, Saunders couldn't really think of any other job that would describe what Kathy did for a living. She had one sole purpose, and that was to try and antagonise the British public. She wasn't a "writer" because she didn't really write anything. She wasn't a "journalist" because her stories didn't offer any balance. "Shit-stirrer" wasn't a valid job title, so Saunders mused that "presenter" seemed to be the only box that her particular profession could loosely tick.

"Flipping heck," said Saunders, as he began to discover another, far-less reported side to Kathy Hopkirk.

She'd done a lot of serious work before becoming a "presenter." She'd held some really good jobs in her career. What age was she? Fifty-five. And she'd been a "presenter" for about ten years, since she appeared on Big Brother. Before that she'd worked in media mainly, at one time she'd been a big boss at Radio One in London, looking after marketing and promotion. It was at the time when the radio station was at its most famous, as well. There was definitely more to this Kathy character than simply behaving like an irritating gob-shite on Twitter.

Saunders was finding this fascinating. He stepped across his city-centre apartment and headed to the fridge. He opened himself an icy bottle of Peroni, shoved a slice of lime down the neck, and went straight back to the computer.

"Balls to cooking. I'll have to ring a pizza now because of you, Kathy."

Chapter 3

In London, at Shepherds Bush police station, the C.I.D. evening shift was just clocking on to start a brand new week of overnight crime investigation in the UK's capital city. Kathy's disappearance had been logged with them, and as she was a Greater London resident, the Metropolitan Police's Hammersmith and Fulham section were in charge of this "Mis-Per" case.

DCI Martin Paxman was standing before his team of twenty seven detectives. He was smiling, and looking relaxed.

"Okay welcome back from the weekend guys." The comment was greeted with groans and chuckles from the staff who were all looking through the paperwork on their laps and trying to catch a snap-shot of what had occurred over the weekend, and ultimately – what they were likely to be working on tonight.

"Well as you may have read, it's been a busy weekend. We've had two murders, one life-changing attempted-murder, a death by dangerous driving and the usual numbers of stabbings, robberies and violent assaults. There is one tiny difference this week though, we've also got a high profile mis-per case, Kathy Hopkirk, the country's most offensive and outspoken person."

There was a moment of rabble and gossip, and one or two sarcastic laughs among the detectives. They'd all heard the news, it had been hard to escape it all day. DCI Paxman continued to brief his team. "She's not been seen since Thursday – but her last recorded movements were up in Manchester where she was working. So despite it being reported to us because she lives on Brackenbury Road, W6, and she generally works from home, I'm hoping that Manchester will pick up the lion share of this case, mainly because of the inevitable politics involved."

"What's that supposed to mean Sir?" asked one confused looking detective near to the front.

"Well, its one of those funny cases where it will play out as a major news story on the telly, but in the real world, like, in here – it's just another mis-per. So we need to treat it like any other mis-per that comes in or else we'll be accused of giving special treatment to celebrities, or worse still, a poorer service to non-celebrity mis-pers. Whichever way we decide to go about this, it's going to be a nightmare scenario. So let us all hope that those thick twats up in Manchester take it on, yeah?"

There was a big laugh, and a couple of minutes of banter before DCI Paxman calmed his team.

"So, I'm going to have to put two of you on this for the night duty, just to make sure that day-shift have covered all aspects of the mis-per paperwork and we've not left any glaring holes. Do any of you wish to volunteer yourselves to take it on?"

DCI Paxman laughed when he saw that not a single hand had been raised. "So, I think that confirms there are no Kathy fans amongst our team! Okay, well, I'll choose somebody over the course of the briefing. Okay, let's get on with things then. On Friday night, there was a life-changing stabbing near Westfield shopping centre, young man, seventeen years old, by the name of…"

The rest of the team briefing took forty five minutes. By the end of the meeting, DCI Paxman had decided to give the Kathy mis-per case to a couple of his more experienced staff members, just in case the horrible bitch turned up and demanded to know what had been done to find her. DCI Paxman wouldn't put that past her, from what he'd heard about the woman over the past few years.

"Okay, that's all for tonight, thank you. You all know what you are doing, so I'll leave you to get on with your work. Detective Sergeant Lynne Robinson and Detective Constable Faryad Hussain, come and see me in my office, please."

The room erupted with the sound of busy activity.

Chairs were scraping across the floor and urgent discussions were starting as the detectives packed away their notes and belongings, looking eager to get on with their individual tasks.

DS Robinson and DC Hussain headed straight into DCI Paxman's office.

"Hi guys, listen, I'm sorry to burden you two, but I started thinking, I need to put two of my best investigating officers on this. It is bound to be picked at by the press, and especially by her, when she turns up."

DS Lynne Robinson looked surprised. "You think she'll turn up, Sir?"

DCI Paxman appeared shocked by the question. "Yes, of course. Most mis-pers *do* turn up, don't they? I take it that you're not so convinced then?"

DS Robinson shook her head. "Sir, this woman has upset practically every section of society. Rich, poor, fat, thin, black, white, Scottish, English, Irish, Welsh. She's even been running a six-month long campaign against immigrants. I've been watching the TV news for most of the day Sir, and there are very, very few people who seemed genuinely concerned for her welfare."

"What, you think she's met with some harm?" asked DC Faryad Hussain, of his senior officer.

"Yes Faryad. I really do."

The look of total belief on DS Robinson's face shocked the other two detectives in the office.

"Well, in that case," said DCI Paxman, "I hope for your sake that Manchester wish to take this on as a solo operation, because I can see right now that this is going to be an absolute bastard of a case."

"Oh you can say that again DCI Paxman," said Robinson, with a cold, steely look in her eyes. "If Kathy has been murdered, then I believe there will be thousands of suspects who have made threats to kill her, and that is only online. She boasts about how many death threats she receives on her radio show. It's like a game to her."

DC Hussain nodded his agreement with the DS's point. "Yes, totally agree with you on that. I remember last year some time, Kathy had been making fun of some soap star who was complaining of being harassed online by trolls. She sent a message to the actress saying something like "if you can't handle the trolls, pack up your two-hundred-grand acting job and go work in Primark, and then send your trolls my way you pathetic, stupid cow!"

DS Robinson looked as though she was about to smile. "You don't follow her on Twitter, do you?"

DC Hussain looked a little embarrassed and looked down at his feet. "Some of the things she says though, I mean, it's funny. It's like things that you should never dare to say, she just comes right out with it. It's entertaining, in a weird way. Like, you have to cringe, but it's still interesting to see the reaction."

"And do you agree with your DS, Faryad? That somebody will have taken her comments so much to heart that they may have killed her?" DCI Paxman wasn't amused by this very much, but he was interested in his officer's views.

"No. I don't think it will have gone that far."

"So what were you agreeing with DS Robinson about a moment ago?"

"I was just saying, there are definitely a lot of people out there who have made threats to kill her, on Twitter, on Facebook, on Blogs and Youtube. I was just agreeing that it will be a large investigation to try and work out who would be responsible."

"Precisely," said DS Robinson. "I actually can't think of any other person that will have received so much vitriolic abuse online. The strangest thing is, it seems to spur her on!" Once again, a smile looked close to appearing on the DS's face.

"Well, listen, thanks. I'm glad I picked you two to work on this. I think your first job is to go through the paperwork that's been compiled today, check that it is all water- tight, I don't want any room for criticism. Treat this as any ordinary mis-per, but be paranoid that the mis-per is very likely to chuck a freedom of information request in to see how her disappearance was treated by the Met. That's my concern at this stage. Come and see me again later and tell me what gaps you've found and we'll work out the next steps from there. Okay?"

"Sir."

"Sir."

Chapter 4

Twitter, the micro-blog site was completely awash with Tweets and conversations about the missing celebrity. The "trending" topics were all about Kathy, and to put this trending into context; there had been over six million posts about the subject within the previous four hour period.

Over on Facebook, where conversations went a lot deeper, and where people could express themselves with many more words, the hot topic of discussion was the same, with over twenty million EU users engaged in some form of discussion or debate about Kathy, according to stats generated from the site's "trending this hour" facility.

Most people in the country had an opinion about Kathy. This was a well known fact. Unlike most celebrities, Kathy wasn't pigeon-holed to a certain audience. She was well known to all generations. From primary school children to old Grandma's in nursing homes, and just about everybody else in-between. Everybody in Britain knew about Kathy, and the kind of things that she said. It came as no surprise to anybody that her apparent "disappearance" was proving to be such a popular topic for discussion.

Kathy originated from Scotland, but the straight speaking Scots don't publicly claim her as theirs. Scottish people are fiercely, famously proud of their stars and celebs. Sean Connery, Billy "the Big Yin" Connolly, The Proclaimers and Mel Gibson are treated like Gods and Saints north of Carlisle. But, as was the case in every other district in the UK, the Scottish folk really weren't very keen on the idea of having Kathy as an ambassador for their nation and as such, seldom mentioned her existence in their lists of "notable Scots."

But for all the negativity that she generated, the cold, hard fact of the matter was unavoidable. For all of her haters, and boy, there were plenty – there could be no denying that Kathy Hopkirk had made an incredible success of what she did. Inside a decade, she had managed to transform herself from being an out-of-work career woman on the wrong side of forty, to a multi-millionaire. She was a hugely successful business woman. It hadn't been easy, as she had reminded every interviewer or critic at every possible opportunity. But through sheer guts, endless determination and an unshakable passion for pissing people off, Kathy had become the nation's number one choice of TV and radio talk-show guest, celebrity interview, or magazine article, and she was earning the very best money as a result. When she wasn't making top fees from media appearances, she was making a fortune from her after-dinner talks, her book sales and her latest venture, a phone app which featured some of her nastiest one-liners, which was topping the App Store download charts.

The fact that Kathy had become so rich and successful did nothing to dampen the flames of the public's hatred. If anything, the fact that Kathy had done so well in life, by basically being a complete and total bitch, added to the vitriolic scorn that was poured upon her at every conceivable occasion. At face-to-face opportunities outside studios and bookshops, Kathy would take enormous delight in openly mocking people for their hatred. "Oh you're only saying that because you're jealous." To ensure that she infuriated the person in conversation to maximum effect, Kathy would sing the last word "jealoouuussss" in a screechy, deliberately odious manner. "Face it, you wish you were me, and you hate me because you're not!" Kathy would then turn away like a camp diva, and laugh to herself.

An enormous row had erupted in the previous few weeks, based on a single, random Tweet that Kathy had sent out one uneventful Tuesday afternoon. It made Kathy's comment the top UK news story within hours.

"In Bradford today. Always amazes me that

people in predominantly Asian areas tend to use their own streets to dump their litter. #AllahHatesLitterLouts"

The Tweet created a huge reaction. Kathy just made fun of the outraged Tweets which flooded her way, Tweets which included death-threats for mocking the Islamic God.

"OMG @KathyHK How can you say that, you racist, hate-crime, ignorant, ugly bitch!!!!"

"Who's being racist? You're just annoyed because you throw your rubbish on the floor and I've called it out! Go and pick it up you cock-waffle."

Despite all of the nasty, and unpleasant exchanges of tweets, at the very heart of the discussion was a real issue, and it was an issue that seldom gets discussed, for precisely the reason that Kathy was being accused of – it was deemed racist to comment that there were very serious litter and fly-tipping problems in certain areas.

"Call me racist all you want. If I'd said the same about council estates, you'd nod and agree. But even teenage mums and chavs know how to operate a bin."

"You have to bring religion into it!!!"

"If I'd said God Hates Litter Louts – would that be as bad or worse or better, you complete and utter moron?"

As was usually the case, a big, complicated row had erupted, and local BBC news crews were on the phones to their local authorities, asking if littering was more of a problem in the BME areas of town. Local authority spokesmen weren't sure if they could answer, and promised to get back to the reporters. This was the kind of thing that local council staff would have to respond to extremely cautiously, and very diplomatically. On this occasion, the story fizzled out, as no local authorities wanted to go on-record to deny the phenomenon, nor did any want to deny that there was some substance to Kathy's volatile observation.

The top BBC 6 O' Clock News story concluded with a phone comment from Kathy Hopkirk. Her famous, unmistakable, patronising voice was accompanied by her smiling, almost charming publicity photo.

"I'm not apologising for pointing out a fact. If any members of the Asian communities in England are so confused by my comments, then I urge them to open their door, take a look outside, and if they can see no litter on their street, I will apologise. But as that's not likely to happen at all, ever, I will say this... black bags are currently buy one get one free at Asda."

"Other supermarkets are available," said the newsreader with a very serious expression on her face, as she segued into the next item.

Kathy Hopkirk had an incredible ability to spark outrage, and walk away smiling. Sometimes it was mildly entertaining, or quite daring. But much of the time, she left people feeling hurt and angry. A couple of months before her disappearance, a Youtube video had gone viral in which Kathy had been approached in the street by a young mum, who'd asked the celebrity for a selfy photo. A passerby had filmed the ensuing confrontation on a mobile phone, and the resulting footage had hit the headlines and created the usual type of stir that Kathy was famed for.

The video was painful to watch, as Kathy began verbally abusing the mother in the street. The mother had been smoking a cigarette when Kathy had walked past, and Kathy began asking the young mum how she was paying for the cigarette that she was smoking. She was shouting at the young woman, yelling "your kids are going to have shit Christmas presents and no holidays because of your selfish, ridiculous addiction to cigarettes. How can you sleep at night, you pathetic human being?" Kathy had then stepped back, and waited for an answer. The woman was scared, and totally speechless. Kathy had continued with her uninvited verbal assault. "I'll stand over here while you answer me! I don't want to inhale your children's broken dreams, in the form of putrid, stale fag breath." The footage ended when the person who had been filming went over to comfort the young mum who was visibly upset by the encounter. Kathy just wandered out of there without a care in the world.

It was this kind of thing that made Kathy so universally unpopular, yet morbidly fascinating to watch. Just who on earth did she think she was? Why did she think that it was okay to behave in the way that she did? These were the questions that nobody could answer, and the questions which fuelled such interest in the self-made star. While there was plenty of interest in her activities, Kathy seemed determined to make headlines from whatever situation she found herself in. "Make hay while the sun shines" was the title of her bestselling autobiography, and her personal motto.

Kathy Hopkirk first came to the public's attention in 2007, when she appeared as a contestant on the popular British television series "Big Brother." She had made a huge impression from the very first evening. After Kathy had paraded up the cat-walk and entered the famous house, she was followed by a sexy looking young housemate called Dana. The attractive young woman entered the Big Brother house wearing a stylish, figure-hugging white dress which attracted a great deal of attention and wolf-whistling from the audience outside.

Kathy greeted Dana as soon as she entered the house, and in doing so provided one of the most notorious Big Brother moments of the show's history. It was a moment that would be played back over and over again on TV "best of" shows and compilations. As Dana reached the bottom step, Kathy reached forward and said "hello my darling, my name is Kathy." Dana leaned in and hugged her new friend and said, "Hi Kathy, my name's Dana." It was at this moment that Kathy announced in a very soft voice, "Dana, my darling, it looks like you've started your period, love."

Kathy gestured to the back of Dana's outfit.

The look of panic and horror on the poor young woman's face was heart-breaking. Her stunning, happy, positive glow disintegrated in a flash. Dana's face froze, and her healthy colour drained, as the thought of her making her beautiful, enchanting entrance to a TV audience of ten million viewers, with a period stain on the back of her dress. It was too much to take. Dana sobbed loudly as she broke down and began to cry. She ran away into the house, but she didn't know where the toilet was so she was just running around aimlessly with her hands covering her tears. There wasn't anything on the dress, and Kathy laughed coldly to herself, stared into the nearest camera and said, "I'm only joking, love. You'll get used to me." With that, she did a slow, psychotic wink at the camera and smiled angelically.

In that moment, TV viewers had found a new rogue. A new villain. Britain had found its new "super-bitch" character. The nation had a brand new person that they could very openly hate.

On a late night, light-hearted TV interview, Kathy had once famously announced that the only reason that she is hated so much, is because the public are not allowed to hate anybody else anymore. "You're not allowed to hate bullies, you have to pity them. You're not allowed to hate foreigners, not even the French ones, you have to tolerate them. You are not even allowed to hate thieves, robbers and tricksters who prey on the elderly. You've got to understand them. Seriously, I'm the only one you're allowed to hate, think about it. So I might as well get you to hate me properly, eh?"

But now that Kathy was a missing person, things were becoming a little trickier, and many people in society were confused by their feelings surrounding the disappearance. A lot of people were beginning to realise that even though they *thought* that they hated her, they actually felt quite concerned, and worried about Kathy.

But not everybody. There were still a great many

people who were making jokes and saying dreadful things about her. It seemed that the media would have a precariously fine line to tread whilst reporting this story.

Chapter 5

"Welcome to Sky News at nine, I'm Vickie Bane and our top story this hour is regarding the announcement from the Metropolitan Police this lunchtime, the news that Kathy Hopkirk has been reported missing. Well Sky's chief media commentator Penny McAllen joins me live from Kathy's home address in London. Penny, this doesn't seem real, does it?"

"No that's right Vickie, the news has left everybody in the country feeling a little shell-shocked and I think, a little worried about Kathy's welfare too."

"This disappearance does raise a number of questions Penny, and I think that right up at the top of the list, the question on many people's lips – could this be a hoax? After all, Kathy is famous for her stunts and pranks. Could this just be another one?"

"Well Vickie, I'm going to say no. I've spoken at length to Kathy's manager Sally King and she is extremely worried about Kathy. Sally has told me that Kathy is the consummate professional, who would never miss a work appointment. Well, Kathy has actually missed two appointments since Thursday evening when she was last seen leaving her hotel in Manchester city centre. She missed a book signing on Friday morning, and of course, the moment when everybody realised that something wasn't quite right – when Kathy failed to appear on ITV's live discussion show, Sunday View Point."

"So if this is a genuine missing person case, what exactly are the police doing to try and get to the bottom of this?"

"Yes, the thing is, this is still a very, very new enquiry. Home Office figures suggest that police in the UK deal with around a quarter of a million missing persons reports each year, and it's important to add that almost all of those people reported missing, do turn up safe and well after a few days. So to answer your question, I don't think that the police are creating too much drama at this point in time."

"Are we expecting any updates from the police?"

"No, I'm not aware of any updates that are scheduled. The official police line at the moment is that they are carrying out their enquiries."

"Okay, thank you. Sky's chief media commentator Penny McAllen there, outside Kathy's home in Hammersmith. On to some other news now, and Joy Rowley's fiftieth birthday celebrations are getting underway in Leek, despite the bouncy castle not arriving on time…"

*****

"She hasn't been abducted. Trust me, if she'd been abducted, whoever had done it would have surrendered by now." The well-timed joke from Joe, the landlord of the Hare and Hounds in Manchester city centre received a loud laugh from all of his regulars, sat along the bar.

"I'll tell you now what's happened, right?" One of the regulars, Fred was holding his hand up, trying to grab the attention of his drinking pals, who were still smiling at Joe's quip, but just wanted to listen to the TV news reports, to be honest. "Ey, listen. Ignorant bastards. Right, I'll tell you. Now, what I'm saying is, that Kathy has been taken abroad by the fucking terrorists that she's been taking the piss out of! Innit! I'm telling you – you can't call them the kind of things that she's been saying, without, you know…"

"Consequences?" suggested Joe.

"Yeah! Exactly. I'm right aren't I? You can't call terrorists names like that and expect to get away with it. She'll turn up on some Alibajeera news channel or summat and they'll chop her fucking head off live on the air. And I, for one, will give them a round of applause to tell you the truth."

Fred's drinking associates said nothing. The silence hung for a few seconds, before Fred concluded his point. "I will. Honestly."

*****

Beryl Butterworth, the famous local radio presenter from BBC Radio Manchester was engrossed in the Kathy story, as she sat on her sofa having watched the entire day's news output. She was absolutely fascinated by the story, mainly because she had worked with Kathy many years ago, and the two had remained in contact. Whenever Kathy had something to plug she'd make a bee-line for Beryl's mid-morning show, and was always a very entertaining, and a very interesting guest, who always boosted the listening figures.

Although it wasn't particularly what people wanted to hear, Beryl had always spoken highly of Kathy. The seasoned radio star who had been a constant of the Manchester radio landscape since the 1970's had met practically every star that had been and gone over a forty-odd year period, and she had said many times on air that Kathy was one of the nicest, friendliest and most professional people that she'd had the pleasure of meeting. Beryl had always been keen to make people realise that Kathy's obnoxious style and manner was more of a character role, than the thoughts and actions of a real person.

"Aw, I wish I was on air today, just to give another side to this." Beryl was talking to her partner, Julie. "These news reports are so one-sided. I wish I could say that there is another side to Kathy. I'd love to be able to say that Kathy donated twenty grand to little Demi's America fund, but she swore me to secrecy."

"Well, you can't mention that, but you can talk about all the positive things that Kathy has brought about. You'll get your chance on tomorrow's show, love." Julie was getting a bit sick of hearing about this now, and was hoping for a different topic.

"Yes, you're right pet. I just hope its not bad news by then."

*****

"Flamin' Norah! Is that our Jodie sat there?" Mike laughed at his own joke as he entered the room, surprised to see his sixteen-year-old daughter sitting in the living room.

"Shut up dad. Obviously it's me, or you wouldn't have said anything. Gizoid."

"Alright, alright, I'm just saying, I'm not used to seeing you in here. You're normally up in your room, staring at your phone, all cross-eyed, smelling of bogeys."

"Well its lovely to see you, anyway love," said Vicky, Jodie's mum, smiling.

"Well don't get used to it. I'm only down here cos my telly doesn't have Sky News on it."

"Course it does. All telly's have Sky News. Who's a gizoid now? Eh?" Mike laughed.

"My telly's broke. I meant to say something, but it was six months ago now. It fell off the side." Jodie looked down at the floor.

"Fell off?"

"Yeah. I swear down."

"For fuck's sake love…"

"Aw don't start – I'm trying to watch this." Jodie turned the volume up to drown out her parents' bullshit about the broken television. A moment or so later, Mike had caught the gist, and was quite shocked to hear about Kathy's disappearance.

"No way! When did that happen?"

"It's been on all day dad, where've you been?"

"I've been visiting your nana in the old folk's home. It's the first I've heard about this, turn it up a bit."

"It's on full blast Mike," said Vicky.
"Fucking hell, can't believe this. Mad or what?"

*****

"And this one is going out to all of the Trolls out there. You know who you are, desperately going through your Twitter accounts looking for the death-threat tweets that you've sent to Kathy Hopkirk over the past ten years. This song is for you, and for you as well Kathy, if you're tuned in. Here's the Talking Heads with Pyscho Killer." Veteran comedian and BBC Radio 2 DJ Jonathan James was joking around as he often did on his Sunday evening slot. He had absolutely no idea that his jovial quip would result in the weekend controller Mark Bannister storming straight into the broadcast studio, demanding that Jonathan removed the song immediately, and apologise on-air for the "outrageous" remark.

"Come off it off Mark, I'm not apologising!" Jonathan James was furious at this unprecedented interruption to his show, a show which was celebrated for its "near-the-knuckle risqué humour." He jumped up out of his seat and looking angry, but a little confused too.

"No, absolutely no way is this going on. Remove it, apologise immediately, or I'll put the emergency tape on Jonathan, I'm not pissing around here!" The two men were stood face-to-face, and neither of them looked as though they were prepared to back down.

"Come on Mark, it was just a fucking gag."

"It's not funny. It's beyond reasonable taste and decency. This is the fucking BBC you know, it's not a bloody pirate radio station. Now last chance, take it off and apologise…"

"Or?"

"Or what?"

"What are you going to do if I won't?"

"Right, seriously Jonathan, you've had your

chance. You've got too big for your boots." Mark Bannister turned and walked out of the studio, leaving Jonathan's bewildered guests sitting awkwardly, with bemused "shit-what's-going-on?" looks on their faces.

Inside the adjoining broadcast suite, Mark pulled some levers and pressed some buttons. The red light in Jonathan's studio went off and BBC Radio 2 ceased playing the Talking Heads. And with that the Jonathan James show was off the air, replaced by the emergency tape, which was a simple hour-long segue of none-stop music and celebrity "you're listening to Radio Two" inserts. It very rarely got played, and on the rare occasions that it did, the senior management team would panic that one of the cheery sounding celebs on the tape may have passed on, after all, most of the decent celebs *had* died in the past year or so.

"You complete and total wanker Mark. Fuck's sake man!"

"Just go Jonathan, you've done your last show on here. I'll personally see to that."

"Oh, is that right? Well I might as well give you this then." Jonathan James lurched forward and punched the radio station's weekend boss right in the face. This was truly unbelievable, and all of it was being broadcast live on the BBC website's studio-cam feature.

Mark Bannister was hurt, and shocked, and cried out in pain as he lay on the floor. Jonathan turned and walked away. He saw the red light sign on the wall and realised that the radio desk was live on air, so he decided to sign off in his own, unforgettable way. He turned on the microphone and spoke slowly and quietly. "This is Jonathan James, and apparently, I've done my last show on BBC Radio 2. Sorry for any offence I've caused, and sorry to my ex-boss for his black-eye, but I love that song. See you again my lovely friends, another time, another channel… it will probably be Absolute Radio to be honest. Chow for now."

Chapter 6

As the evening wore on, and most people were making their way up to their bed, the people who had been following the Kathy case all day on the news were becoming increasingly frustrated. The story hadn't moved at all, the only "development" had been the side-story regarding BBC Radio 2's Jonathan James being sacked live-on-air for "making indefensible remarks" concerning Kathy's disappearance, and then punching his boss in the face, which had proved quite a sensational story in its own right thanks to the visual content supplied via the BBC Radio 2 webcam.

But, despite this rather extraordinary distraction, there was a deep anger brewing amongst many viewers, an anger that was manifesting itself in the form of furious tweets and frustrated Facebook posts.

"Seriously though @MetPolice, are you not arsed that somebody could be in real danger?" asked one Twitter user.

"Kathy could be lay in a ditch with a dagger in her neck and the @MetPolice couldn't give a toss!" suggested another.

"Kathy might be a stupid bitch, but the police should still be looking for her ffs. We pay your wages remember! WTF!" Was another viewpoint.

The mood was darkening, lots of people were desperate to know what had happened. They were eager to find out the next part of this story. They had invested a great chunk of their day into following this BREAKING NEWS on the telly, and via their social media accounts. It seemed diabolical that the day should come to an end without so much as an update or even a comment from the police. It just didn't seem right, and as a result, those that were heavily engaged with the news item were launching all kinds of accusations and conspiracy theories at the police via their Twitter and Facebook accounts.

As midnight came, and the headline remained unaltered, the suggestion that the police were not taking the case seriously, simply because of the fact that it was Kathy Hopkirk, was becoming a story in its own right – and Sky News were the first to formally mention the growing discontent amongst its viewers.

"#FindKathy It seems to me that even the police hate Kathy. They've not done a thing to find her. This seems like a massive conspiracy to me @SkyNews" suggested one Twitter user. In a break from the orthodox, Sky News put the Tweet up on their screen and used it as justification to raise the topic. "Sky News viewers are beginning to contact us in their thousands, demanding to know why there seems to be so little police activity in the Kathy Hopkirk missing person enquiry. We will, of course keep our viewers up to date with all developments, including any response that we receive to the suggestion that the Metropolitan Police don't appear to be taking this case seriously."

But it seemed as though it was in extremely bad-taste. It felt very hollow, and soul-less. The tweet suggested so much more than was simply written. It displayed virtually no concern for the missing woman, but conveyed more of a general nosiness, an anger at the police for not providing the latest juicy gossip on a drip-feed for the nation's news junkies and the celebrity obsessed public.

It all felt like a grubby, fake campaign from the outset, mainly because it was completely lacking in the one ingredient that was required in order to make it appear authentic. Compassion. There was none. Not a single tweet was floating around that contained any concern or emotional investment regarding Kathy's welfare. In short, people seemed much more concerned that the police should be providing a running commentary on the latest details. It felt as though nobody really cared where Kathy was, or what had happened. They just wanted the goss.

Indeed, across the various social media platforms that were using the hash-tag #FindKathy and #KathyComeHome the tweets lacked the most basic of empathy or apprehension for the missing woman's plight. One thing the tweets did do, however, was offer a myriad of suggestions and ideas about where Kathy had disappeared to.

"She's gone to get her big wobbly head reshaped by plastic surgeons, and she is leaving show business now she's made her money."

Another suggestion;

"I know where Kathy has gone, she's gone to apologise personally to all the people that she's upset. She'll be back in about 460 years. #FindKathy"

Twitter was seeing a great number of people making fun out of the situation too, there were thousands of tweets that were simply making a cheap shot about the news story.

"Imagine being Kathy Hopkirk, she's a missing person and absolutely everybody in Britain is hoping that it remains the case! #KathyDONTComeHome #StupidBitch"

"I was upset when I heard that #Kathy had gone missing. Not because she's missing, but because I spilt red wine on the sofa, jumping for joy."

There *was* a very small number of people who *were* concerned, and were offering any kind of genuine concern on Twitter. But their number was so small, their tweets didn't really see the light of day as tens of thousands of anti-Kathy tweets were retweeted and favourited and copied.

If Kathy *was* out there, observing the media reaction - which was the theory many people were suggesting, then she must surely be hurt by the complete and utter lack of compassion and humanity shown towards her.

But then again, this was Kathy Hopkirk. She revelled in her notoriety. Perhaps, if she *was* out there, and this *was* just some pointless attention-seeking stunt – maybe she would be absolutely delighted with this reaction.

Chapter 7

DCI Andy Miller arrived at the police HQ early on Monday morning, getting into the SCIU office by 6.30. He'd been beaten, comfortably, by DI Keith Saunders who was typing away at his laptop. There was a steaming brew on the filing cabinet by the side of the desk.

"Bloody hell Keith, I'm never going to get in before you, am I?"

"Not if you come in this late, Sir." replied Saunders without turning around.

Miller laughed and checked his watch. "What time did you come in?" asked the senior detective.

"Five minutes ago."

Saunders always said five minutes ago. Miller couldn't fault the DI's enthusiasm and commitment to his work, but he did quietly worry that Saunders tended to work *too* hard. It was great news for the SCIU team, and for Miller especially. But it did worry the DCI that Saunders may not have the work and private life balance anywhere near to a healthy compromise.

"Did you get my text yesterday?"

"About the missing celebrity?" asked Miller, as he unlocked his office door.

"Yes."

"No, I didn't get any texts off you yesterday." Miller smiled as he pushed the door with his shoulder and disappeared into his glass walled office in the corner of the SCIU department. Saunders followed his boss.

"Do you know if we're running it yet?"

"Whoah, slow down Keith. Flipping heck, give me a chance to get a brew on."

"I know, sorry, it's just…"

"She disappeared on our patch and you want us to run the investigation ourselves, and not watch on as the Met detectives make a dogs-dinner of it?"

"Well… er, yes. Exactly. I've been looking into her

background and that, I know all the basic facts about her, I just want the nod to get on and find out where she is, what's happened and, well, find out where she is."

Miller placed his bag and laptop case down on his desk and tutted at the sheer size of his workload. "Look at the state of this lot. It never goes down," said Miller, to himself mainly.

"Do you want me to brew up?" asked Saunders.

"I'd prefer it if you threw all this lot out of the window to be honest. Yeah, go on then, nice one Keith. Make it two spoons of coffee. Cheers."

Saunders left the office and Miller turned on his laptop and started familiarising himself with the case-files that had been left on his desk all weekend. He soon remembered where everything was up to, and how things had been left on Friday afternoon. The weekend seemed like a distant memory already, and Miller had only been in the building a couple of minutes. Saunders was soon back with Miller's brew, and looked for a space on the desk to put it down.

"Oh, cheers Keith. Good weekend?"

"Not bad. Didn't do much. Spent most of Sunday watching the news about Kathy."

"Oh, I know, Clare had it on all day as well."

"It's a big deal though, isn't it? I mean, it's a serious job. It stinks of foul-play."

"Do you reckon? I'm thinking she's set it all up herself to see what reaction she'd get. I wouldn't put it past her!"

"Seriously?" Saunders looked shocked by Miller's apparent lack of interest in the disappearance.

"Yeah, listen, if anything dodgy would have happened, we'd have heard summat by now, wouldn't we? I mean, somebody would have phoned in and reported seeing Kathy in a compromising position, something they'd seen but hadn't thought of as odd at the time…"

"How do you know they haven't?"

"Well, ha, good point. I don't…"

"Sir, I want to bagsy this one. Please?"

Miller lifted his cup and took a sip, burning his lip. He looked across the desk at his colleague and held his gaze a moment. Eventually, the DCI spoke. "Okay, fair enough Keith. If the Manchester aspect gets handed to us, I'll let you have it."

"What do you mean *if*?" asked Saunders, looking unsure of whether that was good, or bad news.

"Well, if it does get handed to Manchester, there's a good chance city centre CID will be given it. It might not even reach CID. It's a missing person, at the end of the day. It's not that big a deal. I doubt we'll be involved at all to be honest."

"Gutted! I really wanted to get going on this." The frustration was undeniable on Saunders' face, and in his voice.

"Tell you what Keith, why don't you go and crack on with what you're already juggling, and I'll see if I can find out what the Met's plans are. Okay?"

"Sir." Saunders walked out of the office, tapping his pen against his palm as he went. Miller exhaled loudly, as he watched his second-in-command skulking across the office floor towards his desk.

"For God's sake Kathy, now you've got DI Saunders worrying about you."

*****

In London, DCI Martin Paxman was having an end-of-shift debrief with the two detectives he'd asked to check over the Kathy Hopkirk mis-per file.

DS Lynne Robinson and DC Faryad Hussain looked pleased with their work. Or were they pleased that they were about to go home? DCI Paxman couldn't be sure. He invited DS Robinson to talk through the file.

"We are one hundred-per-cent confident that there isn't a full stop missing in this Sir. It's totally complete with all of the details, but it also has interview outlines with Kathy's husband, Jack Greenwood – who last saw her on Thursday morning before he left the house for work. He last spoke to her roughly an hour before she left The Midland in Manchester, and his phone records confirm that this is an accurate account. He had a colleague round from work on Thursday, they were working until around one am, when she went home. We've had this confirmed by the colleague, and there is also CCTV footage at the entrance to the house that confirms this. The only question mark surrounds the colleague. She was a very pretty, very flirty young friend from what the CCTV shows. Both Faryad and I agree that if Kathy was home, this 'working late' in inverted commas probably wouldn't have happened."

"Hmmm. That's interesting." DCI Paxman was reading the file. He didn't look remotely interested.

"To a certain extent, it is. But it's quite a well known thing that Kathy has a lover of her own, they've been photographed, on one occasion getting the car windows rather steamed up down some country lane. The pictures went in the Sunday papers. So perhaps as a couple, Kathy and Jack are quite relaxed about this kind of thing. Anyway, one thing is clear – the husband isn't responsible for the disappearance in a physical sense."

"What about the lover she had then?"

"Apparently, it's all over, and Kathy is dead-set on rebuilding her marriage. But we've tried to contact the ex-lover. The call hasn't been returned just yet, Sir. We're still waiting to talk to him." Said DC Hussain.

"Has anything come to light that might suggest a reason for Kathy to *want* to disappear?"

"No   Sir, nothing obvious," said DC Faryad Hussain. "We also have an interview with Kathy's manager Sally King, who can confirm that Kathy's professional life is at an all time high. She earned fifty grand in the last month alone, so things are definitely going well for her."

"So on the surface, everything looks okay?" DCI Paxman really couldn't care less, that much was abundantly clear. He was just going through this case-file like he would any other.

"Absolutely Sir. Kathy Hopkirk is doing very well for herself. Her work schedule is none-stop busy for the upcoming three weeks, almost every day has a television or radio appearance scheduled. If it's not a media date, she has several book signing dates diaried in, all over the UK."

"Right, okay, very interesting. So you're happy for me to send this lot up to Manchester?"

"Sir." DS Robinson looked extremely confident.

"You guys can guarantee it's water-tight?"

"Absolutely one-hundred-per-cent, Sir."

"Yes, Sir," agreed DC Hussain. "The I's are dotted and the T's are crossed."

"Right then, that's a great big tick on my to-do list. If she went missing in Manchester, then they can sort it."

Chapter 8

"Good morning, it's Monday, the start of a fresh new week, and we do hope you've had a pleasant weekend," said the stunningly attractive TV host Heather Scott to the camera, and to BBC One's 1.5 million viewers at home.

"Yes, welcome to BBC Breakfast," added her colleague Giles Montgomery, another dashingly attractive broadcaster. "And our main topic this morning is all about that shocking news we heard yesterday, regarding the disappearance of TV's Kathy Hopkirk." Giles looked very sincere as he spoke.

Heather nodded. "It really was shocking, wasn't it? I was trying to think of another time that something like this happened Giles. I can't think of anything else like it."

"No, neither can I. But if any of our viewers can recall a celebrity going missing, please get in touch in the usual ways, the text and e-mail and Twitter details are on the screen." Giles pointed towards his knees, where the information was being displayed.

"This morning, we're hearing lots of people suggesting that the police should be doing more to find Kathy. Now, what's important to point out at this stage, is that we don't actually know anything about the police operation. The only news that has come from the police, was the brief press statement that was released yesterday. So, we decided to look a little more closely at this."

"Yes, we're joined this morning by Peter Evans from the National Missing Persons Bureau, who has come along to demystify the procedure that the police will have to follow in the search for Kathy. Good morning Peter."

"Good morning Giles, and good morning Heather."

"Good morning Peter, and thank you for joining us. This is an extraordinary situation, isn't it?" Heather looked really excited by the story, as were a great many viewers at home.

"Yes, yes it is an extremely unusual situation, but it's not completely unheard of," said Peter, a middle-aged, silver haired man in a freshly pressed suit. He looked very nervous and shaky in front of the cameras. "People disappear all the time. Admittedly, it's not usually celebrities, but we have had many cases of people going missing who you wouldn't expect."

"What kind of people?" asked Heather, desperate for the gossip.

"You name it, we have encountered every kind of person from bankers, school teachers, politicians, even police officers. A lot of people feel the need to get away from whatever difficulties they may be experiencing in their personal lives. It makes things very tricky for the police, who really need to make a decision about the level of risk to the missing person."

"What does that mean?" asked Giles.

"Let's just say that if a three-year old child went missing, the level of risk would automatically be assessed as high, and as a result, the area would be flooded with police officers, the police helicopter would be out, the local media would be asked to assist, all of the local community would get involved, and thankfully, these situations usually always end positively."

"Absolutely, but how do you assess the risk factor for a very rich, hugely successful, fifty-five year-old A-list celebrity?" asked Heather.

"With great difficulty I'm afraid. You see, the most important detail that the police have to consider is that it is within everybody's legal right to disappear. It is not an offence to just walk out of the house and not come back. The other vital detail that also needs to be considered, is that yesterday, along with Kathy Hopkirk, another seven hundred and fifty people will have been reported missing. The police spend almost fifteen per cent of their time on missing person's cases."

"Goodness me!" said Heather, visibly surprised by the numbers.

"That's how many people are reported missing on average, every single day in Britain. So when you put everything into consideration, the police know exactly what they are doing, and just because they haven't updated the press, it certainly doesn't mean that they are not doing anything. In fact, you can bet your life savings that the police will be all over this, and will know a heck of a lot more about Kathy Hopkirk's disappearance than we'll ever know."

"That's really interesting. So, tell us if you can Peter, what do you think the police will be working on at this moment?" Giles looked just as interested in this interview as Heather.

"I would imagine that the police will have spoken to the people who have the closest links to Kathy, and they will have worked out what potential reasons there may have been for her disappearance. From that intelligence, the police officers will have painted a picture, and will act upon the findings of that. Now, we are not even twenty-four hours into this missing persons report, and the good news is that more than eighty per cent of these cases are concluded inside the first seventy-two hours."

"This is really fascinating Peter, I'm sure your expert analysis is answering many of our viewers questions. Now, we wouldn't be very realistic if we didn't mention something that really *has* to be said. The thing is, Kathy *does* have her enemies out there. The things that she's said about gay people, about bin-men, about religion, about abortion, about terrorists, and ugly babies, she has built up a huge army of haters."

"Yes, and to add to that, Kathy is officially recognised as Britain's most hated living public figure by Twitter, who analyse the data of all of the hateful tweets that are sent. Now if we consider that for a moment, that's a pretty scary thought."

"It has to be said, and as far as we're aware it hasn't been said publicly yet, but isn't it extremely possible that Kathy has been abducted, or worse, harmed by somebody who has taken offence at something that she may have said, or written?"

"Well, I have no idea about that, I'm here to comment regarding the missing persons aspect. I have no knowledge about any other lines of enquiry that the police may, or may not be pursuing." Peter was still shaking nervously, and his face was showing signs of unhealthily high blood-pressure.

"But, I mean come on Peter, you must have some idea of what the police will be doing to find out if her disappearance is linked to the fact that she is the most hated person in the country. I mean, this is something that Kathy has actually boasted about!"

"Yes, well, I'm sure that this, along with many other factors will be part of the investigation. But as I said earlier, in most cases, the missing person is usually home and all is well within seventy-two hours." Despite his nerves and his stress, Peter was doing his best, but he was really hoping that this would be over soon, the whole experience was terrifying and the lights were so hot in that studio, he felt as though he was going to pass-out..

"That's not very good news when we consider that Kathy went missing on Thursday evening. I'm afraid that seventy-two hour window is now closed. This is actually the start of day four."

"That is also a factor that the police will be looking into." Peter was now on the verge of a panic attack. Heather knew the signs, and dealt with it extremely professionally.

"Thank you Peter, that was really interesting. Now, let's see if we'll be needing to get that umbrella out today. Here's Jane Risdon with the weather."

Chapter 9

Detective Chief Superintendent David Dixon looked uncharacteristically cheerful as he entered the SCIU department, just after ten. He looked like he'd just been having a right good laugh with somebody on the stairs. It took everybody on the SCIU floor by surprise.

"Are you okay, Sir?" asked DC Jo Rudovsky with a mischievous glint in her eye.

"Of course I am, whatever do you mean Jo?"

"Nowt, er, nothing." Rudovsky coughed and tried to stifle a laugh. She couldn't exactly suggest that Dixon's happy face was a cause for concern.

"I am a little concerned this morning though, I have just heard that a nine year old girl has vanished in Middleton."

"Oh no, what...?"

"Yes, she was last seen applying some anti-wrinkle cream that makes you ten years younger!" Dixon pointed at her and grinned. Rudovsky laughed out loud. Not only was that an awful joke, but the pointed finger prompt to laugh was just as bizarre as Dixon's good mood. Rudovsky stood there, still grinning, unsure of how to move things along.

"Okay, well, crack on then, as you were," Dixon said and clap-clapped his hands together. That unsettling, disconcerting happiness was still plastered right across his face.

Dixon turned away from Rudovsky and caught the new DC's eye. "How are you Helen, are you finding your feet alright?" Dixon was talking to the SCIU's newest and best looking member, DC Helen Grant, who was just starting her second week on the team, after a probationary trial transfer from Trafford CID.

"Yes, very good, thanks Sir." She was in her late twenties, slightly built and smartly dressed. Her stylish, well fitted clothes, along with her long, flowing auburn hair made her appear very elegant and confident. But right now, in front of the top brass, DCS Dixon, DC Grant seemed quite shy and embarrassed. It was amazing how senior staff could make the most confident of people lose all self-assurance. It was this aspect of his rank that Dixon enjoyed the most.

"Good, good. They are a good team here. They can be silly buggers, but you'll get used to them. Thank you, and have a good week." Dixon turned and headed into Miller's office, his weird smile was unmistakeable.

"What the fuck's he so happy about?" asked Rudovsky under her breath.

"He's won the raffle, a new bottle of Mandate!" suggested DC Peter Kenyon, Jo's work-partner, taking the piss out of Dixon's famously cheap cologne that has caused more asthma attacks than the Manchester police issue pepper-spray.

"No he's won an eye-brow grooming kit!" suggested DC Mike Worthington, to a chorus of laughs.

"God, I wish he'd won a nostril fuzz remover! It's like Gandalf is trying to climb out of his nose." The new team member, DC Helen Grant had won the loudest laugh with her cutting remark. "I never know where to look!"

Inside Miller's office, Dixon's good cheer was still clear to see.

"Ah, good morning Andy, good morning Keith, how are you both today?" Dixon was absolutely glowing this morning, and both Saunders and Miller looked just as perturbed by it as Rudovsky had done. Dixon was usually very neutral looking, to put it politely.

"Morning…" said Miller.

"Sir," said Saunders, slightly annoyed that the discussion that he and his boss were having was being interrupted so unexpectedly.

"Now, don't take it out on me, but I'm afraid there's been a bit of a cock-up. Central Manchester CID have had an extremely eventful weekend with a gang fight that's ended in a murder, a shooting which resulted in a critical condition, and there was a double-stabbing last night on Deansgate. So CID are maxed-out."

"Sir, forgive me... but when do you ever come down here and update us on what Manchester CID are doing?" Miller was waiting for the punch-line to this. Saunders looked like he was ahead of the game.

"Well, I'm just trying to explain the circumstances of this job..."

"Is it the Kathy Hopkirk mis-per?" Saunders was trying to speed things up, and had already guessed that this was what Dixon was leading up to. The DCS raised his bushy white eye-brows half-way up his forehead.

"How on earth did you guess that?" asked Dixon, looking amazed.

"Well, I... I'm assuming that Manchester CID would have ordinarily been allocated the job, investigating the disappearance from up here... but they're too busy so you've come to give it to us?"

"You are absolutely right!" Dixon looked like he'd just played the think-of-a-number game for the very first time. Miller and Saunders glanced at each other and fought the urge to laugh at Dixon's bizarre demeanour this morning. "Is that okay then?" asked Dixon.

"Well Sir, to tell you the truth Keith was working all day yesterday on it, just in case."

"My! Really Keith? That's quite something. Well, good stuff. Here's the file, I've had a look through, everything appears to be in order and up-to-date. The big questions are highlighted here." Dixon pulled a piece of paper from the section of the file that needed to be completed up here in the north. "The investigation has not yet managed to find any obvious reason for Kathy to leave the hotel. Her mobile phone use ceased fifty-five minutes prior to her walking out of the Midland Hotel on Thursday night. She left there alone at precisely eight-forty pm. The phone numbers that she rang throughout the day are regular numbers that are all accounted for, her manager, her husband, her newspaper editor. The part of the puzzle that we've got to figure out consists of four key questions. Where did she go? Who did she see? When was it arranged? And why hasn't she been seen since? If you can get those questions answered, you'll have solved the mystery."

"Sir, I was going to request the opportunity to lead this case… if CID *were* doing it. That's why I did some background work yesterday. I really think I can do a good job on this."

Miller and Dixon laughed. Some of the results that Saunders had been getting recently were off the radar, the DI genuinely was at the top of his game with his detective work, and his people management skills were coming on leaps and bounds as well. Saunders had a great future ahead of him at the rate things were going, and it seemed that it was only himself who couldn't see it. Saunders was constantly striving, permanently trying to achieve, to break through the next barrier. He was so busy in this mind-set that he was completely oblivious to the remarkable success that he was making of his work.

"Well, I'd say that this has worked out rather well. I had anticipated coming down here and getting the usual amount of abuse and tantrums!"

"We don't do tantrums, Sir. We just deliver well considered feedback." Miller was smiling.

"Okay. Well, maybe this next one will push you over the edge?"

"Oh?" asked Miller, he looked surprised as he'd been under the impression that Dixon was done.

"We've got a real head scratcher of a case. On Thursday night, a badly battered body was found in the central carriageway of the M56 motorway, not far from Manchester Airport. It was a male, a young body-builder, not from the area. The body had been hit by numerous vehicles before it was reported, in fact, it was so bad that the person who rang it in thought it was a curtain off a HGV trailer. Anyway, to cut a long story short, we have a major mystery on our hands here, as we have no idea why he was on the motorway. The body was discovered a hundred yards away from a footbridge, so he could have been a suicide, and the body has been rolled by the vehicles that hit it."

"Grisly. That sounds like a nasty shout to attend." Said Saunders, he looked pale just thinking about what Dixon was describing. "Glad I'm not a bobby any more."

"Yes, sounds pretty nasty. But we're not having anything to do with it. Case closed on that one Sir." Miller was quite clear.

"I just thought that..."

"There's no way Sir. We won't be able to do it. We were maxed out before you came in and handed us this file." Miller held up the Kathy Hopkirk paperwork.

"You can't even look at it?" Dixon was trying his best to charm his DCI into accepting the extra work.

"No way, Jose. Not on your Nelly."

"Okay, well, if you don't ask, you don't get. I won't say I'm not disappointed."

"Tell you what Sir, why don't you deal with this missing celebrity and we'll do the motorway body?"

Dixon ignored Miller's invitation with a wry smile.

"Nah, didn't think so..." said Miller.

"I'm in the office for the rest of the day if you need me. But thank you Keith for your enthusiasm regarding the miss-per case, I really thought that I was going to be listening to one of Andy's long, boring, rambling rants this morning!" Dixon laughed and turned out of the office, pleased with the fact he got two digs in at Miller during the course of the conversation. Saunders waited until he'd got far enough away from the open-door to be out of earshot.

"What the flipping heck's got into him? As if you

just refused a file and he accepted it with a smile?" asked Saunders with an unmistakable look of bemusement.

"Good question!" laughed Miller. "I think Mrs Dixon must have given him a go on her last night."

"Get away! Aw gross Sir. I need to try and un-think that right now." Saunders pretended to be sick in his hands.

"Right, anyway, before you get carried away with this miss-per, let's get back to where we were before Dixon butted in so cheerfully."

"Yes, well, I think we were almost done, just needed you to read through these case-notes on the Thompson file, it needs your final judgement call.
Rudovsky and Kenyon are making good progress with the violent burglar."

"The Pensioner Puncher? Good, I literally can't wait until he's in Strangeways, getting his head punched in night after night. He'll get his just desserts when they hear about him thumping old women in the back of the skull, the sick fucker."

Saunders nodded. This was a really horrific case, but at least the detectives were getting somewhere with it now, after a frustrating start.

"Oh, and the Whitelands Road stabbing has turned up a new witness. She's an elderly lady, lives across the road, she's been on to Crimestoppers, wants it to remain confidential. She's scared shit-less, but we need her on-side. I've told Chapman and Worthington to make her feel happy and confident, and to get it up the top of their to-do-list, so fingers crossed that's going to mean arrests can be made by tea-time."

"Right, okay. Good. Everything's looking reasonably okayish."

"Yes, and our new starter, Helen, I thought I'd maybe take her along on this, with me. It's a bit of extra SCIU training for her. What are your thoughts on that idea Sir?"

"Well, yes I agree that its good experience, but there's plenty of other jobs that she could be getting on with." Miller was playing. Saunders knew from his face. "How long have you been coveting these ideas for?"

"Eh, what?"

"Of partnering up with Helen?"

"Obviously, you're referring to a purely professional partnership, aren't you Sir? Or are you about to start trying to pull my pud?"

"I'm just saying... she's a bonny lass. And single..."

"Is she?" Saunders seemed surprised. One eyebrow seemed to take a little longer than the other to settle down.

"Yes. So, I'm thinking, you two could go well together. God knows you need a lady friend Keith."

"Sir, what's your point?" Saunders was blushing slightly. Or was it too warm in here? Miller was grinning at the spectacle of his super-confident DI getting all hot and bothered over the new, highly attractive young DC.

"Well, my point is, as a pal, not your boss... if you like her, it might be best to keep her at arms length until you get to know her a bit better. I mean if you take her out within a working situation, she'll not think you're very funny or smart when you're having your road-rage outbursts, and farting in the car then denying it. She's a detective Keith, she'll know it's not a drains problem in the area. That's all I'm saying."

"Well, thanks for the brotherly advice Sir. But I'll take her anyway if that's alright? And, I won't fart. And this road-rage bullshit is five years old now. That only ever happened once, and it's still being talked about none-stop."

"Well, you know what they say Keith, you only have to shag a sheep once, to be remembered as a sheep-shagger."

Saunders laughed, knowing that a laugh would

hurry things on.

"Well, okay, good luck, teach her everything you know. And don't forget, if you need any extra staff, or a raise, or your pool car upgrading, Dixon appears to be in the mood for anything today!"

Chapter 10

Beryl Butterworth's was one of the most famous voices in Greater Manchester. She was a very well known broadcaster, and had been a mainstay of local radio since the seventies when Piccadilly Radio first launched. Since then, Beryl's career had seen her presenting programmes on all of the local radio stations that had come and gone, as well as stints of TV work on Granada Reports and North West Tonight. Beryl was also a famous voice-over on TV commercials and was well known nationally as the voice of the DFS sale, which was now into its 19th year, but must end soon, apparently.

Nowadays, Beryl's daily radio show is on the BBC Manchester station, and her mid-morning slot is one of the station's most popular shows.

"Well, good morning, and today, we're taking your calls about the missing TV celebrity Kathy Hopkirk. Now, just to shake things about a little, we want to hear from you if you have something nice to say about Kathy. Maybe you met her once, and she was really lovely. Perhaps you were stuck in a revolving door with her and she was a right laugh? One of our lovely listeners may have run out of change at the launderette and Kathy lent you twenty pee for the dryer? Whatever the circumstances, we'd love to hear from you this morning. But if you want to slag Kathy off, this isn't the show for you! Here's a classic BBC Radio Manchester song from Simply Red, and Money's Too Tight To Mention."

Beryl smiled as she switched off her microphone and saw the bank of lights on the phone thing light up. Her studio manager began answering the phones while Beryl prepared her next song and checked the BBC News app on her phone to see if any new news regarding Kathy had been released. A few minutes later, Beryl's microphone was back on and the red ON AIR lights around the studio were lit up.

"Simply Red there, a fantastic song that we love here on BBC Radio Manchester. Did I ever mention that Mick Hucknall used to be my paperboy back in the seventies? I did? What, every single time I play a song by him? Ha ha, well, let me tell you, he was a lovely lad then, and he's a lovely man now. I remember him crying one morning because his paper bag was too heavy and his hands were cold so I gave him ten pence for a mix up and that cheered him up. Anyway, enough about me and my superstar paperboy, lets get on with the show, and let's talk to Pedro in Altrincham."

"Hello, morning Beryl!" said a grumpy sounding voice on the phone line.

"Morning Pedro, thanks for phoning love. Is that your real name?"

"No, it's my stage name. I'm a turn."

"Ooh, very nice. What's your best number Pedro?"

"Oh, well, I'd have to say, probably My Way, I'm good at that one."

"Well, it's a hard song to sing. Do you get many requests for that though?"

"Nah, not really Beryl."

"Because it's more of a funeral song, than one you'd get up and have a bop to. Anyway Pedro, not your real name, I hear that you've got a nice, positive story about Kathy Hopkirk to share with us?"

"Yes, well I have actually. I work for the hospice shop, voluntary like, and Kathy turned up one day last year with a car full of stuff that she was donating to us. She was really, really nice, and she said she'd drove all the way up from London with it. So I was helping her to take all the stuff into the shop and she said that her dad had been cared for at the hospice, years ago, and she wanted to give something back, to help out like. Anyway, after she'd gone, they were going through the stuff she'd donated and they found a cheque, in amongst some shoes. It were made out to the hospice, and guess what Beryl?"

"Go on…"

"It were for a hundred grand!"

"Wow! Seriously?"

"I swear down. I don't think she wanted it broadcasting like, but, yeah. We couldn't believe it."

"Well, that's absolutely amazing Pedro. Thanks so much for your call, and your amazing Kathy story! Let's go to line sixty one now, and we've got Mary McGinlay from Didsbury on. Morning Mary!"

"Hiya Beryl, morning love, y'alright?"

"I'm okay, I tell you though Mary, I'm not half worried about Kathy though you know."

"I know, I know, I must admit, I am as well. How come you like her so much anyway Beryl?"

"Well, you see, I know her, or at least, I used to know her very well, she and I used to work at another radio station here in Manchester, way-back-when, in the seventies. She had just come down from Scotland and she was just a really lovely lass, and I've seen her a few times over the past few years when she's been in town, and I'll say it 'til I'm blue in the face, she's a lovely, kind-hearted woman."

"Right, but, thing is Beryl, if that's true, why does she say all these nasty and horrible things all the time?"

"Well, I must say, I am surprised by some of the things that she says. But, I think it's just an act, like it's a character that she's playing. And let's face it, if that's the case, she's doing a pretty good bloody job at it and all!"

"Yes, well, I'll give you that. Aw, I do hope she's alright Beryl. I do."

"So do I Mary. Thanks for your call love. Right, lets cheer ourselves up a bit now, eh? How about a bit of Barry Manilow eh folks? How about a blast of Copacabana to make us all happy?"

Chapter 11

The Midland Hotel in Manchester is voted the second favourite building of the City's residents. Their first choice, quite understandably is the stunning Manchester Town Hall, and anybody who has seen it, inside or outside will know what an extra special place the gothic inspired Victorian building is. It was designed to give Parliament a run for its money, and it certainly achieved that, such is the decadent splendour on show. This beautiful, grand Town Hall was built when Manchester was one of the richest cities on earth, at the height of the Industrial Revolution. Its hard to imagine that this was only one hundred and fifty years ago. But, to make a permanent reminder of the City's greatness, the Town Hall was made to the very best spec. It's often rumoured that the interior inspired JK Rowling's visions of how Hogwarts School of Magic and Wizardry would look.

But the runner up for Mancunian folk's favourite building is the gigantic Midland Hotel, across the road from the Town Hall, down near the G-mex centre. This enormous, terracotta coloured granite structure was built at the beginning of the last century, and again, there was no expense spared. It was one of the world's finest hotels when it was completed in 1903. Since that time, The Midland has provided luxurious accommodation to all of the great and the good that have visited the capital of the north ever since. The guest list includes the Queen, and the Queen mum. And the late Queen singer, Freddie Mercury too. Of the famous and rich, it would probably be quicker to write a list of those that hadn't stayed at the Midland, to be honest.

The Midland has an amazing history. For example, it was the place where a certain Mr Rolls and a Mr Royce first met in 1904, and later went on to make cars together. It was one of Britain's first restaurants to receive a Michelin star award. The Beatles were famously refused entry to the place, because they weren't dressed appropriately. There are hundreds of wonderful stories from the hotel, dating back over a very colourful century.

But everybody's favourite story about The Midland concerns a certain Adolf Hitler, who was a huge fan of the building. In fact, he liked it so much that he had very elaborate plans to use The Midland as the Nazi HQ, once the German forces occupied the British Isles. Hitler was so set on the idea, that Manchester remained one of very few cities that didn't suffer from too much bomb damage in the second World War. Fortunately, Hitler's Manchester dream wasn't to be.

And now, sixty or so years after the end of WW2, The Midland was back in the news. This time, it was down to the fact that it was the last place that Kathy Hopkirk had been seen, prior to her disappearance four nights earlier. The outside of the elegant hotel was besieged with news crews, desperate to grab some footage of police activity at the building.

The media story was now almost twenty-four hours old, and the initial, exciting BREAKING NEWS phase was well past its sell-by-date. The story was now focusing almost exclusively on the Met and Manchester police force maintaining their no-comment stance, deliberately and mischievously fuelling conspiracy theories about their "lack of urgency" and "laid-back attitude" and suggesting that Kathy's outspoken views and opinions were the reason that the police weren't looking for her. Put simply, the media were trying to force the police to speak out, so that part two of the story would suddenly emerge and break the dead-lock.

And the dead-lock seemed to be broken at 11am, when DI Keith Saunders and DC Helen Grant stepped into the crowd, attempting to get through the media hustle and bustle outside The Midland.

"DI Saunders, have you been handed the Kathy

enquiry?"

"DI Saunders, is it true that Kathy has been murdered?"

"DI Saunders, why isn't DCI Miller with you?"

There was a lot of noise and plenty of hustle and bustle in the media crowd as the journalists tried to get a word, and the photographers and cameramen battled behind, trying to take photos and film the footage of these Manchester detectives finally entering The Midland. It now looked as though something was finally happening.

Detective Inspector Saunders was a well-known face amongst the local journalists and presenters, he was regularly seen on TV news reports, appealing for information, or giving statements outside court houses. But his appearance today, alongside the unknown face of DC Helen Grant, offered even more gravitas for the media to pursue their anti-police angle, allowing the news stations and newspapers free-reign to insinuate that Manchester's best known detective, DCI Andy Miller couldn't be bothered to look for Kathy, so had sent down his deputy, and a rookie detective to lead the investigation. That was how this development was about to be reported, as Saunders and Grant disappeared into the famous hotel building.

It was much calmer inside the hotel, and both of the detectives looked slightly overwhelmed as they were greeted by the concierge.

"Hello Sir, Madam, Welcome to The Midland." The man was very smartly dressed in his bespoke tailored uniform, completed with a fine, three-quarter length jacket. The sheer elegance of the concierge's uniform was the first hint at the exclusive grandeur of the place.

"Hi, thanks," said Saunders, shaking the man's hand. "We're detectives from Manchester City Police, we're looking after the Kathy Hopkirk case file."

"Ah, a real mystery, that's for certain," the concierge looked genuinely concerned. "Allow me to contact the most appropriate person for you to speak to. Please, take a seat just here." Saunders and Grant were showed to a leather sofa close to the check-in area.

"God it's pretty nice this place. I must have been past it a million times, but I didn't realise that it was as posh as this!" DC Helen Grant looked mesmerised by the amazing interior and was staring up at the elaborate wall decorations and chandeliers.

"I've never been in either. But it is where Prime Ministers and Presidents stay when they visit the north of England. So its bound to be up to scratch isn't it?"

"Yes, I guess so. I don't think I've ever been anywhere this posh in my life!" The new DC really was in love with the place, and Saunders found her look of awe extremely endearing. He looked across at the hotel's grand staircase once he realised that he'd been taking rather a long look at his new colleague.

A moment or so passed, and then the concierge came back, with a very serious looking lady. "Thank you for waiting, this is The Midland's general manager, Erica Hartley. I'll leave you in her care."

"Thanks," said Saunders, "how do you do Mrs Hartley?"

"Oh, call me Erica, follow me, we'll go along to my office." The manager walked quickly, and headed off with great speed past the reception area and onto a corridor that ran behind the check-in desk.

"Blimey, it's even posh behind-the-scenes," muttered Grant as she struggled to keep up with Saunders, who was having trouble keeping up with Erica Hartley himself.

"Here we are, come on in, take a seat, may I get you a drink, tea, coffee?" Erica was clearly a woman who worked quickly, and had rifled through the pleasantries as Saunders and Grant were still walking into the office.

"No, I'm…"

"We're fine, thanks," said Grant, taking a seat

facing the strict, bossy looking manager.

"So, this is about Kathy Hopkirk?" said Erica, sitting up straight at her desk, her face was set in stone, giving absolutely nothing away. Neither Saunders or Grant could tell if she was happy, sad, angry or calm. She just looked completely neutral and it was rather off-putting.

"Yes, presumably you've been contacted…"

"Yes, the Metropolitan Police have made a number of calls to myself and my assistant manager, but this is the first time that I have met any police officers face-to-face regarding this matter."

"Well, it was only reported yesterday…" Saunders felt that he was getting a back-handed bollocking.

"I know. It's extremely frustrating for ourselves though, particularly concerning the media presence outside. It's extremely alarming for our guests, and I hope that the matter can be resolved soon. After-all, we have had this entourage outside for almost twenty-four hours now."

"With the greatest respect Mrs… Erica, that has nothing to do with us. We just want to speak to you about the CCTV footage of Kathy leaving the hotel, and we would like to know a few particular details regarding the room, how it was left, details of any phone calls that were made, or received on the hotel room's phone line." DC Helen Grant had impressed Saunders with the skilful way that she had shut Erica Hartley up, and had effortlessly assumed authority over the situation.

"Okay… well… if we start with the CCTV, we have several shots of Kathy leaving her hotel room, then we have footage of her in the lift, in the foyer and finally on the steps, leaving the hotel. She turned right, heading towards the tram stop, but our cameras lose sight of her after this."

"Oh, well that's extremely helpful, and it will give us a good starting point for capturing her movements on the city centre cameras."

"Well, if you wish, I'll arrange for Derek, my head of security to take you down to our control room in the basement, where you can review the footage yourselves, and he'll burn it to a disc for you."

"Oh, that'd be good, thank you. What about the phone line?"

"Yes, I can generate those details for you. I don't think the Met asked for the phone records so it may take a little while."

"Okay, well, I'll jot down my e-mail address, and you can forward the records on to me later."

"How was the room left?" asked DC Grant.

"As I understand it, the room was immaculate."

"Can we see?" asked Grant, impressing Saunders greatly with her fast pace.

"Well, we had to remove Mrs Hopkirk's belongings from her room on Friday afternoon, and we placed the items in lost property. Check-out is ten am, you see. We had guests booked in for Friday, and they were booked for the entire weekend. So it left us with no option really but to remove Mrs Hopkirk's items, and get the room ready."

"Is that the usual practice?" asked Saunders, surprised by the rather unforgiving way that Kathy's stuff had been brusquely removed in such an abrupt manner.

"Of course, that's our normal policy. It wouldn't do to turn customers away, because another customer hasn't come back in time. We do this kind of thing most days in fact. There is always somebody who has gone on somewhere else after a night out in the city. It happens quite regularly."

"So when did you realise that Kathy hadn't come back for her things?"

"Well, the bill hasn't been settled, so that was an indicator that something was amiss. But when Mrs Hopkirk's manager called us on Saturday, I think that was when I started to wonder what was going on."

"How was she?"

"In what respect, detective?"

"How was Kathy's manner. Was she happy, was she chatty? Did she seem upset? Nervous?" Grant was still chipping away, making notes at short-hand speed in her pocket book.

"By all accounts, she was extremely pleasant, and staff remarked on how "she wasn't that bad in real-life" and so on. But I didn't meet Mrs Hopkirk personally, so I only have this information in the third person. But she was extremely charming, that's what I've been told by several members of the staff."

"Okay, well, that's very interesting. Thank you for your time. We will probably need to talk again at some point, possibly to staff that dealt directly with Kathy. But I think you've provided enough details to keep us going for the time being." Saunders was disappointed by the conversation. He'd anticipated receiving at least one piece of news that might open a door.

"Is there any chance we can inspect Kathy's belongings please?" asked Grant. "You said they were in Lost Property?"

"Well, I wouldn't normally allow…"

"These are very unusual circumstances, Erica. Those items may hold the clue that we desperately need." Saunders was firm.

"Okay, I'll see that the belongings are brought down."

"Thanks."

"Great. So, can we view this CCTV footage now please?" asked Grant.

"Yes, of course." Erica lifted her phone from its cradle on the desk and dialled. After a pause, she began talking into the handset. "Derek, it's Erica. I have the police here, can you come and greet them in my office, and take them down to your control room so they can inspect the CCTV footage please? We also need Mrs Hopkirk's belongings bringing down from the Lost Property hall as well, if you could organise that please. Thank you."

Chapter 12

"SECOND CLASS INVESTIGATION" Screamed the Manchester Evening News' lunchtime edition headline. Beneath it was a picture of DI Saunders and DC Grant trying to evade the cameras, with outstretched arms concealing their faces. The picture had been taken as the pair battled through the boisterous press-pack on their way into The Midland. But the way that the picture was being used in this newspaper story made it look as though the two detectives were trying to sneak past unseen.

"We demand to know why the Manchester City Police are treating this live, ongoing case with such an obvious lack of urgency" said the editorial comment beneath the story.

"What the hell's got into them?" asked Miller as he read the article, after being handed the paper by DC Jo Rudovsky, when she'd returned from lunch. "I'm not surprised they give this away for free! No-one would pay for it, would they?"

"To be fair Sir, we do seem a bit quiet about it all. I mean, she *is* one of Britain's best known celebs. I'd have expected us to seem a bit more... well, arsed." Jo had a great gift for playing devil's advocate, and she was doing a great job of trying to rev her boss, DCI Miller, up.

"Come on Jo, you know that there are procedures. Just because the press want a bloody update every fifteen minutes doesn't mean that we have to provide one. Seriously, the public aren't that thick. As if they'd believe that we'd ignore this case simply because we don't like the missing person. It's complete and utter bollocks Jo, and well you know it."

"Well, yeah, I know it, of course I do. But I disagree with your view that the public aren't that thick! They *are* that thick most of them, they believe whatever they read in the papers or on the internet. Why else would they vote Tory, or vote for Brexit, if they didn't believe all the bullshit that's printed in the paper?"

"So, you're saying that we should hold a press conference in which we announce that we are doing everything we can to find out where Kathy has got to?" Miller was smiling, he loved these debates and discussions with Jo. She could be a feisty bugger and she wouldn't let go when she had a point to make. Miller thought it was her greatest strength, even if it did land her in hot-water from time to time.

"What harm can it do? At least it would reassure the public that we take this shit seriously… even if it is one of the vilest human beings on the planet."

"You're not a fan? Oh yeah, I forgot, she's had a go at the gays as well, hasn't she? What was it she said?"

"She said 'I don't mind Adam and Eve, but Adam and Steve is taking it a bit too far."

"God, she really is a freak isn't she?"

"I don't know. I think she's just a bit insecure about her own shit, so concentrates on everybody else's. So, what do you say Chief? Are you going to do a press conference and sort this out?" Rudovsky gestured to the newspaper.

"Well, DI Saunders is halfway to London at the minute. So if you are insisting on this, you'll have to chair the press conference yourself."

"You what?"

"You heard."

"Fucking hell Sir." Rudovsky's healthy olive complexion suddenly became much paler.

Miller laughed at the look of horror on her normally happy, cheery face. "I'll organise it, you can give the official line, in DI Saunders' absence. Great idea Jo, well done."

"Well, you're much better at these Sir."

"Yes, I am aren't I?"

"Aw come on boss, don't be a twat."

"I'm not being a twat Jo, I'm supporting your

request. Anyway, why are you so scared, you look great on telly."

"Come off it Sir. You know I feel a dick doing press stuff!"

"I'm ace at press conferences, because Dixon forced me to do all his ones. Stop being a whinge-bag. The camera loves you. I'll organise it for four pm, we'll have a de-brief at three-thirty. Okay?"

"Wanker."

"Hey, that's extremely offensive Jo." Miller raised an eyebrow. He was glad the door was closed, as he'd be cross with her for speaking to him like that in front of any other staff. But Miller had a real soft spot for Rudovsky, and she knew it.

"Thank you Sir!" she said as she opened Miller's door and left the office. Miller looked down at the newspaper and continued to read the story.

"Despite the fact that Kathy hasn't been seen or heard of since Thursday night – London's police, as well as Manchester's police look like they couldn't care less. Kathy Hopkirk may be a controversial character, but her disappearance should be treated just like any other." Read the Editorial Comment section.

"What a load of codswallop this is!" said Miller, chuckling half-heartedly to himself. "You shit-stirring bastards!" he added as he folded the newspaper and threw it across the office, where it landed in a heap a few feet from the waste-paper bin.

Miller looked through his glass walled office in the direction of the staff. Rudovsky looked up from her desk and saw that Miller was grinning at her. He held his thumb up and his sarcastic, cheesy expression made her laugh nervously.

Chapter 13

DI Saunders was driving the silver Vauxhall Insignia CID car down the M6, touching on 90mph at times. His passenger didn't seem too fussed, she appeared to trust her new DI. This made Saunders warm to Grant, mainly because all of the other SCIU team slagged his driving off whenever they had to share a car with him.

"So what first attracted you to the SCIU job?"

"Erm, what... honestly?" Grant bit her bottom lip and grinned. She had a very cheeky look on her face and laughed.

"What?" asked Saunders, laughing at the bizarre response to such a straight-forward question.

"Well, I don't know. You're my DI... maybe I should just respond with an interview answer..." that cheeky grin was still plastered all across the DC's face.

"No, no forget that, I'm definitely intrigued now! What's the honest answer?" Saunders laughed out loud and it made Grant laugh too.

"Okay... but you have to promise that you won't judge me..."

"I will *definitely* judge you Helen, I'm not going to lie!" Saunders laughed again, and now he couldn't wait to hear why the team's newest member had applied for the role.

"Right... well... my ex, Mike, he's a DC at Trafford. We split up last year, he was sha... he was sleeping with a PC from Stretford police station. It'd been going on for a year."

"Shit. Sorry, I didn't mean to..."

"No, no, it's fine, I'm well over it. But we had been together for four years, and we had a flat, so it was difficult, at the time."

"What, and you were both at Trafford nick as well?"

"Yes, same office."

"Shit, God I bet that was awkward."

"It was, it really was – especially when friends and colleagues started taking sides and… aw, well it was awful. Horrible time. Totally shit."

"And that's why you decided to apply to us?"

"Well, sort of…" That mischievous grin was back, and Grant was biting her bottom lip again. She cracked and laughed again. "Oh my God, can't believe I'm saying this…"

"Go on…"

"Well, it was Mike's dream to join the SCIU. So as soon as I saw the job advertised, I got my application in double-quick, and put it all around the nick that I'd been asked to apply by DCI Miller. I decided to get my own back that way. Get the job that Mike had always wanted, and make it sound like I'd been head-hunted for it!" Grant laughed, it was a very naughty, cheeky laugh and Saunders thought that the whole thing was hilarious.

"Oh my God, you bloody psycho!"

"I know!"

Saunders and Grant were laughing about the circumstances of her new job for a few minutes. Saunders was grinning from ear to ear. This balls-out honesty was so refreshing, especially as it was coming from a new member of staff.

"What a story!" said Saunders as he laughed again.

A few minutes passed by in silence. Eventually, Grant asked Saunders how he'd come to working for the SCIU.

"Well, it's not as bloody scary as your reason! I was already working for the boss in CID at Swinton. It was when there was a lot more money sloshing about the police force. HQ decided to start a new department to deal with exhausted cases. Initially, the idea was to work on cold cases dating back ten, fifteen, twenty years."

"Wow, I bet that was fascinating!"

"Yeah, It was really, but we were too good. We solved most of them in the first two or three years."

"And you were in right from the start?"

"Yes, Miller was asked to apply for it, and took me with him, along with a couple of others from Swinton. I've been very lucky to be honest."

"You're very modest. He speaks really highly of you, you know."

"Does he? Yeah, I suppose he will do really."

"Yes, he was telling me that you're probably the best detective he's ever known."

"Shut up!"

"Honestly. He can't say enough about you!" It was Grant's turn to laugh now, as Saunders began blushing and appeared lost for words. "He said that I need to listen to everything you say, watch everything you do. He said he would partner me up with you as much as possible during my probationary period."

"Did he now?" Saunders smiled at the thought of Miller being difficult that morning, when the DI had requested working with the new DC.

"So what's he like anyway, DCI Miller?"

"What do you reckon?"

"Er... well he seems nice. Doesn't seem to be a sexist, seedy gob-shite like most of the DCI's I've met."

"Na, he's not. He's one of the good ones. He can be a right moody bastard sometimes though – especially when he's frustrated. Thing is, you should never take anything personally. He can seem really horrible and off, and a few of the DC's have thought he had it in for them. Trust me, if Miller is pissed off with you, you'd be the first to know."

"Ah, sounds like good advice. Cheers."

"Yes, well, you know – if you ever think he's on a downer with you, he's not. It's just what he's like when he's worried or stressed. And with some of the cases we have to investigate, that can happen a lot."

"Well, I'm impressed so far, and the rest of the team seem really good."

"Yeah, we are, it's a good team, close-knit. Bill's not been himself for a bit now… he's been trying to solve a few problems in his personal life. But I think he's over the worst now. Jo is a good laugh, and she's a bloody good detective too, probably the best in the department to be fair."

"After you?" Grant laughed at Saunders' modesty.

"Well, after Miller, and then me…"

"Oh well, you can't accept praise, can you?"

"Well, it's a team-effort, we don't have egos and all that shit."

"Fair enough. Fancy a coffee at the next services?"

"Yeah, go on then. That's not a bad idea. I'm dying for the loo."

"Me too, I'm bursting. I bet we're over half way now as well, so you'd better start telling me what the plan is once we hit the big smoke."

"Yes, well, its simple enough, I just want to speak to the witnesses that have already been interviewed, that's Kathy's husband, manager and neighbours. I can't trust an interview by reading it, I like to look in the person's eyes and get a feeling for if they are telling me the truth. Hence, this slight de-tour from The Midland back to the office."

"Its fine by me. And I was warned that you fart a lot, so don't hold them in on my account!"

Saunders was blushing again as he hit the indicator and started slowing down for the services.

Chapter 14

The Kathy Hopkirk story was not only big news in the UK and across Europe, the disappearance was making headlines on the other side of the Atlantic as well. Several news stations were leading on the story, as Kathy was almost as well known Stateside for her outspoken opinions, and possibly even more detested than she was at home.

Two years earlier, Kathy had been invited onto the Tonight Show, America's number one late-night talk show which averages ten million US TV viewers each night. Kathy was relatively unknown in the US at the time, but had been visiting New York on a book promotion tour, in a bid to get her name out there. The Tonight Show producers had heard that she was causing quite a stir back home in Britain, and decided to give her a five minute slot.

It was to be an unforgettable five minutes, and Kathy certainly used the opportunity to get her name out there. She used the time to alienate herself from most of the television show's viewers. Usually, the Americans can't resist a British voice on their broadcasts, but Kathy did just enough in her debut five-minutes to ensure that she would never be invited back. The video-clip of that ill-fated appearance was still receiving a great deal of interest on Youtube, and had already racked up an extraordinary three hundred and forty-five million views.

The interview started well, and Kathy was extremely smiley and charming. But when the host asked Kathy what she was doing in New York, he had no idea what she was about to say. The answer was supposed to be about Kathy's book. However, the answer that she came out with stunned the host, and made the studio audience shout abuse at the guest, with many walking out in protest in the middle of the broadcast.

"Well, I had a funny feeling that you were going to ask me that…" said Kathy, very flirtatiously. "So I decided to forget all about the book promotion." Kathy held up a copy of her biography "I Beg Your Pardon" and smiled coyly, which received a huge laugh and a round of applause from the audience who loved the British sense of irony.

"Well, considering that you've aborted those plans, you seem to be doing a great job all the same!" laughed the host.

"No, in all seriousness, I have a deeper message. I'm here, because I want to help the people of America. You know, it breaks my heart when I see what happens over here. It seems that every week there is a news story back in England, about a mass shooting where kids are being killed in college, and at the cinema, by other kids who have picked up a gun and it breaks my heart. It really does. But when I'm in England, I feel so far away, I feel so helpless."

The usually cheery host was nodding sombrely, acknowledging the point that Kathy was making. The studio audience were also silenced, as thoughts of tragedy came flooding back.

"And then, I look on the news another day, and I see reports that half of you guys are eating yourselves to death! Great big fat bastards waddling down the road, holding gigantic bucket sized Diet-Coke's, triple-deck burgers and pizzas the size of a dustbin lid!"

There was an awkward laugh from the bemused looking host, and several audience members, who were struggling to see what this bizarre illustration was leading to.

"Honestly, you guys freak me out. Half of you running around with guns trying to kill one another, the other half of you are so morbidly obese that you couldn't run if your feet were on fire!"

There were a couple of embarrassed, awkward laughs, but the mood was becoming tense in the studio. Kathy knew it, she could feel that she was losing the audience, but she carried on regardless. "So, here's the thing. Here's a plan that will solve all of your problems." Kathy stood up and walked in front of the TV host's desk. She stood there like an air-hostess presenting the safety advice before a flight. It was really, really cringey, and the audience were starting to curl their toes.

"All you fat people, grab hold of these shot-gun owners! Go up behind them, put your giant Coke bucket over their head, grab them, and sit down on them. Put all of your weight on their chests." Kathy kneeled down on the floor, demonstrating her idea. "Just sit there until they die! And then, when these gun-owning morons have taken their last, pathetic breaths, you big fat losers can grab the gun out of their cold, dead hands and shoot yourselves in the mouth! And if you could all do that next Tuesday, that would be great!"

The expression on the host's face, as he tried to segue out of this unscripted, frankly suicidal rant by the British guest was a look of bewilderment. The audience had started jeering at Kathy, and one or two paper cups had been thrown down from the audience's seating area. The NBC studio security team looked extremely edgy as many of the audience members began walking out.

"That bitch is crazy, man!" shouted one rather stout lady as she made her exit.

"Man! That shit ain't funny mother fucker!" shouted another.

This was car-crash TV in its rawest form. The host just watched on silently as the audience members continued to stand and walk out of the building. Over the speakers, a trail for "still to come…" began playing and the red-lights in the studio went off.

"What the fuck was that?" screamed the director, marching across towards Kathy, and the host who looked completely frozen.

"It's just what I do, darling. It's just what I do. Is my car here?"

The Youtube video of this unforgettable TV debut was receiving so much interest in the present climate that many people couldn't access it, the video just buffered non-stop.

Even when Kathy Hopkirk was missing, her content was still going viral, and it was this precise quality which made her so unique. Kathy may be missing, but it almost felt as though she was missed, too. The old clips of her various stunts and monologues were being shared around all of the social networks, as people were reminding themselves of just how outrageous Kathy could be. If this was hatred, if this was a public demonstrating how much they detested the woman, it was a pretty peculiar way of going about it.

Chapter 15

"Bloody eight-pound-sixty for two cups of coffee! I had half a mind to arrest the girl behind the counter!" DC Helen Grant wasn't very impressed by the price of the drinks.

"It's the services isn't it? They can charge whatever they like, where else are you going to go?"

"I know, but... it's still a piss-take."

"Plus, we're getting closer to London now, so the price goes up by a quid for every fifty miles closer you get!"

Saunders pressed his key-fob and the car bloop-blooped as the doors unlocked.

Within a few minutes, the car was back on the motorway, exceeding the speed limit again. The conversation so far had been pleasant and relaxed and Saunders really felt comfortable with Grant. He had to remind himself that he was her superior officer, and that she was a new DC on a probationary trial. He decided that all of the polite small-talk should now give way to work-talk, and the Kathy Hopkirk mis-per case in particular.

"Thanks, anyway," said Saunders, as he took a sip from his Costa cup.

"Pardon?" asked Grant, looking across at the DS, appearing as though she'd been in a daze and Saunders had just snapped her out of it. The look of innocence and wonder in Grant's eyes made Saunders' smile affectionately.

"For the brew, thanks a lot." Said Saunders.

"Oh right, yeah, no worries. Make it last you though, I can't afford to get them on the way back as well!"

"No, I'll get them next time. Well, a can of pop, I'm not made of money. So, what do you think might have happened to our missing person?"

"Oh, right, Kathy? I wondered when we'd get

around to talking about *her*."

"Ooh, I don't like the way you said 'her.' I take you're not keen on her, then?"

"I don't think anybody is keen on Kathy Hopkirk, are they? But anyway, it really doesn't matter about my opinions about the mis-per, does it? My priority is to carry out my duties in a professional and neutral manner, just as I would any other enquiry."

"Good answer."

"I bet that was hard work though, when you were trying to catch Pop?"

Grant was referring to a famous case from a few years earlier, when the SCIU team were trying to catch a gunman who was executing paedophiles in cold, calculated hits all over Greater Manchester. It had been a challenging case, and one that had ended in the most devastatingly tragic circumstances for the SCIU team.

"We don't talk about that case." Saunders' voice was cold, detached. It made Grant sit up a little, wriggling in the passenger seat as she tried to adapt to the DS's sudden change in mood.

"Sorry... I..."

"It's okay, it's bound to come up. But we don't talk about that case. We lost our DI because of that. She was our best mate." Saunders' voice wobbled a bit at the end of his sentence, and Grant saw a tear start to form, which was quickly expelled with a wipe from the back of Saunders' wrist.

Grant felt an urgency to change the subject, whilst making a mental note not to put herself in this difficult position again.

"Well, as I say, I don't have much time for Kathy Hopkirk, but I'll still put a full shift in until we find out what's happened." Grant looked out of her window, the scenery was lovely, the sun was beating down on a farm with lots of grazing livestock, the whole scene stood before a village in the distance with a beautiful church steeple on the horizon. "God, its nice round here, isn't it?"

"It is, it's stunning."

"Gorgeous. It looks like something straight off a margarine tub."

Saunders and Grant laughed, and the ice had been broken from the previous, problematic conversation.

"I think that's the most northern thing I've ever heard anybody say!" laughed Saunders, repeating Grant's comment under his breath.

The rest of the journey into London was spent discussing the case, with Saunders explaining lots of the details that he had learnt about Kathy, her private life, her professional life and now her very public disappearance. Saunders went into greater detail about his plans for this visit. By the time that Saunders' car had left the M25 at Junction 14 and was caught up in stationary traffic near to Heathrow airport, both of the detectives were desperate to get to work.

"Oh, here, a text off the boss," said Saunders, looking at his phone as he sat in the traffic jam. "Jo's doing a press conference at four."

"It's two minutes past."

"Shit, I'd better put Radio Five Live on, they'll be taking it."

After a minute of fumbling with the radio and trying to find the correct station, Grant and Saunders heard their colleague's voice in the car speakers, as the DC who was 300 miles away was addressing the press.

Chapter 16

DC Jo Rudovsky's hands were shaking, it was given away by the piece of paper that she was reading from. She realised how bad her trembling hands looked, and placed the script onto the table top. The media centre at MCP HQ was absolutely ram-packed with reporters, all desperate to hear this first official police report on the number-one news story on all networks.

Jo was doing well, despite her nerves. The popular DC had become something of a media starlet in the north-west a few years earlier, when she'd been severely injured in a knife attack trying to protect members of the public. As a result of her heroics, she had received a number of awards, and as she was so pretty and stylish, her photo was appearing everywhere. The final award in a year of glitzy dinners and ceremonies was to win the "Miss Gay UK" title, and Jo had been a gay pin-up ever since due to her swagger, her wicked sense of humour and her natural confidence and charisma.

But today, her usual media charm was missing. Jo had a very serious role to carry out, and she was determined to make a good job of it. This wasn't the appropriate time to flirt with the cameras.

"Thanks everyone for attending today. I have a statement to read out regarding the disappearance of Kathy Hopkirk. There will be an opportunity to ask questions at the end of this brief statement. I'll start the statement in ten seconds. Thank you."

Jo looked around the hall at the press staff, and checked that everybody was ready. She took a deep breath and began.

"Manchester City Police are currently working with the Metropolitan Constabulary in London, trying to find out what has happened to Kathy Hopkirk, the famous television and radio celebrity. As has already been reported in the media, Kathy is a fifty-five year old woman who lives in London, but disappeared whilst she was staying in Manchester. Kathy has never done anything like this before, and as a result of the missing person report – we are currently dealing with this one, as well as a total of thirty-seven missing persons reports that have been logged with Manchester City Police over the course of the weekend."

Jo stopped and took a sip of water. Her boss, DCI Miller had advised her to take a strategic pause at that stage, to amplify the point regarding Kathy's disappearance being just one of many mis-pers that the Manchester officers were investigating.

"We would not usually call a press conference for a missing person enquiry when the case is still as young as this particular one, and when the missing person is as independent and capable as Kathy Hopkirk. However, there are certain sections of the press reporting that we are not trying very hard to find her. This is simply not true. We are treating Kathy's disappearance just as thoroughly as we are all of the other cases. This would be a very good opportunity to remind the press, and the public, that almost twenty per-cent of police time is spent working on missing persons investigations, and as a result of this fact, we know what we are doing. Now, I am afraid that I do not have any further information about this particular case, but as you will be aware, the Serious Crimes Investigation Unit very rarely get involved in missing persons enquiries. However, the Metropolitan Police have requested that the SCIU ensure that this enquiry is run as efficiently as possible. We would like to echo the message from our colleagues in London, and appeal for any information regarding Kathy's whereabouts. If you have seen Kathy in the past few days, we really want to speak to you. Somebody out there knows where Kathy is, and I am appealing to that person to get in touch. Finally, I am appealing directly to you Kathy. If you can see this transmission, or read these words, please get in touch and let us know that you're okay. Our number is on the tablecloth there, just below my glass of water. We will not be providing a running commentary on this enquiry. That's all the information that I have to reveal today, but I am happy to answer any questions you may have."

Jo took another sip of the water and looked around the room as the journalists and news presenters all started shouting their questions. It was impossible to pick out a single question from the torrent of noise.

"One at a time…" said Jo without much enthusiasm.

"Where was Kathy last seen after she left The Midland?"

"We're reviewing CCTV but we know that she was waiting for a tram. When the tram arrived at Saint Peter's Square tram-stop, Kathy disappeared. We are trying to ascertain whether she boarded the tram, or walked away from the location. The CCTV shot we have was obscured by the arrival of the tram, but we have plenty of other cameras to check in the area, and we have a time frame and a general grid location so we are confident that this detail will soon become much clearer."

"So you don't really have any idea where she headed after the tram stop?"

"That's what I just said, yes."

"Bearing in mind that Kathy is such a divisive character, is the fact that she upsets a lot of people playing a part in the enquiry?"

"Well, that's such a loaded question, I don't really know why you are asking it. But as with all missing person's enquiries, we are looking into every aspect of Kathy's life, and especially her links up here in Manchester."

"Has there been any activity online or on mobile phone by Kathy, since Thursday night?"

"Again, this is a major line of enquiry, and this is something that I am unable to discuss at this moment in time."

"Well, is that a yes or a no?"

"I've just said to you, I'm unable to discuss that at this stage."

"So you don't know?"

"Any other questions?"

"Are the Twitter Trolls that have been making death threats to Kathy for many years being investigated at this time?"

"We have specially trained officers reviewing this kind of activity, but as I have already said, this is very early in this investigation so that kind of matter will be looked at much more seriously if this case escalates."

"What will happen to Kathy if this is a hoax?"

"We are not treating this as a hoax, and I'm not in a position to answer that question as it is not relevant to the enquiry."

"Why is DCI Miller not here holding this press conference?"

"Why, what's wrong with me?" Jo's cocky retort received a laugh from many of the reporters in the hall.

"Nothing, but, with such a major investigation, I'm wondering why Miller isn't here?"

"The gaffer is busy, working on this, and several other investigations – and our Detective Inspector is currently in London, interviewing key witnesses."

"That doesn't sound like the normal level of service. Are you sure this is being treated like any other missing persons enquiry?"

"Well, I'm not sure how to demonstrate that we are taking it seriously, and not, as some of you guys have suggested "ignoring it" so I can't really answer that. Last question please now as I have to get back upstairs and get on with my work."

"Is it true that Kathy is struggling with a mental health condition at the present time?"

"I don't know why you are asking that as you

know that it is confidential information. Right, thank you everybody." Jo stood up and nodded at the press as she stepped down from the small stage and walked through the crowds of cameramen, photographers, sound engineers and journalists, and out of the hall.

"Fucking knobs!" she said under her breath as the door closed behind her.

Chapter 17

"Hello, my name is Detective Inspector Keith Saunders, and this is my colleague Detective Constable Helen Grant from Manchester Police. We would like to speak to Jack Greenwood, if that's possible, please?"

Saunders and Grant were standing in the reception of London FM, the radio station where Kathy Hopkirk's husband presented the afternoon show.

"Oh, I'll check he's still here," said the receptionist as she pressed a few buttons on the phone. "Just a moment please."

Saunders and Grant knew that Jack Greenwood was still in the building, as a number of photographers and reporters were standing outside the famous studios, waiting impatiently to "pap" the missing woman's husband on his departure.

"Hi it's Beth on reception. I've got detectives here asking to speak to Jack. No problem, alright, thanks." The receptionist placed the phone down and looked up at Saunders. "Jack's just doing a phone interview with Phil Collins. He'll be out when he's done. You can take a seat there while you wait."

"Well, how long do you think it'll take?" Saunders wasn't impressed.

"Oh I don't know. Not long, hopefully."

Saunders and Grant shuffled across to the leather sofa and took a seat. The walls were filled with signed pictures of the stars that had visited the famous radio studio over the years, they were all there. Lionel Richie, Stevie Wonder, Michael Jackson and Madonna had the biggest pictures.

"Bloody hell, can you imagine if all these had sat on this same sofa that we're sitting on now?" Grant look quite excited by the idea. Saunders looked less so.

"Doubt it. It looks quite new this sofa. Hard luck!"

"Oh well, maybe one or two recent stars have sat

on here!" Grant seemed optimistic that a tiny little bit of superstar DNA could be ingrained into the leather.

"Coldplay were sat on there last Wednesday," said the receptionist, smiling. "Chris Martin was sat right next to you!"

"No way, that's amazing!" Grant smiled, and with it she had a look of youthful innocence which made Saunders' belly flip over. This type of conversation would normally really irritate the DI. Usually, that kind of pointless waffle would make him change the subject. But the fleeting look of wonderment on Grant's face had really melted him.

Shit, he thought, as he looked down at his bag by his feet and began pulling his notepad out of the pocket. Saunders recognised that he and Grant needed to talk shop, and utilise this time as best they could. He needed to be a strong boss, with excellent leadership skills. Not a flirty, awkward moron, talking shite, he considered.

"Okay, let's just go over this for a few minutes then, while we wait for Jack Greenwood. So…" Saunders began talking through his notes with Grant, and was making a list of questions on the right-hand side of the pad as he and Grant discussed the time-line of Kathy's disappearance in Manchester, and the matters that they wanted to discuss with Kathy's husband.

By the time that Jack Greenwood appeared at the reception door, and invited the Manchester detectives into the radio station, Saunders' notes and questions had filled up half of the page.

Whether it was down to Saunders' lack of concentration due to Grant's presence, or if it was just a general oversight wasn't clear. But one thing was certain; allowing the press to photograph his page of notes through the radio station's window had been a significant error of judgement on his part.

Chapter 18

As the "BREAKING NEWS" banner flashed up on the Sky News screen, announcing that Jack Greenwood was a suspect in the disappearance of Kathy Hopkins, the story suddenly began moving with an incredible burst of life.

The photograph which had been taken through London FM's reception window clearly showed DI Saunders, the detective who had been photographed as he entered The Midland only hours earlier in Manchester, and his colleague DC Grant. The hand written notes were clearly eligible and it was the photograph of the notes which had now become the main story.

"Sky Sources have revealed this incredible photograph, which quite categorically lists a number of damning questions that Manchester detectives wish to ask Kathy's husband, Jack Greenwood, the veteran radio DJ who has shocked many people today, by turning up to present his afternoon show, despite the fact that his wife is missing." Sky News' afternoon presenter Sue Bentley was quite visibly excited by this unexpected scoop, which really did inject a much-needed boost of information to what had become an achingly slow-moving story.

"Well DI Saunders and his colleague are still inside the London FM studios, where Jack Greenwood came off the air just a short time ago. Our reporter, Kerry Gregory is there, Kerry – what's going on?"

"Yes, thank you Sue. We are not quite sure what is going on, but one thing is for sure – Jack Greenwood appears to be very high on the list of people that police wish to speak to about Kathy Hopkirk's disappearance."

"And what did the questions in DI Saunders' notebook consist of?"

"Well, many of the questions in the photograph are standard police questions which you would expect from an enquiry of this nature, questions such as, when did you last see Kathy? Is everything okay between you? When did you last speak to your wife?"

"I can sense a but coming..."

"Yes, that's right Sue. Because apart from these questions that we would expect, there are quite a few that are really quite damning. For example, DI Saunders wants to ask Jack Greenwood why he felt it was appropriate to present his radio show today. He wants to know if Jack had asked for compassionate leave today, and if not, why not?"

"Well, that is a very good question..."

"Yes, some people may believe that it is a reasonable thing to ask Sue, but, there are those people who would argue that surely this should be a private matter, and not something which is now being discussed on Sky News, and every other news network for that matter."

"I imagine that Jack Greenwood is regretting that decision to go to work today?"

"Very possibly. This could end up being a very costly error-of-judgement on Jack Greenwood's part."

"Thank you Kerry, stay there, and keep a close eye on what's happening."

*****

Saunders was inside a recording studio with Jack Greenwood and DC Grant. The radio presenter seemed quite shocked, and extremely hostile.

"Look, I've been through all this bollocks yesterday, with the Met's officers. Why the hell are you turning up here at my work, its unforgivable! It's totally indefensible!"

"We're not here to annoy you. We're trying to figure out where Kathy is. We've just driven down from Manchester."

"I don't give a shit if you've come from bloody

Reykjavik. You don't just turn up unannounced at my workplace! This is massively unprofessional, and I am going to sue the fucking arse off you inept bastards!"

"Whoah, can you just tone it down a bit mate?"

Saunders looked seriously stressed-out with the abuse from Greenwood. Grant was shocked by how forceful Saunders became in his tone and physical demeanour.

"Well, it's unforgivable!"

"What is? We're here to try and find your wife! How is that unforgivable?" Grant had stepped in now to give Saunders a bit of back up.

"Bullshit. I'll tell you what, you can both just piss off back to Manchester, and get out of my face."

"That's not going to happen, Mr Greenwood. Now, you can calm yourself down and talk to us here, or I can arrest you and take you down to the police station, and we can have the conversation there. But I'll advise you to stop your swearing, and aggressive attitude."

"Arrest me for what?"

"Obstructing a police officer. Conspiring to pervert the course of justice. Public order. That's three that you qualify for already." Saunders was talking calmly, but Greenwood just didn't seem to be hearing the DI. He was pacing around the room, getting himself more and more worked up.

"Just calm down." Said Grant, softly. "We'll be done in fifteen minutes."

"I went through all of this bollocks yesterday! Over an hour of my day was taken up by talking to police, and now you want to go over it all again! It's fucking bollocks!"

"Right, Jack Greenwood, I'm arresting you on suspicion of conspiring to pervert the course of justice…" Saunders took his handcuffs out of his pocket and cuffed Jack Greenwood as he read him his rights. Greenwood froze, and offered no resistance at all. It was bizarre, the middle-aged DJ suddenly became extremely quiet and compliant.

"This is so unfair! Do you know who I am?" He said, quietly. He sounded as though he was pretending to cry.

"Can you phone the duty sergeant at Shepherd's Bush and request a van to take Mr Greenwood in, please DC Grant? Cheers."

Jack Greenwood began sobbing, and sat down at the table. Saunders noticed that several of Greenwood's colleagues were staring through the glass, watching this extraordinary spectacle. By the speed that their mouths were moving, Saunders could see that lots of conclusions were being reached by the staff of London FM.

"You could have just answered our questions calmly and there'd have been no need for all this unpleasantness!" said Saunders as Grant spoke on her phone to the sergeant at Shepherd's Bush.

"I'm… this is so unfair! It's got nothing to do with me! How can you frame me for it?"

"Nobody is being framed for anything. We came here to ask a few routine questions. We'd have been on our way by now if you'd just helped us. Anyway, I can't be arsed going over it now, we can discuss it at the police station."

Jack Greenwood began sobbing again, and on the other side of the glass, his colleagues' mouths continued wagging, and one or two were taking photos on their phones.

*****

The press members who had gathered outside London FM were absolutely ecstatic when the police van turned up with blue lights revolving. Two officers raced out of the vehicle and ran into the radio station's reception, and then through the internal door. This dramatic footage was being recorded by several news channels, and BBC News were the first to transmit the pictures, just seconds after the uniformed officers had disappeared inside the famous building. The radio station's receptionist looked extremely shocked and confused by this extraordinary turn of events, and was also wary of the press-pack outside, who were very clearly training their cameras on her. It made her do extra things out of nerves, like touching her hair, double-blinking and raising her eyebrows for no reason. There was a huge TV screen on the radio station's wall, just above the terrified looking receptionist. It was tuned to Sky News, and was showing images of the receptionist, sitting at her desk. It was a good job that she couldn't see what was on the screen as it would have made her even more edgy.

"So as you can see," said one excited reporter to his cameraman, "it looks as though the story we broke just moments ago, regarding Kathy Hopkirk's husband Jack Greenwood, has escalated dramatically in the past few minutes. We have received reports from staff within London FM, and what we are hearing is that Jack Greenwood is currently in handcuffs inside that building, and we understand that he will be taken to a police station for questioning about the mysterious disappearance of his wife. And, yes, here come those police officers with Mr Greenwood now."

The radio station's inner door had opened, and in-between the two uniformed police officers was a man, bent double, with a coat over his head. The receptionist dashed round from her desk and raced to the door to open it for the officers. DI Saunders and DC Grant were following behind.

"Well, this is quite incredible, I can't remember reporting on anything as shocking as this since Rebecca Brooks battered Ross Kemp. The scenes that we are witnessing here, on the steps of London FM are incredible. The man who is being obscured by the jacket is London

FM's afternoon presenter Jack Greenwood. We can only assume that these extraordinary scenes are connected to the disappearance of Kathy Hopkirk."

Within seconds, the police officers had managed to scuttle through the excitable press-pack, and had Greenwood banged up in the back of the van. Just moments later, that police van was pulling off into the rush-hour traffic, a number 148 London bus flashed the police van, its passengers were all staring down at the press wondering what all the drama was about. It wouldn't be very long until they found out.

*****

"Welcome to the ITV tea-time news, I'm Chrissie Hecquet. There has been a major development this evening in the search for missing TV star Kathy Hopkirk." The look on the ITV newsreader's face conveyed the high-level of drama and excitement which surrounded the bizarre development in London. As the broadcasters and online news apps were reporting this sensational turn-of-events, the character of Jack Greenwood was being scrutinised by every single journalist that had been handed the story.

Every hack in the country wanted to be the first to find a story, or unearth a rumour that could have warned the world that Kathy was in danger, before she actually came to any harm, if in fact that was what had happened at all. It was a very, very confusing picture for all of the journalists who had to piece the jigsaw together. The only source of information that they could go on, apart from the arrest, was DI Saunders' hand written notes which had been the hot-topic of conversation in the media just moments before the high profile arrest. This story was moving so quickly, that DI Saunders was still unaware that his notes had been the lead item on this story for the past half-an-hour. For now, at least.

*****

Saunders and Grant were sat in an interview room planning a revised conversation with Jack Greenwood, once he had calmed himself down a bit. Saunders felt his phone vibrate and grabbed it from his pocket.

"Oh hi boss, I was about to ring you…"

"Hi Keith. What the hell is going on mate?"

"Aw, I don't know. This Jack Greenwood started acting all weird, acting like a bit of a diva."

"What are you on about Keith? The press have published photos of your fucking notebook. They're reporting it as though he's killed Kathy, and its all because of your notes."

The colour drained quickly from Saunders' face. His grey complexion had aged him instantly. DC Grant looked concerned.

"Are you alright?" she mouthed.

Saunders put his head down. "Oh shit. Fuck's sake! How's this happened?"

"What's up?" mouthed Grant. She looked really concerned. Saunders was ignoring her.

"It looks like it was at the radio studio, you've been papped through the window. The photos of your notes are all over the news. You circled the word alibi, and wrote double-check, didn't you?"

"Aw shit. This is unbelievable. How the hell have I allowed that to happen?" Saunders was holding his head in his hands. He knew that there was much more written on the page than just the bit Miller had gently mentioned.

"What the fuck is going on?" asked Grant, this time with a snappy tone in her voice. Saunders held up his hand to request silence from his DC, as he continued to stare down at the floor.

"Well, it's not as bad as it could have been. Now he's been arrested it looks a lot neater. Make sure you ask every question that's on your pad."

"Okay Sir, no worries. Fuck, that's a schoolboy error, I can't believe it."

"Why have you taken him in, anyway?"

"Oh, he was playing stupid buggers, wasn't co-operating. I warned him but he just carried on being a gimp. He changed his tune when the cuffs were on, though!"

"They always do. Right, so the next question is going to be about expenses..."

"You what?"

"Well you're not coming back tonight are you? You're going to be there a long time un-digging this grave. So do you want me to book something for you and Grant?"

Saunders was still shell-shocked by his massive own-goal regarding the notebook. He hadn't given any thought to getting back up the road to the north.

"Yes, cheers. Text me the details... and, I'm really sorry Sir."

"It's alright, chill out. It could be a lot worse if he wasn't in custody, so him being a bit of a dickhead has saved your bacon and eggs!"

"Yeah, God, cheers Sir. I'll go and grill him now, Sweeney style!"

Miller laughed. "Lay it on thick with Greenwood, and I'll release a statement that the press have over-stepped the mark. Let's make sure this story goes away. Good man. I'll be in touch later on. Cheers."

"Oh, Sir, is Jo still about?"

"Yeah, she is..."

"Tell her she played a blinder in the press conference. We were listening to her in the car. She was excellent."

"I will do, she'll be buzzing with that. Cheers."

Chapter 19

"Right then, Jack Greenwood. Have you pulled yourself together a bit now?" Saunders wasn't being remotely friendly to the DJ. He was going to have to sleep in London, in some crappy motel or something now, because of this moron. Not only that, the DI was still smarting from that press photographer getting one over him at the radio station. Although he rarely did bad moods, Saunders was in one this evening.

"Yes, I'm sorry about... I don't know what came over me."

"Well, we could have done this hours ago, and you'd be at home now, and we'd be halfway up the M6. But anyway..." Saunders began reading Greenwood his rights, and explained the purpose of the interview. Within seconds the interview was under way.

"Can you tell us where you were on Thursday evening, please?" asked Grant, very politely.

"I was at home. All night. I have CCTV evidence as well, the whole house is covered in cameras."

"Why is that?"

"Because Kathy is extremely cautious. Well, that's what she calls it. I call it paranoid."

"And who were with you on Thursday evening?"

"My producer. We were working on a few ideas for this weeks show."

"When was the last time your producer came and stayed at your house until the early hours of the morning?"

"I... I don't... wait, what's this got to do with Kathy..."

"Just answer the questions Mr Greenwood and you'll be out of here in no-time." Saunders was playing the role of the tough cop. Grant was being really nice.

"I just don't know why this is relevant..."

Grant spoke up. "It's relevant because while your

wife is three hundred miles away in Manchester, you've been entertaining an attractive, ambitious young woman round at your house. If Kathy had been aware of that, it may have upset her. It may have made her go off and do something stupid."

Jack Greenwood smiled coldly. It was a sly grin, completely humourless. He'd changed, he wasn't the prima donna he'd been at London FM, nor the sobbing, pathetic victim that he'd become once the cuffs were round his wrists. Now, Jack Greenwood seemed to be playing an entirely different character altogether, and it was interesting for the Manchester detectives to experience these three different personas inside a few small hours.

"Well, I can assure you," said Greenwood. "If that is how you think about Kathy, that she'd do something stupid because of me - then you are completely wrong."

"Thank you. That's exactly what we're here to find out." Grant was fast with her replies, and was doing a good job of softening Greenwood up, before Saunders would hit him with a hammer-blow. This had been the plan, and Grant was executing her part in the procedure brilliantly.

"Nothing would upset her. She's completely devoid of feelings. She's a unique person, there is nobody else like her."

"Do you miss Kathy?"

"What... how do you mean?" Greenwood looked confused, but in a hammy actor, phoney sense. He looked more as though he was trying to appear confused, and it made alarm bells ring in both of the detective's heads.

"You know, in all my years of doing this job, I've never encountered a partner of a missing person behaving so strangely. They always try and help us with our enquiries... even when they were guilty of doing something wrong! But you're a strange one Mr Greenwood, and I will get to the bottom of it."

"How am I strange?" asked Greenwood, that peculiar smirk was back on his lips. It was almost as though he was getting a bit of a weird buzz from all this.

"Well, considering that you've not shown the slightest hint of concern for your wife's welfare is pretty strange, wouldn't you agree?"

"No."

"Well, it's strange to me. It tells me one of two things. Either you know that she's fine, or you know that she isn't. So which is it?"

"Which is what?"

"Is Kathy fine?"

"I don't know."

"Is she safe?"

"I don't know."

"Have you heard from Kathy since you last spoke to her by phone on Thursday evening?" Grant's softer, friendlier questioning style broke off the frosty exchange between Saunders and Greenwood. It made Kathy's husband change tact.

"No! No, I haven't."

"So why aren't you shitting yourself, wondering where your wife is then?" Saunders was angry, this guy was taking the piss, it was blatantly obvious.

"I don't know."

"How come you went into work today, to do your radio show?"

"What do you mean?" asked Greenwood.

"Well, your wife is missing. Not been seen since last Thursday. The press are camped outside your house. This is usually a big deal in somebody's life. How can you concentrate on talking shit on the radio for three hours under those circumstances?"

"It helps. It takes my mind off my real life."

"Bollocks. You went in because you knew the press would be waiting outside to take your picture!"

"Really? What a bizarre idea!" That smug grin was

back again. This guy was really starting to wind Saunders up. Grant stepped in, and played her part in the routine.

"Listen, Jack, we just want to find out where Kathy is, and then go back and get on with all our other cases in Manchester. But listen, you're our best chance of getting to the bottom of it…"

"And you're being a knob."

Grant shot an icy look at Saunders, before looking back across the table, at Greenwood. "Where do you think Kathy is?"

"I have no idea. For God's sake, I've been through all this yesterday, it's beyond a joke now."

"Do you think that if she was okay, she'd have been in touch?"

"I don't know!" Greenwood slammed his hand against the table, it made Saunders and Grant jump. "I DON'T FUCKING KNOW!" Greenwood stood, he was shouting at the top of his voice, his eyes were popping out of his head, staring up at the ceiling. But it felt insincere, it sounded fake. It was creepy.

"Interview suspended at nineteen forty-eight hours." Saunders turned off the recording machine. Grant sat quietly, taking notes. Greenwood was still stood, his bulging eyes were now staring straight at Saunders. He looked like a bad actor.

"You're going to have to stay the night mate, you're taking the piss. We'll talk to you tomorrow morning when you've had a chance to sort your head out." Saunders stood and opened the interview room door.

"No! That's not fair!" Greenwood wasn't impressed by this news, and for the very first time, he seemed genuinely affected by this announcement. Suddenly, the weird, wooden acting was replaced by a real, seemingly genuine concern. "I can't stay here. Please, come on, seriously. I'll answer anything you want. Just, please, I need to get out of here. I'm begging."

"Sorry pal, you've been taking the piss since we came to ask a few routine questions. Something is going on with you, and I'm going to find out what it is."

Chapter 20

"And this news, just breaking in the last few seconds... Kathy Hopkirk's husband Jack Greenwood will be spending the night in a London police station. This press release has literally just come in to the BBC News Centre, and, well it confirms what many commentators have been suggesting for several hours now. Mr Greenwood has not been charged, but he is not being released either, while he "helps police with their enquiries.""

The stressed-looking BBC News presenter was quite clearly adapting to the fast-pace that this story had been picking up over the past few hours. News could be a notoriously slow beast, but could often set off at an extraordinary pace, and leave everybody chasing. This afternoon's sensational developments in the Kathy Hopkirk story were a classic example. For the news staff, it was hard work, but also a huge relief to see so much activity following the frustratingly slow start to this story the previous day.

"Let's cross live now to our senior crime reporter, Owen Daniels, who is outside New Scotland Yard in central London. Owen."

"Thank you, and yes, I am standing outside Britain's most famous police station, reporting on one of the most exhilarating cases of modern times..."

The top story in Britain, and the second top story in the USA, was exciting, and was certainly creating lots of interaction and opinion amongst viewers and social media users who were all keen to suggest their own theories on what was going on.

But annoyingly for the broadcasters and journalists, and especially the police, the story had come to a dead end for the night.

*****

"Hi Keith, what's going on?"

"Hi Sir. We've just left the police station now. We're going to let him stew overnight because he's just being a dick."

"How do you mean?"

"He's acting. One minute he seems like he's playing ball, the next minute he's taking the piss. I can't read him, I can't suss out if he's involved in the disappearance, if he's sad, or worried, or happy even. He's a right knob! But his mood changed when I told him he's having a sleep-over."

"So what do you think you're going to get from him in the morning?" Miller sounded quite stressed and tense. It was hard work running this, in the Met's back yard as well. It was a totally inside-out, upside-down way of working and if Miller had anticipated this kind of development with Greenwood, he wouldn't have allowed Saunders and Grant to go down to London. Things would be a lot easier if the Met had this headache on their own. Still, Miller was grateful that all of this meant that Saunders was off-the-hook for his notebook blunder. At least there was that.

"So what do you reckon about Greenwood? Do you think he's involved?"

"Hmmm, not sure. He's totally bananas. But like I say, he didn't seem remotely concerned about any of this until I said we'll keep him in. And after all, Kathy is worth a good few quid. It's quite reasonable to suspect him, he's due a windfall if Kathy doesn't come home."

"That's a good point. A very good point. He's still got a watertight alibi though, hasn't he?"

"The CCTV you mean?"

"Yes, and the work colleague as well. All seems rather perfect. I always worry when an alibi has two rock solid layers."

"Any developments on Kathy's movements in

Manchester yet?"

"Nah. Not had anything, and I thought we'd have got something back since the press conference. But no, nothing has come up yet."

"And do we know if she got on the tram?"

"Nah, still waiting for Metrolink. It turns out they had a bit of a power outage in a few trams over the weekend, and the CCTV clocks went tits up. So they can't get to the right time."

"They say that crap all the time. Why don't they just admit they can't work their CCTV?"

"They need to admit that they can't work their trams first. Don't worry though – we'll get there. We always do. It's still only day one for us lot and we've already made the top story on the international news!"

"I have!"

"Ha ha, yeah, but only for being a fucking dipstick!"

Miller thought that his comment was funny, but he could tell that Saunders wasn't amused from the awkward silence.

"Right, anyway, me and DC Grant are going to try and find our hotel. Then I think I'm going to find a Wetherspoons and treat me and the DC to a nice Mexican Monday!"

"Ooh, Mexican Monday. Lovely! Give me a call in the morning so we can go over things before you reconvene with Mr Greenwood. Oh, and that hotel booking I text you – they only had a double room left."

"Aw Sir, for fu… are you taking the fucking piss?"

Chapter 21

In the wake of her disappearance, Kathy Hopkirk's ten years of regular television work was coming under the microscope like never before. It came as quite a shock to the average TV viewer to learn how much broadcasting Kathy had actually done since bursting onto the nation's screens just a decade earlier. All of the rolling news reports were being inserted with clips from her appearances on all manner of British programmes.

Clip after clip was being pulled out to keep the news story interesting. In one short video, Kathy was seen talking to the agony aunt of "Britain's Got Issues" the popular daytime chat-show. There was also some light-hearted footage of her being custard-pied on Children In Need, a stunt that had raised over £1,000.000 for the kids charity.

Viewers were also being reminded of Kathy's infamous appearance on "Bake That" five years earlier, when she'd had a row with another celebrity contestant, and had then thrown her competitor's cake mix on the floor. Kathy had been expelled from the competition for her behaviour, but the subsequent, explosive publicity had ensured that she was the hot-topic of conversation through-out the land, and she had remained the UK's number one Twitter topic for three days. She'd also had over a hundred death threats. The British were well-known for taking their baking programmes extremely seriously.

But Kathy Hopkirk's most memorable television appearance which was now being revisited, had been the six-part Channel 5 documentary, arrogantly titled "Let Kathy Show You A Better Way." In this series, Kathy spent each episode with a different family from an area of high deprivation. It was part of the TV channel's "Poor Folk and Cigarette Smoke" season.

Kathy's idea was to spend one week with six

different families, and try to help them to manage their finances better, teach them how to clean their houses and then keep on top of stuff, including how to tidy their gardens. It was Kathy's idea to make the show, and it had been her dream to turn around the fortunes of the families that she was sent to stay with each week. Kathy had famously said at the start of each episode, "if I can't help these people, nobody can."

In reality, it was a very gripping, very real and "gritty" programme, but Kathy didn't quite manage to turn the families lives around. Despite the good, albeit naive intentions, the series just became a weekly slanging match between Kathy and the families that she'd gone to help. The most memorable moment had come when Kathy slapped a husband who had spent all of the family's weekly benefits in the bookies. He shouted that if the cameras weren't there, he'd "fucking smack you one, and then let the fucking dogs eat you." The series won "Best Factual Entertainment" at the TV Quick Awards.

What was becoming apparent from these constant reminders of Kathy's various TV projects and appearances, was that this woman had absolutely dominated the TV landscape for the past ten years, and nobody had really noticed that she was doing it. It was only in retrospect that you could see what a richly diverse "show-reel" she had created for herself.

Outside Kathy's home in Hammersmith, West London, the media crews were starting to wind-down their activities as it became increasingly apparent that this story was done for today. The final reports were being read-to-camera.

"And now, as the search for Kathy Hopkirk closes on its second day, with her husband spending the night in a police station, and with still no word on her whereabouts, concern is continuing to grow for Kathy's welfare." Said the ITV news reporter. And it seemed, over these past few hours, that people were starting to forgive

Kathy.

All the high blood pressure that she had caused, all the arguments and broken TV remote controls suddenly seemed forgotten about. The news channels had spent the day reminding everybody that they had taken a great deal of entertainment away from Kathy's various stunts and activities. The mood in Britain was changing, just a bit, and those cries of "well I hope she's dead" from the previous day were turning to "I hope she's okay that Kathy. She's alright really. Salt of the earth, isn't she?"

Chapter 22

"Hi, I've got a booking, it was done online about an hour ago by Manchester Police." Saunders was standing at the check-in desk of the Premier Express, and still hadn't plucked up the courage to inform Grant that Miller had booked them into a double room. He was just hoping and praying that there was a settee in the room, which he'd offer to take. But he had a feeling there wouldn't be a settee.

"Ah yes, is it Mr Saunders?"

"Yes, well, its Detective Inspector Saunders, and Detective Constable Grant," said Saunders, politely, trying to tell the receptionist that a double room wasn't really appropriate, using only his eyes.

"And it's a double-room, is that right?" asked the receptionist. Saunders' eye message hadn't worked.

"A double?" asked Saunders, trying to sound surprised, and failing. "That's not really appropriate... it's a business, I mean, we're work colleagues..."

"This is the booking, Sir."

"It must be a mistake," Saunders was going red in the face, and it wasn't anger or irritation. It was just good old fashioned shyness and embarrassment. Grant found it very charming.

"It'll be alright, we can top and tail, Sir!" Grant had a cheeky grin on her face and the receptionist smiled coyly, pretending that she couldn't hear.

If a hole could just open up and swallow Saunders up right there, that would be a perfect end to this cringey situation.

"Are there no other rooms available?"

"I'm sorry Sir, we are completely booked. The room that has been booked was a cancellation."

"Right, well, can you sort out some extra bedding please? I'll bunk down on the floor."

"Yes, of course, I'll organise that for you. Now if

you can just sign here, your room is on the second floor, number two-two-nine. Breakfast is served from six until ten, and checkout is at eleven o clock. I hope you will enjoy your stay with us."

"Right, cheers." Saunders took the keys and walked off sulkily towards the stairs. Grant smiled at the receptionist as she followed.

"Cheer up Sir! It's better than driving home all night!" she said as she walked just behind her DI.

"I know, it's just... I don't... doesn't matter." He looked around at Grant and her face was full of colour, and that smile was there, just as refreshing and irresistible as it had been all day.

"Just what? Come on Sir, cheer up, we're on an unexpected holiday!"

"Yes, well, I mean..."

"I need to find a supermarket, to grab some pyjamas and some fresh undies. Don't suppose you know if there's one nearby?"

"There will be, we'll find summat. Let's get a look at this room first, and we can go and get some tea, have a wander around. Hopefully, they'll find a spare bed they can lend us while we're out."

*****

Even after 9pm, the human activity within London seemed relentless. The traffic, the cyclists, commuters, tourists and revellers were all around. There were thousands of people out in the streets, and every one of them looked busy and focused on what they were doing, and it was Monday too.

The traffic jams were still in full flow as though it was rush-hour. Big red buses full of people, all of them looking miserable and isolated. Black cab taxi drivers were honking on their horns and shouting at one another. The business people were rushing past, heads down, staring at the ground.

"Why are they so robotic down here?" asked Grant. "Nobody ever looks you in the face. It's scary."

"They're all busy aren't they, trying to get home. I bet they're a bit more friendly in their local communities."

"It's a shame though, it's such a buzzing place, but its just lacking that human interaction."

"What like Manchester you mean? Excuse me mate, my wife's just text me to say she's gone into labour and in my excitement I dropped my wallet down a grid. You wouldn't lend me a tenner for a taxi would you?"

Grant laughed at Saunders example of a typical Manc blagger. The Mancs were too cool to beg, they preferred to tell you a load of bullshit until in the end you just submit and hand them a tenner just to get them away from you.

"The difference between Manchester and London is mad. It's like two different countries!"

"Have you not been down here before?" asked Saunders.

"No. Well, I have with school, on a trip years ago. But not as an adult. It's amazing, isn't it?"

The look of wonderment in Grant's face was as charming as all of the other facial expressions that she'd made throughout the day. Saunders had a really giddy, happy feeling when he looked at her. He could only compare it to a teenage crush he'd had on a girl in the year above. The girl in question, Annette Thomas, never even looked at Saunders, she didn't even know who he was. But it didn't matter, he still loved her. And the dizzy way that he'd felt for Annette Thomas, twenty years ago, was how he was feeling towards his new DC. Pure, undiluted infatuation. It was great, and fun and exciting and such an unexpected change from normality. But at the very same time, it was a total headache. It was a complete disaster. Saunders had a responsibility to be this newly recruited detective's boss, and mentor. How could he be a decent role-model if he was going to be flirting and giggling and making daft comments because of nerves? This had all of the ingredients of a complete and utter nightmare, but Saunders didn't want it to end *just* yet.

Grant was looking all around, up at the buildings, lost in her own thoughts. Saunders was planning to find a Wetherspoons or a Yates', and a chance to relax over some cheap grub. But the moment took him, and he found that he'd grabbed Grant's arm and was running up towards the traffic lights with her.

"Come on, let's get on that sight-seeing bus!" he shouted as he ran. Grant was giggling as she tried to keep up with her DI. She was having an amazing time, it was just what she'd needed.

Half an hour later, Saunders and Grant had seen the sights. The Houses of Parliament, The London Eye, Buckingham Palace and Tower Bridge, and Grant had loved every minute of it.

Now, they were in a gastro-pub, waiting for their food order and enjoying a beer. The first pint, which Saunders sank pretty quickly loosened the DI up a little.

"I was a right dickhead today."

"Eh? You what? What are you on about?"

"Oh, I've had a frightful day. I can't believe I let the bloody press take photos of my notes." Saunders knew that it was all because of Grant distracting him. It wasn't her fault of course, and he'd die if she found out what a massive impression she was making on him.

"Sir, no way was that your fault! Those windows were covered in adverts and branding. You couldn't see the press outside, so it's perfectly reasonable to let your guard down. You shouldn't beat yourself up about that!" Grant seemed passionate, and genuinely wanted Saunders to stop dwelling on his mistake.

"I know but… well, I'm meant to be showing you how the elite detectives of the SCIU do things, and it's just been a pile of shite."

Grant took a swig from her glass, and thought carefully about her response before she started to speak. "Well, I have loved today. You must be really OCD about your work if you get this upset by a tiny bit of bad luck."

"It's not just that though. I was so pissed off with myself, I screwed up that interview with Greenwood. So, I just want to say, sorry, my performance has been pretty dismal today. I hope that normal service will resume tomoz."

Grant let Saunders' comment hang in the air for a moment. She didn't fancy becoming an emotional crutch, so she decided to let his self-absorbed unhappiness wash away by itself. After her boss had drained his pint, he spoke again, and she was pleased to hear a much more positive inflection to his speech.

"So, anyway, I've had an idea. You were bloody brilliant with Greenwood today…"

"Was I?" Grant's face transformed from a neutral, comfortable expression to a wonderful, bashful, self-confident smile. She leant forward and began twirling a length of her long auburn hair around between her fingers as she blushed. Saunders felt his insides turn over again, a full 360 degree rotation which made him smile himself.

"Yes, you did brilliantly. So, I've been thinking. How do you fancy looking after the interview with Greenwood on your own?"

"What? Seriously?"

"Yes. I've got a really shit chemistry with him. My own fault I suppose. But I think you'll have him around your little finger in no time."

A waitress came across to the table, interrupting the conversation, just as Grant's face beamed another beautiful, belly-flipping expression in Saunders' direction.

"Mixed grill?" said the young lass, she looked like a student who was just doing the job to make ends meet.

"Yes, cheers, that's mine." Said Saunders.

"And this is the fish and chips" she said as she

placed Grant's plate down. "Watch it, the plates are hot."

"Thanks a lot," said Grant.

"Can we order the same drinks again please?" asked Saunders.

"Sorry, you'll have to order drinks at the bar, Sir."

"Right. Okay, thanks. Back in a minute." Saunders stood and headed to the bar. "And I know how many chips are on my plate, so don't nick any!" he said as he left. Grant laughed, and gestured her hands at the mountain of chips that she had on her own plate.

Saunders was stood in a queue at the bar, and Grant couldn't decide what the correct etiquette was. Should she get stuck in and start her meal? After all, she was starving and the smell of the fish and chips, and the big chunk of lemon was making her mouth water. Or should she wait until her boss came back with the drinks?

Grant found that she had no idea what to do for the best. This wasn't a date. It was just a working tea. She glanced across and saw that Saunders was still waiting to be served. He looked around at Grant, and as their eyes met across the crowded pub, the DC grabbed a chip off Saunders plate and threw it in her mouth. It made Saunders laugh really loudly, and she burst out laughing too.

Grant took her phone out of her jacket pocket and looked up her best friend Steph in the contacts.

"OMG, I'm in London working on the Kathy Hopkirk case with my hot new boss! We're staying in a hotel and it's a double room! How bloody awkward is that! LOL." Grant smiled as she pressed the send button.

It was only a matter of seconds before Grant's phone pinged with a reply from Steph. "OMFG! I saw you on telly before! I'm trying to get a stain out of my pants. Why are you always doing better stuff than me??? PS don't screw your boss LOL X"

Grant was still laughing at the reply when Saunders suddenly appeared at the table, holding the drinks.

"What are you laughing at?" he said, still smiling from Grant's shameless chip theft.

"Oh, just a text off my friend. She's trying to get a stain out of her pants."

Saunders placed the glasses down, and had a bemused look on his face, wondering what was so funny about that. He was tempted to ask what kind of stain, but decided to just leave it. He grabbed a chip off Grant's plate and ate it, grinning as he sat down. They both laughed, and then started to eat.

"Good?" said Saunders, pointing down at Grant's food.

"Mmm, yeah," she nodded, her mouth was full so she didn't want to provide too much detail.

"Cheers!" Saunders held his glass up and Grant bashed hers against his. They were feeling merry thanks to the ale, and both were glad of the food. But at the back of both of their minds remained the difficult situation regarding their hotel room. Grant decided to put it back on the agenda, and then swiftly move back to the matter of Kathy's disappearance.

"So listen, Sir, I've got no problem about the double bed... except, I just want to say... this is really embarrassing right, but sometimes, when I'm asleep... I fart. A lot." Grant was smiling and Saunders was mesmerised once again by the sheer innocence of her face.

Saunders blushed. He was clearly embarrassed by the conversation. Grant thought it was very charming that her boss was so shy. Most senior officers were very much the alpha-male type of gob-shite who would have comeback with some shite, acerbic reply. DI Saunders was a breath of fresh air.

"Listen, its fine, I'll sort out another hotel. I'll put it through expenses. I've got that Late Rooms app on my phone."

"You don't have to... its fine!" Grant almost

sounded as though she was begging Saunders to share the room.

"Well, let's have a look anyway." Saunders took out his phone and opened up the app. He clicked on the "nearby" button and looked genuinely gutted to see the "0 availability in this location" message.

"What's it saying?" asked Grant, through a mouthful of fish batter. Saunders showed her the phone.

"Cool! That's it settled then. Come on Sir, don't be a big wuss!"

"I'm not… I'm not… I just… I'm not keen on the idea of you farting all night!"

Chapter 23

Grant and Saunders arrived on foot at Shepherd's Bush police station just before 8am. Neither anticipated the considerable media presence outside the building.

"Shit!" said Saunders under his breath.

"Flipping heck," muttered Grant. As the first press photographer started clicking, the rest followed. As the detectives made their way closer to the front doors, the deafening sound of camera clicks, pops and flashes was being drowned out by the shouts from the journalists and reporters.

"Has he killed her?"

"Why's Greenwood been kept in?"

"Why isn't Miller handling this?"

"Have you found a body?"

"Why aren't the Met investigating this case?"

Saunders and Grant managed to push their way through the scrum and were soon inside the building, although the camera flashes continued to strobe through the windows.

"They're such dicks!" said Saunders, brushing himself off. "Are you okay?" he asked of Grant. She nodded, but she looked a bit shook up by that unexpected, stressful start to the working day. That one had been a bit too physical compared to the previous days experience outside The Midland.

"See, I'm bloody losing it. It was obvious that the press would be camped out, and I've not even considered it. I'm going to be back in uniform in no time!" Saunders was joking, but it was pretty obvious that he was pissed off with himself. Worst of all, he couldn't make light of the reason his mind wasn't fully functioning. Grant was the reason. Saunders' heart skipped a beat every time he looked at her. The thought panicked him, for a variety of different reasons. He decided that he needed to try and put this latest balls up to the back of his mind for now, but he knew that it would be easier said than done.

After agreeing an interview room and suitable time with the custody sergeant, followed by a strong cup of tea in the canteen, and a long discussion on the way that the questioning needed to go, it was time for Grant to speak to Kathy Hopkirk's husband. Alone. It was all agreed. Saunders was to wait outside the interview room, where he would be eaves-dropping on the conversation. If he needed to prompt or direct her, he was going to do it by text message.

By 9am, Jack Greenwood and DC Helen Grant were sitting face-to-face across the desk in interview room three. Greenwood was in very low spirits, and seemed extremely annoyed.

"Are you okay to be interviewed?" asked Grant, with a kind, caring edge to her voice.

"Of course I am. I just want out of this shit-hole."

"Well, if you can answer the questions that I need to ask, we'll be done in no time."

"And I suppose these are the questions that I could have answered at work yesterday?" Greenwood was being sarcastic, but it wasn't clear why. The answer to his derisive question was self-defeating. Grant just looked at Greenwood, and gave a gentle, sympathetic nod.

"So where is the Detective Inspector this morning?" Greenwood appeared to be quite indignant, thought Grant, and she wondered why he seemed to believe that he had the moral high ground. It was his own stupidity and bizarre behaviour the previous evening that had earned him his night in the cell.

"DI Saunders is interviewing another witness this morning. I said I'd like to finish things off with you, and get you on your way."

"Is that so?"

"Well, if you prefer I can wait for DI Saunders to finish up with what he's doing, and we can start then?" Grant was so lovely about it, the veteran DJ was completely wrong-footed.

"And in the meantime?" asked Greenwood, staring down at the table-top, deliberately avoiding eye contact.

"Well, you can go back to your cell, and..."

"No, forget that, lets just get on with this bullshit!"

"Okay," said DC Grant, calmly. She started the recording, and read Greenwood his caution for the benefit of the tape. All the time that she was reading out the familiar paragraph, she was wondering why Greenwood hadn't asked her if there'd been any news about Kathy. She wondered why he'd not said "so she hasn't turned up yet, then?" or something like that. It was strange, and it reinforced Grant's view that this man knew perfectly well where Kathy was, and what had happened.

On the other side of the interview room door, Saunders was thinking precisely the same thing.

"So, if we can just pick up where we left off yesterday. We need to know if you've had any contact with Kathy since you spoke on the phone just before eight pm on Thursday evening."

"Not spoken to her."

"Have you communicated in any other way... text, internet, face-to-face?"

"No. Not heard from her since Thursday. Said all this to the police on Sunday. We're just repeating ourselves dear."

"Have you *tried* to communicate with Kathy since Thursday?"

"And what's that supposed to mean?"

"Well, have you phoned her? Have you messaged her via text, or Facebook or whatever?"

"No. Well, yes, I phoned her a few times on Friday, to see what time she'd be home, but she didn't answer."

"Okay, so when did you start to think that something was wrong?"

"In what respect?"

"Well, the fact that Kathy was missing."

"Oh, right, oh I see. No, you don't understand. Kathy's work takes her all over the place. She doesn't keep a diary with me, and I don't keep a diary with her. It's quite normal that we don't see one another for a week, often two at a time."

"But even if she is working away, I would have thought that you'd talk to one another, on the phone or over a text."

"Why?" Greenwood wasn't being sarcastic now. And he didn't seem to be doing the hammy acting that he'd been performing in that very same interview room the previous evening.

"Well, I just... it's what a normal couple would do."

"Honey, Kathy and I are not a normal couple! Not by the most elasticated stretch of the imagination!" Greenwood laughed, but it was a cold, fake laugh full of bitterness.

"Well, as I said to you. We need to locate Kathy, we want to check that she is okay. In normal circumstances, the next of kin is the person who can unlock the mystery. We really hoped that you might have a piece of information which would help us to reach the next stage of this inquiry."

"And with the greatest respect detective, I have already answered the questions. On Sunday, and then last night. And now, here I am again."

"You didn't answer the questions last night. And the answers you gave to the officers on Sunday were just as vague as the answers you're offering me."

"How can you possibly say that?" Greenwood suddenly threw his hands in the air. It was all very camp.

"I've got their report, here." Grant pulled the missing persons form out of her file. "Let me see, ah yes, it says here in the comments 'husband seemed quite

unwilling to assist. Very snappy remarks. Quite rude.'
Does that ring any bells?"

"No. Look, I'm just about done with all of this
nonsense. Can I go home now?"

"Not yet Mr Greenwood. I have some more
questions for you to answer."

*****

Saunders was standing in the corridor outside the
interview room, listening intently. He could feel his blood-
pressure rising. This Jack Greenwood was a complete
tosser. He was playing some sort of a game. Saunders'
mind was racing with ideas of why this man would
behave in such an odd manner. Thoughts of different
scenarios were flying into his mind. Maybe he's trying to
land a big newspaper deal. "Why the police think I've
killed my wife! EXCLUSIVE" would be worth at least six
figures. But then again, this guy already had plenty of
money. He'd been a famous DJ since the seventies. He had
been a regular presenter on Top of the Pops in the eighties
too. God, he was probably mates with Jimmy Savile back
in the day. The thought made the DI shudder as he
continued to listen by the door.

Saunders was racking his brains, desperately
trying to come up with an idea of how to move things
forward, but he was beaten to it by Grant.

*****

"We haven't been entirely honest with you,
anyway." Grant was watching Greenwood's facial
changes like a hawk. This statement suddenly made the
muscles in his neck contract.

"I beg your pardon?"

"Well, we're one step ahead of you in this
inquiry."

"Oh, so you are playing silly games now?"

"Mr Greenwood, I am not playing games. I'm trying to find your wife."

"Well, locking me up in a police cell is not helping."

"Have you got any theories about what might have happened to Kathy?"

"Who said anything *has* happened to her?"

Grant was starting to get really frustrated now. This man was just taking the piss, and it was really hard work. She took a deep breath. She had to remind herself that she was working on Britain's most talked-about case, in her capacity as a probationary applicant to join the SCIU. There was a hell of a lot at stake as far as her professional obligations went. That short internal dialogue helped to put this peculiar man and his equally strange behaviour into perspective.

"At this moment in time, Kathy is the biggest celebrity in Britain, her disappearance is on every front page, it's the main story on every channel. It's the number one topic across the internet. Now if we let you go out of here, and release a statement that says that you are not co-operating with the police, I can assure you Mr Greenwood, you'll be begging us to bring you back into the police station, so you can get away from the press! They will hound you from that moment until this case is resolved."

"You can't do that?"

"What, can't do what?"

"Say that to the press."

"Mr Greenwood, of course we can. We have a duty to report our ongoing investigations to the press, they help us to get our information out into the community. We can, and we will reveal important details, especially details as important as the fact that the missing person's spouse isn't helping with the enquiry."

"So, it's a threat?"

"What is a threat? That we'll mention true facts in

our press conference?"

"Look, for heaven's sake alright, I don't know where Kathy is. If I knew where she was, I would have told the officers who visited on Sunday. I've not spoken to her since Thursday night, as I've said. I've not communicated with her by any other method." Greenwood suddenly went silent, when Grant thought that he was about to say something else.

"And at this precise moment in time, you have no idea if your wife is alive or dead?"

Greenwood just stared down at the tabletop and exhaled his breath loudly, as though he was a huffy teenager. After a few seconds he spoke. "No, I don't."

"And, forgive me for asking, but its extremely important. Do you want Kathy home?"

"I'm not bothered."

"But you hope that she's okay?"

"Well, yes, for God's sake." Greenwood slammed his hand down on the table. "Of course I hope she's okay. But she is never happier than when she is pissing people off. It's what makes her tick. So, there is a very good chance that she is *not* okay. Do you understand?"

Grant had returned to her kind, compassionate character role, and was nodding slowly.

"Now, if you told me that she'd had her head stamped on by a crazy, angry, overweight woman who had taken offence at Kathy's endless jibes and insults for the past ten years, it wouldn't come as a great shock." Greenwood was tapping his foot. The pace was quickening and Grant felt that some progress was finally being made here.

"Well, if that's the way you feel, why haven't you mentioned any of this?"

"Would you? If you were married to one of the biggest circus freaks in the land?"

Grant let a silence hang. Suddenly, it seemed that Greenwood wanted to talk. He was considering his next sentence, that foot tapping was in full flow.

"Every day of my life I get abuse and insults because of her. I've been spat at, kicked, my car tyres have been slashed. I even had a young girl punch me in the face when I was coming out of a shop in Camden. All her friends were laughing, and I went off in tears. This girl, she shouted 'pass that on to your fucking horrible cunt of a wife!'

Grant was listening intently, and nodding sympathetically. She seemed very genuine, and in many ways, despite Greenwood being a dickhead, she did feel for him. Grant could imagine how intimidating it must have been, and how embarrassing, being attacked like that. But despite the natural feelings of sympathy that Greenwood's story had sparked within her, Grant still felt that the man sitting before her was in some way involved in Kathy's disappearance.

"That sounds awful. Did you report it?"

"What, to the police? Are you joking me?"

"No."

"They wouldn't be interested in that. It's just part of the job of being Kathy's husband. I just have to try and keep out of the public eye as much as I can."

"Do you love her?"

Greenwood looked up, and exchanged eye contact with Grant. That question had come from nowhere, and it appeared to have confused the interviewee.

"That's a strange... I didn't know that you asked things like that..."

"Well, from what you've said, you don't really appear to be very concerned for her welfare. I just wondered if your marriage was..."

"Was *what*?"

"Valid."

Greenwood fake laughed, throwing his head back as he did so. It was a lame, embarrassing, pantomime cackle, and Grant wondered if he was about to revert back to the bizarre behaviour again. But no, he soon straightened up, and it looked as though he was really feeling sorry for himself. His eyes were becoming very moist.

"Valid! That's such a peculiar word to choose, but my God, it's very apt. No, Detective Grant, to be perfectly honest with you, my marriage is *not* valid. My marriage has not really been valid for the past ten years, maybe longer. Kathy has made me the last on her list! That's how I feel, I feel as though I'm the last on the list!"

Grant was beginning to wonder if Greenwood was mistaking this interview for a visit to his therapist, but she kept her gentle, sympathetic nods going.

"Don't get me wrong. It was great in the beginning, in the early days. She used to work at Radio One, she was the head of marketing and promotion. She was behind the scenes at some of the most famous events in the eighties and nineties. Live Aid, Comic Relief, The Brits. She was funny, happy, and she had thousands of friends. But then, one day out of the blue, Radio One decided to aim at a younger audience and Kathy lost her job. Suddenly, she went from being a really big part of the biggest radio station in Britain, to being flung out on her ear. They offered her a similar role at GLR, which she declined. It was like going from a starring role in a Hollywood blockbuster, to a walk-on part in Hollyoaks. That is how she describes it, anyway. That was in ninety-five. She's been horrible ever since that day. We *are* married, but it's only because neither of us can be bothered with moving out. I suppose it's more a case of *when* we get divorced rather than if."

"But surely, under those kind of circumstances, you must see that you need to help us as best you can. We need to eliminate you from our inquiry one hundred per cent, and you're not making that possible for us at the moment. You avoid answering questions, and then when you do answer, you say things that could potentially implicate you. I mean seriously, think about it. Kathy is missing, and you say that you don't like her and things like that. It isn't helping at all, is it?"

"No, I suppose not. But I'm not sure how I can be implicated in this when I have a witness who can confirm that I was at home three-hundred miles away from where Kathy disappeared. I also have CCTV footage that confirms this. How can I possibly be made to look guilty under those circumstances?"

"Nobody is saying that you are involved. But I'm trying to explain to you why it would make a lot more sense if you were trying your very hardest to help us."

"Okay, point taken. But I've still got a shit-storm coming from the press after you kept me in all night. There was no need for all this."

"To be fair Mr Greenwood, you could have talked like this yesterday, at the radio studio. We'd have been gone within half an hour."

"Okay, okay, I don't want to go over all that again now."

"Fine. Well, I want to know about any theories you have about where Kathy is, what's happened. Regardless of how irrelevant they might seem. We really need a leg-up right now, because looking for Kathy with absolutely no idea where she could be is an impossible task, and if she's in danger, it's absolutely crucial that you help us."

"And who do you plan to interview next?"

"We have a few people we want to talk to, including Kathy's manager, Sally King."

"Well, she's already been interviewed as well. You're just wasting your time, just going over old ground."

"Well, give me a few more names, a few people we've not interviewed yet."

"And then I can go?"

"Yes."

"Okay, well have you spoken to Greg Hughes? He was her toy boy. Works at Channel Five. She's been making life difficult for him recently. Then there's Phillip Young, the squeaky clean TV presenter. He's been having a bit of trouble with Kathy, she says she has some compromising pictures of him from years ago with rent-boys and cocaine. She teases him about it all the time. There's also a page three girl, God what's she called she's one of Kathy's regular sparring partners, Jo Abbott, that's it. She's well connected with a few gangs in Essex, and it's not beyond the realms of possibility that they could be involved."

"How do you know all this?"

"I'm married to Kathy Hopkirk. It's my life. Can I go now please?"

"Yes, come on."

Chapter 24

"Morning Andy." DCS Dixon had silently appeared in Miller's office.

"Jesus! I wish you wouldn't do that Sir!"

"Pardon?" His bizarrely good mood from the previous morning seemed to have dwindled, and the DCS looked more like his usually grumpy, stressed-out looking self.

"You, when you sneak up on me like that. It shits me up."

"Oh, I can't stop doing that Andy, that's police training from the old school. Sneak about and you catch people at it!"

"Yes, well, it's a fair cop, you've caught me at it! You've caught me wondering how the hell I can manage with Saunders and Grant down south. They've just had to let the husband go, ran out of time, nothing to charge him with, unless being a complete dick is something the CPS would rubber-stamp."

"Ah, so Jack Greenwood isn't our man?" Dixon raised his famous white eye-brows, and the gesture told Miller that in his bosses mind, Greenwood had already been sent down.

"Nah, nothing with any substance. He's got an excellent, bomb-proof alibi. Got to admit, we're struggling here Sir. It's a real mystery."

"Well, maybe I'm your saviour this morning then!" Dixon sat down, which suggested that the old boy was planning to stay for a while. Miller sat up in his chair and faced his DCS.

"Oh?" Miller tried to make it sound more enthusiastic than he actually felt. He seriously doubted that Dixon was likely to be his saviour any time soon. All Dixon ever did was create extra work. Never less work, it was always more.

"I've had the social media team scouring the

Kathy Hopkirk profile pages. Her Twitter is the main platform she uses, she's got more than four million followers on there, and over half a million Facebook fans. Well, anyway, the stats have just been put together with in-depth analysis. You'll get a bigger, more in-depth report in due-course. But I wanted to give you the heads up that the social media team have identified over six thousand instances of death threats against Kathy Hopkirk, made over the past three years."

"Fucking Norah! That's a lot of death threats!"

"Yes, quite. So, that's in the pipeline, its going to add a very dynamic and interesting angle to your enquiry, no doubt."

Miller exhaled loudly, ending with a raspberry. "Well, that's even more bullshit to empty on my carpet. Seriously Sir, who in their right mind would make a death-threat on Twitter, and then follow it through?"

"Well, a counter-argument would be who in their right mind goes around killing people?"

"Well, we don't know that Kathy's dead yet, do we?"

Dixon sensed that Miller was about to get moody, so he stood up and decided to get out of there before he was forced to become a sympathetic ear. "Well, just be on standby that a list of more than six thousand potential suspects will be with you in the next few hours!" Dixon smiled and mouthed "you're welcome" as he turned to leave.

*****

Miller was dismayed by the Social Media Team's report into instances of hate and threats against Kathy over the previous thirty-six months. There was an endless list of Twitter account names, with the date and time of the offensive communication, followed by the message in full. Miller felt depressed as he read through a random page of the pointless, nonsensical messages. "@KathyHK I read what you said about people from Birmingham I think you crossed the line . Ur dead meat bitch."

The messages on that first page were basically as idiotic and pointless as that. But Miller noticed an anomaly on one message. It was clear that the word "dead" was one of several which had been used to search out these messages. But in the north of England particularly, the word "dead" was often used instead of "really" to add emphasis. So, it was common for a northerner to say "God, I'm dead tired" or "You looked dead fit last night."

Miller noticed that one of Kathy's so called "death threats" was in fact just a bit of stupid banter.

"@KathyHK Your head has disappeared so far up your own arse that it's going to be dead easy for you to roll down the stairs now." That remark had been made by a user called @AndyRoss on 15th January 2015 at 2:17pm. There was no further information available. It didn't say anything about who Andy Ross was, or where he lived. There was no IP address for where the tweet had originated. This was completely pointless, and Miller wondered why Social had passed it on.

Opening Twitter, Miller realised that he could use the search bar to place keywords from @AndyRoss's tweet, in order to locate the Tweet himself – despite it being several years old. "Bingo!" said the DCI as the exact same Tweet that Social had reported appeared on the screen. It had been re-tweeted more than six hundred times by other users who'd found it amusing or inspirational, or whatever. After a couple of minutes digging around, Miller had discovered that Andy Ross was a radio DJ on Sheffield's Hallam FM. He was followed back by Kathy, and the two had several interactions over Twitter. Indeed, Kathy had replied to Andy's Tweet on the same date. It read, "Wait until I get my hands on you @AndyRoss – I'll break that big ugly nose of yours!"

Andy Ross had retweeted the reply, and

everybody lived happily ever after. Miller wrote on the list; Highly Unlikely Suspect. He blew out an exasperated breath when he thought of the prospect of going through six thousand of these inane, pointless interactions, in the unlikely hope of finding a person who genuinely did wish harm on Kathy.

Miller began to realise that this was no more than a banquet of bullshit, which had been placed on his desk. He stared at it, and tried to work out where he could send it to be refined. After a minute or two, he threw it in the bin.

*****

Beryl Butterworth was dedicating her entire Radio Manchester show to Kathy's disappearance for the second day. The previous day's programme had concentrated on a rather leftfield topic, people speaking nicely about the missing woman.

Today, Beryl was standing by her desire to promote a more positive message about Kathy Hopkirk, but her main focus centred around the fact that Jack Greenwood had spent the night in the police station, and furthermore, hadn't been released. Mainstream media was going crazy with speculation of why Jack was still in police custody. The difficulty for them was to report the facts, and leave the wild speculation to the viewers, readers and listeners at home.

"So as we have been hearing all morning," said Beryl Butterworth, "there is still no sighting of Kathy. And as things currently stand, Kathy's husband is still, to quote the official statement 'helping police with their enquiries' at Shepherd's Bush police station. It's turning out to be one hell of a mystery, and if I'm being honest, I really did think that all of this would have been resolved by now. But what are *your* thoughts on Kathy's disappearance? And what ideas have you got for how police could track her down. Get in touch with the studio, and if we think you don't sound too crazy, we'll talk to you on the air. Okay, here's a song by one of the loveliest people I've ever been lucky enough to meet, a true legend, who I still can't believe is sadly no longer with us. It's George Michael."

As soon as Beryl switched her microphone off, she turned the volume up on the studio TV, which was showing the BBC News channel. Something appeared to be happening, and the news reporter on screen was getting in a bit of a tizzy as the story suddenly began to have some fast moving developments.

Just after 10.30 am, Jack Greenwood was driven away at speed from Shepherd's Bush police station in an unmarked police car. The silver Audi estate was moving quickly, but not too fast for several press photographers, who managed to take snaps through the rear windows. Inside, leant forward and trying to cover his face with his hands, sat Jack Greenwood. He was out of jail, and not wearing handcuffs.

The Kathy story now had its next element, and the pictures were on TV screens within moments of the car leaving the police station.

"Well, now, we'll have to stop you there, George," said Beryl Butterworth into her microphone, "As we bring you some breaking news from London, and in the past few seconds, Jack Greenwood has been driven away from the police station where he has famously spent the night, since being arrested yesterday at the London FM studios. So, that would seem to spoil a lot of the theories that are banding around today, especially the ones on Twitter, which I can't repeat for legal reasons!"

This dramatic new development was just what the media people needed. It wasn't exactly the outcome that many had planned for, but none-the-less, it was good for them to have a new aspect to concentrate on for the time being.

But the time being was to be much shorter than

anybody could have anticipated. The story had a completely different headline by twelve noon. By the time that Beryl Butterworth's show was going off air, the Kathy story had a sensational new development.

Chapter 25

Just before noon on Tuesday, the mystery was solved. Kathy Hopkirk sent a Tweet from her Twitter account. It was a simple link, which opened up a video in Youtube.

"Hi, hello everyone. I'm sorry I've not been around for a few days but I've had a lot of thinking to do." Kathy Hopkirk was talking into a video camera. She looked relaxed, and quite happy, though slightly nervous. She had an unusually serious edge to her voice. This was an absolutely incredible end to the mystery of her disappearance.

"I've decided, after a great deal of thought and consideration, to retire from my job as the most hated person in Britain. It stops, right now. I've realised that my actions, my words, my thoughts, they all have consequences. I'm not perfect, yet I seem to try and portray myself as such to you, the public, while trying to infuriate you as I do so. But let me set the record straight right now, if you would kindly indulge me for a few more minutes before I sign off." Kathy looked sad, possibly a bit regretful as she looked straight down the lens of her camera. "I'm not brave, but I have said things that have offended many brave people, people who have gone to war, people who have overcome incredible challenges, people whose lives I could never be strong enough to live." Kathy leant over towards the camera, checking it was in focus, before leaning back. Her hands were trembling noticeably.

"I'm not somebody who eats a perfect diet, I'm just lucky that I have been born with a metabolism which prevents me from getting fat. However, these facts have never stopped me from upsetting and offending people who do have to watch their diets. I'm not religious, so in all honesty, I don't really qualify for an opinion on religious matters. In fact, for all the things I have said, on all the topics that I've caused offence, upset and outrage with, I am truly, truly sorry." Kathy stared down the lens, and it looked as though she was becoming tearful. This was a unique moment. Publicly, Kathy Hopkirk had never shown the slightest hint of human emotion before.

"So, I'm being honest. I'm filled, no, totally absorbed with hatred. Its not that I don't like seeing fat people stood at bus stops... it's the smile, the laugh, the happiness they have that upsets me. Its not fatness, its happiness that offends me. I'm not even bothered about religious fanatics. It's the sense of community and togetherness, and love that so many religious people share amongst one another that totally breaks my heart. I guess I'm jealous of it. I'm hateful of the Scottish people because I miss home, but nobody invites me back. I'm offensive to Americans because I haven't been accepted there. I'm, look, I'm just a mess. I've found a way to make a lot of money, by just being hateful. By just being downright nasty, and offensive and as unpleasant as possible, and it's made me incredibly rich. Human beings have an unbelievable appetite to hate a common enemy, but many of those people... you're not allowed to hate them anymore. You can only hate the person or thing that it's okay to hate, a person or thing that the media say it's okay to hate, like Honey G. I saw that as an opportunity, and I've made several millions out of it. But I've made my money, I'm done. Now, I'm finally confessing, I'm owning up, and I'm retiring. The Kathy Hopkirk show is over. Thanks for the opportunity guys, and please, I want you all to know, I'm not joking around here. This will be my last public appearance. I'm not going to be in the UK anymore, so my most passionate haters can have a fantastic party this evening, and I wish you all well. Thank you everybody."

With that, Kathy smiled sombrely, leant forward and turned off the camera.

Chapter 26

"Fuck me dead! It was all a load of shit about Kathy, she was taking the piss!!!!"

"Put the TV on, Kathy's turned up. It was a hoax!"

"Gutted for you mate, she isn't dead after all lol!"

Text messages, online alerts and phone calls were spreading the word as fast as the excited, giddy British public could pass it on to friends and relations who were not in front of televisions or i-pad screens. At times like these, everybody wanted to be the first to "break the news."

For those who were already watching the news update on TV, many were left with mixed emotions. They weren't entirely sure how to react to this unlikely outcome. It had been thought that every potential scenario had been catered for in all of the thousands of discussions and arguments that had taken place over the past forty eight hours. But now, here was Kathy with a conclusion that nobody had anticipated. For one final time, she had run rings around the Great British public, and had the last laugh. Kathy was retiring, and not only that, she'd wanted to ensure that the world's attention was firmly on her as she said her goodbyes. It was nothing short of genius, and even the most passionate haters had to smile at the incorrigible audacity of Kathy Hopkirk.

But those smiles quickly turned to anger, and irritation, as people began to realise that they had been part of the stunt themselves. They had personally invested their interest in the disappearance, and now, as they began to realise that Kathy had just been taking the piss all along, not only over the past few days, but since she had first appeared from nowhere a decade earlier. As the minutes wore on, and the trick became clearer, people got angrier. In homes and factories up and down Britain, similar conversations were taking place.

"It's not funny that! I can't believe someone would

deliberately do that! What a dick."

"I tell you what, I might be six foot three, and a bloke, but I'd still kick her down an escalator for that. Stupid bitch. Innit though?"

"You'd have to be sick in the head to try summat like that though wouldn't you though?"

Many British people decided to express their thoughts through Facebook status updates and tweets to their followers.

"To think I was starting to worry about the bastard! Rot in hell Kathy you total bitch!!!"

"Well, what a terrible thing to do. Honestly! Still, I'm glad she's okay… but only just!"

Kathy's video was the only topic of discussion. The public were expressing their views in the best ways they knew how to, and one or two lucky ones had managed to get through to BBC Radio Five Live, and were enjoying having the nation's airwaves to vent their frustration on.

"We're joined on line five by Simon in Sevenoaks. What are your thoughts on Kathy's incredible announcement Simon?"

"Yes, hi and thanks for putting me on the air. What I want to say is that I am absolutely disgusted by the behaviour of Kathy, and I would just like to know what the police are going to do about this complete and utter waste of time?"

"In what respect Simon?" The presenter sounded slightly confused.

"In the respect that we've had two police forces, in fact, two of the biggest police forces in the country out looking for this stupid little madam for the past two days! How many police hours have been wasted on this?"

"Well, that is a fair point Simon, but, well it wasn't Kathy who reported herself missing, it was her manager who was becoming worried about Kathy's welfare."

"I don't care who phoned up, I'm saying charge

her with wasting police time! Take all this money she's so delighted about, and give it to the police forces involved!"

"That might be a slightly hysterical reaction Simon!" the presenter was clearly amused by the caller's bizarre demands.

"And that's exactly what's wrong with this country! It's that kind of attitude that encourages this kind of nonsense!"

"Simon, for goodness sake man. Nobody is encouraging this kind of behaviour. I tell you what, following your logic, I think they should take your house off you for making ridiculous comments to the British radio listeners!"

"Well, I think you're a cunt."

The remarkable thing about this latest news announcement, was that nobody was actually bothered about what Kathy was saying. Nobody was coming out with comments of regret that Kathy had decided to call it a day. Not a single Tweet was sent out begging Kathy to reconsider her decision. As had been the case on Sunday, when the disappearance had first been announced – it wasn't about Kathy so much, it was about people voicing their opinions on Kathy. People just couldn't resist sharing their point of view.

There were a lot of people who were just hoping that this was true, and that this really was the last the British folk were going to see of Kathy Hopkirk.

Chapter 27

Miller was not amused by the news. As soon as he heard, he rang Saunders.

"Hi Sir, alright?"

"Hi Keith, I take it you've heard?"

"About Kathy? Yes. What's the plan?"

"The plan is get your arse back up the M6, and I'll take my flipping blood pressure tablets."

"Yes, I thought that would be the plan. Right away Sir. Grant's just in the police station finishing off her arrest notes. I'll go in and tell her it's all over and we'll head back. It'll be tomorrow by the time we're back in the office though."

Miller looked at his watch. "Shit, is that the time? Right, well, no worries, I'll tell the Met that they can have this shite back and we'll get you two back up here working on proper stuff!"

"No worries. I'll tell DC Grant that we're folding down the investigation."

"How's she been getting on?" asked Miller, sounding as though the question was an after-thought.

"Yes, very good. I'm very impressed. She did a really good job on the husband this morning. I couldn't get anywhere with him. So yes, good reports Sir."

"Did you both sleep okay?" Miller was laughing down the phone.

"That was a twattish thing to do by the way Sir!"

"Hey, don't blame me!"

"Don't worry, I'll get you back for that. Right, anyway, I'll go and grab Grant and we'll get ourselves sat in the traffic."

"Cheers. Right. See you tomoz then." Miller pressed the red button on his phone and ended the call. He looked at his e-mail folder on the laptop and tried to find his colleague in London's e-mail.

"Ah, there it is. DCI Paxman." Miller opened the

e-mail and pressed the reply button.

"Dear DCI Paxman,

In light of today's news regarding Kathy Hopkirk's reappearance, I am writing to inform you that I have stood my officers down from the enquiry, and I am formally handing over full responsibility for the case to be finalised and closed by yourselves in the Met Police Division.

Best

DCI Andy Miller"

"Right, that's a job done. Now to get back to proper crime stuff." Miller pulled out his LIVE file, and had a scan over which investigations his officers were currently overseeing. He wanted to curse Kathy Hopkirk for losing the SCIU department two officers for two entire days. Miller could have done without this when his live case-loads were relentless at the moment. As Miller continued to study his department's workload, he felt a presence in the room. He glanced up and saw his boss, DCS Dixon hovering by the door.

"Two visits in one day Sir? I'm truly blessed!"

"Bad time?" asked Dixon.

"I'm a bit pissed off to be honest Sir. This Kathy Hopkirk mis-per was a load of bollocks."

"Yes, I've just heard." Dixon wandered in and sat down facing Miller's desk.

"So I've lost a few days of real work time. Could have done without that to be honest!" Miller was still looking over his file as he spoke.

"Silly woman!"

"I know, she needs her head testing that one. But, anyway, it is what it is."

"I meant to mention earlier. That was an unfortunate incident with Saunders, wasn't it?" Dixon was finally rewarded with a glance from Miller.

"Oh you mean the paparazzi. Yes, he was pretty pissed off about that. It serves as a reminder to everyone though, you've got to keep your guard up at all times."

"It's just not like Saunders though, is it?"

"No. No, it's not. I'll have a word."

"Yes, well, I was going to have one with him myself. I'm sure there's a perfectly good explanation. It's just…"

"Its just it looks like the northern pillocks go down south and everything goes tits up?"

"Well, yes, it's a tad embarrassing."

"I'll have a word when he gets back."

"Thanks. And how is the new DC getting on?"

"Very well. She's fitting in very well, and Saunders had a lot of good praise for her. So, it's all very positive, thanks Sir."

"Good, good. She's a bonny young lass as well, isn't she?"

Miller looked up again, and laughed. "Kin 'ell Sir, that's a pretty creepy thing to say!"

"I know, but… well, you know. I bet Saunders likes her!"

"Yes, I bet he does. Right, well, anyway…"

"Yes, of course, I just didn't want this business with Saunders sweeping under the carpet."

"No, no, of course. I know the drill Sir. You have hundreds of amazing days of successful, productive work with brilliant results, and nobody says jack-shit. But if you make one little cock-up, its time for a chat."

"Well, you do put things in a funny way, Andy."

"No I don't Sir. I say things how they are." Miller stared hard at Dixon, prompting him to retaliate. But Dixon knew very well that a closed-mouth policy would save a lot of fuss.

"Just mention that I've mentioned it please. That's all. See you later."

Chapter 28

DI Saunders and DC Grant were sat on the motorway, in their unmarked CID police car, stuck in traffic. They were on the M25, trying to make their way out of the Greater London area.

"Couldn't live like this. Could you?"

"What in all this traffic you mean?" Grant looked bored, and a bit fed-up.

"Yeah. It's shit. I hate it me. Hate traffic."

"What time do you think we'll get back?"

"Well, this... plus four hours."

Grant checked her watch, it was half past two. "So in the best case scenario, if this traffic jam started moving now, we'd be back for about half six?"

"Ah, yes, say about seven-ish."

"Nice one, I might just get back in time for the pub quiz then. Starts at half eight, so a quick wash, quick change and out the door."

"Well, let's see how we go on first. It's four hours, after this."

"Yes, but come on Sir, we don't *have* to sit in this." Grant was smiling, and that funny, indescribable thing that kept happening to Saunders happened again. It was as though his heart was beating a bit harder. His belly flipped over and he could feel that he was blushing a bit. Trying to act cool when this kept happening was proving to be very difficult. He was grinning at Grant's lovely, cheeky, contagious smile.

"You mean?"

"Yes, you know exactly what I mean Sir!" Grant led forward and pressed the red 999 button on the dashboard. Suddenly, the under-cover police car began sounding a siren, and the front and rear blue lights hidden in the bodywork were flashing on and off. Saunders looked over his shoulder, then in front, checking that there was a pathway between all of the stationary vehicles.

A few seconds later, the Manchester detectives were negotiating through the traffic jam, as the parked cars all slowly moved over and created a gap which Saunders and Grant could inch their vehicle through.

"You're going to get me shot, you!" Saunders was laughing at this ridiculous situation, as all the cars up ahead were trying to make a gap for the emergency services to get through.

"Just get me to the quiz! That's all that matters Sir! Hey, I tell you what, why don't you come along?"

"What seriously?" Saunders was buzzing.

"Yeah, why not? As long as you're not thick, you'll be great!"

Saunders was trying to get the car across to the hard shoulder, so he could get his foot down and get the speed over 5 mph.

"Yeah, go on then, that'll be ace that. I've not been to a pub quiz for ages. Who else is in your team?"

"Well, you'll be the only bloke. So I hope you can handle yourself around lots of boisterous bitches!"

"How many?"

"Only three others. You'll be alright. Aw, are you coming then? Please!"

"Yeah, why not? Go on. Cheers."

Saunders had finally made it across to the hard-shoulder and was now in a position to press his foot against the accelerator. Within seconds, the unmarked police car was whooshing past the traffic jam, and Saunders was thinking of getting to the pub quiz, an opportunity to spend even more time with DC Grant. He had a massive smile on his face as he drove along the motorway's emergency lane, feeling pretty good. Saunders realised that he'd not felt this good for a long time, and the thought troubled him. In his private life, things always had a habit of turning to shit. But he had a very, very good feeling about his new colleague. That thing happened in his tummy again.

Chapter 29

The media frenzy was almost over. The press-pack which had quickly gathered outside Kathy Hopkirk's house on Sunday afternoon was now thinning and dwindling. There was no way that she was going to turn up at her house anytime soon, after announcing that she was finished with the media life for good. A few "glass-half-full" reporters stayed put, just in case, but most had headed off now, despatched to other stories or back to their offices and studios.

The debate was raging on across the British radio talk shows, about whether this was a real hoax, or a publicity stunt, or whether Kathy had actually, genuinely disappeared for real. Radio phone-ins were the ideal place to really vent some anger and frustration, and many people were waiting "on hold" to get on air, and express their thoughts about the whole affair.

Sky News had demoted the Kathy story to second in the headlines by five pm, and it was third by six. The energy that had surrounded the "what if" nature of Kathy's disappearance had now been replaced with a deep sense of anger and irritation. People were angry and irritated for various reasons, and as the newspaper website and Facebook comment boxes filled up once more with the odious thoughts of a duped British public, the editors and producers realised that this story had become too toxic to give any more airtime or column space to.

Suddenly, there wasn't very much of an appetite for this story, and the fact left a huge void in the news. There wasn't very much happening, so it was a very tricky situation to try and manoeuvre out of. But one newspaper had found the perfect angle, and while it was a God-send for the media outlets, it was likely to be a difficult situation for DI Keith Saunders and DC Helen Grant to wriggle out of. But the press care very little about little details like this, and as such, they had a great new story.

The London Evening Standard had been contacted by a London Tour Bus driver who had supplied CCTV footage of DI Saunders and DC Grant having fun, laughing and joking on a tour bus the previous evening, when they were supposed to have been in London looking for Kathy Hopkirk. For the London newspaper, this was a golden opportunity to take the piss out of northern coppers who had ventured onto their manor, especially as the same officer had provided press photographers with a photo of his investigation notes. The journalist who was excitedly writing the story was Googling Saunders, looking for any other errors that could be "revealed" in the story.

DI Saunders was on the M6 motorway, just north of Birmingham when the Evening Standard Online went live with their "exclusive" story, headlined; "IS THIS BRITAIN'S MOST USELESS DETECTIVE?"

Chapter 30

Saunders and Grant had been making good progress of the journey north. It was almost seven pm as the car approached Knutsford on the M6, but it looked quite doubtful that they'd make the pub quiz now, after half an hour of stop-start traffic just north of Birmingham. This had knocked their timings out, but none-the-less, they were in good spirits and enjoying a light-hearted chat and lots of banter all the way home. The pub quiz wasn't the be-all and end-all. Grant was planning to invite Saunders to have a drink with her anyway, if they missed the quiz.

Despite the long drive and the traffic problems, the mood in the car was good natured and fun. The radio was on, playing some good stuff and Saunders had been entertaining Grant with stories from his early days as a uniformed policeman, back when he'd been trying to attract the attention of the CID. He was sharing some of his slightly auspicious experiences, in a bid to show a more modest side to his professional image. Grant was hugely entertained by one particular story that Saunders recalled.

Saunders was just a young PC then, in the late 1990s. His beat was the Salford area, a tough place with plenty of crime and difficult social-issues at that time. A 999 call had come in, it was a man claiming that he'd been robbed in his own home in Little Hulton, and that the attacker was still in the house, reportedly having a toilet-rest. Saunders drove the Ford Escort "jam-butty" police car on blue lights and sirens, and arrived with his partner within minutes of the call. They were quickly let into a run-down, decrepit council house, and were faced with a very skinny, very angry man in his early thirties, wearing nothing but a pair of SPX shell-suit bottoms.

"I've bin robbed, I've bin robbed!" Saunders was doing a very amusing Salford-scally accent, which made Grant roar with laughter. Saunders continued explaining what he and his colleague were confronted with when they reached the grey pebble-dashed house.

"Calm down, and just tell us what's happened!" said Saunders to this crazy guy, who looked like he was struggling with some addiction or other.

"My dealer's stolen my fucking crack man!"

"Is he still here?"

"Nah man, is he fuck!" Saunders was really enjoying himself, doing the character voice for Grant's entertainment. "He's fucked off with my gear! I want him arresting, I want my fucking gear back!" The man was worked-up, shouting and sweating profusely. He was getting into a real state. Saunders and his partner were struggling to understand what the actual issue was.

"Right, just listen to me. Why has your drug-dealer stolen your drugs?"

"Because I haven't paid him."

"And how much do you owe him?"

"Forty quid."

"So if you had forty quid, would he bring it back?"

"Yeah, course he would, why?"

"What's he called, your dealer?"

"Tez Sanderson."

The name rang a bell, and Saunders hatched a plan, deciding to utilise this unbelievable opportunity to try and impress his colleagues in the CID. After all, that was the only place that he wanted to work in the police force. He hated the uniform job, chasing after the same yobs and dickheads night after night.

At this point in time, the local Detective Sergeant was a certain DS Andrew Miller. The young Saunders phoned Miller and explained the situation. The dealer was a man that Salford police had been after for a while, for various drugs offences, robbery and violence. Saunders told his partner to drive the police car off the estate, and then gave the complainant forty pounds, telling him to ring his dealer, and ask him to bring back the crack. The man was so desperate for his drugs, he got straight on the line. A couple of CID officers were at the scene within minutes and Tez Sanderson was locked up.

A year later, Saunders was offered a position in Miller's CID department, and it was probably all thanks to that lucky encounter with a desperate addict and a thick dealer.

Grant loved the story, and began making fun of the guy who had shopped his own dealer. "What became of the drug addict?" she asked.

"Oh, he got nicked. When he realised what was going on, he started kicking off so we took him in as well. It was for the best, or he'd have been murdered for being a grass. And I got my forty quid back too."

*****

Miller arrived home a little after seven pm. Clare was stood at the door with Leo by her side, Molly was inside, chilling on the settee with her i-pad.

"Hello my darling, what a lovely surprise to see you before bedtime!"

"Hello Daddy!" said Leo, waving. Clare was laughing, and whooping to herself. Andy could now look after the worst part of the day. Bedtime. The time of day that just when you thought you were done, the kids want to drink water. Try giving them water in the daytime and there's no chance. When you want them in bed, it's all they can think about.

"Hiya, nice to see you! I got finished on time today, I'd have been in a lot earlier but there's been a pretty bad smash on the East Lancs, its took me an hour to get here from Swinton you know."

Miller kissed his wife, and ruffled Leo's hair. "Do you want to carry Daddy's bag in for me?"

"Nah, its okay," said Leo, before laughing and

running into the house. Miller laughed at the cheek of his four-year-old, as he closed the front door and placed his bag down by the bottom of the stairs.

"Brew or beer?" asked Clare as she walked off towards the kitchen.

"Beer. Definitely a beer. Just one though! Cheers love."

"Hi Daddy!" said Molly, dropping her i-pad onto her lap. She threw her arms open for a hug.

"Hello gorgeous! How are you?"

"Tired!" Molly wobbled her head and blew a raspberry. Miller smiled and leant down to kiss Molly's forehead. He stood back up, groaning at the sudden pain in his back, before heading towards the kitchen. He grabbed the ice-cold bottle of lager off the worktop. Clare had taken the lid off.

"Cheers love. Oh, by the way, forgot to say, Keith has got himself well and truly obsessed with that new DC we've started."

"Is that the girl he's been on telly with, down in London."

"Yeah, that's her. Well, she's not a girl, she's nearly thirty. But yeah, he's bloody crazy over her."

"Aw, that's so cool. She's really pretty too. I hope she likes him back."

"She does apparently! That's what Jo Rudovsky was saying. She's a bit obsessed by him as well. So this is going to be absolutely brilliant, or absolutely awful. Only time will tell!"

"Aw, bless him. Aw that's so cute! Keith Saunders with a woman. God, she'll soon get sick of his twenty-four hour shifts!"

"Or his guffy farts!"

"Andy! Why do you always lower the tone?"

Miller didn't reply, his mind was suddenly elsewhere as his work phone began vibrating in his pocket. He grabbed it, but didn't recognise the number.

"DCI Miller" he said as he answered. He took a swig of lager from the bottle.

"Ah, Mr Miller, hello, my name is Ann Walker, I'm with the Daily Express."

"Oh, right." Miller was cold, and deliberately unwelcoming. These journalists were always getting his number from somewhere. Miller was about to read the rehearsed line about contacting the Manchester City Police Press-Office when Ann continued.

"It's about the misconduct story surrounding your Detective Inspector. I assume you're aware of it?"

Miller turned around and stared out of his side-window, trying to figure out what this lady was talking about. "No, what. Wait… I've not got a clue…"

"There's a story that has come out in the past hour about DI Saunders, apparently using Kathy Hopkirk's disappearance as an excuse to go on a jolly around London."

"What? Listen, that's such a load of nonsense…"

"It's the Evening Standard who broke the story. But, the thing is, its pretty quiet today, now that the Kathy mystery has been solved, so quite a few of us are using it too."

"Okay, thanks for letting me know Ann. I owe you one."

"No, wait, I…"

Miller hung up, then looked at his call logs. He blocked the number that had just called him, before pulling up the London newspaper's website on his phone. Sure enough, there it was, a full "exclusive" and "revealed" story about DI Saunders and DC Grant, accompanied by a really cheesy "exposed" photograph of the pair, looking as though they were on a fair-ride or something. As Miller began reading the report, Clare called him through to the living room, with a tone of voice that made him think that he wasn't going to like this.

The same story about Saunders and Grant was

making BREAKING NEWS on the Sky News channel.

*****

"Hi Sir, how's it going?" Saunders had Miller on speakerphone.

"Alright Keith, where are you?"

"Just approaching the best city in the world…" Saunders was waiting for a daft reply from Miller, such as "What Swansea?" or something similar. But Miller didn't make a joke, he sounded pretty tense. Grant picked up on the bad vibes too.

"Fucking hell Keith, I don't know what's going on, but you're all over the news! Some journalist has come up with a story, saying you and DC Grant have used this trip to London for a knees-up!"

"You what?" Saunders looked across at Grant. He wanted to laugh, assuming this was a wind-up.

"Yes, I know, don't worry – I know it's a load of shit. But listen, if any press contact you about it, just say nowt. Act like a crook and say no comment. In fact, don't answer your phone to anyone except me until I've sorted this out. Is Grant with you?"

"Yes Sir, sat right beside me."

"Hello Sir!" said Grant, her voice wobbled as she struggled to find the correct pitch for the seriousness of the situation.

"Hi, listen, did you hear what I just said?"

"Yes Sir, all of it."

"Okay, don't answer your phone or reply to any text messages until I give the all-clear. I need to nip this shit in the bud before it gets silly."

"Of course Sir, no problem."

"Right, Keith, talk me through your diary for yesterday, and tell me about any parts where you might have been photographed having a good time with DC Grant."

"Flipping heck Sir! Yesterday was a total pain in the arse from the minute we arrived in London. The only time me and Helen would have had a smile on our faces would have been long after we finished, we didn't even check into the hotel until nine pm. Oh, and on the way to get some tea we saw a daft tour bus so jumped on that for half-an-hour. Other than that, it was a totally frustrating, ball-breaking day with Kathy's bell-end husband.

"What time did you go to bed?"

"We got back to the hotel about eleven, after a couple of beers in the pub where we ate. This is totally ridiculous Sir. We both did about six hours over-time each yesterday."

"I know, don't worry about it. Go home, and stay put until I ring you. If there's any press outside your house, just smile and be polite but don't say nowt. Right?

"Right, Sir."

Chapter 31

"Kathy Hopkirk has turned up safely, but there are growing calls this evening for a senior detective in the case to be removed from duty." The BBC 9'0'clock news presenter looked really disappointed by Saunders' actions as he read the bulletin. "Let's cross live now to Catherine Appleby who has the details."

"Yes, thank you. This has been a very unexpected development in the Kathy Hopkirk story. The detective who was responsible for trying to find Kathy can be seen very clearly on video footage, relaxing and having fun with his colleague on a London Tour Bus. This came just hours after Detective Inspector Saunders, from Manchester Police, allowed press photographers to take pictures of his highly confidential notes relating to the disappearance." The reporter also looked really disappointed.

Saunders was sat in his apartment in Manchester city centre, trying to take this ridiculous story in. Grant was sat beside him. They both looked utterly confounded. Not a word was said between them as the BBC national news ran its lead story.

"Officers from the Met Police Force are tonight said to be angered by these images, particularly as they had been informed that Manchester police were taking over the investigation. However, Detective Inspector Saunders' superior, DCI Andrew Miller has been very quick to defend his staff, and try to rubbish the claims."

The screen changed from the head and shoulders shot of the dissatisfied looking reporter, and was replaced by a photograph of Miller, with a telephone graphic in the corner to tell viewers that this was a phone call. Miller sounded bemused, rather than annoyed.

"Well, course I'm rubbishing these claims. This is probably the most ridiculous thing I have ever heard in my entire life, and I've heard some bonkers stuff, let me tell you. DI Saunders is the most dedicated, hard-working and obsessive detective that I have ever known. I can confidently say that this news story is a complete and total joke!"

"With respect DCI Miller, it doesn't seem like a joke. In fact, it looks extremely serious, and there are growing calls for DI Saunders and DC Grant to lose their jobs over this scandal."

"Scandal? Are you being serious? Honestly, is this a prank call?"

"No DCI Miller, it is not a prank call. The public are extremely alarmed that a leading officer can treat a missing persons enquiry with such a flagrant display of disinterest." The reporter looked outraged now. Miller just laughed mockingly.

"Listen right, I've spoken to DI Saunders, and he's told me what happened. I'm happy with it, and that's all that matters."

"And can you tell the British tax-paying public what happened, as they surely have a right to know."

"Yes, no problem, if you don't mind finishing your report with a load of egg on your chin. Right, so, this bus ride took place at half past nine at night, some, what, fourteen hours after my colleagues clocked into work in Manchester. You can't dispute that, when this tour bus footage you've broadcast has the time in the corner. So they were off duty, and having a bit of a laugh after a long, hard, stressful day. That's it."

"Could they not have been working on something a little more productive?"

"Listen, you're obviously desperate to make something out of this, but it's a load of nonsense. They'd put in a fifteen hour shift. They'll not be paid any extra for that either. In those fifteen hours, they travelled to London, arrested a suspect, questioned him, and then locked him up for the night because he wasn't co-operating. They then found a hotel, and went out for some tea. That's dinner down your way isn't it? Sorry, they went out to dinner, oh and they went on the London tour bus as well, enjoying a bit of down-time. They got back to the hotel around eleven pm. As your own reporters showed this morning, live on air, they both entered Shepherd's Bush police station just before eight am and looked very smart and professional."

"DCI Miller, thank you for your…"

"No, wait, I just wanted to add… If I'm annoyed about anything to do with this, it's that DI Saunders and DC Grant failed to bring us back a souvenir. Like, one of those little red London Buses or a Beef-Eater ornament, or summat. Anything, you know, a memento, just a little bit of tat. But quite frankly, that doesn't surprise me because it's a well known fact that DI Saunders is as tight as a drum. I had to use a spanner to get fifty pence off him once! Honestly, I've never known anyone as mean as DI Saunders! I went round his house the other day and he was stripping wallpaper. I asked him if he was redecorating, and he said, no, I'm moving house." Miller laughed loudly, and the news reporter looked completely wrong footed. She stalled as she looked into the camera.

"Anyway, is that all? I want to ring my excellent colleagues and ask them about their trip. Oh aye and I'd better check they don't claim that bus fare on expenses, or you'll have another world-exclusive on your hands!"

"Well, DCI Miller, thank you for your time. It's quite clear that you're not concerned by the unprofessional conduct of your officers."

"You're welcome. Good luck with finding a proper story to report on."

"Back to you in the studio."

*****

Saunders was laughing, properly, right from the bottom of his gut. That cheeky TV interview had been just the tonic following the previous few, frustrating hours.

"Aw, what a legend! I can't believe DCI Miller can be so cheeky on the news! Bloody brilliant though, weren't he?"

Saunders had tears running down his cheeks, he'd been laughing so much. "God, I needed that!" He started laughing again, the comment about him being tight, on the main BBC news programme was just so surreal, it had really put everything into perspective. Saunders was grinning as he was typing a text to his boss.

"You legend. Cheers Sir!"

A few seconds later, a reply pinged on Saunders' phone.

"Ha! Doubt Dixon will be quite so pleased about it, but glad you liked it. And I meant every word, you tight sod!"

Saunders was beaming. He looked really chilled out and relaxed. Grant was looking at him, smiling.

"Right, well, I'd better get off."

This was awkward. Saunders didn't want Grant to go. Grant didn't actually want to go, Saunders could hear it loud and clear in her voice.

"Well, wait, what about... I bet you're starving aren't you? Do you fancy going out, grabbing something to eat. Subway might still be open."

Grant laughed loudly. "So *it is* true, about you being a tight get!"

"What?" Saunders had a fresh look on his face now. Confusion.

Chapter 32
THURSDAY

Saunders was already in the office when Miller arrived. That in itself wasn't particularly unusual, but the fact that he was sitting there watching Youtube on his computer screen certainly was.

"Morning!" shouted Miller. It had the desired effect and Saunders juddered visibly in his chair.

"Fuck sake Sir! Nearly had a frigging heart failure then!" the DI looked seriously pissed off.

"Soz. Dixon keeps doing it to me. Anyway, what are you doing there, watching telly?"

"It's Kathy Hopkirk's video, the one she announced her retirement on the other day. I'm not happy with it."

"Well, you must be the only one! Everyone else is absolutely buzzing that they won't be hearing from that daft cow again!" Miller had a confused look on his face.

"I'm just wondering if this investigation has been formally closed down yet?"

"I gave it back to the Met. It's their problem Keith, nowt to do with us."

"Yeah, Sir, I know. But I'm a bit worried about something."

"Okay, well I'll fire the computer up and check my e-mails. And I'll make a brew as well, not had one yet. Give me ten minutes."

"Cheers."

Saunders returned his attention to the computer screen, and started watching the short video from the beginning. He was staring obsessively at Kathy Hopkirk's face, her mouth, her body language as he listened carefully to her confession, and shock announcement about retiring from the media business.

Saunders was still studying the footage a quarter of an hour later when Miller appeared from his office and walked across to his DI's desk.

"God, we finally get shot of her, and you develop a fetish for her. What's going on?"

"That's what I'm trying to find out. Something very weird is going on. Have the Met formally closed it down?"

"I don't know yet. I had an e-mail that just politely confirmed that they were taking back the ownership of the case. I've not had anything since."

"Well, I'm not saying anything yet, because I'll never live it down if I'm wrong. But I need the Met to confirm they've formally closed the mis-per enquiry before I'll share this with you."

Miller understood what Saunders was talking about. To close down a live mis-per enquiry, a police officer has to formally identify the missing person, confirm that they are safe and well, before the case can be closed. Saunders was asking if Met officers had actually seen Kathy, in the flesh.

"I'll get in touch with them now and ask."

"Cheers Sir."

"Listen, you're not still pissed off with the press for that bullshit the other night are you?"

"Yes."

"Is that what this is about?"

"No Sir, trust me. Try and get the information for me please."

"Okay." Miller turned and headed back to his office. He lifted the phone from its cradle and checked the clock. It was just before eight. He wondered whether his colleague in London would still be in the office as he was working the night-shift. Miller found the number on an e-mail and dialled. It was picked up after a couple of rings.

"Paxman."

"Ah, DCI Paxman, it's DCI Miller up in Manchester."

"Oh, what's wrong?"

"It's about Kathy Hopkirk. Have your guys spoken to her yet?"

There was a pause, and then a hefty gust of air.

"Just a sec DCI Miller, I thought that you had passed this back our way?"

"Well, I have. But it's a pretty reasonable question. What's the issue?"

"It's a confidential matter."

"It's not. You can just say yes or no. It's as simple as that."

There was a pause, and then another gust of air. "No, we've not actually identified where she is. There has been no formal contact with her, all we know is that she put the video online on Tuesday dinnertime."

"So is somebody looking into that?"

"Well, I assume so, but it's slipped down the to-do list at the moment."

"Okay. Well, thanks, and if you can just drop me an e-mail or give me a call when it's formally closed, I'll knock it off my to-check list."

Miller put the phone down and huffed. He wasn't quite sure why there was such a tension between the two DCI's. It had all been pleasant and professional when Paxman was offloading it onto Miller's desk. It seemed that Paxman was spitting his dummy out now that it was back on his desk.

"Knob head." Said Miller under his breath. He noticed that Grant was in the office now, looking at whatever Saunders was looking at. Rudovsky was just arriving too, noisily.

"God, get a fucking room you two!" She said extremely loudly.

"Jo!" said Saunders, blushing.

"Just saying!" said Jo, laughing. She started unzipping her jacket and smiled. Grant was blushing as well now.

"Jo, come off it, don't be a dick."

"Ooh! Get you! The worst detective in Britain is calling *me* a dick!"

"Jo, shut your gob!" Miller was raising his voice just one volume notch enough to let everyone know that he wasn't in the mood for any daft banter this morning.

"DI Saunders, the answer from the Met is no. Nobody has spoken to her. All they've got is that same Youtube video you've got."

"Well they can't close the mis-per on the strength of that."

"I know. And he's not too happy that I'm sniffing about it now. He's got a right mard-arse on him. But anyway, now you'd better tell me why you want to know."

"Right. Okay. So, here, look at this picture of Kathy walking out of The Midland last Thursday night. Now, we've still not had a positive sighting of her anywhere until this video popped up on Tuesday dinnertime."

Miller, Rudovsky and Grant were nodding, listening intently. "Now then, I've got three stills of Kathy walking out of The Midland. Look at the pictures, and watch the video."

Saunders pressed play and Kathy Hopkirk's voice started playing through the speakers. Rudovsky was studying the pictures, and her eyes were flicking up at the video on the screen. Saunders paused the video after twenty or so seconds had passed.

"Anyone?" he asked. All three of his colleagues shrugged.

"Come on guys. Look." Saunders pointed at the freeze-frame video clip on the screen. "Her hair is shorter in The Midland, than it is on the video. How can her hair grow two or three inches in four days? Can't be done."

"Bloody hell. No way!" Jo Rudovsky looked impressed by Saunders' observation and sat down beside her DI.

"Now, if you want a second opinion, watch this." Saunders grabbed the computer mouse and opened the BBC I-player app. He had a clip paused. "This was last Tuesday morning on BBC Breakfast. She was on there, flogging her new book. This was two days before she went missing. Just concentrate on that hair length, focus on her neck and shoulder area. Use this big mole or whatever it is on her neck as a marker." Saunders clicked the play button on the screen's video-player. Suddenly, the sound of Kathy Hopkirk's voice filled the SCIU office.

The detectives watched for a few seconds.

"Yeah, definitely." Said Miller, nodding.

"There's no doubt about it... it's a good two, maybe three inches longer than on that other video. It's as clear as the nose on her face." Rudovsky needed no further evidence.

Grant stood by, nodding and agreeing with the rest of the team.

"So here, I have produced a print-out of Kathy's head and shoulders from this BBC broadcast last Tuesday." Saunders put the A4 picture on his desk. "And here, I've printed a picture at a similar angle, from Kathy's Youtube video." Now that both pictures were side-by-side, the evidence was undeniable. "Now, I've been looking into this a bit deeper. A woman's hair grows on average four inches per year, so that's one inch every calendar quarter. It's roughly a quarter of an inch a month... which is... God I'm shit at maths... it's about a tenth of an inch a week. Bottom line is this; that video where Kathy is resigning from working in the media was made at least six months ago."

Chapter 33

DCI Miller decided that the media's behaviour regarding Saunders and Grant's tour-bus shenanigans had created the perfect circumstances to rub the media's collective face in this. He'd even written in the press invitation, that the press conference would be presented by "Britain's Worst Detective," which amused him greatly. He deleted that bit just before he sent it, but he was still in a silly mood as he headed out of his office.

"Tell you what would be funny!" said Miller, laughing to himself as he strode across the SCIU office floor heading to Saunders desk.

"What's that Sir?"

"If we organise the press to assemble at Blackpool Pleasure Beach, and you enter the press conference after just getting off the Big One!"

The office erupted in laughter. Saunders wasn't that impressed though. He'd been pretty hurt by the story in the papers, and he thought it was unforgivable that the press could just print and report that kind of nonsense without any foundation at all.

"Too soon?" asked Miller, grinning. Saunders nodded sombrely. "Well, don't worry, you can take the piss right out of them with this discovery you've made. He who laughs last…"

"Laughs loudest!" shouted Rudovsky with great enthusiasm.

"You can't make an omelette without breaking a few eggs!" suggested Bill Chapman, enjoying this familiar office banter.

"Never look a gift horse in the mouth!" offered Rudovsky, grinning widely at her contribution.

"Hope for the best, but prepare for the worst!" laughed Saunders, finally snapping out of his grumpy mood. DC Grant just stood there, looking a little confused.

"Oh, we need to get a book of English Proverbs for

DC Grant! She looks a bit lost."

"Here, she can have mine," said Chapman, pulling his tatty book out of his drawer. "I know them all off by heart." Chapman stood up and walked across to Grant's desk. "Here you go love. Birds of a feather flock together." There was another big laugh, and Saunders realised that this silly conversation had really relaxed him ahead of the press conference.

*****

"Thanks everyone for coming. Well, considering your terrible behaviour the other day, I'm sure you'd all like to apologise to my colleague DI Saunders, before we continue?" Miller looked out across the Manchester City Police Media Centre, at a sea of bemused looking faces. There was an awkward silence.

"Well, I'll tell you now, we're not going to start this press conference until you do." Miller was smiling sarcastically at the uncomfortable people before him. He folded his arms and began his battle of the wits.

"Sorry," said one reporter, quietly.

"Yes, sorry DI Saunders!" said another. It wasn't a very convincing performance.

"Sorry Sir! Even though we didn't even cover the story!" said one stronger, more confident voice from within the pack. It attracted some mirth amongst the press representatives.

"No, that's very poor. It lacks conviction. I'll tell you what guys. We've got a major announcement about the Kathy Hopkirk case, stuff that's going straight on your front pages and number one on your top of the hour stories. But I'm not starting this press conference until my colleague gets a proper, heartfelt apology for being stitched up by all you lot." Miller was messing with his phone as he spoke. "Remember when you were little kids at school and you had to say good morning to the teacher in assembly? Well after three, I want you all to say sorry Detective Inspector Saunders. Okay?" There was another judder of awkwardness swelling from within the group. This was about as cringey as it got, and Miller was taking enormous delight from it. Saunders was sitting beside his boss, looking extremely embarrassed by the whole carry on, but enjoying his moment none-the-less.

Miller held his phone in front of him and clicked the video camera button as he counted the media folk down.

"Sorry Detective Inspector Saunders!" came a great, chorus of embarrassed voices. Miller stopped recording, and looked absolutely delighted with the resulting apology.

"Do you accept their apology?" Miller looked across at Saunders. He was determined to take the piss out of the press, just as blatantly as they had attempted to with Saunders. The DI nodded, and smiled, and looked a bit ashamed by the whole performance.

"Right, okay, thank you. But for the record, my colleague, DI Saunders is the most gifted detective in this city, bar none. He is the most committed, hard working and conscientious detective in the business. I know the press are famous for always getting it wrong – but I'll tell you, you couldn't have got it more wrong in this particular case. There are plenty of crap, lazy coppers out there that you could be exposing, so next time, go after them, and leave this absolute superstar detective alone. Right, end of lecture." Miller was grinning, and he felt that he'd won the war. Everybody in the room was just pleased that he'd finally shut the fuck up. He stepped down from the small stage and left DI Saunders alone on the tiny stage, sitting in front of a gigantic police emblem as his back-drop.

"Hello everyone, thanks for that. Okay, we'll go live in fifteen seconds if you're transmitting or recording, you need to get your fingers out. Ten seconds." Saunders checked over his notes, before looking up and choosing the Sky News camera to focus on.

"Good afternoon. My name is Detective Inspector Keith Saunders, from Manchester's Serious Crimes Investigation Unit. I'm here today because I wish to make a fresh appeal for information surrounding the disappearance of Kathy Hopkirk."

This announcement didn't make much of an impact on the press employees. They assumed that Saunders was just looking for info that would help to tie a few loose-ends up. But his next sentence would certainly stir things up in the Media Centre.

"I have discovered a serious concern regarding the video which Kathy Hopkirk supposedly published on Tuesday lunchtime, and I would like to share this concern with you all, and then re-launch our appeal to speak to anybody who has seen, or heard from Kathy Hopkirk at any time since last Thursday evening, when she left The Midland in Manchester city centre."

That was it, that was enough to fire up the media-storm. There was a sudden burst of energy from the group of one hundred reporters. A barrage of inaudible questions, gasps, and excited comments filled the room. Saunders just stared down at his paperwork until the members of the press calmed themselves down.

"I'll take questions at the end, alright?"

The press staff were quiet now, desperate to hear the rest of this announcement.

"This afternoon, Kathy Hopkirk's husband Jack Greenwood has been taken into police custody by our colleagues in London, and we are currently organising a joint-investigation with the Metropolitan Police to establish exactly what has happened to Kathy."

Again, this news was met with the fervent excitement of the reporters, journalists and technicians who filled the room.

"At this stage, our investigation centres around two key facts. Fact one is that Kathy Hopkirk has not been formally interviewed by police. Until such time as a police officer has identified a missing person, and found them to be fit and well and in a place of safety, we cannot close a missing persons enquiry down. The second fact is slightly more concerning. On Tuesday lunchtime, shortly after we released Kathy's husband from our custody, a video appeared online, supposedly uploaded by Kathy Hopkirk. We now know that this video was recorded at least six months ago." There was another burst of noise as the media crews realised just how monumental this announcement was. The Kathy Hopkirk disappearance had never been resolved, and now it was even more suspicious than ever before. Saunders allowed the excitable noise to subside once again, before continuing.

"By examining Kathy's hair length on Thursday evening from CCTV footage gathered at the Midland Hotel, and from a television appearance last Tuesday morning, I have discovered that if the video in which Kathy claims that she is safe and well, and retiring from show-business is legitimate and a trustworthy piece of evidence... then it means that Kathy's hair has grown three inches within one week."

Saunders held up the photographs. Several members of the press could be heard to gasp. This case had just taken a bizarre, unbelievable twist.

Miller was sitting on a chair, close to the TV crews at the front of the stage. "Not bad for Britain's worst detective!" he shouted, loud enough to be broadcast on Sky, BBC and CNN news channels. "None of you spotted that. Did ya not?"

Saunders rounded up the rest of the press conference, reiterating the appeal for any sightings of Kathy to be called in. Finally, Saunders kept his word and invited questions from the press.

"Kelly Fisher, Granada Reports, isn't there any other CCTV footage of Kathy after leaving The Midland?"

"Hi Kelly, no, well, I mean, we *were* making

progress on this, but then the operation was halted completely on Tuesday lunchtime, as we all assumed that the case was closed. We will of course pick those enquiries up again now, but it means we've lost a few days, and if there is forensic evidence to be gathered, that's been a really unhelpful delay."

"How can a city centre the size of Manchester not be able to track a single person down?"

"Well, it was night time, and Kathy was wearing a very neutral coloured outfit. It was a black jacket, black pants, grey handbag. I'm sorry to say but there are literally thousands of women walking around in very similar clothes, and that's what has caused a lot of difficulty on this investigation. It's almost like looking for one silver car on Motorway cameras, when most of the cars are silver. That is the best way to describe it I'm afraid. One CCTV operator told me that it was as though Kathy just upped and vanished from the Metrolink stop. She was seen there on CCTV, and then a tram arrived, obscured the CCTV footage, and then about ninety seconds later, when the tram left, she was no longer stood there. There was no credit card payment made by Kathy, so she didn't buy a tram ticket with her card. She could have paid cash, but she didn't do that before the tram arrived. So, we have to start our enquiries once again, at Saint Peter's Square tram stop."

"It's a bit embarrassing all this, isn't it?" shouted one journalist. The remark seemed to attract some agreement from others in the Media Centre.

"It wouldn't be appropriate for me to comment on that." Saunders looked down at his paper work, satisfied that from his response, every member of the press knew that Saunders agreed, and that he was laying the blame squarely at the feet of the Met officers who hadn't wiped their bum with this one.

"You must be frustrated though!" shouted another correspondent.

Saunders nodded. "Yes, it is frustrating, but on a more positive note, we now have the video, which has been put online to wrong-foot us. So, with this new piece of evidence, the search for Kathy's whereabouts just got much more interesting. Before I stepped in here I was waiting for Youtube to identify the location where the video originated from. I'm encouraged that we know of the address, and that we have the person that we believe responsible for publishing that video in police custody. My over-riding concern now is to find Kathy, and over and above that, I want to find her safe, and well. Thanks a lot everyone." Saunders stood and headed quickly out of the Media Centre, with questions still being shouted at his back.

"Has Greenwood been charged with anything?"

"Where do you think Kathy is?"

"Are Manchester Police taking sole responsibility for this case now?"

Saunders disappeared behind the double-doors, walking with a meaningful stride which left no doubt in anybody's mind that he was in a hurry to get on with his work.

Chapter 39

"Well, that was... I'm lost for words. I can only say, that was an absolutely startling press conference from Manchester." Sky News' afternoon presenter Sue Bentley looked visibly rocked by the revelations which Saunders had just read out, and those candidly truthful answers which he had given to the questions posed. It was literally unbelievable.

This news was even more earth-shatteringly sensational than the original story, which had broken four days earlier, on Sunday. It was Thursday now, so give-or-take a few hours, it was almost an entire week since Kathy had left The Midland, and hadn't been seen nor heard of since.

"Well let's cross live now to our North of England correspondent Paul Mitchell who is still in the press office there, Paul, what the heck is going on?"

"Yes, absolutely Sue – that is what every single person inside this room is wondering!"

"And everybody here, at Sky Centre, and everybody else out there in the UK. This is just unbelievable!"

"Definitely." Paul was just nodding into the camera. He had no idea what to say, and it seemed that like Sue, he was also completely bowled-over by these sensational developments. After a couple of seconds of silence, Paul panicked and decided to ad-lib for a moment, sure that Sue would be getting all kinds of information fed into her earpiece, and could use a little breathing space.

"Not one of us had any idea what today's press conference was about, until we arrived here. Well I can honestly say Sue, that you could hear a pin drop in here, as all of the members of the press tried to get an understanding of what developments had been made in the search for Kathy Hopkins, a search that we were all under the impression, had ended two days ago."

*****

Pat and Joan, two work-mates from the McVities biscuit factory in Stockport, were sat in the familiar rush-hour traffic jam on Wellington Road, listening to the radio.

"I hate working there. I just smell of ginger all the time. You know what, I'd leave, but I knead the dough."

Pat groaned at the familiar joke. "I'm after a new job. I fancy becoming a mirror cleaner you know."

"A mirror cleaner?"

"Aw yeah, I could really see myself doing that."

The workmates laughed at Pat's daft joke.

Pat turned the radio up as the news headlines came on. They sat in silence whilst the newsreader excitedly, breathlessly announced the big news regarding Kathy.

"Wait a minute, summat just doesn't add up here with all this. It's dodgy as anything!" Pat turned the radio off.

"God, that is weird though isn't it? They thought she were safe and now they're saying it was all just a lie. God, what do you think must have happened to her Pat?"

"Well it sounds to me like her husband has killed her, and well, this video, he must have made her record it for a laugh, or a prank or summat?"

"Yes, I bet you're right. I bet he's tricked her into doing it, saying summat like, let's pretend you've gone missing, and we'll see what the public make of it. But he's actually done it for real. Fucking psycho mate! Absolute fucking psycho!"

The traffic finally started moving, Pat put her foot down as she turned off the main road and onto Broadstone Road towards the estate where she and Joan lived opposite one another in Reddish.

"He looks the sort though, doesn't he?"

"He does, proper wrong 'un that Jack Greenwood, I've always said it. He makes my skin crawl. He used to present Top of the Pops as well didn't he, back in the day? I bet he was in on all that what Jimmy Savile was getting up-to. They reckon Savile murdered a few kids as well you know."

Patricia started indicating, and slowed the car down. She parked on double-yellow lines.

"Right, I just need to bob in Bargain Booze a minute, if you see the traffic warden press the horn loads of times."

"No worries. What you getting?"

"I'm gonna watch Sky News with a bottle of plonk. I'm gonna ring myself a curry for tea and I'll give the kids money to piss off out for their tea. Heaven. See-you in a minute.

*****

Behind the paint-faded front-door of a small, run-down looking terraced house in the Heybrook district of Rochdale, this latest news update was causing a blazing row.

"Nazir, you're going to have to tell."

"I cannot Sadia! I am in deep trouble already. It has been too long, and now I will be implicated in this. I must never speak of this again. AND YOU MUST NEVER!" Nazir was towering over his wife of twenty-six years. His body language was intended to scare his wife, but it didn't work. Sadia was more terrified by the prospect of her husband facing prison, than she was of a slap for back-chatting.

"You're no good to us in jail Nazir! If you won't tell, I WILL!"

Nazir Sardar was a private-hire driver. The previous week, he had been called into the office by the boss, Nazir's cousin. Based on how much trust existed between the two men, Nazir was to be offered an excellent opportunity. He was asked to pick up a fare from

Manchester, and take the passenger to a rural address close to Ashton-Under-Lyne. It was explained to Nazir that there would be a fee of two hundred and fifty pounds for the fare. However, this was an extremely sensitive matter, and it was to remain top-secret no matter what. That was why such an impressive sum of money was involved.

However, Nazir had let himself down. On Sunday, when it had been announced on the news that the person he had picked up, and had driven to the drop-off point had been reported missing, Nazir began to realise that he was in trouble. He needed to talk to somebody, needed to share that after dropping a passenger off at her destination, she had not been seen or heard of since.

Whether it was panic, or shock, he wasn't sure. But Nazir confessed all to his wife. He told her of the arrangement, where he took the passenger, and how it was all to remain a top secret. Nazir and Sadia talked it through, and decided to sleep on it.

The following day, Monday morning, they were both nervous-wrecks, but decided to wait and see what happened. "They will find your car on CCTV Nazir. You can't hide!" Sadia had pleaded with him. They agreed to sleep on it once again, though to be honest, neither of them slept very much at all, due to the strain that they were both feeling. It was a long, stressful, panic-stricken night.

But then, on Tuesday, when it was announced that Kathy had posted her video on Youtube, everything was okay. Panic over. Thank heavens that the couple had not spoken to police, they'd considered. Nazir had done a few of these dodgy fares before, usually it was young girls being moved around from one location to another. Rochdale to Burnley runs were the most common, but never before had the money involved been so handsome.

The girls that he had moved around were usually teens, from some Eastern European country or other. There was always a menacing looking man in the car on these journeys too. Nazir never asked questions, he just did as he was asked, and accepted the money afterwards. It wasn't any of his business, and he preferred for things to remain that way.

This trip had been very different though. For a start, Nazir recognised the lady, but he couldn't remember why he knew her. That small detail had soon been explained though, when the photographs were all over the news programmes, the press and the internet a few days later.

It had been such a massive relief on Tuesday, with the story ending the way that it had. Now, the feeling of terror and paranoia was back, and it was worse than ever. Sadia just wanted her husband to wake-up to the seriousness of his position, and call the police.

"No! I won't do it! And neither will you Sadia Sardar! If you disobey your husband I will fucking break your back and put your body in a wheely-bin, and then I will push it into the river. Be warned!"

But Sadia would not be swayed. She was going to tell the police about this, the first chance she got. She knew that Nazir would go out soon, to do a few more hours in his private-hire car. He would be out at least two or three hours, taking the drunks home from the pubs. Although she promised her husband that his secret was safe with her, Sadia could not wait to release this burden from herself.

Chapter 35

It was quite busy. Thursdays were always a good night for taxi drivers. The blokes play pool on Thursday in the north, a very old tradition dating back to the days when working men were handed their wages in a little brown envelope on Thursday afternoons. Traditionally, the mill-workers, miners, steel-workers et-al would tip-up the wife's house-keeping, put the bill money in the bill-jar and then go off and have a few pints and a game of billiards with the lads with what little bit of cash was left. It was the highlight of the working week. Pool night still happens to this day, and is one of very few traditions that remain from a time when the industrial north was the powerhouse of the world.

Pool night also results in a lot of taxi work, taking the "away" teams to pubs in other districts in their league. There was also plenty of work afterwards, for the return journeys. On top of all this, there were usually plenty of men that had enjoyed one or two too many, and they required a cab to get home. It could mean rich-pickings for taxi drivers.

It was just after nine, and pretty quiet. This was the lull between taking teams to pubs, and picking them up again later. Nazir Sardar was on duty, parked up at the taxi-rank in Rochdale town centre, waiting for a fare. His window was down and he was smoking a cigarette whilst looking at something on his phone, when he caught sight of a police car pulling up alongside his.

"Shit. Something is happening!" he said to himself as he saw that the police car had been parked in a way that blocked him in. He threw his cigarette out of the window.

"Hello Sir, can you give me the keys for your vehicle please?" said a young PC as he reached Nazir's window. He looked like a friend of one of his own boys. Nazir was stunned.

"What's going on?" he pleaded. He looked scared.

The PC leant in and took Nazir's car-key out of the ignition.

"Are you Nazir Sardar?"

"Yes Sir, I am!"

"Sir, I am arresting you on suspicion of perverting the course of justice..." The PC looked pleased with how easy this arrest had been. The call had only come over the radio two or three minutes earlier. As the officer was on patrol in the town centre, he decided to drive past the taxi-rank, just to see. Bingo. It had been a nice easy one, the taxi driver looked as though he was about to break-down in tears.

"What am I done for?" asked Nazir, his voice was faltering as he spoke, the emotion and fear was taking over.

"No idea mate. All I know is what I said, perverting the course of justice. Come on, jump out of the car and let's get you down to the station."

"But I am not a pervert officer! Not at all."

"Come on. Let's lock your car up!"

"But wait, I'll get a ticket if I leave my car here."

"Well to be fair mate, that's the least of your worries at this moment in time! Come on."

*****

"Right, I don't have any time for bullshit Nazir. I want straight-forward answers to my questions. You can make this easier for yourself, you might even get away without a charge if you answer my questions. If you don't play ball, you're going to be living in Strangeways prison for the next fifteen years. Do you understand me?" Saunders was being extremely harsh towards the taxi-driver, who looked small and scared as he huddled over the interview room table at Rochdale police station. Nazir was nodding.

"You need to speak, for the tape."

"Yes, yes Sir, I understand."

"Okay, is this a photograph of your taxi?"

"Yes."

"And does your taxi have a false number-plate on it in this photograph?" Saunders presented another picture. He placed it in front of Nazir.

"Yes Sir."

"Can you please tell me why you had a false plate on your taxi?"

"I stick it on sometimes, it's just in case I go through speed camera."

"Well when my colleague arrested you a few hours ago in Rochdale town centre, those plates weren't on your vehicle."

"No, that's right, that's what I mean, I took them off."

Saunders exhaled loudly and shook his head. He wasn't impressed. "Right, listen to me Mr Sardar. I just told you not to bullshit me, and you stand the better chance of avoiding prison."

Nazir was nodding manically.

"Why did you put the false plates on?"

"I have them for... sometimes, I am asked to do jobs that are... well, they are a bit..."

"Dodgy?"

"Yes, yes, dodgy."

"So let me show you this photo. Is this your car?"

"Yes."

"This photo was taken on CCTV in Manchester city centre last Thursday night. With your dodgy plates on."

"Yes Sir, I am truthful."

"And this photo here. It's your car, in the city centre with a female passenger. We believe that passenger to be Kathy Hopkirk. Is this the case?"

"Yes Sir. I confess all. This is her, but I know nothing about her disappearance. I just pick her up, and drop her off. Nothing more."

"Well that presents two vital questions Mr Sardar. The first one is why were you even in Manchester city centre picking up a fare when your private-hire license is Rochdale. And it also makes me wonder why you had fake number plates stuck over your vehicle's real plates."

"I can explain all. I was asked the pick up the lady. I was told I had to make my car invisible to the cameras."

"Is this something you are asked to do often?"

"Sometimes I do. Sometimes I do long journey jobs and I have to put the plates on. The man who pay me, he insists on this. I do as I am told."

"And the man who told you to pick up Kathy Hopkirk told you to put the plates on?"

"Yes, it was part of the deal."

"Where did you drop Kathy Hopkirk off?"

"In Ashton, it was countryside near Ashton and Mossley. I was told it was a secret business meeting. I was paid a very good fee. I was happy Sir, very happy. But then, I see on Sunday that my passenger was on the television and she was missing. I have been scared about this. I was going to speak to police about this. But then, they said everything was okay, that the lady turned up so I felt relief. You must believe me."

"So you dropped her off in Ashton?"

"Yes, well, it was Mossley really. It was in the country, a place called Hartshead Pike. I drove there, as far as I could get along the track. And then the lady, Kathy, she thanked me, gave me a twenty pound note and got out. And that was all I know. I went straight away."

"Who organised this fare?"

"Sorry Sir, I cannot remember…"

"Mr Sardar, who told you to put your dodgy plates on, and pick this woman up in Manchester city centre?"

"I must not confess to this, I will be in great danger."

"Mr Sardar, calm down, and listen to me. Whoever organised this fare has information that we need urgently. If you do not give me this information right now, then you will take all of the blame, and all of the responsibility for this crime. I would advise you to tell me, right now, who organised this fare?" Saunders was not messing, he had his most intimidating stare drilling into Nazir's eyes.

"Okay, okay, it was my boss man, my cousin. He owns the taxi company. He trust me not to mess up. He's going to make trouble for me now."

"Don't worry about that. What's he called, your cousin?"

"Shamim Sardar."

"And what's his taxi firm called?"

"Central Cars."

Saunders stood, and went to leave the interview room, but Nazir continued to speak. "But he has gone away, very suddenly. He has gone home to Bangladesh."

Chapter 36

Suddenly, things were starting to happen, and Miller couldn't be happier, despite the fact that it was gone 11pm. He was at home, on the phone, orchestrating the operation now that this new information had come to light. The DCI was speaking quietly in his study, because the twins were asleep in the next room. He was talking to Saunders, who was at Rochdale police station.

"Right, we need his taxi bringing in for a full forensic search, I mean inside and out."

"That's already in progress Sir, his taxi is still at the rank in Rochdale town centre. We're waiting for a lorry to take it to CSI."

"This taxi driver's car... has he got a dash-cam in it?"

"Don't know."

"Well find out, if it has, see if we can pull that out before it goes down to CSI. You never know, Kathy's journey might still be in the memory."

"No worries, I'm on that now." Saunders sounded enthusiastic, despite the fact that he should have gone home hours earlier.

"As soon as those phone numbers come back, e-mail them across to me please. I'll get on to Tameside police and request an exclusion zone around the Hartshead Pike area, and we'll get a crime scene search going at first light. If anything else comes in, let me know."

"No probs Sir. What am I doing with the taxi driver?"

"Bang him up for the night. It might be enough to make him remember something else."

"Are you sure? He's been an absolute star, he's answered everything."

"Well why don't you just tell him it's for his own protection."

"Are you sure, Sir?"

"Yes, of course I'm sure. He's only going to go and batter his wife for grassing him in, so it's best all round if he spends the night there. We can get specially trained officers to assess the situation in the morning. One thing is for certain, I'm not being blamed for a dead wife, I can't be arsed with all that shite at the moment, I've enough on."

"Okay Sir. Cheers."

*****

By eleven PM, the hills above Ashton and Mossley were being illuminated by revolving blue lights. It was quite a spectacle for the people in the town beneath the famous hill, and this sudden burst of police activity had lots of local folk talking.

Facebook was bursting alive with community reporters speculating on what this extraordinary blue light show up at Hartshead Pike was all about.

"Our Dan's just been up for a nosey but police have closed the road. They wouldn't let him go in the lane." Said one commentator on Ashton Buy and Sell page.

"I think they've found a drug stash up at the Pike. There's meant to be hundreds of stashes up there!" suggested a group member on The Tameside Hangout page. The activity was certainly creating lots of debate, and people were desperate to know what was going on. Especially the really nosey ones.

"It'll be a helicopter crash. I bet it's that Noel Edmonds."

"I'll bet you a tenner it'll be an unexploded bomb from the war. There's thousands of them up there."

"I'm telling you, it's a rave. They'll have closed the lane so no more ravers can get up there. There used to be raves all the time up there in the nineties you know. That's where I met my ex-wife."

From over one hundred comments which suggested various explanations for this most unlikely of places to have such a heavy police presence, not one of the commentators linked this exciting activity to the disappearance of Kathy Hopkirk, which was quite surprising as it was still the main news topic in the UK, and especially in Manchester, the city where she was last seen.

The Tameside police officers had secured the entire area around Hartshead Pike with police cordon tape, and had closed the area to the public. This was a huge undertaking, particularly in the pitch-dark. The second phase of the police activity was to reassure the locals. This involved knocking on the doors of the dozen or so farmhouses and cottages dotted along the mile long country lane from Mossley Road, the main road which links Ashton through the rural climb to its neighbouring, and much prettier town, Mossley.

"Its nothing to worry about," said one officer to a rather bemused, middle-aged home-owner who was standing at his front door in his pyjamas. "We've launched a police investigation here this evening, and the road is closed to the public. But there is no risk to any people or property. We just want you to be aware."

"What's the investigation about?"

"That's classified information I'm afraid Sir."

"Aw go on. My wife will get a right cob on her if I don't tell her what's going on."

"I'm afraid I can't add any further comment to this Sir. We just want you to be reassured that you are safe and that you are in no immediate danger. Goodnight."

Things were very neat and tidy, and the residents were extremely calm and relaxed considering the circumstances. By midnight, just a couple of police vans remained at the site. The road was closed from the junction with the main road, and everything was calming down. However, somebody within the Manchester police community had tipped off the press, and reporters began arriving at the scene in the early hours of the morning.

It wasn't clear what they had heard, but it soon became apparent that they were pretty convinced that they were reporting from the final resting place of Kathy Hopkirk.

*****

Saunders was the only person working in the SCIU offices. It was almost one am when he accepted that he had finally had enough for today, and decided that it was time to get himself home and grab some sleep. He headed off on the short walk across the city centre, to his apartment on the Piccadilly side of town.

As he walked through the brightly lit, bustling and noisy centre of Manchester, his mind was racing with thoughts, but for the first time that he could remember, these thoughts weren't about work. Saunders' mind was focused solely on his colleague, DC Helen Grant. She'd smiled at him earlier, and his mind was replaying that smile, that look she gave him, over and over. He realised he was walking really quickly, and it made him smile when he noticed what he was doing. Saunders felt an inexplicable urge to punch the air, or jump for joy. It was so weird, so corny how he felt. But it was the idea that Grant was also interested in him that really kept him going. Usually, Saunders would start analysing this type of scenario, and would start trying to think of reasons why it wouldn't or couldn't work out.

But as far as Helen was concerned, he couldn't think of a single pit-fall. Saunders couldn't think of anything negative to put in the way of pursuing a relationship with his new DC. Tonight, he had worked late, as he often did when a major case was live. He had made the conscious decision that he was going to focus on his work, and that the distraction of his thoughts and feelings for DC Grant were not going to get in the way of his work. It had been a personal test, and Saunders had passed. He was absolutely buzzing with the results.

As he walked past Piccadilly train station, and got closer to his flat, he was feeling delighted that he had managed to put a really productive shift in at work, that he had managed to play it cool with Grant, as well as his other colleagues. This proved to him that he was capable of managing a relationship with the stunning, beautiful, gorgeous, funny, cute and sexy new team member. The thought made his guts somersault.

Tomorrow, he *had* to make his move, and the thought gave him such a buzz, he almost walked past his apartment block.

Chapter 37
FRIDAY

"Good morning, and welcome to Britain's Breakfast news. Our main story this morning centres on that continuing search for Kathy Hopkirk, and those sensational revelations yesterday, when it was announced that Kathy's infamous resignation video was not genuine, and that police are treating the video with great suspicion, a fact that was demonstrated with the re-arrest of Kathy's husband, the veteran radio DJ Jack Greenwood."

The newsreader almost gasped for breath, as she tried to keep up with her autocue. "This morning, Mr Greenwood remains in police custody. And, there have been even more dramatic developments overnight, as a police cordon line has been erected around a popular beauty spot in Greater Manchester. Police haven't provided full details yet, but here are the aerial camera views taken from our helicopter in the past few minutes. These images really show the extent of police activity at Hartshead Pike, one of the most popular viewpoints across the Manchester area."

Breakfast TV viewers were being treated to some stunning, sweeping views across the lush, green countryside at the edge of Greater Manchester. This is where the sprawling urban metropolis which is home to three million people, finally gives way to the Pennines, the place where the moors and mountains gradually take-over the land and build their hardy divide between Lancashire in the West, and Yorkshire to the East.

Hartshead Pike is still a very popular picnic spot for walkers, boasting one of the best viewpoints in the region. This spot is famed for its seemingly endless views of the four counties, Lancashire, Cheshire, Derbyshire and Yorkshire. On a very fine day, visitors to the pike can see as far away as the Welsh Mountains. The Pike itself is marked by an imposing, gothic looking construction. This imposing, circular, stone built tower, looks very similar to a church spire. The building's prominent position at the top of Hartshead hill dominates the horizon from the city below.

The tower was first built in the late 1700's, and rebuilt in the 1800's after the tough Lancashire weather had worn it down. It became a hugely popular walking location and between the two world wars, it served as a sweet shop for the thousands of visitors who ventured up there for the magical views, in an age before video-games, TV or app-stores.

The breakfast viewers continued watching the footage from the helicopter, as the presenter updated the public on the overnight developments in the story.

"So, this is the area known to most people in Manchester, Hartshead Pike. There is growing speculation this morning that this location holds specific interest in the Kathy Hopkirk mystery. Our pictures clearly show that all of the investigating officers from the Serious Crimes Unit are at this location as we speak. DCI Miller and DI Saunders can be seen discussing something, these are the two detectives who are leading the Kathy Hopkirk investigation." The newsreader looked as though she was struggling to catch her breath as the director panned away from the Manchester beauty spot, and focused the camera shot on her face. "And, it does look like the police officers will be working there all day, so let's see if the weather is going to be favourable for them, here's Julie Prole with the forecast."

It was the only news item on every channel, on every radio breakfast show and on the front of every newspaper in the land. Nothing like this had ever happened before. This was the most enthralling news story that the presenters and journalists and editors could remember covering, and it all seemed a step closer towards reaching some kind of a conclusion this morning. A real conclusion this time.

The lack of information from the police was extremely frustrating for the media. The papers, the TV, and radio journalists were desperate to know what this heavy police presence was all about. There were three separate news helicopters roaming around the area, desperately trying to figure out what had prompted all of this activity. But there were no obvious clues. There was plenty of police vehicles, and several detectives on site. But there was no digging taking place, no forensic tents had been erected. Without any explanation of what this police activity was, the media had no choice but to ad-lib, and try to create a plausible reason for the dramatic pictures which clearly showed the Kathy Hopkirk detectives, and a huge police presence, but very little else.

Sky News were the masters of making-it-up-as-they-went-along. Especially with these types of breaking news stories. And, in their inimitable fashion, they broke away from the pack with their 9 am headlines.

"Our top story this hour is the breaking news that police in Manchester believe that they are close to finding Kathy Hopkirk, and the information that we are receiving from the north is extremely depressing news. We are told that police officers are currently awaiting the arrival of mechanical digging machines, and that they are soon going to be excavating an area in the vicinity of the tower which you can see from our Sky-copter pictures. We will of course bring you the latest as soon as we have it. But the breaking news from Manchester this morning is the very grim news that police are expected to start digging, in the search for Kathy Hopkirk's remains, at some point in the next hour."

Chapter 38

Miller was standing on the visitor's car park at Hartshead Pike, roughly two hundred metres away from the famous tower on the peak of the hill. He was just outside the exclusion zone, standing at the edge of the police tape, which was flapping furiously in the wind. The tape was whipping and clapping against it self, creating a hell of a noise. He was on the phone, trying to hear what his colleague in London was saying.

"Jo, speak up, I can't hear a word. It's blowing a gale up here!"

"Sir, can't you go and sit in your car or summat?" Rudovsky sounded irritable.

"You what?" said Miller, becoming tetchy himself.

Jo hung up. "He's a dud sometimes you know. Does my fucking head in!" She was talking to her partner, DC Peter Kenyon who nodded as he looked at her.

"Why have they sent us down here? It's a piss-take. Can't the CID down here sit here and listen to this prick saying no comment? It doesn't make sense."

Kenyon exhaled loudly. The two DC's from Manchester were sat in a disused office in Shepherd's Bush police station. Miller had sent the pair down the previous evening. It was still a mystery to the pair, who had been pulled off their own case.

"It's bollocks Pete."

"Well, I guess DI Saunders and DC Grant will have had a hand in this. They've spent hours interviewing him. Maybe they thought we'd be able to get somewhere?"

"Or maybe we've been stitched up! If Saunders knew that this guy was such a tit, why didn't they leave it to the Met to deal with?"

Kenyon shrugged. "Jo, I don't know."

Rudovsky's phone started ringing. It was Miller. She pressed the green button to answer the call, and pressed the loudspeaker function too, so Kenyon could hear the conversation too.

"Jo, soz, I've got a better line now. What's up?" Miller sounded pretty wound-up. At least that blast of wind was gone now.

"Oh, this guy is just taking the piss Sir. He's no commenting everything. We've done three hours with him, over three separate sessions because his brief keeps saying he needs a rest. The brief is interrupting everything we say as well. We're no further forward."

Miller couldn't hide his disappointment. "Well if *you* can't break him Jo, I don't know what to do for the best." It was a well-meant, and well earned compliment. Jo Rudovsky was absolutely first-class at cracking no-commenters. The SCIU had a list as long as Miller's arm of instances where she'd managed to encourage the most obstinate people to talk and answer questions. She had a variety of tactics that she used, from being over-friendly, to being downright provocative and antagonistic. Rudovsky had excellent intuition for how to play her interviewee. Many detectives had quizzed her about how she'd learnt the knack to do it, how she could work out in twenty seconds what her opponent would respond to. Jo couldn't answer it, she just put it down to an instinctive gift. Miller always said it was because she was a sociopath herself, and it was commendable that she used her mental health problems for the benefit of Manchester police. Jo didn't mind, it was quite a compliment.

But today, Miller was quite clearly surprised that his secret weapon hadn't managed to chink Jack Greenwood's armour.

"So what's going on up there?" asked Rudovsky, despite wanting to say "so can we come back home now?"

"We've had India Nine Nine up with their thermal imaging, they've been combing the area." Miller was referring to the Manchester Police helicopter, and the sophisticated machinery on board which could detect any disruption to the countryside. If a grave *had* been dug, and Kathy Hopkirk had been chucked in it at some point within the past seven days, the thermal equipment would show it up as though it was a red car in a snow-covered field.

"But there's not been anything to report on the Pike. It looks like the taxi-driver has dropped her off here on this muddy little car park and headed off. Kathy must have got into another car, but we haven't got the foggiest."

"There's a pub up there isn't there? I used to go with me Mam and Dad when I was a kid."

"Nah, the pub shut down years ago. It's been converted into a house now. Why?"

"Nowt, I was just reminiscing."

"Oh."

"Well, I was going to say, the pub will have CCTV."

"Yes, we've got uniform officers talking to all of the home-owners up here. There's about ten farm houses and barn conversions along the track. There's a chance we could get a CCTV clip of the other vehicle leaving, but its still a fucking nightmare job this. I can't believe we've not had a single phone-call in from someone saying they've seen her somewhere. It's unheard of."

"I know. So... well, I'm not sure what me and Peter are..."

"Do you want to go in again?"

"He's not talking Sir. Honest, he's a fucking psycho, he's just staring me out. Everything I say, everything Peter says to him, he just stares straight through you and says "now comment" in this weird voice. It's as though he's trying to take the piss out of my accent or summat."

"Do you think a shock tactic might move things on?"

Jo thought hard for a few seconds, whilst staring at DC Kenyon. Her colleague nodded enthusiastically, persuading Jo that he still had some patience left.

"What are you thinking?" asked Rudovsky of her boss.

"I've not... I was just thinking, last throw of the dice... you could go in there and talk a load of shit. Say she's just been admitted to a hospital in Stoke with head injuries or summat. Ask if she knows anyone in Stoke. Ask if he knows what she was doing in Stoke. Talk shit Jo, see if he starts getting a bit agitated or confused or summat. I don't care what you say, I just want to see if you can shake his foundations a bit. Figure out whether he knows what's going on with Kathy, or not. If he knows there's no way that Kathy is in a hospital in Stoke, you and Kenyon will be able to read it loud and clear. Go on... please mate, I'm not having you leaving London without sussing this douche-bag out. Right?"

There was a pause before Rudovsky answered. "Okay Sir, I'll see what I can come up with. But he's as smug as Gary Barlow singing at the Inland Revenue Christmas do."

"Come on Jo. I'm on the ropes here. I need you to turn this around. Is Peter there?"

"Yes, he's listening."

"Alright Sir?"

"Hiya Pete. Right, just keep your eyes trained on Greenwood please. Any odd actions, involuntary movements, tensing shoulders, foot-tapping, sweating, twitching, gurning, dismissive gestures. We need to know if he's in on this, or if he's just playing some kind of game with us."

"No problem Sir, I'll monitor him very closely. But..."

"What?"

"Well, Jo's right in what she says... he's impossible to engage with. It's as though he can't hear what we're saying. But then he just says 'no comment' when your lips stop moving. He's a creepy fucker."

"That's exactly what DI Saunders has said. In fact he got so frustrated that he left DC Grant to interview him alone."

"He's a bell-end Sir, of the highest order."

"But I know you can sort this Jo. Come on, don't be a loser. I can't believe an old crud like Jack Greenwood can get the better of you. Sort yourself out Jo. Jesus, even the new DC got further than you, what's happened to you? Where's your self respect?"

"Right. Shut up. You've pissed me off now Sir! We're going back in."

Rudovsky hung up on her boss and shot Kenyon a look of anger. "God, he knows how to push my buttons."

Kenyon just nodded. He knew that Miller was the master of getting Jo revved up. It was as though she had a clockwork winding key on her back, and only he could turn it to full tension.

*****

"So, here we are again." Rudovsky was going for a softer, friendlier approach this time.

Greenwood just stared at her, that smirk was still present on his face. All Rudovsky could think about was slapping him so hard, he'd struggle to pull that wretched expression for a few days at least. Deep breaths, she told herself. Deep fucking breaths.

"Just to remind you Mr Greenwood, you are here because we have reason to believe that you have some involvement in the disappearance of your wife."

Greenwood just stared ahead, looking beyond Rudovsky's shoulder.

"And the thing that is baffling us all, is that you don't seem to have anything to say about it."

"No comment."

"Exactly. It makes absolutely no sense that you would say no comment when we are trying to locate your wife. We are trying to help you, trying to help Kathy, and basically, well, its so bizarre how you are behaving that I'm beginning to worry that you are not mentally well enough to continue."

There was no reaction from Greenwood. Not an eyelid flutter, not a blink. The solicitor didn't look too impressed with Rudovsky's choice of phrase however. She couldn't care less, and she demonstrated it by returning the solicitor's hard stare straight back at him, which unnerved him visibly as he looked down urgently at his notes.

"No comment."

"But the thing is Mr Greenwood, there's something you don't know. You're sat here in the belief that you're holding all the cards. But it's us who are holding the trump mate." Rudovsky smiled, and made a quiet snort noise. We've got something. And we know for a fact that you can't possibly know about it."

Kenyon's eyes were trained on the aging DJ. There wasn't a flicker of concern, not a hint of interest on his face. This was a very cool customer. But Rudovsky was about to put this to the test with maximum pressure. Her knee tapped against Kenyon's leg under the table. This was the signal. She was going for the reaction.

"We're in touch with Kathy."

Greenwood's hand began to shake on the tabletop. It looked like an involuntary twitch, but it carried on for a second or two. Kenyon saw it peripherally, despite keeping his eyes transfixed on Greenwood's face. There was a shimmer appearing, enveloping his head. This announcement had made him react, no question about it.

"Is there anything you'd like to say to her? Through us I mean. A message you'd like us to pass on?"

Greenwood's jaw began vibrating and he leaned back heavily in his chair. This was good, Kenyon was making mental notes. Rudovsky was getting somewhere. His ridiculous smirk was gone now. It was being retracted slowly, but surely. The solicitor didn't look impressed at all. The no comment tactic was hanging in the balance here, it was all about to go tits up for Greenwood and everybody in the interview room sensed it. Rudovsky could taste first blood and was ready to pounce, ready to kill her prey.

"You're in a lot of trouble Mr Greenwood. So I'm glad you've stopped acting clever, because when it comes down to it, you're not clever at all, are you?"

"IT WASN'T ME!" shouted Greenwood, his eyes were filling with tears, his voice betraying the calm, confident posture that he'd tried so desperately to portray. It was a pretty spectacular reversal, from grinning psycho to panicky infant.

"Why are you choosing to tell us that it wasn't you? You've had all morning to say this to us."

Greenwood's solicitor looked as though he was getting nervous, and placed his hand in the air, his client was losing the plot, and fast.

"We need to take a break." Said the brief. There was a sense of panic in his voice as well.

"I'm not talking unless I get police protection. I mean it."

"We can promise you police protection, we can get you all the protection you need. I guarantee it. But you need to tell us what the hell is going on."

Greenwood grabbed his solicitor's plastic cup of water and drank the contents in one. His hand was shaking violently, his eyes had an unmistakable fear within them. The room began to smell rotten, and it quickly became obvious that Greenwood had passed wind. Kenyon was satisfied by observing Jack Greenwood, that Rudovsky had destroyed him inside a couple of minutes, and it was all down to one tiny fib.

"Let's have a break for ten minutes. I'll talk to witness protection and alert them that we need their services. Interview suspended at… eleven thirty five.

Thanks."

Rudovsky stood and headed to the door, as Kenyon followed, leaving a very scared, very broken man sitting with his solicitor in a room that stank of egg and body odour.

Ten minutes later, the Manchester detectives returned to the desk of interview room six at Shepherds Bush police station.

The solicitor began talking on his client's behalf. Greenwood was just staring down at the tabletop, his arms hugging around his waist. It looked as though a great weight had been lifted from his shoulders, but he looked somewhat humiliated by the situation too. He was in a state. Rudovsky and Kenyon had no sympathy, and felt a great sense of pride for the part they'd played in creating this transformation.

"My client wishes to make a phone call. Can this be arranged please?"

"What, now?" asked Kenyon.

"Well, when it is convenient." Kenyon and Rudovsky looked at one another. This was interesting. Rudovsky nodded to Kenyon, letting him know that she had no objections.

"Yes, I'll organise for an officer to take you down to custody." Kenyon stood and left the interview room. Rudovsky looked down at her notes and used the time productively, adding notes to her paperwork.

A few minutes later, Kenyon returned. He was accompanied by a uniformed police man. "The phone is free, so you can go now. We'll just wait here."

Greenwood nodded as he stood, and followed the policeman out of the small, grey room. There was a slowness about him, he seemed to shuffle more than stride. For somebody who'd displayed such a cocky, arrogant demeanour, Jack Greenwood looked like a different person. It was as though he knew that his game was up, just when he'd least expected it.

Chapter 39

Sally King had lost half a stone in the time that Kathy had been missing. That was a hell of a lot of weight to lose for such a small woman. She'd been stressed out of course, but also worried. The anxiety had sent her metabolism into hyper-drive. She'd hardly eaten in the seven days that Kathy had been missing, and what little food that she had managed to eat had gone straight through her. She didn't look her usual, well-presented self as she sat at her desk.

Sally King Associates was her trading name. She was the manager of one of the most successful talent agencies in London. She had more than twenty A list names on her books, and as many B and C listers too. Kathy Hopkirk had started as a C lister a decade earlier, straight out of the Big Brother house. It hadn't taken her long to step up to the B list, and during the past five years, she'd remained a strong A list member of Sally's team.

And now this. Jack Greenwood was phoning her from his police cell.

"Sally, it's Jack. I'm voluntarily entering into the witness protection programme. I'm confessing to everything I know about Kathy's disappearance. I just thought that you should know the state-of-play. I'm sorry if this puts you in a difficult spot, but I have no choice."

Greenwood put the phone down on its cradle. As he did so, he could hear Sally shouting "Wait! What are you..."

Sally King held the phone to her ear, even though the call was disconnected. This was the worst case scenario. This meant only one thing. Sally King would now have to hand herself in, and join the witness protection scheme too. It was game over. Her life would never be the same again.

"Kathy you stupid woman!" she sobbed as she stared out of her office window and across Covent

Garden, knowing that this would be the very last time that she would be able to. The life that she knew and loved, that she had built for herself from nothing, was over now.

PART TWO

Kathy Hopkirk's notoriety had presented her with some excellent showbiz opportunities over the years. As radio had been her first love, she had been over-the-moon when an offer came in from the national station Talk AM. The Sunday night slot, from 7pm until 10pm was offered to Kathy, with only one condition. The condition being that she attracted a whopping-big audience. The pay cheque was extremely generous, and Kathy laughed at the amount of noughts on her weekly fee. She loved radio so much that she would have happily done the show for free.

Talk AM is a very serious, high-brow radio station, broadcasting none-stop news, sport and current affairs twenty-four hours a day. Kathy Hopkirk isn't their usual type of presenter by any means. But the radio station's bosses had worked out that Kathy attracted such a huge following, it was an unmissable opportunity to get the radio station's brand out there at the very least, and the adverts and trailers throughout her three hour slot would hopefully sell the rest of the station's output to Kathy's listeners.

It paid off. The listening figures for Kathy's show were close to the million mark. It was beyond compare for a Sunday evening slot, and the programme was the most listened to off-peak radio show in Britain. Listening numbers had swelled on every other slot on the schedule too, as new listeners discovered the stations various selling points off the back of Kathy's involvement.

The "No Empathy, Just Kathy" show had caused several high-profile stirs in its first twelve months on the air. The most memorable suggestion that she'd made was that all new parents should be required a license in order to keep their children. If they smoked, or drank, or were unemployed, or had a criminal record, they should be refused a license, she'd suggested. "You need a license to drive a car, or to run a pub. You even need a bloody license to sell clothes on a market stall," she suggested, "but any old ugly-faced moron can procreate without a single questionnaire being filled in? It's not right, and we need better systems to thin out the amount of arseholes that are walking our streets. Especially around Grimsby."

To be fair, the suggestion was made with Kathy's tongue firmly in her cheek, but it went viral anyway. This was great news for Talk AM, and had secured several minutes of the radio station's logo time on all of the news networks as the nation's most hysterical people took great offence at this latest suggestion. The suggestion had even ended up being referred to at Prime Minister's Questions in Parliament.

"Who the hell do you think you are?" came the familiar outrage from the listeners who jammed the radio stations switchboard. Thousands were desperate to get on the air and tell Kathy what they thought of her outrageous suggestion.

"You're no oil painting yourself darling!"

"Maybe not, but I'm not a useless moron who can't put a nappy on a child without getting fag-ash in its eyes, lovey. Am I?"

It was entertaining radio for the most part. Kathy Hopkirk revelled in her "shock-jock" role, and had a running death-threat count throughout each show. She even had a jingle made, to make her online abuse into a regular feature on the show. The most death-threats that she'd received via text, e-mail, tweet or phone call in a single show was fifty-five, a figure that Kathy was delighted with, and had even contacted Guinness Records to see if she could be included in their book.

And that was what made Kathy so bloody infuriating. Instead of piping down, or trying to wind her neck in a little, The more insults, outrage and even death threats she received, the more contented she became.

"You don't hate me!" she'd explain to her army of weekly listeners. "You think you hate me, but then you tune in to my show! That's not hate you morons, it's adoration. You adore me! Now, let's go to line seven... Phil, what do you want to talk about lovey?"

"I want to know why you think you're so clever?" asked the angry, irritable sounding cockney.

"I don't think I'm clever Phil. What makes you say that?"

"You come on here, shouting the odds, saying that folks need a license to fetch kids up. You're off your bonce mate."

"Phil there, on line six. License application rejected. Those poor children, stuck in a house with a man like that. Run away kids, go now, flee...while he's still trying to figure out why he can't hear anything in his phone."

The programme was entertaining, there was no question about that. It was also highly controversial at times, and in Kathy's inimitable style, she encouraged her listeners to be as divisive and near-to-the-knuckle as they could. Kathy Hopkirk had no intention of allowing this radio show to become just another "what's your favourite kind of biscuit" phone-in. Kathy was determined that it should be edgy, but more than anything else – interesting.

As she closed the show one Sunday night, around a month before she'd disappeared, Kathy had made her familiar appeal for topics to discuss on the following week's programme. The Tweets and Facebook comments came in as usual.

"Next week, why not discuss people going to Mars on a one-way rocket? It might cost ten-million dollars, but I'm sure everyone will chip in to pay for it if you promised to go Kathy, you awful old boot." Was one typical suggestion.

But in amongst all of the hatred and the bile – one person had a good idea for a discussion. A woman called Janet Croft contacted the radio show's Facebook page. The most interesting messages from listeners were forwarded onto Kathy by the radio station's producers. Janet Croft's message was certainly interesting, and heart-breaking. It was sent to Kathy with the red "high priority" label illuminated.

From opening and reading the message, Kathy realised immediately that she had a very, very good story to focus on. But the more she read, the more she realised that this was absolutely heart-breaking. Kathy wrote back immediately, thanking Janet Croft for her message, and telling her that she was extremely brave for getting in touch about such a traumatic experience.

The messages went back and forth between Kathy and Janet for several days. Then the two moved onto phone calls. Eventually, after a few more days of communications, Kathy arranged to meet Janet at the office. The office was the place Kathy used for formal meetings, and discussions that she wanted to remain private, and out of the lenses of paparazzi photographers. The office was actually Sally King's office, and Kathy would regularly take a smaller office for a few hours for such business. "You take twenty per cent of my earnings, darling!" she would remind Sally if she seemed a little annoyed. "And besides, it's not as if I'm taking a shit in your toaster."

By the time that Janet Croft had left Sally King's offices in Covent Garden, Kathy Hopkirk felt as though she had known the woman for years. As she waved the hard, but kindly looking woman away, Kathy broke down in tears, and made a pledge that she would help that woman. As Janet Croft turned the corner and disappeared into the bustling London rush-hour, Kathy knew that her life had just taken on a new meaning. Kathy was going to help that poor woman get justice for the appalling life that she had endured.

*****

Janet Croft left school with excellent O level grades, and started working for London Television as an admin apprentice in the 1970's. It was a very exciting, very respectable first job, and her parents and friends were delighted for her to have such a glitzy and glamorous opportunity at such a tender age. But it wasn't quite what it appeared. She told Kathy that she was used as a sex toy by TV stars and executives at the corporation, for three years. And then, as her apprenticeship came to an end when she was eighteen, she was dismissed. Another fifteen year old girl was brought in, to take her place. This cycle was normal in the sixties, seventies and early eighties.

Janet Croft's life had been ruined by the time that she'd reached eighteen. The disgusting abuse and degradation that she'd suffered on an almost daily basis caused her to suffer a great number of mental health issues. The issues began with self hatred and self loathing. She felt that she was weak, that she should have walked out, should have reported it. She should have stood up to the fucking perverts and rapists and bullies. But she didn't, and the reason was, because she had been very skilfully tricked. She'd been made to believe that it was normal, it was fun, made to think that it was *her* who was weird for not enjoying it.

Another reason that she didn't do anything about it, was because she didn't want to upset her parents, who were so proud of her amazing achievement. She couldn't do anything, she just put up with the abuse and the awful, degrading treatment in the hope that it would all stop soon, and that at least she would have a job at the world famous broadcasting station in the end. But it wasn't to be.

One Friday afternoon, a lady from the big offices upstairs came down to Janet's desk and announced quite ceremoniously that it had been a pleasure having her on the apprentice scheme, and wished her well for the future.

To Janet, it felt like a wall had been pushed on top

of her. She felt stunned, winded, she couldn't catch her breath. She looked around the office and her colleagues were all smiling and offering the young lass a round of applause.

Most of them were men, and all of them had had some fun with Janet. And now, it was all over. Thanks, now clear your desk and go. Just like that.

The more thought that she put into those awful, terrorised teenage years, the more mental health issues she suffered. Her self confidence and self esteem were broken, and she struggled to find the courage to even think about the next step in her career, let alone start to apply for jobs. Janet felt that she was such a dirty, useless little slag, and that everybody would know about her. By the time that Janet was nineteen, she was extremely unwell. She had begun to self-medicate against her mental health problems, and had a very worrying alcohol dependency by 1981, the time she'd reached twenty.

Her parents despaired. They had no idea what had happened to their pretty, funny, outgoing and sporty young girl. She had aged incredibly since losing her job at the television station. She'd lost her friends. The light in her eyes had gone out. They tried, they tried so hard to help, to try and get to the bottom of what was going wrong with Janet. But every time, it just ended in a blazing row, her parents would be stressed, hurt and frustrated. They felt completely lost and confused. Janet would just head back to her room, and continue drinking.

Life never improved for Janet whilst her parents were alive. When she attended her father's funeral in 1989, she was twenty-eight years old. Most of the family, friends and extended relations failed to recognise her. Janet had become a weak, frail, unhealthy looking woman who didn't look like she was long for this world.

The heartbreak of losing her husband of almost forty years was too much for Janet's mum, who passed away just a month after her man. The death was recorded as a sudden cardiovascular death, more commonly known as a heart-attack. But everybody who knew the family, knew that Janet's mum had died of a broken heart.

The cycle of despair and self-loathing, self pitying and drinking continued. Before Janet knew it, she was thirty-five years old, and the Spice Girls were just coming into the charts. A whole twenty years had passed since she'd started that exciting, wonderful apprenticeship which had promised so much, and had warmed her parent's hearts.

Another ten lonely years passed, the Spice Girls came and went and Janet's alcoholism continued, funded by her weekly giro-cheques from the incapacity. The rent on her council flat was paid by the DHSS, so she was an ideal tenant, who had a no arrears, and her desire to be left alone meant that she never presented any anti-social problems. Because she was such a quiet tenant, Janet Croft was practically forgotten about by the authorities, and her local community. Her only contact with the outside world was her daily trip to the shop for her drink. The cycle continued for years, and years. On the day that Oscar Pistorius was charged with the fatal shooting of his girlfriend, Reeva Steenkamp, Janet's life changed forever.

Janet was an extremely weak and feeble lady, and on the night of February 14th in 2013, returning from the corner-shop with her three-litre bottle of cider, Janet had collapsed in the stairwell of her block-of-flats. The resulting fall had been so violent that she'd suffered a broken arm, a sprained ankle and a nasty head injury. An ambulance was called, and the paramedics who attended the shout didn't think that the lady would last the night. They were shocked, and saddened to learn that she was fifty-two. They'd guessed at eighty. And an unhealthy, gravely-ill eighty at that.

But it was the best thing that had ever happened to her, that nasty fall. The pain had been quite bad, but she'd been so pissed, it all felt just the same as everything else in her life… fuzzy, and not quite real. Janet spent her 53rd birthday alone, in the hospital. She was completely isolated from all friends or family now. She had nobody. She'd locked herself away for over thirty years, and had spent all of that time drinking, and wishing she was dead.

The nature of her injuries prevented her from being able to leave the hospital, so her fall down those stinking concrete stairs turned out to be a blessing.

Over the course of a long, torturous week, Janet Croft had no option but to sober up. It proved a very unpleasant and difficult week, but by the time that it had ended, she was glad of it. The hospital ward became clearer, and sharper in her vision with each passing day. When she visited the bathroom at the end of the ward, she didn't recognise the old, wrinkly woman who stared back at her from the mirror. Janet was confused, she thought that there had been some sort of mistake. Some kind of a mix-up.

But there had been no mix-up. It all soon came flooding back. That endless cycle of waking, hating herself, walking down to the shop for booze, drinking it, hating herself, falling asleep, and repeat. She was stuck on a loop, and throughout all of that time, all those years, almost thirty-five sad, lonely years, the routine barely changed. In the eighties it had been Thunderbird wine. In the nineties, she'd acquired a taste for White Lightning cider, a product which was later discontinued by its brewers Heineken, due to its links with ill-health and anti-social behaviour. In more recent years, Janet had been taking advantage of the unbeatable value of Frosty Jacks super-strength white cider, which cost just £2.99 for three litres.

Janet would buy two, often three bottles every-day, drinking it none stop until she fell asleep with the last sip of the last bottle. The only food Janet ate was baked beans or pot noodles. She was very rarely sober enough to organise anything more than toast or crumpets for breakfast, and that was only when she had any bread in.

Janet Croft was gravely ill when she'd entered the hospital. Aside from the injuries that she'd sustained on that miserable, stinking stair-case, there were a number of serious, life-threatening issues which needed to be dealt with. Most significant of all was Janet's weight. She was painfully thin, almost skeletal, weighing just over five stones. The malnutrition was causing dozens of negative effects to her vital organs, and the doctors wanted to tackle the malnutrition first, and monitor Janet's progress based around specialist dietary care. It was a starting point.

This form of treatment involved being fed by a tube, the fastest and most effective way of ensuring that Janet was receiving all of the correct nutrients and supplements. It was the start of a long road, but within days, Janet was making positive progress. A month after she'd been rushed into hospital, Janet was beginning to look much better. Her skin had lost its latex look, and the blue tinge around her eyes was making way for a healthier complexion. Her eyes looked less sunken into her skull now as well. Most noticeably, she'd started putting some weight on, and had the beginnings of a bum growing behind her. She'd been a model patient, very polite and undemanding, and Janet was well liked by the NHS professionals who were nursing her back to health.

"I... I don't want to go home..." she said quietly to a nurse one night. The nurse had cheerfully announced that Janet would be ready for discharge soon, possibly within the next few days. The prospect filled her with an intolerable terror. She couldn't even bear the thought of imagining what her flat must be like inside. She had fuzzy, whoozy flash-backs of the place. It was dark, cold, there was mess everywhere. No electric, the supply had been terminated years ago. It was a miserable place, and she didn't want to go there again. Big piles of mess, rubbish, clothes, junk was everywhere. The memories began stuttering back. A cold sweat began enveloping her frail, pale face, her bony, scabby arms and body.

"Of course you want to go home Janet!" said the nurse cheerfully, playfully mocking her patient. But the tears, the panic and anxiety that this suggestion fuelled told a different story. Those sad, lonely, yet kind, loving eyes were desperate and the nurse saw the pain that Janet was in. The nurse contacted the mental health intervention team, asking them to take a look at this patient's situation. Luckily for Janet, she had landed at the right place, at just the right time.

It took many months of rehab and counselling, and several other care packages that Janet had to engage with. By the time that ten months had passed, Janet was absolutely desperate to get out of the hospitals and clinics and day-centres that had saved her life. She didn't want out of there because she was unhappy with the constant meetings, support sessions and awareness exercises. It wasn't that, she was sure she'd miss it, miss the friends she'd made, the camaraderie. The laughs. No, Janet wanted out because she was absolutely desperate to get on and start her life, her new life. Janet's life, version two. It was all she could think about. The past was the past, and that was shit. But throughout the rehab sessions, she'd learnt that you don't *have* to go back and revisit the past. You can treat the past like you'd treat a shit holiday resort. Never go back there again. Most importantly, Janet had been taught that the best days of her life lay in front of her, and now, going off to explore those best days was all that she craved.

The mental health professionals had worked miracles with Janet. And Janet had worked miracles with them too. At the very start of the journey, when Janet was heavily doped up to cope with the various side-effects of quitting alcohol, there was very little that she wanted to do, other than pass away.

Janet had really upset a nurse, albeit unintentionally. She'd said that it wasn't fair that the hospital should have her taking up a bed, that it wasn't fair on other people who needed the treatment, and she said that it would be better if she could just die, and let someone better have this bed. It was desperately sad, to see another human-being in such a sorry state, and it made a lasting impression on the nurse that had to hear such sad words that night.

But the NHS staff had been truly amazing, and they had provided ten months of delicate care and considerate, dignified support to Janet Croft, and they had turned her into a different lady. The major turning point had come quite early on in the recovery. A meeting had been called, for the alcohol and substance addicts on the ward. The subject of the meeting was to try and identify triggers that made the addicts do what they did.

Janet began talking quietly, and slowly, and through tears of pain and tears of shame, she began to tell her story to the group. She explained how thrilled she had been to land the apprenticeship at London TV Centre. She talked about how proud everybody was of her, how exciting it all was. But then she spoke of the horrific abuse and humiliation that was forced on her from practically the first day. She spoke of one day, a managers meeting was taking place, and Janet had been asked to go through to the Boardroom. The manager who was running the meeting explained to Janet that she needed to undress and stand on top of the table.

She asked why, in her shy, scared, fifteen year-old voice. She was told that it was because the meeting was boring, and that it would be more fun if a pretty young thing was stood on the table, wearing nothing but a smile. The Boardroom had erupted in laughter. Janet had told them, the adults, that she didn't want to do it. In reply, she was told that she had two options. Option one was to do precisely as she was told, showing gratitude and with a smile on her face, and option two was to leave the TV station right now, and never return.

Janet broke down in tears in front of the group of recovering addicts, as she described how valueless and vulnerable she felt taking her clothes off in front of all those guffawing, chain-smoking old men. She struggled through, talking about that day, and how it had ended, with her on her knees whilst several of them abused her in the most degrading and unspeakable manner.

It was tough. It had been harder to speak of that event, to re-live that horrific day, than anything else that Janet had ever experienced. It had been harder to undress her secret, than that day had been, all those years ago, taking her clothes off while all the old men stared at her, smiling and winking and making lewd comments to her. But her thirty-eight-year-old secret was out now, and there was no turning back. Janet's crippling, self-destroying, torturous secret had finally been unburdened from her, and the relief that she felt was life changing. Gone was the shame, the self hatred, the self-pity, the low self-esteem.

The months off the drink had cleared her mind. The counselling staff had taught her that she had baggage which needed letting go of. The mentors had taught her that she had to deal with the issue that was causing her to drink. The psychiatrists explained that finding vengeance for her abuse would be a positive step to take going forwards.

As impossible as it had always seemed, Janet had found a way out of the living hell that was her useless life. It had been a positive way-out too, it wasn't the way that she had hoped for, for so many years, that she wouldn't wake from her next drunken sleep on the settee in that stinking, stone-cold flat.

On the day that she took over full ownership of her day-to-day care, Janet took a bus from her new flat in Tower Hamlets, to the town where she grew up. She felt happy, and giddy, ridiculously excited, with butterflies in her tummy, as she remembered the old places and the fun-filled days of her childhood. She stood outside her childhood house for a few moments, happy, joyful memories came flooding back as she stared up longingly at her bedroom window from all those years ago. Janet realised she was smiling, from ear-to-ear, as she walked along the very same route she had covered every day to her school. She walked all around the district, finding joyful memories of her early years. Happy memories on every corner, at every shop or café.

Janet found herself in the cemetery, surprised and rather impressed that her sober mind had been able to use her drunken mind's memory, to find her parents' final resting place. She stayed there a lot longer than she had imagined that she would. She spoke for a long time to the dirty, weathered marble headstone. She apologised for her behaviour towards her beloved parents. She thanked them for giving her a wonderful childhood, and a very happy life. She talked of blissful memories stirred up on this most enchanting of days, chattering away like a mad woman.

Janet then gave a rather vague explanation as to what had happened at the TV station. It was vague because she felt embarrassed, despite being alone in this deserted cemetery, telling her dead parents about the horror that she had endured, while they thought that she was having the time of her life. "The time of my life, Mum, Dad, was with you. You were the best parents, and I hate that I never told you what happened. I'm sorry."

Janet ended her visit with a promise to come back and clean all the moss and dirt off the gravestone, and to try and tidy up the weeds and nettles round the back.

It had been an exhausting day, and Janet had nodded off on the bus home, missing her bus-stop by about two miles. But this made her laugh as well. "What am I like?" she asked herself as she limped along the road. It had been a great day, and so what if she had to walk back a few miles back to her sheltered accommodation scheme? At least she was alive.

Life was looking good, for the first time that Janet

could remember, and that prospect filled her heart with joy. She felt cured of her alcoholism now, and never was this better tested than now, as Janet made her way past dozens of Off-Licenses and Mini-Marts on her way back to her new home, and her new start.

Janet arrived home, back to her flat. It wasn't in the best of conditions, it needed a good clean-up, and a redecorate. But Janet was looking forward to getting stuck-in, and sorting the place out. It would be a project to focus on. She was thinking positive now, looking forward.

She went through into the living room and took a seat on the settee that her support-workers had got for her from the second-hand shop. There were tears in her eyes. Tears of joy, of relief, of regret. It had been a very emotional day, but she was glad that it was over now, she needed her rest. Day one of Janet's life version two had been an overwhelming success.

The tears continued to sting Janet's cheeks, as she realised that there was bound to be some difficult days ahead too. Especially if she was to keep her pledge about bringing her abusers to justice. The way that her heart suddenly started jolting high in her chest whenever she thought about her teens told her that there was unfinished business to attend to. The thought scared her, but also brought a peaceful feeling too. Those heart-jolts settled down as a wonderful, settling calmness flowed through her. The tranquil, easy feeling came from deep within her, and a confidence in the knowledge that she was going to win in the end.

*****

Kathy Hopkirk had spent several hours with Janet, learning about her tragic back-story. Over the course of two-weeks, Janet had poured her heart out via e-mail, phone conversations and face-to-face chats at Sally King's office. And now, in the third meeting that had been arranged at the prestigious Covent Garden offices of Kathy's manager, Janet was prepared to reveal the reason that she had shared all of this private, personal trauma baggage with a complete stranger.

It hadn't all been depressing. For the most-part, Janet and Kathy had had a laugh, and talked about other stuff, like how freaky it is that Facebook has started showing you adverts for things that you've looked for on Google.

"Honestly, I can't believe how lovely you have been to me! Its as though they're talking about a different person when they talk about you in the papers," said Janet, as the two sat in Sally King's spare office and talked over a skinny mocha frappucino in Kathy's case, and a tea, two-sugars in Janet's.

"Oh, there could be no Super-Bitch career if people thought that I was nice really. It wouldn't work."

"No, I guess not. But I had no idea…"

"People who know me genuinely help me to remain successful by ignoring the nasty stuff, and keeping quiet. It's all a big con, there's loads of us out there. Simon Cowell is a great example. He doesn't know anything about music… so he gets five million TV viewers to tell him which singer to hire."

"Yeah, God, I suppose you're right. When you strip it back like that…"

"Besides, it's not a total secret. Most of the journalists already know I'm not totally subhuman really. They know it's just an act, a stage persona. But I need to make a bit more money before I can retire, so let's hope nobody finds out that I'm okay really!"

Janet laughed loudly, and it was a really joyful, squeaky sound, that came right from the belly, which made Kathy laugh too.

"Anyway, I've got a plan. Don't tell anybody, right – but I am going to retire one day, by completely disappearing."

Janet laughed, but then stopped laughing when she saw that Kathy was being deadly serious.

"You can't tell anybody though. Swear to God."

"What, why... I'm surprised that you're telling me this..." Janet was stunned that Kathy Hopkirk, one of the most famous, most unpopular people in the UK, was sharing such a private, bizarre conversation with somebody that she barely knew.

"Well come on Janet, if I can't trust you, someone who's just told me every private, painful detail of your life story, then I can't trust anybody, can I?"

"Yes, I suppose. So what are you going to do?"

"Well, I'm going to whip up the hatred to level ten..."

Janet threw her head back, and another huge roar of infectious laughter filled the room. "So what level is it now, just out of curiosity?" asked Janet once she'd simmered down a bit.

"It's only level six, six and a half. But I'll get it up to level ten no trouble..."

"And disappear?"

"Yes. That's the plan. I'm serious, don't breathe a word of this to another soul..."

"I've not made a promise for a long time..."

"How long?"

"Well, let's just say, the last promise I made was to promise that I will do my best, to be true to myself and develop my beliefs, to serve the Queen and my community, to help other people and to keep the Brownie Guide Law!"

The two women laughed, and smiled for a minute as an air of nostalgia filled the room.

"No, honestly, I promise, of course I won't say a thing..."

"Thanks. Well, the plan is, I get the hatred level maxed out, and then I disappear, into thin air. The papers and TV channels will be in a frenzy! I'll keep it up for a day or two... and then..."

"What?" Janet was really excited by this bizarre idea, but she thought it was hilarious none-the-less.

"Then I'll pop a video on Youtube, announcing my retirement, and I'll apologise to everyone that I've pissed off, and say I only did it for the money! Then I'll say goodbye and that I've left show-business and the media for good, and that will be the end of that!"

"Oh my God! That's absolutely mental!"

"Well, that's the plan, go out on any almighty thunder-clap of hatred. Then move to my new house in a secret location. I've already recorded my departure speech, well, it's a practise run... but I just need a couple more big jobs, and I'll have made enough cash to live comfortably for the rest of my time. I fancy a little cottage by the coast. Somewhere pretty remote." Kathy's eyes glazed over and it became pretty clear to Janet that this was quite an established plan.

"Wow... I'm, I'm really shocked that you've told me. Thank you!"

"Oh, don't be daft I know you'll keep shtum, especially now that you've said the Brownie promise!"

The two ladies chatted about nonsense for a while, until the conversation returned to Janet's story.

"So, anyway, we need to work out where we are going with everything that you've told me. You see, I think we could get a lot of goodness from this."

"Goodness?"

"Yes, I'm talking money. There'll be a book, a TV dramatisation, endless media interviews. I've spoken to my manager Sally and she's..."

"What, no, sorry wait Kathy. I think you've got the wrong end of the stick here."

"Eh? How do you mean?"

"I'm not here for money..."

"What? I don't understand." Kathy looked genuinely confused. This was an unexpected announcement.

"I'm not... making money was never my intention. I contacted you because I just had a feeling that you'd be able to help me."

"Help you to do what?"

"I want to get the bastards that abused me. I want them in prison. That's what I have to do... then I can have my peace. It's not a cottage by the sea that I'm craving Kathy. It's closure, revenge, a settling of scores. "

Kathy looked across at the window, and gazed out over the London skyline. Eventually, after an awkward silence, she spoke. "Janet, love, where do I come in to that?"

"Well, I was out of my head when all the Jimmy Savile stuff came out. I missed it all, the celebrity child abuse scandals. I was completely off my nut on cider."

Kathy looked deep into Janet's eyes. She could see, as well as feel, the sadness flooding back.

"I knew nothing about any of it until I was in the Cuckoo's Nest. They told me all about it, after I'd opened up about my apprenticeship at London TV."

"Shit! Oh my days that must have been horrific?"

"Well, no, it was, I don't know. I'd spent most of my life pissed up-to this point, so it just felt, I don't know... I wasn't surprised anyway. But the staff, the mentors, they were telling me to sue, to get my name down with the thousands who have complained against Savile and Rolf Harris and Stuart Hall, and all the others. But I don't want money. No amount of money can buy me the thirty odd years I've lost."

"What are you saying?"

"I want to name the others. Some of them are still working today. One of them you'd not believe... I want to name and shame him, and get him locked away, behind bars."

Kathy looked shocked, and moved, but also a little bit excited by this.

"Wait... why are you only telling me this now?"

"Because, if I'd told you that first, you'd never have heard about my story."

"Well, I..."

"And if you'd never heard my story, you wouldn't want to help me now."

"Makes sense. But why did you choose me? I mean, I'm the worst bitch in the UK! It seems a little bit bizarre that you'd approach the hardest, nastiest woman in the media to help you."

"I told you, I heard you on the radio. You said if there was anybody who had an interesting story to tell, to get in touch."

"Yes, but I meant, I don't know, someone banged a car into you on purpose to get some compo, or someones wife cooked a pie made out of dog food for her cheating husband... I never imagined that... well, anyway, it doesn't matter. I'm really glad you did get in touch, it's a really heroic story."

"There's nothing heroic about lying in your own piss for thirty years Kathy!"

"No, no, of course not. But I mean, the ending!"

"It's not ended yet."

There was a weird silence, and suddenly, both women felt awkward.

"But you can help me to get to the end."

"Taking your abusers to prison?"

"Absolutely right. So what do you say, are you in, or are you out?" Janet looked nervous. A lot, an immeasurable amount rested on the answer to this question.

"Course I'm in! Fucking hell Janet, I wouldn't miss this for the world!"

There was an audible sigh of relief from the vulnerable, weak looking lady.

"You've not heard who I'm talking about, yet."

"I can probably guess..."

"You can't."

"Well, okay, that sounds like a challenge?"

"You'll never guess."

"Okay… I'll trust your instincts. Give me a name."

"Bob Francis."

Kathy's eyes widened as her brain visibly struggled to compute the name with the deviant sex-acts that Janet had described. At first, Kathy seemed a shade paler, and then a moment after that, she seemed to be heating up, as a rosy glow filled her cheeks.

"Bob Francis? Like, *the* Bob Francis?"

Janet nodded, to confirm. But as she did so, Kathy noticed that her eyes were moistening, and that her hands were trembling. In that split-second, this stopped being an unbelievable piece of juicy gossip about one of Great Britain's best loved entertainers, and Kathy was reminded of the horrors that Janet had described in their earlier conversations.

"Fuck!"

Janet nodded again. This was quite a shock, quite an unbelievable, head-wrecking moment.

Bob Francis was one of the UK's most famous, and best-loved entertainers. He'd been a British institution almost as long as HRH Queen Elizabeth II. He had been a household name since before The Beatles were famous. He was so well-known, it seemed as though he had presented every big-hit television and radio show that had ever been on the air in Great Britain since the end of the Second World War.

The fifties teds, sixties swingers and seventies punks had all grown up with him. As had the eighties posers, nineties ravers, right through to today's idiotic, brain-dead millenials. They all knew who Bob Francis was. As 2016 claimed an extraordinary amount of famous British names and celebrity stars, a Facebook group had been set up called "Please Keep a GP, an Ambulance, an Intensive Care Bed and a Transplant on Standby for Bob

Francis Until 2016 Is Over PLEASE." The page had over a million likes. It may have been a joke, and a bit of sarcasm, but those million plus people wanted to put their love of Bob Francis out there anyway. Put simply, the man was the most celebrated legend of light-entertainment in the UK.

To ask the British people to associate this national treasure with nasty sex crimes against a fifteen-year-old girl, over a quarter of a century ago, was quite frankly going to be a very, very big ask. It was possibly *too* big an ask, not least because he had recently been on a variety of TV shows celebrating his ninetieth birthday, where his kindness, his charitable work and "all-round-good-guy" image had been given a fresh lick of paint by every single department which made up the national media.

Kathy Hopkirk was thinking fast. She was trying to figure out if there could possibly be any substance to what Janet was saying. It was remarkable that a man so famous could have kept such reprehensible behaviour quiet, especially throughout the past few years. This particular point in recent history felt as though every single British celebrity was a suspected nonce or a rapist. The press had groomed a blood-thirsty nation of outraged TV viewers, who were absolutely desperate to know who the next sex-monster would turn-out-to-be.

But Kathy couldn't recall Bob Francis' name being mentioned, not once, not ever, in the long list of beloved British stars whose names had been suggested in the press. In most cases, celebrity names cropped up simply because they had "links" to some of the accused stars, many of whom had been arrested, and then put under investigation and suspicion for a year at least - before finally being cleared of whatever accusations had been made against them in the first place. It had been a very dark time in British show-business.

"I'm really, really struggling to get my head around this Janet." Said Kathy, calmly, and kindly.

Janet looked disappointed, but not surprised.

"I know, I get it."

Kathy looked across the London sky-line, and recalled how sad and shocked, and completely confused she had felt when the news was announced that Rolf Harris had been found guilty of sex crimes against children. It was so unbelievable, it was as though it was one of the satire news websites that had made it up. Rolf Harris had been one of Britain's best loved celebs. He'd enjoyed a hugely successful career spanning forty years. He was rich, popular and was widely regarded as one of the kindest personalities in the country. At the time that Harris was sentenced, it seemed beyond belief that he had committed the sex crimes that had been heard in court, some of them involving children as young as six or seven.

And now, several years after the jail term was handed down to the shame-faced, disgraced entertainer, it still seemed surreal. Kathy reminded herself of how upset she had felt for Rolf Harris' family and friends, who were left to pick up the awful pieces when his G4S van took him away to prison, pelted with eggs.

Kathy looked back across the room at Janet, who was waiting patiently for the conversation to continue.

"Listen… I don't think I can take any more today. Can we take a break, let me try and get my head around this?"

"Yes, yes, course. It's a head-fuck, isn't it?"

"It is… in lots of different ways. Can I give it some thought, and get back to you… say tomorrow?"

Janet looked a tiny bit embarrassed, and maybe a little bit let down too. Judging by the expression on her face, this hadn't been the response she'd expected. She didn't look thrilled by Kathy's "I'll get back to you," remark, but she accepted it gracefully.

"I don't want you to mention this to anyone…" said Janet, as she stood.

"What… not even…"

"Nobody. I have never told a single person about this. Not consciously anyway. I might have blurted it out when I was in drink, but nobody would have taken any notice of a sad old drunk. That's if I did say anything on the very few occasions that I've been in the company of anybody else." Janet was stood over Kathy, waiting for a nod, or a smile to acknowledge the request to keep quiet about Bob Francis.

"Okay, I'll not say a word. I just want to mull it over, think of a way that we could do this."

"How do you mean?"

"Well, the thing is... no. Look, I'll phone you tomorrow. There's no point in me saying this now." Kathy had a gentle, reassuring look on her face. It wasn't an expression that she was famed for.

"No point in what?" Janet sat back down, across the table from Kathy. "You're starting to worry me. You don't think I'm lying, do you Kathy?"

"No. No, of course, that's not. Okay, listen... I know you're not lying, I can tell a mile off when somebody is telling even a tiny lie, let alone a massive one. I'm just really worried about something."

"Go on."

"Bob Francis is a very well protected man, in terms of his reputation, his history, and let's not forget his back catalogue of shows. Now that all of the TV companies have been named and shamed in the years after the Jimmy Savile scandal... I'm just really worried that you'd be dismissed, you'd be ignored or made out to be a liar. And I'm just not confident that you'd be able to take that treatment Janet."

"No. Neither am I. That's why I came to you. I knew that you'd be able to help me." Janet's eyes looked as though they were filling up with moisture.

"Go on, get yourself off home. I'll buzz you tomorrow. Okay?" Kathy stood up and hugged Janet's frail little frame. Janet turned and left, and cut a tragic figure as she did so. Kathy could feel the hot swell of tears fill up in her own eyes.

"Shit. This can only end badly!" she said as she flicked the tears away, trying to protect her mascara.

*****

Even though Kathy had promised not to say anything about Janet's incredible announcement, she just couldn't keep it to herself. Her husband of twenty two years, Jack Greenwood sensed that something was troubling Kathy, as she prepared the couple's dinner ready for tea time.

"Why the long face?"

"Jack, stop calling me horse-face!" Kathy threw a mock look of anger before smiling coyly.

"Come on, out with it. We had a deal, remember. If something is playing on our minds, we speak out about it before it becomes an issue."

"Oh, I've got into something... something that's troubling me."

"Should I prepare for a shock?" Jack looked worried.

"What... oh, no, nothing bad. About us, I mean." Kathy blushed, as she realised that her "fling" which had been covered by every newspaper in the land was once again the elephant-in-the-room, completely by accident. As the burning in her cheeks got hotter, Kathy decided to swerve this unfortunate scenario by asking Jack for his opinion on what Janet had disclosed earlier that day, at Sally King's office.

"Open a bottle... I'll throw this in the oven and then I'll tell you all about it."

Half an hour later, Kathy had shared much of Janet's tragic tale with Jack. As the last of the bottle of wine was shared between the couple's glasses, Kathy announced that she was about to break a promise that she'd made to Janet earlier.

Jack was saddened, and shocked by the circle of tragedy that this poor woman had endured all of her adult life. But that shock and sadness didn't put him off wanting to hear the rest of the tale.

"Listen, I'm being really, really horrible for repeating this. I promised her that I wouldn't tell anybody. She told me that I am the only person that she has ever trusted enough to say this to, you know."

"Well its safe with me, I'm not exactly going to announce it to London's drive-time audience tomorrow evening, am I?"

"I don't know Jack... perhaps once you've heard what Janet told me, you might be tempted!"

Jack let the silence hang, and allowed his wife the opportunity to think about what she was about to say.

After a big slurp of the wine, Kathy blurted it out.

"The worst offender at London TV was one of Britain's best loved national treasures."

"Who, Ed Balls?"

"No. Stop being stupid. Who instantly pops into your mind?"

"Well... national treasures, let's see... Bob Francis..."

"BINGO!" shouted Kathy, making Jack jump with fright. His face turned from panic to shock as the idea of Bob Francis being a sex offender struggled to form in Jack's mind.

"Bob Francis was one of this woman's abusers?"

"Girl, Jack. She was fifteen years old."

"Still, it's ... I can't believe... Bob Francis?"

"Good, well, I'm glad you said that Jack, because that was exactly my reaction when she told me.

"It just doesn't ring true. It's too shocking to imagine. I mean, it wasn't a shock when it all came out about Savile."

"What do you mean, it wasn't a shock?"

"Well, in exactly the same way that it wasn't a shock when Amy Winehouse died. We all knew that Amy was playing a dangerous game, and it ended in the most tragic way. It was sad, it was heart-breaking… but it wasn't exactly a shock was it? Same goes for Savile. Everyone knew he was a deviant, every BBC employee from lighting to accounts had heard the rumours. It was an open-secret that he was a child abuser. When it all started to come out, a few days after his funeral, there were a hell of a lot of people who were genuinely surprised that it was a big announcement. Do you know, he asked the BBC bosses every year if he could help out with the Children In Need appeals, and every year he was told no, and he was ordered to stay away from Television Centre when it was transmitted. That says it all for me. Its like an admission that they all knew what was happening, but they were all too deeply implicated in looking the other way, that they had to continue looking the other way for the rest of time."

"So you don't think that they looked the other way whilst Bob Francis was raping and abusing this young girl?"

"Honestly, no. It would have been said, or at least whispered. Especially in the last few years."

"But I believe her. She's telling the truth."

Jack exhaled loudly, and drank some more of his wine. "So, what's the problem then?"

"I don't know. I've just got a really bad feeling about the whole thing. My instincts are telling me to stay the hell away from it."

"And, being Kathy Hopkirk, you always do the opposite of what your instincts advise?"

"Yes. Aw come on Jack, help me out love. How can I say that I don't want to help her? How can I say that I'm not interested. She has chosen me as the only person in the world to off-load this awful shit onto. I can't just say thanks, and good luck, can I?"

"Kathy, you're paid handsomely to be the nastiest bitch in Britain. Of course you can tell her you're not interested. And I advise you, that you should."

"Well, what's the worst that could happen?"

Jack laughed as he stood to grab another bottle of wine from the rack. "Well, I don't know the answer to that, do I? But Bob Francis is a very well protected man. A lot of people have a lot of vested interests in him. He is the face of a dozen charities. He advertises more stuff than I could remember. He is mates with the Queen for God's sake! This man is probably the worst person to have been abused by, if that *is* what happened. I'm strongly advising you to walk away, because if you don't... the worst *might* just happen Kathy."

With that, Jack pulled the corkscrew up, and poured a generous helping into his glass, and then an equally large portion into his wife's.

"You didn't answer me Jack. What is the worst that could happen?"

Jack thought about the question for a few seconds. "Okay, well, your earnings at the moment are at an all time peak. If the media feel that their loyalties lie with Bob Francis, which they most definitely do, then you'll be looking at one thing in your diary for the next twelve months. Celebrity Cash In The Attic, for seven hundred and fifty quid. You'll be finished love. Game over."

"Well, I'm nearly ready for the big finish anyway... I'm only looking at a few months more work and I'll have three million in the bank, plus my assets. So it doesn't matter, in fact, if anything Jack – this could make for a better way out than the disappearance!"

"Well, I've said my piece Kathy. I think you would be better advised to stay well away, this is another league altogether, and the cynics will just think that this is a stunt, the most unpopular British person versus the most popular one."

Kathy opened her mouth to speak but Jack got in

first.

"But, all that said...I wouldn't want to try and convince you, it's just my opinion. I know that you do your own thing, and it's what I admire about you the most."

"But?"

"Well, I think you should talk it over with Sally first. And whatever she says... that's probably going to be the best advice."

"Oh shit!" Kathy jumped up from the seat.

"What? What's wrong."

"I've burnt the dinner!"

*****

"Hi Sal,

Just wondered if you had a thirty minute window at some point today? I need some advice.

Let me know, I can be there with thirty minutes notice.

Chow for now

K x"

Kathy clicked send on the e-mail, and felt relieved that it had sent, and there was no turning back now. A problem shared is a problem halved she reminded herself, as she looked in her handbag for some pain killers. That third bottle of wine with Jack had been a stupid idea. Still, the take-away was nice enough – probably a lot nicer than the meal that had been cremated.

The laptop dinged with a new e-mail notification.

"Hi K,

I'm not too busy between three and four, so I'll see you later. I'm quite perturbed that you need *my* advice! But I'll wait it out, with baited breath.

S x"

*****

It had taken fifteen minutes, by which time, Kathy was nearing the end of Janet Croft's story. Sally had listened to it all, from beginning to end. She'd also had the benefit of meeting Janet, briefly, during one of Kathy's meetings with her, so she also had a face in mind, which gave greater depth to the harrowing story. And it *was* a harrowing story – Kathy didn't try to play any of it down, she didn't try to gloss anything over. She was worried that it could be seen as just another hard-luck story. It was so much more than that, and Kathy had been determined to present it in a passionate manner.

Janet's life story was a tragedy, and it was this aspect of it that had affected Kathy the most. It was the sheer misery that most of Janet's life-time had been wasted, completely and utterly lost, because of the abuse that she had suffered, abuse which had been mixed with such indignity and degradation which ultimately ended with the sudden rejection from her apprenticeship. The sheer audacity of Janet's abusers really made Kathy angry.

Sally King was shocked to see Kathy so worked up. Kathy was not known for showing her human side. It was a big surprise, and Sally found it very endearing.

But the big shock was still to come. The headline of this story was the real jaw-dropper, and Kathy had expertly explained Janet's life-story as an epic tragedy. Now the stage was all set to reveal the name of the sexual deviant responsible. Kathy sat back in her chair and took a deep breath.

"So, here's the reason I'm stressed. This is the reason that I wanted your advice…"

"Oooh… not sure I like the sound of this!"

"The man who abused Janet Croft at London TV, the man who instigated much of the sexual abuse, who made her do the most unspeakable things for his pleasure, his colleague's pleasure and, basically just for his own twisted amusement was a big star at the time, a very big star."

"Go on, stop teasing Kathy. Do I know him?"

"I don't know. Do you? He's called Bob Francis."

Revealing the name had the same jaw-juddering effect that it had had on Kathy. Sally King, the well respected media-mogul, the woman who managed more than fifty-percent of the UK's top forty A-List celebrities looked stunned, and winded as though she'd just been kicked in the stomach.

A few seconds passed-by before she spoke. When she did, Sally's voice had an unmistakable wobble to it. "Bob, Francis?" she asked, as though she'd imagined it.

"The very same," said Kathy, her voice completely flat and emotionless.

"I can't believe that. Seriously… I just can't take that in."

"That's exactly how I felt. But I believe her. I can tell that it's true. I've looked at Bob Francis' career, he definitely worked at London TV for nine years. Britain's cuddliest old man is a fucking sex monster Sal."

"But how, I mean, how can we possibly. Shit, I don't know what I'm saying. This is unreal!"

"I want to out him. Out the sadistic old bastard in an unforgettable, unforgiving way. I've got an idea, listen to me Sal, I've got this idea where we set up a kind of an awards thing, all his cronies and fans are sat around in a big TV studio, and we have all these video clips of the great and the good talking about what a wonderful old boy Bob Francis is. And then, from nowhere, we say, 'here's a clip of somebody you've not spoken to for a *very* long time!' And then a video of Janet comes on, describing what he did to her, she is describing all the things that he made her do, all the mates he made her do things to. She can describe the way she felt, and describe the way that her life became one long, lonely, hazy bender by herself."

"Oh, I'm not so sure about this Kathy…"

"Just to have a camera on his smug face while his

horrible, slimy past comes out, and he's revealed as the disgusting little cunt that he is. That will be a great antidote for Janet. Then the police come in and cart him off, and he dies in prison. It'll be amazing."

"No, I'm... listen I'm having seriously bad feelings about this."

"Why?"

"Well... look, I know this is your kind of thing, I get that. But seriously, Bob Francis is a very powerful man in the media world. He might be ancient, but he's still the royalty of this business. He's untouchable, Kathy."

"Nobody is untouchable." Kathy looked as though she was getting annoyed with her manager.

"Bob Francis is. He'll have more secrets on more people than anybody else in the industry. That's how this business works Kathy, you know that. If this is true, what Janet has told you,"

"It *is* true. I know it is."

"Okay, so there, that kind of helps me to prove my point. If it *is* true, that will explain why Bob Francis' name has never come up. Look at all the legends that were accused and acquitted after the Savile story broke. People like Jimmy Tarbuck, Paul Gambaccini, Bill Roach, Cliff bloody Richard! These are some of the biggest stars in the land. There were dozens upon dozens of big names being accused, but not once did Bob Francis' name come up."

"So..."

"So, I'm telling you Kathy... he's untouchable. Completely and utterly untouchable."

"Not to me. Nobody is above-the-law as far as I'm concerned, or as far as Janet Croft is concerned either, for that matter."

"Well, listen to me Kathy. I'm strongly advising you to steer clear of this. If it *is* true, then I agree that Bob Francis is a despicable man. But you'll never get to him. He's too far up the chain. Please, just leave it." Sally leant across her desk and grabbed hold of Kathy's hands. "You need to walk away from this. It will end badly."

Kathy looked straight into her manager's eyes.

"The only person that this is going to end badly for is Bob Francis. And my mind's set."

Sally blew out a gust of air, a little too loudly. "Kathy, I thought you told me that you wanted some advice."

"I did."

"Well I'm advising you, *strongly* advising you to leave well alone. This is my professional, and personal advice."

"So I'm on my own?"

"As far as this thing is concerned – it has absolutely nothing at all to do with Sally King Associates, either."

Kathy looked annoyed, and hurt. "So you are sacking me?" She pulled her hands out of her manager's embrace.

"Wait... hey – I didn't say that Kathy."

"Well I take it to mean *that* Sally. I'm really disappointed with you. This is the biggest issue of our time, and you want to do what everybody else in show business has done for the past fifty years – pretend its not happening. I thought you had a bit more about you Sally. I really did."

Kathy stood and walked out of Sally's office. Sally remained seated, her mouth was open as though she wanted to speak – but no words came out. Kathy closed the all-glass door behind her and walked off briskly towards the reception, and the way out of Sally's, and the place that she thought of as her own, office."

Sally sat there a moment, mulling over what Kathy had just said. It was terrible, sure, no-two ways about it. What had happened to Janet Croft was despicable. But as Sally thought it over, she reasoned that it wasn't her fight to get involved with. There was far too much at stake, far too many professional relationships that would be damaged irreparably if Britain's best-loved entertainer was outed as another sordid, creepy sex-case. And in his ninetieth year too. This really was better swept under the carpet, as far as Sally King was concerned.

Sally had one loyalty, and that was to her company, Sally King Associates. With that in mind, she lifted the phone and rang her old friend and colleague Piers Marshall, the managing director of London TV, the television station from where these alleged activities took place forty years earlier.

"Piers, hey you! It's Sally!"

"Sally King! The woman I should have married! Why didn't I?" Piers was chuckling.

"Because I wanted to marry a much less successful man with a far smaller... erm, personality!"

Piers laughed very loudly, forcing Sally to hold the phone away from her ear. She was nervous, and stressed, but Piers couldn't tell as the two former work colleagues talked shit for a couple of minutes.

"So, anyway Sally King, why have you phoned me today? Have you found me a fresh new face to host Britain's Worst Restaurants?"

"No, actually, I'm not pitching anything..."

"Oh? Are you feeling okay?"

"Yes, I'm fine, I'm just a little stressed out about something."

"Stress is no good for a woman of your vintage. What's the matter?" Piers sounded genuine, the silly flirting had stopped, and it sounded as though there was real concern in his voice.

"Well, its Kathy... she's just been in and told me something. Something about Bob Francis."

The line went quiet. Silent. Sally wondered if the connection had dropped.

"Piers?"

"Yeah, yeah, I'm here. So, what exactly did Kathy say about Bob?" Now it was Piers' turn to sound stressed.

"Well, a lady called Janet Croft, she was an apprentice at your place forty years ago. She's approached Kathy. She has said some things that don't paint Bob Francis in the usual light."

"Okay, well, I hope you've advised Kathy to keep out of it?" Piers sounded extremely anxious and uptight.

"Of course. But… well this is Kathy we're talking about, it's not always that straight-forward."

"Well I want to make this as clear as I can. This stops now. Tell Kathy. It stops now."

"Okay. I've already… she's… she won't listen to me." Sally had gone from sounding stressed and emotional, to sounding scared. Piers was being very hard with her. She'd never heard him speak to her, or anybody else in such a bossy, unpleasant way.

"This is very bad Sally. I hope I can depend on you to help me to get this back in the box?"

"What, well, I mean of course. Yes."

"Okay, I'll come and collect you now. We'll go and face Kathy together. She has to realise the danger that she is putting herself in. I'll be at your office in twenty minutes."

"Okay… thanks Piers." Sally put the phone down and realised that she was trembling. She felt weak, and noticed that she was sweating. "Shit shit shit, what have I done?" Sally tried to work out if she had screwed up. Had it been good idea ringing the boss of London TV? From Piers' response, it seemed like he already knew that Bob Francis had another side to his public personality. The public personality that puts him at the top of every "beloved national treasure" and "best-loved stars" list, time-after-time.

The more Sally thought about it, the clearer it became that Piers knew exactly what was going on with Bob Francis. She'd barely said anything about it. Sally was trying to remember exactly what she had told Piers. She was frustrated that she couldn't remember the exact words she had used, but she was confident that she had only hinted at what was being alleged by Janet Croft. Then it came back to her. She had said that Janet had said something that didn't paint Bob in a good light. That was all. Shit. There must be something in this, to attract such a reaction.

Sally was agitated. She was fidgeting, rocking in her chair, messing with her skirt, constantly checking her watch. This was scary, and Sally didn't want any part in it at all. Piers' response on the phone had really given her a cold-chill down her spine. The way that he had spoken in that snappy, nasty style told her a lot. It reminded her of a newspaper story that she'd read about Manchester Police a year or two earlier.

The legend had it that throughout the seventies and eighties, the Manchester Police Training School instilled a piece of wisdom in all of the new recruits. It was along the lines of "Remember that nobody is above the law. Nobody. Oh, except for the MP for Rochdale, we just have to leave him to it." The remark was about Cyril Smith, the big fat disgusting former MP who sexually and physically abused lots of children over a forty-year period, and everybody knew about it. It was an open-secret in the north of England. The police, the schools, the council, the care homes that he visited for sex with little boys, as well as the Scout groups, the holiday camp staff, and even, its rumoured that the Prime Minister of the 1980's, Mrs T knew about Cyril Smith and his perverted desire for small boys. Smith's crimes were practically committed in broad daylight, under the noses of the powers-that-be and nobody had the courage to do anything about it. It was so blatant that trainee police officers were told about it as a black joke.

And that's just what this felt like for Sally King, as she waited for Piers to appear at her office. It seemed as though Piers was Manchester Police's equivalent in this, only it wasn't a dead MP that he was covering up for, it was a living celebrity. The biggest celebrity in the land. Sally was beginning to regret making that phone call now.

The moment that she saw Piers' face when he pulled up outside the office, she knew that there was trouble in the air. For the first time, Sally got a real sense of danger.

"Shit."

PART THREE
Chapter 40

"Okay, this had better all start making sense now Jack." DC Jo Rudovsky was standing over the husband of the missing TV star, Kathy Hopkirk. "I've given you a letter there which confirms that you will be treated as a prime witness, and when you sign it, it basically means that you will be under police protection from that moment onwards."

Jack Greenwood was scanning the contents of the letter which confirmed that he was now a member of the Witness Protection programme. Eventually, he nodded.

"Is anybody else being put on this?" he asked. He looked scared, and slightly emotional.

"I have just been informed that Sally King, Kathy's..."

"Yes, I know who she is," snapped Greenwood, in a bid to hurry things along.

"I've just been informed that she has volunteered herself into Charing Cross police station, and has formally requested to join the Witness Protection scheme. We are presently making plans to transport her up north."

"And what about me?"

"You'll be travelling north as well, with us."

Greenwood had a sudden look of panic in his eyes. "We'll be followed, you bloody maniacs. As soon as a police car leaves here with me inside it, we'll be followed by a hundred reporters and paparazzi goons."

"Don't worry about all that," said DC Peter Kenyon in a firm, but fair tone of voice.

"Well I DO FUCKING WORRY ACTUALLY!" Jack Greenwood was shouting at the top of his voice. This unexpected outburst made both Rudovsky and Kenyon jump with fright. The hysterical eruption made Rudovsky angry, and she shot a furious look across the table at Greenwood.

"CAN YOU FUCKING NOT?" she bellowed back, as loudly as she possibly could. The radio DJ looked stunned, and mildly embarrassed, being shouted at by a detective half his age and size. It worked though, Rudovsky snapped Greenwood out of his self-pitying before he'd even managed to go there.

"There's no need for acting like a big diva pal. We'll have none of that bullshit, right?"

"Okay… I'm sorry."

"Well knock it off. If you make me jump like that again, I'll rip that piece of paper up and you'll be on your own."

"I'm sorry. I'm just a bit tense. I'm tired as well, I've not slept in days."

"DC Kenyon, do me a favour please, go down and ask at reception if they've got a violin I can play for this one."

"Oh, for God's sake!" Greenwood wasn't in the mood for Rudovsky, and the feeling was completely mutual.

"Oi, I just told you, zip it. Have you got any idea how irritating it is to be sent down here, to sort you out, when me and him were this far off nicking a violent burglar who punches old ladies in the face and then shits on their stairs?" Rudovsky held her thumb and forefinger up. "We got some concrete DNA evidence back from the labs, it's a case we've been on for weeks. We've sat and held the old ladies hands, tried to comfort them in hospital, we've promised them we'll catch this bastard."

Greenwood looked totally disaffected by Rudovsky's frustration, but she carried on telling him anyway. "We were planning to go and arrest the suspect, and take him off the streets for a good while. We were looking forward to going around and telling the old ladies the good news, try and build them up a bit. And then this happens!"

"Oh I *am* sorry my wife has gone missing!"

"That's not what I'm on about Jack, and well you know it. I'm talking about you acting like a dick all week. You've frustrated our Detective Inspector so much, we've been lumbered with coming down here to listen to you shouting and acting like Elton John with no tea-bags. Meanwhile, our suspect could very possibly go and punch another old lady in the face tonight!"

"Are you done?" Greenwood was staring down at the floor.

"Do you not even feel bad about what I just said?"

"No. I've got my own problems."

"See DC Kenyon. I told you. This is why Saunders has sent us here. Well this cock-splurt can come up north, I'm not staying down here a minute longer!"

"Wait Jo, we've got to start a new interview, there's been some new information. Miller has text me." DC Kenyon was not saying anything that Rudovsky wanted to hear.

"Could this lead to us finding Kathy?"

"I'm not sure. He's the only one who knows that." Kenyon nodded in Greenwood's direction.

"Okay, right, sit down then Pete, lets get on with it. Start the tape, let's get cracking." Rudovsky sat down and there was no mistaking her eagerness to get started.

Kenyon introduced the recording with the official legal jargon, before getting straight into the prepared questions that DCI Miller had text through.

"Okay, Jack, in the interests of trying to find out where Kathy is, we need to know why you have requested to sign the WP?"

"Because basically, Kathy was about to reveal some very uncomfortable facts about a major celebrity. These were not facts that the celebrity would want to be revealed. If Kathy's disappearance is connected to that, and I strongly suspect that it is, well… I'm very probably going to be the next to disappear."

"Well, now *that's* interesting!" said Kenyon, who

finally looked like he might be getting engaged with this investigation for the very first time.

"And to think you could have said this on Sunday, Jack!" said Rudovsky, there was no attempt to hide her discontent. "I think you need to tell us the full story."

For the next twenty minutes, Jack talked about the situation that Kathy had found herself in, following the Talk AM show. Both of the detectives were intrigued by the speed in which this had escalated. They allowed Jack to talk until he was done. The story ended when Kathy went off to Manchester by train the previous Thursday morning.

"And you've not heard from Kathy in any way, shape or form since your phone call with her at seven forty-five pm on the night that she disappeared?"

"No. I've not."

"What was the lady called, the lady who contacted Kathy about the abuse?"

"Janet Croft. She is an old drunk, well, she's sober now, has been for a few years. But I told Kathy that this was going to be a nightmare, I told her to leave well alone."

"Does anybody else know anything about this?"

"As far as I know, only Sally. Sally told Kathy to leave it alone as well. They'd had a big row. Kathy stormed out of the office and they haven't spoken since."

"So in theory, the only people who know about the abuse claims are you, Sally and Janet Croft?"

"As far as I'm aware."

"Are you sure Jack?" asked Kenyon, softly.

"I don't know if anybody else knows. I certainly haven't said a word about this, until the last few minutes. That's the truth. If anybody else knows, then it has come from Kathy, or Sally, or Janet Croft."

"Interview suspended at," Rudovsky looked at her phone. "Fifteen hundred hours."

Rudovsky turned off the recording device and scribbled down some notes on her pad. Kenyon also did some paperwork.

"Right, Mr Greenwood, that's very helpful. We'll have to leave you here while we go and have a look around, but I'm going to ask my boss to release a statement saying that you've been released from police custody earlier today, without charge. That should get rid of the media circus outside. I'll tell the desk sergeant to find you somewhere comfortable to sit until we get back."

"So I'm not going back in that cell?"

"No. Not yet anyway. We need to go and check that your story adds up."

"It does. Seriously, I'm not making this up."

"I believe you. Right stay here, I'll get someone to come and sort you out. Order you a take-away or summat. Cheers." With that, Rudovsky and Kenyon dashed out of the interview room and headed through the maze of corridors towards the custody desk.

"Are you thinking what I'm thinking Pete?"

"Go and find this Janet Croft?" asked Kenyon.

"Yes, you are. That's weird!"

"It's a pretty common name I'll bet. There's going to be a few of them in the Greater London area.

"Well, she's going to be aged fifty five, fifty six, if she was fifteen and did her apprenticeship forty years ago."

"Fucking hell, check out Sherlock Holmes here."

"Plus she's bound to have had some scrapes with the law being a piss-head for all that time. If not, we'll soon find her via the NHS database, Watson."

"Ha ha! You're getting sharper you Pete! I can see you as a DS in fifteen, twenty years!" scoffed Rudovsky as they left the police station's back-door which led into the car park. They were quick getting into the Manchester CID pool car.

"I'll be retired by then Jo. Believe me."

"Or poached by the National Crime Agency."

*****

Rudovsky and Kenyon were driving onto the Boundary Estate in Bethnall Green, just forty-five minutes after finding Janet Croft's address details on the PNC. Janet's flat was on the estate. She lived on the second landing of Hurley House, a once grand, two-tone, red-bricked four-story tenement block which was built during Queen Victoria's reign. The Boundary estate, also known as Arnold Circus, was the world's very first council estate.

"I've always wanted to come here," said Kenyon. Rudovsky laughed.

"What?" he asked. He looked surprised by Rudovsky's reaction.

"You, you're tapped Pete. I could understand if we were stood at the Colosseum in Rome or summat. But I'm intrigued now, why have you always wanted to come here, to some shitty council estate in London?"

"Oh, it doesn't matter." Kenyon looked out of the window at the tall, impressive buildings as Rudovsky drove around the estate. They still looked rock-solid today, over a hundred years since they'd been built.

Building this estate had been a grand experiment which had worked so well, tens of thousands of similar schemes were built all across Europe in the years which followed. The buildings at Arnold Circus were very ornate, and had been built to last. Affordable housing had been in great demand back then, at the height of the industrial revolution, mainly because of unscrupulous landlords renting out slum properties with no regard for their tenant's health or well-being. The workers didn't earn enough money to buy a property, so affordable social housing was required urgently. It shows how slowly society is progressing, when the very same situation is happening again, over a century later.

The enormous success of the Boundary Estate taught Britain's and subsequently, the world's local councils that if they built good quality housing to rent to low paid, working people who couldn't afford to buy their own homes, there was an enormous amount of profit to be gained from it. Like all council estates that came after it, the Boundary Estate had required a hefty investment at the time, but it paid for itself twenty times over, generating extra funds for other council activities such as social services, children's and youth services as well as parks and recreation.

Council estates are still the main bread-winner at most UK town halls, although this fact is never publicised. The current trend is to demonise people who live in social housing. Unfairly, the media, particularly Channel 4, Channel 5 and the Daily Mail have been running a "hate your-local-council house-tenants" campaign for a number of years, desperate to convince the general public that people who reside in social housing are scum-bags who sit at home all day watching TV and laughing at all of the "normal" people who go out to work, and who subsequently fund the council-scum's lifestyle. It's total nonsense of course, and the vast majority of council house tenants are in full-time work, and pay their rent just like any other person who lives in any other type of rented accommodation. But the media don't mention that, it wouldn't help them demonise the working-class. They actively encourage the public to believe that people on council estates are no good. It's no different than saying that everybody from Ireland is thick, and that everybody with brown skin is a terrorist.

Yet, no matter how ridiculous it is to smear people who live on council estates, the media is guilty of doing this, on a regular basis. Despite the brainwashing media trying to convince people otherwise, council estates have been a good thing, and as a result of their success, they have been recreated all around the world. And it all started right here, in Tower Hamlets.

As Rudovsky and Kenyon parked their unmarked CID car outside Hurley House, Janet Croft's tenement building, there were lots of people loitering around the area, groups of men and gangs of youths standing on corners, smoking pungent smelling joints and laughing loudly. Music was booming from several different flats. Drum n Bass from one window, mellow Reggae from another. There were people of lots of different ethnicities and age groups, mostly men, but there was also a group of boisterous teenage girls by the shops, who were attracting lots of cat-calling attention. Rudovsky and Kenyon felt quite stressed, intimidated even, as the locals openly viewed these two outsiders with suspicious eyes.

Once inside the relative safety of the tenement's stair-well, and away from so many prying, inquisitive eyes, the Manchester officers breathed a sigh of relief. As they made their way up the stinking, decaying stairwell, Rudovsky decided to go about her business in as loudly and as confidently a manner as she could. There was no other way, she felt. Kenyon looked quite nervous as well, and he was famously as soft-as-shite if anything *did* kick off - so she decided that she was going to pursue this enquiry at full volume, just to tell the spectators that their visitors were police officers, and that they were here on business. Business that didn't concern any of them. Hopefully, this would be enough to keep the peace, she reasoned to herself. But even though they were from Manchester, both Kenyon and Rudovsky were acutely aware of the tension and distrust that existed between the Metropolitan Police, and its multi cultural communities.

After inhaling the foul, stale-piss stench of another stinking, stone-cold staircase, the detectives found themselves standing outside Janet Croft's front door.

"POLICE, open up Janet, we need to speak to you urgently!" shouted Rudovsky. She started slapping her hand against the door. There was no sound from within the flat, but the constant thud-thud of some distant music in an adjacent flat was pumping at the same speed as the two detective's pulses.

"Janet – this is the police! Open the door please!" shouted Kenyon. Rudovsky slapped her hand against the door, harder this time. There was no activity inside the flat. The place felt deserted. A glance through a small net curtained window beside the door showed that there were several letters on the doormat, several days worth, at least.

Rudovsky turned to Kenyon. She began speaking quietly, through the corner of her mouth. "Thing is Pete, if anybody should have rung us up about Kathy's disappearance, its Janet. She knows exactly what's gone on, doesn't she?"

Peter Kenyon nodded. He had a sombre look on his face, as though he was reading his colleague's mind. There was an excellent chemistry between the two DC's, and they had a very strong connection. As they stood at this eerily silent doorway, they both knew what the other was thinking.

It wasn't *just* Kathy Hopkirk who was unaccounted for. Janet Croft was also missing.

Chapter 41

"Good evening, and welcome to Sky News, I'm Alison Morris. Our top story this hour... the search for Kathy Hopkirk continues, but the operation at Hartshead Pike beauty spot in Greater Manchester has been scaling down all day. It would appear that whatever led police officers to this isolated, rural location through the night, was a red-herring. We are currently waiting for the latest press update from Manchester police, but in the meantime, here is a brief update of the situation right now."

The Sky News screen changed from Alison Morris's serious looking face, to a shot of Kathy's publicity photo. Words began appearing on the screen, as the newsreader gave an update on the day's events.

"Kathy's husband Jack Greenwood remains in police custody this evening. Police should have charged him, or released him by now. We are trying to get confirmation on this matter... and, well..." Alison Morris suddenly looked flustered as some BREAKING NEWS graphics appeared on the screen, joined by loud "whoosh" sound effects. "...we are hearing some vital news, this just coming in..."

The newscaster suddenly sounded extremely stressed and concerned as she updated the nation's news junkies on the very latest developments.

"I'm joined by satellite from Manchester, by our north of England correspondent Paul Mitchell. There's been a significant development this evening Paul, what's happening?"

"Yes Alison, thank you. I have in my hands a press release from Manchester City Police, which states quite categorically that Kathy Hopkirk's husband has NOT been arrested by police, and that he has been helping police with their enquiries in a voluntary capacity. It goes on to say that Mr Greenwood is not being charged with anything, and that he is a free man, and that he is no longer in police custody. It goes on to repeat, quite categorically that Jack Greenwood is out in the community, and that he is not, as the press have been reporting all day, in police custody."

"Well, that's quite an unexpected announcement Paul, many people here in the press, and our viewers at home were anticipating quite a different outcome with regards the missing woman's husband."

"You're quite right Alison, in fact, it's clear that police want to end any speculation in this regard. They have put a sentence in the press release which states quite emphatically 'Mr Greenwood is going through a most difficult time, and we would ask the press and the public to respect his privacy, and his feelings at this uncertain time.' So it almost reads as though the Police anticipate that Jack Greenwood, Kathy's husband is likely to face a hard time."

"Well, this story has more twists and turns than any other I can remember Paul. Did the police say anything about the video which emerged on Tuesday, claiming to be posted by Kathy?"

"No, there is no mention of that in this press statement, Alison."

"Presumably then, if Mr Greenwood has not posted the video on Youtube, then it would suggest that somebody else is responsible?"

"Quite, Alison, and I would imagine that this factor will be a major element of the investigation. But to confirm what I have in writing here from the investigation team looking into the disappearance of Kathy Hopkirk… Jack Greenwood is not connected to this mystery. They have also asked us, the media, to stop speculating about this case."

"And why do you think that they want us to stop speculating?"

*****

This news story was getting more and more complicated with each passing day. The news companies had pretty much sentenced Jack Greenwood to life for murder in the past two days, with no chance of parole. Now, he was the innocent, unfortunate soul who had been caught up in everything through no fault of his own.

"I can't keep up with this!" Ken Watson, a retired engineer was getting sick of the news channels constantly changing their stories. "Half an hour ago, they were suggesting that this bloke had killed his wife, and now they're saying he's totally innocent! The other day, they said she's turned up, and now they're saying they don't know where she is. I can't make me mind up what's going on with all this, so I'm putting the football on!"

"You are not Kenneth!" shouted Shirley, from the armchair. She placed her knitting down on her lap and gave her husband a harsh stare, despite knowing that he was joking.

"Oh, come off it Shirley, this is absolutely crackers! Next they'll be saying that Kathy Hopkirk's come back from the dead as a big zombie and she's going to bite Prince William's nose off, but then Gazza comes along with a fishing rod and three cans of Fosters and sorts it all out."

"Have you washed them pots yet Kenneth?"

"No, I'll do it in a minute. They're soaking."

"They've been soaking for two hours now you lazy old turd! The water will have gone cold now. Go and do them, and make me a cup of strong tea while you're in there."

"Right. I will, anything to get me away from this pissing Kathy Hopkirk bollocks!"

"Language Kenneth!"

"Sorry Shirley. Right you are."

*****

Outside Kathy and Jack's home in Hammersmith, the press pack was beginning to swell again, the reporters and cameramen were returning to their spots, hopeful that Jack would be at home, or at least, would soon be there. There was a lot of anticipation for getting something from Jack, maybe a clue as to where the police investigation was centred. Following Jack's bizarre entrance at work on Monday, the day after the news broke that his wife was unaccounted for, the press had good reason to believe that he would turn up. Newspaper reporters from the big four papers already had budgets from their editors, and were feeling anxious to get to Jack Greenwood first, and secure an exclusive agreement. Texts, e-mails and phone calls were all being made to Jack's mobile, all of them very positive in tone.

"Jack, Hi, it's Mal Donoghue from the Mirror, fantastic news that you are cleared of any involvement mate, result! How about you sign an exclusive interview with us, there's a 75k pay day involved. Best, Malc."

"Hey Jack, Susie Walker, The Sun. Talk to us exclusively for £100,000. Ignore any other offers, they only pay in instalments. Hurry with a reply. Oh and huge congrats."

"Dear Jack, so sorry to hear about your ordeal. I feel now is the right time to offer you a few shifts on BBC Radio 2. Ken is off for half-term in a few weeks. Zoe Ball usually covers. She is okay but she can't do Pop Master very well. Fancy the gig? Let's meet and have a tall skinny soy frappachapacinno and discuss. Best Regards Bob."

Dozens of texts were being sent to Jack Greenwood's phone. None of the messages were receiving replies.

As the time wore on, the positive expectation began turning to negative scepticism, doubts were beginning to panic the media staff who felt that they were missing the big story, because it certainly wasn't taking place here. The weather was miserable in London, it had been a gloomy, wet day where everything looked grey and uninspiring. Outside the Hopkirk / Greenwood residence, the mood was tense, and turning quite hostile as the media crews, and general public grew increasingly disappointed that Jack wasn't offering "his side of the story" which was now the most urgent thing that the Kathy story needed for continuity. There was literally nothing to say about this mysterious case now. It desperately needed a new angle.

Chapter 42

On the Boundary Estate, outside Janet Croft's flat, Rudovsky and Kenyon had been trying to engage with the local community to find out if any of the neighbours had seen Janet around over the past few days. The response was dismal, very few doors were being answered, and any that did open contained confused looking people who seemingly had no idea who Janet Croft was.

Rudovsky had a morbid fascination with Janet Croft's front door, which made her keep revisiting the old, decrepit red painted door. She had lifted the letterbox several times, and had caught a strange scent from in there. It wasn't a pong, it didn't pinch at her nostrils – but there was certainly an unpleasant whiff coming from inside the property, and Rudovsky had a strong suspicion that the smell was that of a decaying body.

It was an extremely frustrating situation for the two Manchester officers, as they couldn't perform their duties in the manner in which they would do back at home. Because they were in the Metropolitan Police area, they were required to follow the procedure book to the letter. This meant that Rudovsky's instinct to boot the door in and get inside to check if somebody was indeed rotting away was a none-starter. Rudovsky had to liase with DCI Miller up in Manchester, who in turn had to liase with the Met CID, and for all involved, it was an exasperating, red-tape dominated circus. Matters weren't helped by the fact that there existed a very strained relationship between Manchester's and London's police services at the present time.

However, despite the anger and bitterness which existed between the two police forces over the handling of this case – there was still a very important job to do. At this moment in time, that job was to try and discover if the premier witness to Kathy Hopkirk's activities over the past few weeks was alive or dead. The more Rudovsky lifted that letterbox and sniffed the cold air from within the flat, the more she was convinced that Janet was dead.

As soon as the Met CID and SOCO teams arrived and closed off the area, Rudovsky and Kenyon were asked to go and stand outside the block of flats.

"Are you taking the fucking piss?" asked Rudovsky, of a greasy, sweaty DCI who looked like a divorced, demoralised alcoholic with low self-esteem.

"Just go outside, this isn't your crime scene!" He snapped back, waving his arm dismissively. Rudovsky did exactly as she was told, she raced down the stinking, concrete, echoing steps as fast as she could. It was that, or kick that stupid ugly bastard right in the balls. Kenyon followed his colleague, albeit at a noticeably slower speed. DC Kenyon walked down the stairwell, dreading the abuse that he was about to endure. Luckily, as he got to the entrance of the tenement, he found that it was Miller who was taking the abuse, via mobile phone.

"Oh my God Sir, I'm going to have a fucking stroke Sir! What the fuck are we doing down here, it's a complete fucking shambles!"

Miller was stressed out as well, and this outburst, however understandable, wasn't a positive contribution.

"Jo, just chill out!"

"No, *you* chill out! We're having the piss taken out of us. Can we just hand this case over to the Met Sir? It's a joke, I'm ashamed to be involved in this enquiry. It's total chaos Sir from beginning to end, and I want out."

"Jo, just calm down. I know you're pissed off, but you need to deal with this in a professional manner." Miller was talking calmly, and slowly, trying to put forward a measured reply to Jo's outpouring of exasperation.

"I can't calm down Sir! Me and Pete have just got the first concrete lead, and now the Met have kicked us out – I'm so fucking angry Sir, I just want to twat someone."

"Don't twat me," said Kenyon, quietly. Miller heard it down the phone and smiled.

"Jo, listen to me, this sort of bollocks is normal. Trust me, if it was the same scenario, and the Met were up in Manchester, we'd have to follow the same procedures, and ask them to step aside while we investigated the scene. Just go and grab a brew somewhere, chill out. You've done a blinder on this job Jo, both you and Peter, so just think about all the positives. DI Saunders was absolutely buzzing when I told him that you'd cracked Greenwood. You know what he said?"

"What?"

"He said, 'told you Jo would nail it.' So think of how many arguments you're going to win because of that, eh?" Miller thought he heard a smile down the line. "Seriously mate, just take five, calm down and you'll be back in the driving seat in no time. Okay?"

"Okay. Thanks Sir. Sorry, Sir."

"It's alright, we all get wound up. You should be absolutely buzzing with yourself though. Right?"

"Right. I'll high-five myself the minute I get off the line."

"Well, you'll look a bit of a dick doing that, but whatever floats your boat."

Rudovsky and Kenyon took Miller's advice, and headed off towards their car. They knew how notoriously slowly these kind of investigations ran, and in all honesty, they knew that it could well be several hours until all of the people were on the scene to break into the flat.

The two detectives decided to have their tea, and use this inconvenient interruption positively. They drove around the area, and parked up when they found a fried chicken shop.

"Are we sitting inside?" asked Rudovsky.

"Might be better sitting here, in the car. We might be overheard. Don't want any of that shit Saunders had to put up with the other day!"

"Fair enough. Right well, I'll have a zinger meal with a coke. It's your shout."

"Sake! It's always my shout Jo!"

"Stop moaning! And get me a few extra wipes please mate. I just need to ring the wife."

Kenyon stepped into the busy KFC while Jo phoned her partner, Abby, who was at home in Chorlton.

"Hi babes, how are you doing?" Rudovsky still sounded tense and wound up, and Abby picked up on it straight away.

"Oh, you sound stressed. But at least you remembered that I existed!"

"Don't be like that. I'm more pissed off than you are, looks like we're gonna be down here another night…"

"Aw Jo!"

"I know, it's the pits this case. I hate it."

"I miss you like mad, hate it when you're not here."

"I know. I was crying this morning."

"Aw were you? What's up chick a dee?"

"I was just thinking about how much I love you and it just made me cry, in a happy way."

"That's so cute. It's clearly a lie, but it is very cute though. I haven't cried myself, but I am missing you. I hate not being with you."

"Well think of our reunion! I'll take you out for tea when I get back!"

"Wetherspoons?"

"Better than that! Somewhere in town! Fancy?"

"Somewhere proper, with table-cloths?"

"Might do. And then a few cheeky drinks in the village?"

"Oh aye, go on then, that sounds alright!"

"Nice one. Well, I'll have to go. Just wanted to say I love you, and I'm missing you."

"Well it's lovely to hear your voice. Don't worry about me, just get Kathy found, dead-or-alive and get yourself back home to me, safe and sound."

"Alright. Love you."

"Love you more."

"Love you the most."

"Right, shut it. Seeya."

Kenyon arrived back to the car carrying a huge paper bag.

"Aw that smells fit!" said Jo, the sudden whiff of the KFC made her mouth water.

"Get stuck in, there was no-one looking so I filled my pocket with lemon wipes for you."

"Aw, you're a good egg you Pete! Cheers mate."

"Who was on the phone? The boss?"

"No, Abby, I was just telling her that I'll probably be staying here again tonight."

"She alright?"

"Yeah, well, a bit pissed off about me not coming home, but I've told her I'm going to treat her to a night out in town when I get back so she's suitably chuffed about that."

"God, Tracey loves it when I don't come home. Bed to herself, no farting, no snoring, no kicking off at the kids. She whinges at me for coming home, not because I'm staying out!"

Jo laughed out loud as she grabbed her food out of the bag.

"Aw, Pete, do you want a hug?"

"No, I want my chips to go in that gravy so get the lid off. And if you spill it again, you're cleaning it up."

*****

Thirty minutes later, Rudovsky and Kenyon were back at Janet Croft's flat. It wasn't good news.

"There is a body inside," the DCI explained quietly. "It's looking around about a week since her passing."

"Suspicious?"

"Yes, very much so."

"Shit. Fuck's sake. It's a week since Kathy disappeared," said Rudovsky to Kenyon.

"Is it definitely Janet Croft?" asked Kenyon of the DCI.

"We have not had any opportunity to carry out a formal identification at this stage in the investigation, but it's looking as though it *is* the tenant."

"There's no way that it could be Kathy Hopkirk?" asked Rudovsky, of the DCI. The question seemed to confuse him, and the two Manchester detectives saw very clearly that this DCI wasn't the sharpest knife in the drawer.

"Kathy Hopkirk?" he asked, as though he was trying to buy a bit of extra time.

"Yes, you know, that internationally famous woman that we're down here investigating the disappearance of?" Rudovsky had no humour in her voice whatsoever. This DCI looked like he was struggling to recall what Kathy Hopkirk even looked like.

"I'm sorry, I'm not familiar with…"

"Does the dead body look like *this* person?" Kenyon held out his phone and showed the senior officer a photograph of the missing woman.

"No. No I don't think so."

"Can we come and check please?"

"I'm afraid that's not really…"

"I will put it on the news that you might have found Kathy's body, but you are deliberately obstructing us from finding out…"

"Are you threatening me?"

"Did you drive here, Sir?" asked Rudovsky.

"Yes, I did, but what the hell…"

"Well, you seem pretty pissed to me Sir, and that's an instant dismissal, regardless of rank. So let us past and stop being a pain-in-the-arse, or I'll demand that one of these uniformed officers organises a breathalyser, and I'll film it all on my phone and post it on Youtube, you smug, greasy haired, irredeemable old knob-head."

The DCI was offended, but it was as though he was working to some kind of a delay system. Maybe Rudovsky had hit the button, and the DCI *was* under the influence. Whatever it was, he suddenly jerked into life.

"For fuck's sake, come on then." The DCI looked crest-fallen as he led the way into the cordoned off stairwell. He had no choice, and he looked ashamed as he led the way up the stairs, coughing uncomfortably as he went.

Once the three detectives reached the doorway, Rudovsky stepped past the DCI and walked into Janet Croft's flat. That scent which she had picked up was certainly stronger, and much more pungent now.

"Hey, watch it, this…"

"I've entered a crime scene before, Sir." Jo didn't hide her contempt for the bedraggled senior officer. "I know I'm a northerner, and I'm meant to be as thick as pig shit. But you're the one that's leaning against the door frame, probably wiping prints off there with your grubby coat."

The Met DCI was beginning to hate this cocky little Manc madam, and the strikingly obvious fact pleased Rudovsky very much. Both her and Kenyon turned away from the senior officer and began walking into the dark, depressed looking flat. The red and yellow carpet looked like it had been down since the seventies, and the paint-work on the skirting boards and door frames was also very dated. Everything seemed to be either beige, orange or brown, colours that hadn't been in home-décor fashion since Bullseye was on telly on Sunday afternoons, and the star prize was a coffee-coloured Mini Metro.

The smell inside the flat was getting stronger with each step forward, there was no mistaking the pungent, morose scent of a decomposing human being.

"Right, what have we got?" asked Rudovsky of two white boiler-suited SOCO officers who were taking photographs and making notes in the living room.

"She's been here for about a week." Said the female SOCO officer, in a broad cockney accent. "The smell's been contained because this internal fire-door was shut. As soon as it was opened, it smelt like an open grave in here."

"What makes you certain that it's a week?" asked Kenyon, holding his hand in front of his nostrils, and silently fighting back his gag reflex. He and Rudovsky were stood around the back of the body, and could only see the back of its head.

"See how her skin is blistering? It's ready to fall off. That usually occurs within six to eight days at normal room temperature."

The two detectives stepped around the settee, and were shocked by the sight of the dead woman. Her eyes were bulging out, and her tongue was also stuck out of her face. Her skin was a dark green, but with a purple tone, in her extremities, such as her fingers, ears and nose, it was a very dark purple, and it looked as though it was getting darker still.

"Why are her eyes popping out like that?" asked Kenyon, sure that it had something to do with how this person had met their end.

"Have you not seen a decaying corpse before?" asked the SOCO officer in her broad East End accent, talking so matter-of-factly that she might have asked if Kenyon had ever been to WHSmiths.

"Not this advanced, no."

"Well, this is the most active time of decomposition. All of the internal fights and wars between billions of different bacteria have all been fought now, and much of the bacteria is dying off, at a rapid rate. There is very little value left in this corpse, most of the gases have escaped now. The biggest clue is the advanced state of the decomposition. It's going very nicely. Once we reach this rotting egg smell, mixed with that unmistakable whiff of tooth decay and a bold hint of vomit and diarrhoea, we know that at least six days have passed for the body to have become so putrefied."

"Lovely." Said Rudovsky, trying very hard to breath through her mouth and not allowing the overpowering smell to penetrate her nostrils. It was no good, and the SOCO officer kindly handed Rudovsky and Kenyon a face mask each.

"That'll help, but it won't block it out completely," she said, once again displaying a complete disregard for how grotesque, and unsettling this situation was for the two detectives.

"Cheers."

"Thanks a lot. Good of you that." Said Kenyon, who couldn't put the white nose and mouth cover on fast enough. He just pressed it against his face, in too much haste to put the elastic round his head.

"Any thoughts about the identity? This person looks a lot fatter than the description we have for Janet Croft. Her GP's notes state that she is of a very small, frail build."

"We're waiting on a pathologist. Should be here soon. We'll have a better picture once they've done their stuff. We're pretty confident that this *is* Janet Croft, though."

"Really?"

"Yes. And that's not fat you can see, it's just bloating, it's all the gas in her body looking for a way to escape. It blows you up like a balloon. The smell gets much worse once that gas finds an outlet."

"What's the fastest way of finding out the identity?"

"Finger-prints. We've already had a go, just waiting on a match. It looks like we haven't had any dealings with this person before."

"Really?"

"Yes. Why, what's wrong?"

"Well, Kathy Hopkirk has had several altercations with the police. Mostly for theatrical effect or to get on the news. We've got her prints on the PNC."

"So…" The SOCO looked lost.

"Well we were kind of hoping that this was Kathy Hopkirk, and not Janet Croft."

"I think it's fair to say that this *is* Janet Croft… I'd bet you those nose protectors."

"How can you be so sure?" asked Kenyon.

"Her bus pass is in her pocket."

Chapter 43

Saunders and Grant were in Busaba, the Bangkok themed restaurant inside The Printworks. The plan was to eat, and then watch the latest Tarantino film next-door in the cinema. The Friday-night atmosphere was buzzing in the venue. The loud oriental music, the stylish eastern decor and the mouth-watering smells of the food really made this place feel like it was a million miles away from Manchester city centre. The SCIU colleagues were smiling like teenagers.

"Okay, so the rule of date night is, there's no talk about work allowed." Grant was sipping at her glass of prosecco and realised that she'd used the wrong word there. Shit.

"Date night?" Saunders grinned awkwardly and began blushing.

"Well, you know... not date night, but... you know..."

Saunders coughed and looked down at his lap. Shit.

"Tell you what, let's cut the crap, and just be honest about it. It *is* a date night. We can both pretend its not... but it is." Grant surprised herself by the forthright nature in which she took control of this situation. She'd normally try to giggle something like this off. Maybe it was courage from that glass of fizzy wine. Whatever it was, she kept going. "Look, I like you, and you very clearly like me. So let's stop hiding behind this work relationship. Let's stop pretending that we're here because we share a mutual appreciation for Quentin Tarantino's work. Let's just cut the crap! It's a date night, and I'm here because I really like you." Grant was staring at Saunders who was sniggering and looking down at the floor. This was torture. Grant sensed the cringe-factor was on full power, so decided to push it off the edge. "And I just wanted to add, I think you're really fit."

Saunders burst into laughter, slapping his leg as he did so. God, that was just about the most cringe-worthy moment of his life, but he'd loved every single second of it. He knew that Grant was being mean on him, she could see him squirming, and she'd kept going. Saunders decided to bat it back, and make his colleague cringe for a moment.

"Ah shit, this is really… I don't know how to say this…" Saunders' face was bright red, you could warm your hands on the heat from his cheeks. Grant was smiling as he spoke, her flirty, provocative stare was inescapable. She really was the dominant one here, a casual onlooker would never guess that she was sat with her boss.

"See the thing is Helen, you're a nice enough girl…"

The carefree look on Grant's beautifully made-up face suddenly began to harden. What was Saunders about to say? This wasn't in the script. Shit.

"…and I really like you, you know, to get a long with. But I'm just not sure about dating you and stuff. You're just not my type…"

Grant's eyes began to well up, and the scorching shade from Saunders' cheeks was very quickly transferring across the table. Now it was Grant who looked embarrassed, and scared, and vulnerable. She opened her mouth to speak, and the look of mortified devastation washed her assured, confident expression away.

"I'm joking! I'm joking!" Saunders laughed loudly, and Grant juddered visibly as the penny dropped that he'd been having her at it. "You seemed to enjoy taking the piss out of me before… I thought I might make you squirm for a minute!"

"You little bastard!" Grant laughed and took a greedy slug of her wine. She laughed again at Saunders' smug expression. He was extremely pleased with himself, and Grant was just relieved that it was a prank after-all.

That could well have been the most embarrassing moment of her life if it had been for real.

"I think we'll call that one-all. Fancy another?" Saunders pointed at Grant's glass.

"Yes, I bloody need one!" Grant threw the remainder of the wine down her throat.

Saunders decided to be a bit nicer. "So, it's a date. I feel very privileged. Thank you."

"You're welcome." Grant tapped her empty glass against Saunders' beer bottle.

"And we're going Dutch... yeah?" Saunders waved his arm and caught the waiter's attention. He gestured for a re-fill.

"No. You can definitely pay after pulling that trick. You tight sod!"

"Hey, do you mind? That's an urban myth about me being tight. I'm very generous I'll have you know."

"Give me an example."

"What, how can I give you an example that I'm generous."

"Okay, what was the last amount you donated on Just Giving?" Grant's confidence was back now. That charming vulnerability from a few minutes earlier was all gone.

"I don't think I've got Just Giving." Saunders had been nut-megged. He coughed and looked away.

"Bullshit! Everyone has Just Giving. Everyone has a mate, or a relative, or a colleague who sends a link to their fundraising page. Now at least if you said you'd donated a fiver I could call you a mean, tight-fisted old scrooge. But the fact that you haven't even managed to donate a bloody fiver to one of your mate's sponsored runs or swims leaves me speechless!"

"I wish it would!" said Saunders, pleased with his wise-crack.

"So, you have never sponsored anybody's Just Giving page. Okay, I'll give you the benefit of the doubt."

The waiter arrived and filled Grant's glass. Saunders still had more than half of his bottle of beer left, and declined the offer of another. He looked slightly nervous about this tightness interrogation and was trying to think of a subject that he could segue into.

"Thanks a lot mate," said Saunders as the waiter turned to leave. "Hey, I'll tell you what, that guy has probably only lived in this country for a matter of weeks and he still speaks better English than half of the students at Manchester Met!"

"Ooh, that's not a very effective attempt to divert me away from the business in hand!" Grant raised her glass and smiled smugly. "I'm offering you the opportunity to prove that you're not a tight-wad, and your response is to change the subject! I'm beginning to have very serious concerns about this date night!"

Saunders smiled. He didn't know why he'd acquired the "tight" tag. He preferred the words "careful" or "thrifty."

"What's the most generous thing you've ever done?" asked Grant, playfully. Saunders groaned and rolled his eyes to the heavens which made his date laugh loudly.

"What's the most generous thing *you've* done?" he asked.

Grant began to blush. She looked a little bit embarrassed as she spoke, and it seemed as though she suddenly regretted asking the question. Saunders was definitely intrigued.

"Well, do you remember that massive earthquake in Haiti? It was awful, it wiped the capital city out, killed about two-hundred-thousand people?"

Saunders looked serious now as well, he nodded sombrely.

"I'd been out with some mates, and I came home and it was on the news. I was pissed, and I was watching the footage, this total devastation. Three million people had been made homeless in the blink of an eye. I sat there bawling my eyes out, it broke my heart."

"Yes, it was awful that. I remember thinking, what the hell would we do if something like that happened in Manchester."

"I know! Exactly! So, anyway, I was watching it, crying at all the people stood next to the rubble of their homes when this number came up on the screen, it was an appeal for the survivors. So before I knew what was going on, I was on the phone, reading out my long card number."

Saunders raised his eyebrows. He was beginning to realise that this generosity story was about to nuke any ideas he had for his. "Go on…" he said, eager to hear the end of the story.

"So, next thing I know, I wake up on the sofa. My head's banging. It was daylight, I open one eye and see a bottle of wine that I'd opened when I'd got home. It had about a glass left in it. I groaned, knowing I was already hammered when I'd got in. I started wondering how long the hangover was going to last. Then I was desperately trying to work out what day it was, trying to figure out if I was working. No, it's Sunday, calm down, I thought. I closed my one opened eye and tried to get comfy and that was when I had the biggest 'aw no! what the hell have I done?' of my entire life."

Saunders smiled widely, enjoying the animated expressions which accompanied Grant's drunken tale.

"Come on, seriously, I'm desperate to know. What had you done?" He didn't know if it was okay to laugh, or not. He didn't. But he really wanted to, just because of the look of utter horror on Grant's face. It was years ago, surely she should be at peace with herself by now. He could feel a grin forming.

"So I looked in my phone, the last number I'd called, it was at half two in the morning. I'd been on to them for six minutes. I had this panic, I started sweating and shivering. I'm thinking 'oh shit, oh shit' I just knew it wasn't a tenner I'd donated. The other part of my brain was going 'don't worry, it'll only be fifty quid."

"You piss can! How much did you donate?"

"Well, that took me a while to find out. I had to get my shoes on and go down to the cash point. I stumbled out of my flat, praying I'd donated a tenner. Praying that fifty quid was a worse case scenario... I was saving up for a mortgage at this time. But deep down, I had this feeling that I'd donated a wee bit more."

Saunders took a long, meaningful swig from his beer. It was all he could do to stop himself laughing at Grant.

"So, I got down to the ATM at Spar. I was shaking, my fingers were trembling. I didn't know if that was because of this or just the amount of booze I'd had the night before. Then I couldn't remember my pin number!"

Saunders finally cracked and laughed loudly. A few customers looked around, the ferocity of his laugh had made them jump.

"Finally, I calmed myself down and put the pin number in, and then I fell to my knees in shock." Grant looked down at the table-top and shook her head. "I'd donated all my savings to the earthquake appeal. Three grand!"

"Holy shit!" Saunders stopped laughing now. "Wow! Shit!" he said again.

"I wandered home in a daze, couldn't believe I'd done it. I phoned them back up and explained what had happened, but they just fobbed me off, said that there's nothing you can you do. But I wouldn't take no for an answer. I got put onto the manager, and he agreed to refund me. I said I meant thirty quid, not three grand!"

Saunders did his loud laugh again.

"So, luckily, they refunded me, and I said I'll phone back and donate the thirty quid once the funds have cleared in my account. It was the most excruciating phone call of my life. I could tell from his voice that he didn't believe me. I started panicking, thinking I'd lost my deposit. Luckily, my last throw of the dice was to mention that I was a police officer! That was what swung it, I think."

"And did you ring back, and donate the thirty quid?"

Grant looked down at her glass and shook her head. "No, I forgot."

There were tears running down Saunders' cheeks, he was laughing so much. Grant look confused, she didn't think it was a particularly funny experience.

"What's tickled you?" she asked as Saunders eventually started to simmer down.

"Aw, that's just the best thing I've ever heard. And once this gets around the office... I think it'll be you who takes over the role of the tight bastard! The woman who donates her life savings to a disaster fund, and then demands the money back the next day! Bloody hell Helen, you'll never hear the end of this, I'll make sure of it! Swear down!"

"Aw stop it. You mustn't speak a word of this to anybody!" Grant smiled flirtatiously and took a huge gulp of her wine. She had an unmistakable "stop-it, I like-it" look in her eyes as she placed the glass down. Saunders smiled widely, as he realised that things were going extremely well. But then his phone began vibrating in his pocket. He reached to get it out, and looked down discreetly at the screen. It read "MILLER" and Saunders' heart sank. It was almost half-seven for fucks sake, thought the DI.

"What's up?" asked Grant, she noticed the sudden mood change.

"What, oh nowt. Phone call off the boss." Saunders put the phone back in his pocket, reminding himself of the technique that Miller uses when Saunders tries to contact him, and he can't be arsed. But it started vibrating again.

"Soz," said Saunders to Grant. He answered the phone.

"Where are you?"

"I'm in town Sir, what's up?"

"It's all getting going. We're going to London – air support are just fuelling up and organising a landing and refuelling spot for India Nine Nine in the capital. We'll be going in the next thirty minutes, so get your arse to HQ. Where's Grant?"

"She's sat directly across the table from me, Sir."

"Tell her. It'll do her good to come along."

"What's going on?"

"Lots. I'll tell you in the helicopter. Get your skates on, we need to be in the air."

Chapter 44

"Okay, listen closely everybody, we've got an extremely big case on our hands here, and this Kathy Hopkirk thing has turned very dark, very quickly." It was 9pm, and DCI Martin Paxman was briefing his officers at the start of Friday's night-shift. His team of twenty-seven detectives were staring straight back at him, eager to learn more.

"This case has been fraught with difficulties, due to the fact that she is a London resident, who went missing in Manchester. We had, as many of you know, handed the case over to Manchester police. When the fake video surfaced on Tuesday lunchtime, Manchester handed the file back to us." Paxman checked his watch. "However, due to a number of issues, Manchester are now running the bulk of this enquiry – here in London."

There was a loud groan from the detectives. They knew that life was hard enough having to contend with the red-tape and procedure that accompanied ordinary, every-day detective work. Working in tandem with another force was going to make it even-more, unbearably frustrating, especially if it was going to be with people from up north.

"Now listen, let's give our colleagues a chance. You all remember that at the start of this week, I put DS Robinson and DC Hussain on this case – and I told them that I wanted Manchester to take over the reigns, just to give us an easier life. Well, they did, and it's back-fired for us. I'll apologise now for that. But DCI Miller is going to be landing with his team anytime now. This case is so important to Manchester that they are flying their team in on their helicopter.

One of the detectives couldn't resist a wise-crack. "Bloody hell, didn't know they had helicopters up north yet!"

The room erupted in sarcastic laughter as the old

rivalry between the south and the north was brought up as standard.

"Okay, okay. Calm down. Now, on a serious note, I want a full and professional response to this enquiry, and I want you to show the Manchester lot how polite, helpful and smart you all are. Don't give them a chance to complain about us. The pressure is on full power tonight, across both of our police forces, and I want you all to make me proud of your professionalism. Okay?"

There was a chorus of "Sir!" and "Yes, Sir!" It was an awkward position to be in, but they were in it now, and it made sense to just get on with things and try and make the best of a bad job.

"Thank you all. Okay, while we wait for DCI Miller and his team, I'll give you an overview of today's eventualities…"

*****

DCI Miller wasted no time in explaining the situation to the unknown team of detectives that sat before him. The atmosphere in the huge conference room was electric. If Miller was nervous, talking to all of these people that he had never met before, he didn't show it.

"So, I know it's a lot to take in, but let me explain the situation as we understand it, in a nutshell. We've discovered that in the days before she vanished, Kathy was planning to out Bob Francis as a sex offender. Yes, *THE* Bob Francis, as a sex abuser who systematically abused a fifteen year old girl in the seventies. This was a prolonged campaign of sexual abuse and rape that took place over a three-year period."

There was a sharp intake of breath amongst the team in the room. That *was* a shock. Asking people to think of Bob Francis in *that* way was a very big ask. It was like asking people to imagine David Attenborough punching a penguin. Or to imagine Robbie Williams standing quietly in a queue. It was a very, very surreal suggestion.

Miller could see that the Met detectives weren't convinced on the idea.

"You're looking at me as though I'm crackers. Fair enough...I totally understand. I struggled to get my head around this myself earlier on. But, let's think about this objectively, with an open mind. If there's nothing in any of this, then we must put it down to a shit miracle that Kathy disappeared just before she could announce her scoop to the public. It must be another shit miracle that the individual that Bob Francis allegedly abused has today been found dead."

There was an audible, collective intake of breath. Miller could see that his audience were beginning to see that there could well be something in this unbelievable scenario.

"The girl who was abused forty years ago, who only just announced it a matter of weeks ago, to Kathy Hopkirk, and Kathy Hopkirk alone, has been found dead. I've seen some bizarre coincidences in my time – but this one is off the radar."

Once again, the room was filled with the sound of restlessness and surprise. The detectives were becoming more and more engaged in this extraordinary turn of events, and were also finding Miller's confident, straight-to-the-point and honest style very endearing.

The CID boss DCI Martin Paxman was standing beside Miller, listening intently. He raised a hand to speak.

"Yes Sir?" asked Miller.

"This is gripping stuff DCI Miller, but how have we suddenly arrived at such an enormous amount of information today?"

"Good point. We've been messed about all week on this, especially by Kathy's husband, Jack Greenwood. He's been a pain in the fucking arse all the way through this to be honest. But today, whether it's because the gravity of the situation has hit-home at last, or maybe he's just shit-scared of being the next person to vanish… whatever it is, Kathy's husband has finally started talking…"

Once again there was a restlessness amongst the detectives, they were finding this a very compelling briefing.

"…but only after we promised him a place on the witness protection scheme. But now, as I have alluded, things are becoming very, very sinister." The detectives were silent, and totally engaged in Miller's briefing. They were desperate to hear the next detail in this enthralling investigation. "The woman who Bob Francis allegedly abused was called Janet Croft. She approached Kathy Hopkirk about the matter a few weeks ago, and was found dead earlier this evening at her home on the Boundary Estate, Tower Hamlets. Time of death looks remarkably similar to the time that Kathy Hopkirk went missing from Manchester, last Thursday evening."

Miller ignored the inevitable whispers and surprised glances as they spread throughout the room. Miller allowed a few seconds grace, this was, after all, quite an extraordinary situation – and the detectives needed to get their heads around the sheer magnitude of what was being suggested.

"Now, I know that this is a very live case – and we need to get cracking if we want to get to the bottom of it. However, there's a slight problem standing in our way now. Can anybody guess what that is?"

Miller stood and looked at the faces before him. None of them volunteered a suggestion.

"Well, put simply – we've all been in a lot of trouble for the way we have handled sex complaints against celebrities over the past five years. The public are sick to death of it now, they have been disgusted by the way that we have treated a lot of stars. Stars who had no case to answer. There is no appetite left for these kind of revelations. Just look at the reaction that you lot gave me when I suggested that Bob Francis was a wrong 'un! Five minutes ago you were all thinking that this was bullshit."

Miller took a drink from his can of Coke. "So we find ourselves in a very delicate position in this regard. I'm sure you are all aware of the damage our investigations have caused to the reputations of innocent celebrities. Paul Gambaccini, Doctor Fox, Jim Davidson, Jimmy Tarbuck, and many others have been dragged through the gutters by the press, and guess who got the blame when it turned out they were innocent? That's right, us." There was another moment of informality as the team looked around and nodded their agreement with Miller's assessment of the way that the press play their games.

"However, there is a chance that Kathy Hopkirk is out there, being held against her will. Its an absolute priority that we act immediately - even though the Cliff investigation made us all look like muppets, particularly when it transpired that the poor guy had no case to answer... I'm going to have to ignore the advice of treading carefully. I want Bob Francis arrested, right now, and I want to know who else was told about this." A wave of restless excitement washed over the group, manifesting itself as wriggling, fidgeting and frantic doodling onto pads. This was an exhilarating conclusion for all of the detectives in attendance.

"DCI Paxman, can you organise your officers to investigate Bob Francis' closest working circle please? His manager, his PA, his security manager, his driver, his cook, his cleaner, his butler. We need to bring them all in, at the very same time. It's now..." Miller looked at his watch. "Half past ten. I want the top tier of people around Bob Francis inside police vans by four AM, and this is obviously a very, very secretive investigation. No press releases please, formal or informal. Okay, DCI Paxman, I'll leave this part of the investigation to you. I'm now going to interview Sally King, Kathy's manager, to try and learn what she knew, and who else may have learnt about the Bob Francis situation. Jack Greenwood has insisted that Kathy kept very tight-lipped about it, and the only person he knows that Kathy spoke to about it was Sally King. The reason I'm telling you this… is because the people that you bring in tonight will know where Kathy is. At least, one or two of them will anyway. Good luck, and thank you."

Chapter 45

"OMFG... I've got the biggest exclusive of the decade. Twenty-five grand and it's yours."

The text message was sent from the staff toilets of Shepherd's Bush police station. A minute passed before the text message received a reply.

"Must be good for that much. Provisional yes... but depends on story."

"Fuck that. Put 25k in my account in the next five minutes and you will want to double it. Hurry up."

A few minutes passed before the next text message pinged.

"Okay. It's in."

"I'll just check my internet banking, two mins."

Another short delay passed before the next message was sent.

"Great stuff okay. First of all, you need to get your paps round to Bob Francis' house. There's going to be a dawn raid, 4am. Him and all his staff in relation to paedo sex offences, murder and the disappearance of Kathy."

A few seconds passed before the reply came. "Fuck!"

"Make sure the paps are discreet."

"Sure. That's a mind blowing story."

"Want to double the 25k now?"

"Yes. But not doing. Cheers."

"Make sure it can never get back to me."

"Usual rules apply. Cheers."

*****

As the night wore on, DCI Paxman was left in charge of organising the police raid. This was going to be a significant operation, involving three separate addresses, in two separate police force areas. It was going to involve over forty uniform officers, twelve operational vehicles;

which mainly consisted of police vans for the purpose of removing the detainees from the addresses, and keeping them separated.

Such spontaneous demand for uniformed staff and their vehicles was always unpopular. It was highly likely to cause a headache for the various neighbouring borough forces that would inevitably pick up the knock-on effect. But regardless of the bitching and moaning that DCI Paxman's requests were causing, the procurement of the resources was non-negotiable. Frustratingly for the inspectors and duty sergeants who were signing off the resource requests, it was all top secret too. None of the officers could know anything about the operation until it was getting under-way.

DCI Paxman's team were putting in a superb shift. After an initial "brain-storm" session, followed by some intensive research via Google, the Inland Revenue and Companies House, the CID team identified the key members of Bob Francis' team. It had quickly become apparent that Bob Francis was not just an internationally famous entertainer who was loved by millions. Bob Francis Ltd was also an industry, consisting of dozens of close staff members who looked after the star's daily routines, and dozens of arms length staff who worked at his television and radio production companies. Besides these significant numbers of staff, there were even more regional freelancers who worked on Bob's tours and public appearances, employed casually as and when required. All in all, the Shepherd's Bush CID team found that in total, Bob Francis employed almost one hundred people.

The "A team" of employees was the list that the detectives really wanted. They needed to refine a definitive list of those staff members who were closest to Bob Francis – and those who were paid significant sums of money. It didn't take long to arrive at eight names. Eight key people who were employed to protect all of their bosses interests. It was absolutely crucial that every single one of the team were rounded up and brought into custody at the same time. This aspect of the planning was causing the most difficulties, and DCI Miller wasn't available to communicate with at the present time – a fact that DCI Paxman found most frustrating.

*****

Miller was in an interview room at Shepherd's Bush police station. Joining him were DI Keith Saunders and Sally King.

Over the previous hour, Sally King had been as open and honest about Kathy's disappearance as she possibly could. Miller and Saunders were extremely impressed by how helpful she was being. After all, she could have kept herself out of this. But now that she had volunteered herself onto the witness protection scheme, she seemed eager to cleanse her conscience and offer a full and frank account of everything that she knew. Miller and Saunders had sat there in relative silence, allowing Sally King to speak at her own pace, and offering encouraging gestures of smiles and nods when the pace slowed slightly. They had resisted several opportunities to burst into her version of events and ask questions. Now, Sally had neared the end of her story.

"So what happened when you told Kathy that you didn't want to be involved?" asked Miller.

"Well, she looked hurt, and angry. And, well I guess she felt betrayed too. That's how I would describe the look in her eyes."

"What did she say?"

"Nothing much. I told her that there could be no formal agreement between what she was planning, and my company. I told her that it wasn't in my name."

"And what made you say that?" asked Saunders. It didn't make any sense to him. Sally King looked a little embarrassed, maybe a little bit ashamed too, as she spoke.

"I told her that it was dangerous. I said that it was going to be more trouble than it was worth."

"What did you mean by dangerous?" asked Saunders.

Sally exhaled loudly. "I suppose that sounds quite sinister. I didn't mean it in that way, I mean even at that point, I had no idea that it could be dangerous from a physical perspective. By dangerous, I was talking about the knock-on effect for Kathy's work… and my own too, I guess."

"But, what Kathy was telling you, what she was saying was that a crime had taken place, a crime which had scarred this woman so badly that she's been a drunken, outcast, prisoner in her own home for, what forty years. Did you not think that Kathy was doing something good?" Miller wasn't bollocking Sally, he was just trying to understand the mentality.

Sally thought about the question for a few moments before replying. She had tears in her eyes as she spoke. "Okay, okay, hands up, I didn't care about the same thing as Kathy. I just saw this as a mess, and it was a mess that I didn't want any part in cleaning up. So, okay, I admit, I'm not a very good person. I wish Kathy had never told me."

Saunders was about to speak, but Sally King had a little more to add. "You see, maybe I'm a little bit dehumanised, or whatever by the industry I work in. I have to ignore a lot of things that are morally questionable on a daily basis."

"Such as?" asked Miller with an eyebrow raised.

"Oh my God, there are millions of things. One of my top clients has a thing for cocaine which is going to destroy him, his family and his career. But I cannot say anything about it, because he is very highly strung, and he'll leave my agency, and subsequently I'd lose my twenty per cent. He earned five million last year. That's a million pounds which I would have lost, if I had stood up and done the right thing, which would be to check him into the Priory and save his life. Now, what I'm saying is, that's morally indefensible. But it's the way it works in show-business. We are all two-faced, lying, cheating beasts who are just out for ourselves and our careers. Anything real, anything like emotions and morality, they come second. I'm not apologising for it, it's just the way it works in a superficial industry."

"But presumably, Kathy felt differently?"

"Yes. She did. I can't say what her motivation was, however."

"What's that supposed to mean?"

"Well, Kathy has never done something which hasn't been a headline grabber. In the years that I have managed her career, we have never had a conversation where we discussed something that hadn't worked. I have a joke with her, that she holds only one dart, but she always hits the bullseye."

"And as far as Janet Croft is concerned…"

"As far as Janet Croft *was* concerned, well, I'm sure that her plight would have been a great motivation. But I doubt that it would be as great a motivation had the person responsible for the sexual and emotional abuse been a Night Casino Live presenter from Channel Five."

Miller looked at Saunders who was sitting beside him. They understood the point that Sally King was making. Saunders spoke.

"So, in theory, Kathy's greatest motivation in all of this, was to bring Bob Francis down?"

"Yes, I'd say that was a fair assessment, to be honest."

"So, after Kathy left your building, did you hear from her again?"

"Yes. I went round to her house, practically straight away."

"Alone?"

"No. With a colleague."

"What's the name of the person you visited Kathy with?"

"He is called Piers Marshall. You'll be aware of him, a very influential player in the media. He is the MD of London TV."

"And how did Piers Marshall become involved in this?"

"I phoned him, I wanted to ask him, off the record, if there could be any truth in the claims."

"Why?" asked Miller, this wasn't stacking up to the DCI. "If you told Kathy that you weren't interested, and that your company would have nothing to do with this... why then would you try and investigate it further?"

"I don't know... I just, I guess I was stunned that Bob Francis could be responsible for something like this."

"So you phoned Piers, and said what exactly?"

"I said, I asked him if he knew of any unsavoury comments surrounding Bob Francis. All of a sudden, he changed. He got really angry and nasty, and said that he was coming round to see me, and told me to wait for him."

Saunders opened a new page in his notebook and wrote "Piers Marshall" in the centre of the page. He circled the name slowly.

"And that was all you asked, if he knew of any unsavoury comments?"

"Yes."

"You didn't state what the comments were about?"

"No. I said that Kathy had uncovered another side to Bob's personality, and asked if Piers knew of any unsavoury comments that had ever been made."

"Sounds like you touched a nerve, then?"

"Absolutely. I knew the way that he had put the phone down that I'd made a mistake. Twenty minutes later, Piers was outside my office in his Range Rover, beeping the horn. I went straight out, and got into the passenger seat beside him. He seemed weird, nervous. I've known him for nearly thirty years, I'd never seen this side to him. I was scared."

"And where did Piers take you?"

"He drove straight to Kathy's house. He was driving really recklessly, it was alarming, and all the time I was thinking, why is Piers getting so stressed out about this? It made no sense to me. Then, suddenly, he began to calm down, he returned to his usual relaxed, charming self."

"Did he say anything on this journey?"

"Not much. He just said that some people in our industry knew the rumours, and that he would be happy to help Kathy in doing the right thing. But he needed to know who else knew about it first."

"That was a bit of a U-turn, wasn't it?"

"Well, yes, looking at it now, retrospectively. But at the time, I was just glad to hear that Piers was going to help. I had thought that he was going to end her career right then and there."

"And could Piers Marshall really do that? Could he honestly put a stop to her career? Realistically?" Saunders didn't seem too convinced that one man could put a stop to such a successful career.

"Oh yes. Of course. Don't underestimate the power that these people hold. It would only take a few calls from Piers to his network of friends, and she'd never be in front of a TV camera again, unless it was presenting Night Casino Live on Channel Five."

"So you arrived at Kathy's? Then what?"

"Piers told me to phone her, and ask her to come outside and speak to us in the car."

"And did she?"

"Yes, she came straight out, she looked really pleased to see me, I think she thought that I'd changed my mind. But then she saw Piers, and looked a little less enthusiastic. But anyway, Piers asked her to get into the car, he said that he had a proposition for her. Typical Kathy, she was completely fearless, and jumped in. Piers set off driving, and said that he wanted Kathy to tell him everything that she knew about Bob Francis."

"And did she?"

"Yes, of course she did. This is Kathy Hopkirk we're talking about. She couldn't give a shit. Piers seemed sympathetic towards what was being said. After the whole story had come out, Piers told her that he wanted to be part of the deal."

"What deal?" asked Saunders and Miller at the same time.

"There was an idea that Kathy had for outing Bob Francis on a live TV show. Piers said that it was genius, and that he wanted to make the show. It was all concluded within about an hour – and Piers pulled up outside Kathy's home, made her swear to secrecy that she wouldn't breathe a word to anybody else about it. She agreed, and seemed really excited that things were moving in the right direction. Piers was very charming, and he was talking about Kathy receiving a BAFTA Life-Time Achievement Award off the back of this. Kathy was horrified by the idea, and said that it wasn't about her, or about receiving awards. She seemed really genuine. Finally, Piers said that none of us must communicate about this over the internet, under any circumstances. He told us to watch out for a parcel the following day, he said he would send us both a phone, but only he would have the number. He said that we could only use that phone to discuss this, as our ordinary phones could easily be hacked. Piers seemed really pumped up in the end, reminding us that if this was leaked, it wouldn't be possible to present the live, trick broadcast that Kathy had suggested, where they pretend Bob Francis is getting some amazing award, but instead, we call out him as a seedy, nasty little sex monster. Piers told her again that she would go down in history for this. Kathy got out, went into her house and Piers then drove me back to the office. I'll be honest with you, I needed a lie-down by the time I'd got back to the office, my mind was all over the place."

"When did you next hear from Piers?"

"The next day, a deliveroo man came to my office. I signed for the parcel, opened it, and inside there was a phone and a charger, and a small box of Belgian truffles. The phone was one of those old Nokia bricks from the nineties. It had a text message on it, it read something like "these phones are the hardest to hack as they work on older technology. Keep it charged, and keep it on. Love P."

"And then what happened?"

"Well, nothing. I kept the phone in my bag, kept it charged, but nothing else happened. I assumed that Piers was communicating directly with Kathy, and that I was surplus to requirements for the time being."

"And when was this exactly?"

"Two weeks ago. In fact, it was the Friday before Kathy went to Manchester. So it's, what six days before her disappearance."

"Well, this is amazing stuff Sally. It's a real shame that you didn't step forward with this earlier..." Saunders sounded disappointed in Kathy's manager.

"I know... I wanted to, honestly... but once I thought about it, well, I just thought that it was quite clear what had happened. I didn't want to put myself in any danger."

"Has Piers been in touch with you since Kathy went missing?"

Sally looked scared, all of a sudden. She nodded. Eventually she spoke. "He called me, on Monday morning, on my mobile."

"The one that he sent to you...?"

"No, no. *My* mobile. He seemed in good spirits. He told me that he was shocked and saddened by the news, and said that he hoped that it wasn't connected to the stuff she'd been saying about you-know-who."

"Is that what he said, you-know-who?"

"Yes, word for word."

"And that was it?"

"He just said that if I needed anything, that I knew where he was, and he said that it would be wise, under the circumstances, to forget all about that other programme idea that Kathy was working on, for the foreseeable future and beyond."

Chapter 46

"Okay, how's it going?" Miller looked shattered, his usually healthy, tanned complexion was drained and grey. There were dark bags under his eyes and he looked like shit. However, there was still plenty of enthusiasm in his voice, and lots of activity in his eyes. He wasn't ready for bed just yet.

"Oh, DCI Miller, good to have you back." DCI Paxman had been desperate to speak to his opposite number, but hadn't wanted to interrupt the interview with Sally King.

"How is everything going?"

"Well, not too bad... but there are a few issues, I'm quite sure that we are going to have to put this operation back by at least one hour."

"Really, why?" Miller opened another can of coke and tried to remember how many he'd had now. They always caused him a bad bout of IBS if he had too many, and he hated it when his teeth went furry too. But, despite the downsides, when he was on these frantic all-nighter jobs, the thirteen spoonfuls of sugar in each can certainly helped to keep him going.

"There are a number of issues. The main one is a lack of resources in a neighbouring borough. Kent say that they can't spare any bodies."

"And who is in Kent?"

"That's the property of Christine Mason, she's Bob Francis' P.A."

"And what is her domestic situation?"

"She lives with her husband, they have a couple of big dogs too, from what we can gather. But that's not the only difficulty."

"Oh? Go on..."

"Bob Francis' house is on a huge country estate in Hertfordshire, so it's also on another force's manor. I'm waiting for the necessary permissions from Herts' Chief

Inspector. Assuming that's just a box ticking exercise, we are then faced with several operational difficulties at the address."

"Oh?"

"Yeah, basically the gaff is like a fortress. To get to the property itself, you need to get through the perimeter gates, and drive half a mile through his country park, where he keeps a herd of deer and God knows how much game. Once you've got through there, you then encounter a nine-foot high wall and another set of electronically controlled security gates, behind which is his mansion, and his staff's quarters."

Miller took another slug of the sugary drink, and began to realise that plan A was beginning to sound like a non-starter.

"So you're saying that there's no way that we can just spring up and surprise them?"

"Absolutely no way. The first gate will alert them that we are on site, the CCTV will give away the amount of vehicles we are taking in. There will be absolutely no element of surprise. The operation is just not going to work in its current format."

"Okay, well, good work on figuring this out. I'm glad we're learning this now, and not while we've got a convoy of police vehicles locked outside the gates. That could have been very embarrassing."

"So what do you suggest we do?" Paxman was really leaning on Miller to call the shots. Miller had a head full of other thoughts regarding the new prime suspect in all of this, Piers Marshall. This was a development in the case that Paxman was still unaware of.

"Well, the interview with Sally King has been extremely productive, and my DI, Keith Saunders is just doing a few back-ground checks on a couple of queries which have cropped up from Sally's interview. There's a delivery driver that we need to interview, and a couple of other loose ends which need tying up to check that her information is reliable. But if all that checks out okay, we may need to look again at this whole operation. Potentially cancel the dawn raid, and apply a completely different tact."

"Oh? That sounds like a major breakthrough. And, well, its music to my ears to be honest because this raid at Bob Francis' house is going to be a total nightmare. It's almost as though he's got himself prepared for such an eventuality!"

"He probably has, to tell the truth. Sleeping must have been pretty hard work for him over the past few years. Whether the allegations are true or not… he's one of a very small number of superstar celebrities that haven't cropped up on Operation Yew Tree."

"True. God, how depressing, to imagine that his security system is designed to keep out the police! But like you say, he must have been expecting us, sooner or later."

DI Saunders came bounding into the incident room. There were no greetings or salutations, he just came straight over to Paxman's desk in the corner of the huge room, beneath the case-file wall which was littered with various photos of Kathy Hopkirk, and some random notes and comments that had been pinned up by the pictures in the past few hours. It looked as though it was more for effect, than any useful, operational benefit.

"What's up with you?" asked Miller when he saw his side-kick. Saunders looked annoyed, livid.

"Sir, Sir, can we please go somewhere private to talk?" He was talking to both DCI's, which made him sound as though he'd suddenly developed a stutter.

Paxman stood straight away, "Of course, follow me." Miller stood too, and started following the London DCI as he headed out of the incident room and onto the stair-well outside the office. Saunders took a good look around the incident room to see if any of the detectives had been eaves-dropping on the conversation that he'd just burst into.

"There'll be an interview room available at this time of night, we shouldn't be disturbed there," said Paxman as he strode up the stairs to the floor above.

"What have you just said, in that incident room?" asked Saunders, quietly of his boss.

"Nowt really. DCI Paxman was doing the talking, mainly."

"Have you said anything about what Sally King told us?"

"No... I mean, I was about to. But I couldn't get a fucking word in edgeways."

"Good. Well, can we just keep it that way, for the time being at least?"

"Why, what's up?"

"I'll tell you in a minute. Just keep that whole new angle to yourself for now, okay?" It was hard to believe that this was a DI speaking to his senior rank. But Miller knew his DI well, and trusted him implicitly. Saunders wouldn't take the role of the gaffer if it wasn't absolutely necessary, and he was clearly onto something here. Miller understood that he would have to keep shtum about Piers Marshall, for the time being at least.

DCI Paxman was standing at the doorway, holding open the door. He wondered what the two Manchester detectives were muttering about, and the look of wariness was clear on his face.

"Problem?" he asked, as Miller grabbed the door handle, and held it open for Saunders.

"Yes, actually, there is," said Saunders, before Miller had an opportunity to think up some kind of well-mannered explanation for Saunders' whispering.

"But let's get into the interview room first."

"Okay, well... just on the left here, and... interview room six is free." Paxman held open the door and gestured Saunders and Miller through.

"What's going on?" asked Paxman, as he sat down.

"You've got a snide in your team." Said Saunders. Paxman looked confused.

"A what?"

"A snide, a grass, an underhand little twat, who has informed the press about the forth-coming raid that's due to take place at Bob Francis' house."

"You… what? There's no…"

"I've sent three of my officers, Rudovsky, Grant and Kenyon to do a reccy around Bob Francis' estate, their brief was to have a drive about, find the easiest route in, and out. I told them to look for a tradesman's entrance, the place where the staff enter and leave. Well they've got up there and they've found at least four photographers and cameramen hiding in bushes."

"Aw for fuck's sake!" said Miller, there was the clear sound of condemnation in his voice.

Saunders was furious, he couldn't hide his anger.

"Hey, now just a minute…" Paxman had raised his hands in the air.

"Don't start any of that denial shit DCI Paxman. It's one of your team – they've tipped off the press. This is going to be a fucking disaster now."

"How do you know it was one of my…"

"Because we do. It's not going to be one of ours, is it? We're both here, and Rudovsky, Grant and Kenyon are at Bob's house. Besides, we've never had anything like this happen before, for fucks sake, and we've run some of the most publicised cases in modern policing history – such as the search for Pop, the paedo killer." Miller was fuming, not just because of this totally unnecessary complication – but also because the opposite DCI had the audacity to question Saunders' and his own team's integrity.

"So, what are we supposed to do now?" asked Saunders, of Miller.

"Fucking hell bollocks." Said Miller, completely lost as to what the plan was going to be now. "How many press did they say were there?"

"At least four separate photographers, stood in different bushes, long lens cameras all set up, night vision aids. It's the professionals. They saw our officers, but didn't look remotely arsed."

"Has anybody said anything to any of them?"

"Yeah, Rudovsky went over to one of them, showed her warrant card and asked them to leave. They said 'no way,' they said that pictures of Bob Francis being arrested will be worth anything between twenty and thirty grand, at least."

"So they definitely know something's going on. It's only come from one source."

"Hey, this still doesn't mean that my team…"

"Yes it does DCI Paxman. One of your team has tipped off the press, and now we'll have a nightmare making the arrests. It's a fucking disaster."

"What do you suggest we do now then DCI Paxman?" asked Miller. The London officer looked confused, and embarrassed. He had nothing to say, this was a real bolt-from-the-blue. Miller looked disappointed, but what Paxman didn't know was that this under-hand activity by one of his team had created an excellent opportunity for the Manchester detectives, who were now beginning to feel that they had absolutely no loyalty to show towards the London force.

"I don't, I can't believe one of my team would do that. Genuinely guys, I want you to believe me." Paxman really did look upset by the revelation.

"Look, we're not blaming you. I can tell by your reaction that it wasn't you. But it's happened now, and it's going to be your problem to deal with. We'll be off to the north as soon as we can, away from here, but you'll still be left with a rat in your team."

"Okay, well, I'm sorry…"

Miller wanted to spare Paxman's blushes now, despite the fact that he'd been acting the dick all week with this unfortunate case. Saunders on the other hand was still visibly angry. He hated this kind of nonsense getting in the way of his work, especially after all the crap that had been printed in the press about him and Grant already this week. This job had been a nightmare from the very beginning, and none of the men in the room felt particularly enthusiastic about the Bob Francis arrest now that it was practically going to be televised live.

There were a few moments of quiet, while the three senior detectives lost themselves in their own thoughts. Eventually, it was Miller who broke the silence.

"Listen, try not to beat yourself up about it too much, you've got a bloody massive team of officers. It's hard to be tight-knit when there are so many personalities involved."

Paxman didn't say anything. His pride was very openly bruised in front of these two northerners. Not only were they from the backwards north, they were also significantly younger than him, and they dressed much more smartly. It wasn't supposed to be this way. It was supposed to be the thick-twat northerners getting out-of-their-depth in the big smoke, where policing is done much better and with greater sophistication. That was how it was supposed to have been anyway. It certainly wasn't supposed to have worked out that the northerners come down here and make the southerners look like useless fucking morons. But that's how this was starting to pan out, and DCI Paxman was beyond embarrassed.

"Listen," said Miller. "I've got an idea, how we can make this work. You need to call your team in, and tell them what's happened. You never know, the culprit might just go bright red." Miller smiled, in an attempt to lighten the dark mood. "But the bottom line is this, one or maybe two of your team have created this problem, so I think it's only right that your team take full ownership of the problem. You guys carry on with this plan, as you intended. You can have the extra hour. You need to bring in the eight names that we previously discussed, but the number one priority is Bob Francis. So I suggest you revise the approach, and you send in just one undercover car with four officers in. You then go in with a new car, every few minutes, and take the next person out...."

"And what exactly will you be doing while my officers are carrying out these raids?" asked Paxman. He looked quite sad, and embarrassed.

"Well, I can't really say, under the circumstances."

Chapter 47

The greed and unprofessionalism of one of Paxman's detectives had actually worked out extremely well for Miller and Saunders, and the other three SCIU members, who had just arrived back at Shepherd's Bush police station.

Miller and Saunders met the car as it pulled into the car-park at the rear of the police station.

"Oh my lord, who's been grating parmesan in here?" asked Saunders, knowing full well that the pungent smell was DC Peter Kenyon's feet.

"I can't smell that DI Saunders, all I can smell is Jo's farts. Hanging Jo!"

"Ey, come off it, you're smelling this car out of context Sir!" said Rudovsky. "There are several smells in here, including goody-two-shoes DC Grant here, who's been ripping plenty of eggy farts out."

"That's such bullshit!" said Grant, with a great deal of passion. It gained a laugh, and this daft banter cheered up Miller and Saunders especially. They were just glad to be out of the station, and back amongst familiar people. People they could trust. "Well open a window anyway, give us a chance!"

Miller and Saunders slammed their doors shut. Saunders was over-the-moon to be sitting in the back with Grant. He'd almost forgotten all about her lovely face while he'd been getting wound up with Paxman's CID circus.

"Right, just drive aimlessly, there's lots to talk about." Miller tapped Kenyon on the shoulder and the DC eased his foot off the clutch, reversing the car out of the car park that he'd only just driven into. As the car drove past the side of the building, both Miller and Saunders saw the silhouette of DCI Paxman, and another colleague, standing by the window on the stairs. Both of the officers looked deeply dissatisfied as the car drove away.

"Well guys, I'll tell you what, I've seen some bullshit in my time, but these southerners take the trophy. They haven't got a Scooby doo!"

"Why is it, right Sir, that southerners hate us so much?" Jo Rudovsky was leaning round from the front seat, "we've just been going on about this. We can't suss it out!"

Saunders decided to answer. "It's just jealousy, innit?"

"Is it?" Rudovsky didn't seem too convinced.

"Yeah, definitely. Think about it, best football teams, from up north. Best bands and music, from up north. Best celebrities, from up north, best comedians, best telly shows, best inventions, best everything. But if you ask a southerner what comes from up north, they just say mushy peas and diseases." Everybody laughed out loud at Saunders' quip, including himself.

"Northerners are a lot friendlier as well!" offered Kenyon. "These Londoners just walk around looking paranoid and confused."

"The southerners are just massively inferior, they're all like the school bully picking on the ginger kid. And if you come from the north, you're the ginger kid."

"So we're all sort of like ambassadors for Mick Hucknall!" suggested Grant which received a good laugh.

The conversation continued for a few more minutes with more light-hearted references to the north-south divide.

"Right, anyway, drive to an all night café and let's sit down and have a catch-up. Find the most southern themed café you can please DC Kenyon, and we'll stop and have some fackin' laaavly cockles!"

*****

Miller and his team soon found themselves tucked away in the corner of an all-night McDonalds on Uxbridge

Road, tucking into some traditional cockney Big Mac and Fries.

Speaking quietly, Miller and Saunders told the rest of their team about the bizarre turn-of-events regarding Sally King's tell-all interview. Rudovsky, Grant and Kenyon were stunned, but re-energised by this exciting announcement.

Although the media tip-off had presented a ridiculous situation, and a very embarrassing one for the London detectives, Miller explained how it had proved extremely fortuitous, and helpful for the Manchester team. Armed with Sally King's bombshell revelations, the SCIU team could now leave the ball-ache operation of bringing in Britain's best loved national treasure to the snidey sods who'd sold the story on already.

This left Miller, Saunders, Rudovsky, Grant and Kenyon with the big, secret task to themselves. Bringing Piers Marshall in, and all the while, the media eyes would be looking in Bob Francis' direction, and watching the sensational news developments in the heart-stopping hunt for Kathy Hopkirk.

"These southern detectives have scored a hat-trick of own goals on this case. From day one, last Sunday, they've tried to dump it on us, knowing it would be a nightmare case. And guess what, we've managed to break away from them completely now. They are off doing the dawn raid at Bob's, whilst we are going to be working on something much more interesting and exciting!"

Over the next forty-five minutes, in the corner of that deserted McDonalds, the SCIU team planned the operation of bringing in Piers Marshall. It was decided that this was going to be a "dumbo" operation. For the benefit of the new DC, Helen Grant, Miller explained what a "dumbo" job meant.

It was a very familiar operation in the SCIU, throwing a dumbo – it was just an extremely polite and well mannered affair with a chief suspect, a simple "we were just wondering if you might be able to help us please," type of introduction, usually aimed at the prime suspect. A few dumbo questions would be asked, along the lines of "have you heard about the disappearance of Kathy Hopkirk?" which would warm up to, "have you heard any rumours within the industry?" and then the carefully planned, but deliberately dumb conversation would lead to the officers revealing that they "haven't got the faintest idea what is going on," and "nobody really gives a toss anyway, let's be honest."

In this situation, in theory at least, this manner of behaviour should begin to empower Piers Marshall with the notion that the detectives didn't have a clue. From some unexpected police attention rattling his cage, to then realising that the detectives running the investigation were about as much use as a handbrake on a canoe, it was planned that this tactic would enable Piers Marshall's confidence to get sky-high.

"Over confident people are very easy to break down, because they make silly mistakes." Explained Miller, "people with less confidence always do their homework, they always dot the I's and cross the T's. Folk with plenty of confidence are always a bit too arrogant to waste any time on such nonsense."

"How do you mean?" asked Grant, looking as though she wasn't quite following.

"Well, look at David Cameron. Perfect example. Through his arrogance and over-confidence, he called the EU referendum, believing that the British people would do as he told them, and vote remain. He was so over confident in himself, so caught up in his own sense of power, he forgot to check if it was a good idea first."

"And it turned out he was a total bell-end, and lost his job that day?" asked DC Kenyon.

"Precisely. Case in point! He lost his job as Prime Minister because he was too confident and arrogant to dot his I's or cross his T's."

"He did cry on the news though, doesn't that count for owt?" offered Rudovsky, to a wave of mocking laughter.

"Over-confidence and arrogance, a failure to do your homework, they are the main signs of weakness. And for us, as investigating officers, they are the greatest qualities we can ever wish to find in people, because we trap them every time, especially when we act dumb."

"Okay, I get it," said Grant.

"So what we try to do is lead suspects down a path which actively encourages them to think we are all as thick as David Cameron."

Grant raised her hand, and Miller nodded to give way. "I've got a slight problem with all this," she said, without much conviction in her voice.

"Oh?" said Miller.

"Well, from what we've seen with the paparazzi guys at Bob Francis' house – it's not going to have escaped Piers' attention that Bob Francis is in custody. I don't care how thick we are supposed to be acting - when we get to his house, he's not going to swallow it. It's way beyond any coincidence. He's going to know that the game's up."

"Yes, she's right," said Rudovsky.

"Shit, yeah. Didn't think of that." Said Saunders.

"There's no way that Piers will be able to avoid the news. The news is absolutely everywhere now, on phones, tablets, even Facebook. If Piers Marshall is awake, he'll be aware that Bob Francis is in police custody."

"So what do we do?" Miller looked surprised by this obvious announcement from his newest member of staff.

"Call off the arrest of Bob Francis?" suggested Grant.

"What? Why…" Miller looked lost by the idea.

"Well, lets be honest, he's not going to be charged with anything, is he? The girl that he allegedly abused has been found dead. Are there any witnesses? Do we have any forensic evidence? The CPS won't let us charge him, even if he confessed to it all. It'll never happen without at least one supporting witness. From what you've said, the only person who could possibly offer any supporting evidence is Kathy Hopkirk. And nobody seems to know where she is!"

"Now that is a bloody good point!" said Rudovsky, and it was appreciated by Grant, who felt that her only female colleague wasn't really a fan.

"Go on," said Miller, he was most intrigued by the new DC's point of view.

"I say, best all round if we call the whole Bob Francis thing off. And the police officer who phoned the press will get a red face as well, when it doesn't happen." Grant was growing in confidence, and this suggestion had just given her a great deal of kudos amongst her colleagues. It was an excellent suggestion, and nobody thought otherwise.

"But, just to throw caution to the wind – the press that we saw up at Bob Francis' estate will have tipped off others. Even if we don't bring Francis in this morning – it's going to get out there very soon that police are linking him to a murder, and the disappearance of Kathy Hopkirk. It's too sensational to keep a lid on."

Grant stopped talking, and took a suck of her chocolate milkshake. Saunders looked pleased by the reaction on the rest of the team's faces.

"Bloody hell, she's going to be our next DCI, this one." Said Rudovsky, patting Grant gently on the shoulder. She then pointed across the table at Miller. "You, get a bin-bag and clear your fucking locker out!"

There was a bit of laughing and banter for a few minutes while Miller got another round of drinks and a share box of chicken McNuggets in. When he arrived back at the table, he looked like he was ready to get things sorted.

"Right, it's now half-past-four. There is half-an-hour until Paxman and his team raid Bob's house. I'm going to suggest that we carry out our own raid at Piers Marshall's house, at exactly the same time."

"That's going to cut it fine, Sir." Said Saunders. "Piers Marshall's house is thirty minutes away according to the thing on my phone."

Miller smiled. "For God's sake, what are the chances? Right, okay, everyone get in the car, I'll drive. And don't forget those McNuggets."

Within seconds the SCIU team were sitting inside the unmarked Vauxhall Insignia, and were racing away from the McDonalds, headed up Wood Lane, past the world famous BBC Television Centre, and in the direction of Piers Marshall's city home, seven miles away in Belsize Park, at the foot of Hampstead Heath.

Chapter 48

A fresh, misty dawn was breaking as DCI Paxman's team gathered on the Fox and Hounds car park, roughly a quarter of a mile away from the gates to Bob Francis' country estate. Despite the sweet sound of birdsong and the fresh country air - there was an uptight, snappy atmosphere amongst the London detectives, all of whom viewed one another suspiciously. Paxman had made no secret of his anger that one of his officers had contacted the press, and the friction was all around. His officers were keen to discover who the rat was, so they could divert any suspicion from themselves.

Paxman didn't know who he could trust. It was a difficult enough operation to organise and carry out, without the added complication of being paranoid about who he could depend on amongst his staff.

"Okay guys, time to put the negative energy behind us. Stop sulking about the bollocking and let's all focus on the job that we have come here to do."

The considerable crowd of detectives and uniformed support officers were standing in front of Paxman, who was addressing them from his vantage point, stood on top of one of the pub's bench-tables.

"We are going in there one car at a time, the first car, my car will arrest the home-owner. Once we have that individual in our custody, the next car will be ordered to attend. Each incoming car will be four-up, and each outgoing car will leave two-up, with one suspect. We have five suspects, so this will result in a surplus of ten officers inside the property. Okay then, off we go. Good luck."

A window opened above DCI Paxman's head. An angry looking woman in her fifties stuck her head out. She had a face like a melted welly. "What the hell is going on? Why are you filming Midsummer Murders on my car park? It's five o' clock in the morning, you gormless bastards. Fuck off!"

*****

"Right, here we are. That's his house... and that's his car. Look." The registration plate of the Aston Martin Vanquish read "P1ERS"

"Now, *that* is a car!" Kenyon's eyes were popping out of his head as he gazed at the graphite grey supercar, as the stinking fart, feet and chicken McNugget infused CID car pulled up alongside.

"They cost two hundred grand them! More than my flipping house!"

"Shut up Pete. God no wonder your wife wishes you were dead." Rudovsky pushed her partner in the ribs.

"Geddoff."

"Nice gaff Piers." said Miller, gazing out of the windscreen in awe at the immaculate row of four-storey town houses. "Look at the state of these houses! It's like something off one of those posh films. Four Weddings and a Funeral or summat. Proper nice!"

"Chris Evans lives round here somewhere. He'll have an even better car than that," said Kenyon, still in full ogling mode.

"God Pete you are such a dud."

"Kenyon and Rudovsky, stop bickering you pair of knobs, it's like being in the car with Basil and Cybil Fawlty."

"Not old enough to know that one, Sir." said Rudovsky. "Pete is though!"

"Right, you two can do this one. Hurry up, make it all seem rushed. And don't forget, you're going to tell him that his name has come up in conversation, along with another thirty or so, so it's just a process of elimination. Convince him that you're just here ticking boxes, ask him where he was last Thursday night, has he got anyone that can verify it, and don't forget to feed his ego, just as we discussed. After a few minutes of talking shit and putting his mind at ease, ask him to come and talk

- 314 -

to us at the station, say we need to see him ASAP because we need to head back to Manchester."

"Yeah, but he's not going to buy all that Sir. We'll be banging him out of bed. He's going to know that it's a load of shite, asking him to attend the police station after he's had his brew."

"Jo, shut up, you'll be right. You're the biggest bull-shitter I've ever met. If anyone can talk absolute crap, it's you. You wipe your mouth after taking a shit."

"Right, well, cheers. That's a pretty shambolic compliment, but I'll take it." Rudovsky pulled a sarcastic face.

"What he means is, you're a cunning linguist." Saunders was sniggering at his own, familiar gag.

"Fuck off Sir," said Rudovsky, starting to get annoyed by the onslaught of piss-taking.

"Right, jog on. If he starts being arsey, just text me and we'll be right outside the front door."

"Right, no worries."

"Good luck."

"It's not luck I need, it's a method of spraying breath freshener in his mouth. I hate interviewing suspects who haven't had chance to brush their teeth yet. Smells like Janet Croft's flat."

"Come on Jo, stop waffling. Let's get this done." Kenyon was almost out of the car, urging his partner to get herself together.

"Right, go and park up. See you in a bit."

*****

The first arrest that was made was carried out at exactly 5am. The address was in Bromley, Kent, the person taken into custody by two of Paxman's detectives was fifty-seven year old Christine Mason.

Christine Mason had been Bob Francis' PA for almost thirty years. It had been a job which had served her well, judging by her opulent home and idyllic gardens. She was a kindly looking woman, who spoke as though she was an announcer for BBC Radio 4.

"What on earth is this about?" she asked as the detectives entered her front door.

"I'm afraid that we have to ask you to come with us to Shepherd's Bush police station, to help us with our enquiries."

"What, Shepherd's Bush. What in God's name is going on here? Is this a hoax?"

"No, Mrs Mason, I can assure you that this is not a hoax. We can ask you to join us voluntarily, and we can clear this matter up very quickly, and drop you back off here in a few hours."

"Or?" Christine Mason was standing in her dressing gown, her arms firmly folded across her chest. Her husband was standing behind her, he looked shocked and confused by this incredible situation. Police had never been at this door, not even to offer crime reduction advice, let alone to carry out a dawn raid. It really was quite preposterous.

"Or, we can arrest you, and take you against your will. But that will only make things take longer as there'll be more paperwork and procedure involved."

Christine Mason couldn't hide her anger. She stood there, shaking her head as her husband caressed her shoulders.

"Really Mrs Mason, there is no need for any unpleasantness. We would strongly advise you to co-operate."

"And would you mind telling me what I'm supposed to have done wrong?"

"This is a very sensitive matter. We cannot disclose any information until you are in our police station. All I *can* say is that you or your family are not under any suspicion for any crimes. This is purely relating to an ongoing incident which you may have information regarding – most probably unwittingly. That's all I can say at this time."

Christine turned and looked at her husband. He nodded to her, offering her encouragement to submit her hostility and surrender to this absolutely ridiculous situation.

"The sooner you go, love, the sooner it will be done. At least then you'll know what it's all about, eh?"

"Can I at least get dressed?" asked Christine, huffily of the detectives.

"Of course. My female colleague will escort you though, if that's okay?"

"For heaven's sake! WHY?" Tears were running down Christine's cheeks as she struggled to cope with the anger and frustration and downright confusion from this bizarre early morning wake-up call.

"Yes, come on officer. For God's sake!" Christine's husband was losing his temper.

"I'm afraid you must be escorted while you get changed. It is just so that we can ensure that you do not contact anybody while you are out of our sight. This is a very sensitive enquiry, and the fewer people who are aware of it, the better. Now, this is normal procedure."

"Okay, I just want this over and done with!" Christine walked briskly towards the stairs, the female detective followed.

"Seriously, this is most outrageous!" said the husband. The detective gave a stock look of sympathy before expertly driving the conversation on.

"Are you going to follow behind?"

"What, yes, well yes I will have to be there for her. I can't think of a single time we've had any dealings with the law. And now this, a dawn raid. It's quite something."

"Well, I'm sure that once you are made aware of the facts surrounding this matter Sir, you will appreciate the reasons."

"Okay, well I'm just worried about what the

neighbours will be thinking."

"To be honest with you Sir, I imagine that they are fast asleep and know nothing about this. Now, you can follow directly behind us if you like, but won't that attract suspicion from your neighbours, if any of them *are* awake?"

"Yes, yes, I suppose so."

"As far as anybody else is concerned, this could be a taxi company, taking your wife off on a business meeting. There is absolutely nothing to worry about."

This comment, delivered in a kind and apologetic manner seemed to satisfy Christine's husband. He walked off quietly towards the stairs.

"I'll just get myself dressed. Thank you."

Within five minutes, the London CID car was pulling off Christine Mason's neat drive, with the home-owner sat in the passenger seat, a deal that had been brokered to try and keep things civil and appear less like a police matter.

The first staff member of Bob Francis' team was in custody.

*****

The huge metal gates which protected Bob Francis' enormous country estate were locked shut. One of the stone built walls which supported the gates had an intercom device, upon which DCI Paxman had been trying to get an answer for several minutes, without success. There was no noise when he pressed the button, so he couldn't be sure if it was working correctly. One thing that was certain was that his every move was being filmed by CCTV cameras, one of which was moving slightly, which suggested that it was being operated remotely by somebody.

Paxman pressed the buzzer again, holding his ear close to the unit to try and hear any click or fizz of connection when his finger pressed against it. He thought he could hear a faint sound in there. Paxman stood straight and looked through the railings of the gates. He could see a strobing, flashing white light coming from the side of a tree, halfway up the lawn.

"Bleeding paparazzi!" said the DCI under his breath as he stepped once again towards the intercom, and pressed the buzzer.

Inside his CID car sat three of Paxman's detectives. They didn't seem too impressed by how this operation was going, and it hadn't even begun yet. Not properly anyway.

"This is a complete farce."

"It's a bit of a bodge job, got to admit."

"Well it fucking wouldn't be if it weren't for the tit that told the bastard press."

"True."

Suddenly, without warning, the gates started opening. The unusual sound, and the unexpectedness of it made Paxman jump. There hadn't been a voice on the intercom, just a loud clunk and then the whine of the motor. It put him on edge and he felt his adrenaline flick up another notch, but he was still pleased to see the pathway opening up. This had had the potential of being the most embarrassing police raid ever, caught live by the vultures who were filming it from behind bushes and magnificent oak trees further up the dew covered lawns.

"Right, right, we're on," said Paxman as he raced into the passenger seat. "That wasn't in the script!"

His driver eased the car through the gates, and they began a steady 10mph drive up the half mile driveway, which led to the next set of perimeter gates.

"Did they not say anything on the intercom, Sir?" asked one of his team.

"No, not a thing. I just saw the gates start opening and jumped in the car."

"This is so bizarre. I can't believe they didn't ask

who you were?"

"Maybe it's just set up for the milkman or something." Suggested another colleague.

"Well, we'll see once we reach the next gate. We're only half way in."

A couple of tense, slow minutes passed before the undercover police car reached the next obstacle which stood in the path of the CID officers, a huge twelve foot wall covered in ivy and other climbing espalier plants. This place looked and felt like a fortress. As the car approached the gateway, Paxman took a deep breath. The driver began slowing to a stop, and the DCI took off his seat belt, ready to jump out and press the intercom.

But the double gates just opened. Those huge, solid wooden gates began opening very gracefully.

"What the actual fuck is going on with this?" asked Paxman as his driver pressed gently against the accelerator and eased the car through the gates, and into Bob Francis' courtyard. This was so weird.

*****

Rudovsky and Kenyon had been knocking at Piers Marshall's house for a couple of minutes, but the door wasn't being answered. Kenyon had spotted a curtain twitch upstairs, so there was somebody home. But whoever it was seemed reluctant to open the door.

Rudovsky double pressed the door-bell again, as Kenyon slapped his hand repetitively against the front door. Still, there was nothing.

"I'll ring the boss." Said Rudovsky. "He's in there but doesn't want to answer. I'll see what Miller suggests." A few seconds later, she was speaking into her phone. "Hi, someone's in, we saw activity in the upper left window. They don't want to open the door though."

"Okay, well, it'll be a shame if you have to, but if you felt it necessary to announce that you are police officers, at a very high volume, and grab the whole neighbourhood's attention, that might hurry things along."

"Sir."

"What did he say?" asked Kenyon, still knocking at the door. Rudovsky answered him, and executed Miller's suggestion at the same time.

"POLICE, OPEN UP! POLICE!" Shouted Rudovsky at the top of her voice. Suddenly there was the unmistakable sound of activity behind the door.

"COME ON, WE KNOW YOU'RE IN THERE! OPEN THIS DOOR! POLICE!" Shouted Kenyon, unable to resist joining in with this most mischievous tactic. It seemed to be working though, both officers could hear urgent footsteps coming towards the door.

A big, heavy sounding bolt could be heard being unlocked behind the door. And then, with a turn of a key, the door began opening slowly. Rudovsky and Kenyon were not prepared for the sight that greeted them once the door was fully opened.

*****

"Harry, darling, wake up."

"Eh? What?"

"Harry, quick, wake up. Something's happening over the street, at Piers Marshall's house!" Wendy Hudson was standing at the bedroom window, trying to figure out what all the commotion was in the street.

"What?"

"Harry, come here, at once!"

Harry, a fifty-two year old barrister was most dissatisfied by this alarming disturbance to his sleep. "What on earth is it?" he asked as he stood and walked across the enormous bedroom, and joined his wife at the window.

"These two people have been banging on Piers'

door for a few minutes now. I saw a curtain move upstairs, so they are definitely at home."

"His car's there. What time is it?" asked Harry, wiping the sleep from his eyes.

Wendy walked across to her bedside table and took her phone. "It's five, just gone."

It was a ridiculous hour to be awake, and she hoped that the children didn't hear this antisocial noise. The kids getting up and starting their Saturday at this hour was the last thing she needed. She began recording the commotion on her phone.

"I'll send this to the council. It's absolutely outrageous!" The phone couldn't really pick out the two characters who were hammering on Piers' door, so Wendy pressed the zoom button and the images became a little clearer.

"They might be plain clothes police officers Harry!" she announced. Her suggestion was confirmed as accurate a second or two later, when one of the people started shouting; "POLICE, OPEN UP! POLICE!" It was a woman shouting, and then the other person, a man started shouting too.

"OPEN THIS DOOR! POLICE!"

Wendy zoomed her camera in even further. The images weren't very sharp, and her trembling hands made the video look quite wobbly. But Wendy and Harry could see the two officers very clearly on the phone screen. And then suddenly the door opened and the two officers were confronted by a woman.

"Oh my God, Harry! Who is that standing at the door? Is that... no, it can't be?"

*****

"What the..."

As DCI Paxman got out of the vehicle, he was instantly greeted by two security officers. Paxman's own officers alighted the vehicle and suddenly, the confidence of the two security men looked dented. The six people were standing in the courtyard car park, close to the front entrance of Bob Francis' stunning country mansion.

"What's happening here?" asked the older looking security man.

"We're police officers, from the Met. We need to have a few words with Bob Francis."

Both of the men looked surprised. From the look on their faces, it wasn't a regular occurrence for police to come up here, asking to speak to Britain's best loved TV personality.

"Have you made an appointment?" asked the younger of the two security men.

"No Sir, this is an urgent police matter. Can you get Mr Francis here for me please?"

Suddenly, another person started walking across the courtyard towards the six people on the car park.

"What's going on here?" It was a young woman, early thirties, she was wearing her pyjamas, and she looked extremely annoyed.

"Who are you?" asked Paxman.

"I'm Jen, Bob's personal secretary. Who the hell are you?"

"They're police," said one of the security men, quietly.

"We need to talk to Bob Francis please, as a matter of urgency. If you could go and get him please, that would be most helpful."

"But Bob is asleep right now, it's five o' clock in the morning for goodness sake!"

"Well I'm afraid you will have to wake him madam, this is an urgent police matter."

Jen turned sharply and started walking quickly back towards the house. "Tell them to wait in the summer house!" she snapped in the direction of the security guards, before disappearing into the lavish, stunning property. The security officers gestured the police officers to follow them, as they headed away from the main entrance to the house, and headed around the side of the building.

Bob Francis' home looked like an exclusive country hotel, the kind of which that was reserved for only the very super rich. Every part of this property looked like it was made from the very best that money could buy. The main building was painted brilliant white, and had a conical blue slate roof, the kind rarely seen in the UK. The gardens were pristine, and the whole place looked like a palace. This man was very clearly intent on living out his concluding years in the most resplendent comfort.

This place had been in the news several times through the years, most notably for Bob's summer garden parties. These private parties were the highlight of Bob's annual charity work, and he would invite hundreds of sick and disadvantaged people to come along and meet the stars of TV, film and music throughout one spectacular day of fun and happiness. Bob Francis' garden parties were the talk of the media, mainly due to the fact that the media were locked out. Bob didn't want his big charitable day being broadcast and published in magazines, so if you were invited, you were made aware that you'd be letting everybody down if you sold photos or made films of the event.

People from all over the UK were invited along. There were children with terminal illnesses, teenagers who'd done heroic things in their communities, adults with learning difficulties who'd achieved special goals in their lives. Ordinary people who'd done extraordinary things for others, were entertained for the day by the very cream of the UK's musicians and comedians, telly stars and celebs. Attendees were picked from nominations which were sent into Bob Francis' Charitable Trust by teachers, carers and support workers throughout the year.

"Nice place!" said one of Paxman's officers as they

followed the security men through a picturesque, never-ending garden which was bursting with colour and life.

"The gardener must work a few hours on this!" remarked another officer.

"There's a team of them." Announced the older security guard, in quite a sniffy manner.

"Yes, I'll bet," replied the detective, trying to keep relations cordial.

After walking around the entire perimeter of the house, the four police officers were led into a smaller house, which looked like a miniature version of the main property, complete with blue slate conical roof.

"Okay, if you can wait in here, we'll bring Mr Francis to you once he is up and dressed."

Paxman didn't seem happy with this. "No, I'm sorry, we're not here for a cup of tea and a natter at Mr Francis' convenience. We need to see Bob Francis as a matter of the utmost urgency, so please take us to him, right now."

"Jen's getting him now. He's fast asleep. He's ninety years old for God's sake!" snapped the security guard, who clearly held his boss in a very high regard.

"Right, I'll give you five minutes. No longer."

The security guard headed off in the direction of Bob's house, leaving the younger one standing outside the summer house with Paxman and his detectives.

"They must think they're above the law if they've got a bit of money!" said Paxman, for the security man's benefit more than anybody else's.

A few minutes passed by, and then the older guard, and Jen appeared, pushing a very familiar looking man in a wheelchair. It was Bob Francis, although he looked different sitting in this wheelchair. He certainly didn't look like the happy go-lucky entertainer from Saturday night TV. His famous white hair was all up and frizzy, and he looked furious, his face was so red.

"What the hell is the meaning of this?" he shouted

as his wheelchair was pushed nearer to the uninvited guests. "How DARE you come here unannounced to speak to me! I demand that you leave here at once!" Bob Francis was getting extremely worked up, pointing his finger and waving his arm about.

But then he grabbed his chest with both hands, and fell forward. He made a gasping sound, before jerking forward. He jerked so much, it made him topple out of the chair. It all happened so quickly.

"Bob!" shouted Jen, as she rushed around to her boss's motionless body that was lay out on the ground.

"Shit!" said the security guard that had been pushing the wheelchair. "Do something!"

"Oh my God," said Paxman as he fell to his knees, trying desperately to revive Bob Francis.

PART FOUR

Kathy Hopkirk always enjoyed visiting Manchester. For a Scottish child, growing up in seventies, Manchester was the exciting, exotic city in England that her family would visit for a day-trip every year during their annual "Wakes week" holiday to Blackpool.

Home of the Bee Gees, Coronation Street, Georgie Best and the Arndale Centre, Manchester was usually the closest that working-class Scottish families got to visiting England's capital city. Arguably, it's a much better city anyway, and its close proximity to Blackpool, and its rich industrial heritage, along with the areas exciting cultural achievements are largely the reason that so many people of Scottish heritage have settled in the Greater Manchester and Lancashire areas today. Put simply, Manchester is much better than London in many Scot's eyes because the people are friendlier, there are plenty of off-licenses around and haggis is available at many Mancunian Butcher shops. Plus Manchester is "nearer tae hame" than the capital city is.

And now, many years on from those wonderful halcyon childhood holidays and day trips to Manchester in the seventies, here she was. Kathy Hopkirk wasn't looking up at the building from the pavement anymore. Now, she was inside the place, she was staying at The Midland. This enormous, Victorian era hotel, built from red granite, and the almost indestructible Accy red brick had captivated her imagination as a child. Her eyes would be drawn to the attention to detail around every window, every hand-carved cornice and finial. She'd stand there as a little girl and dream of the film-stars and pop singers and Kings that were relaxing inside all those big, elegant rooms.

It was always her first port-of-call when visiting Manchester, still to this day. That big posh hotel which had offered accommodation to the world's most famous and gifted people for over a century was her idea of paradise. By just standing outside, looking up above the double archway entrance, it made her feel young, and innocent, carefree and happy once again. She felt extremely grateful that she was now financially comfortable enough that she could stay there whenever she found herself in the north west of England. Kathy used this childhood dream of hers as a barometer of her success in life. In this case, dreams really did come true, and Kathy was mindful to never forget that she was once that poor, penniless child standing outside and admiring this place, dreaming of one day entering the fine looking building. It always made Kathy thankful for her lot, when she thought of her younger self in that way.

The following day's engagements were in Kathy's diary. The plans included an interview for Granada TV's local news magazine show, a book signing event at Waterstones in the city centre, then she'd need to write her newspaper column for The Mail at some point, and then the day would end with a visit to Piccadilly Radio, where she was going to record something controversial for the late-night talk show. She wasn't sure what she'd say just yet, but she couldn't possibly leave this city without making a big splash on the front page of the Manchester Evening News. Anything less would be viewed as a wasted opportunity.

As Kathy phoned down to room-service and ordered a bottle of House Red, and one glass, she was planning to relax in the Jacuzzi, watch a little television, and grab an early night. As the clock reached 8pm, Kathy Hopkirk could have had no idea that none of her appointments for the following day would be fulfilled. Shortly after this time, the telephone that she had been sent by Piers Marshall began ringing.

She rummaged around in her handbag. She'd almost forgotten all about that phone. After a few seconds of frantic scrapping through the piles of junk that she kept in there, Kathy found the old, retro mobile.

"Hello?" she said, she sounded nervous, and slightly awkward. She'd never answered a call on this phone before, and she had no idea what the protocol was when answering a secret phone.

"Kathy, its Piers. Where are you?" he sounded quite stressed, thought Kathy, as she told him where she was, and what her itinerary consisted of for the following twenty-four hours. She rounded off by explaining "but I'll be back in London around this time tomorrow, so we could meet up and have a chat then, if you like?"

"No, Kathy, I'm not in London, I'm in the north myself, Yorkshire. Look, I need to speak with you, face-to-face. Tonight."

"Oh?" Kathy sounded very concerned.

"Something unexpected has cropped up. I need to check a couple of things with you, before I can book the studio for our big show."

"Well, you can ask me now, on the phone?" Kathy really wasn't in the mood for altering her plans for the evening. By the sound of his voice, Piers wasn't really in the mood for altering his plans either.

"No, listen, time is tight. If I don't book that studio by midnight tonight, we'll be looking at six weeks until it's available again. I'm not prepared to chance it. And I'm not prepared to risk this leaking by talking over a phone connection. You never know who could be listening in."

"So you want to see me in person?" Kathy sounded a little bit pissed off, but all the same, she wanted that studio booking more than anything. She wanted this most outrageous, most shocking sex abuse outing of Bob Francis to take place ASAP. Yesterday, if it was at all possible. After all, he was ninety years old. There was no way that she wanted a six week delay hanging over this.

"Yes, I need to speak face-to-face. I'm at a shoot for a new crime drama we're filming in Huddersfield at the moment, it's about an hours drive to Manchester, but

I'll organise a car to pick you up, and we'll meet up half way. What do you say? I won't need you for long, and then you can get back to what you're doing in Manchester, and I can get back to this."

"What I was planning to do was relax!"

"Sorry! But you know what these things are like…"

Right. Okay. No problem."

"Where are you staying?"

"The Midland."

"Ooh, very nice. I've spent many a lovely night there, enjoyed the divine food at Mr Cooper's House and Garden, too."

"Oh, I must try Mr Cooper's. I always eat at The French."

"Love it! Okay, give me a couple of minutes please to organise transport, and I'll call you back with the details."

"Okay, thanks Piers. I'm really glad that you're doing this."

"Me too Kathy. Give me five and I'll call you back."

"Give me ten if you will, I need to shower."

"Okay, no problem. Speak to you soon."

*****

Ten minutes later, Piers called.

"Hi, I've got you a car, it'll pick you up at Saint Peter's Square, just across the road from the Midland at quarter to nine. The driver says that it takes an extra ten minutes to get out of town around the one-way system at the Midland, so walk across the square, just wait at the tram stop and he'll let you know when he's there."

"Quarter to nine. Saint Peter's Square tram stop. Okay, no problem. Thanks Piers." Kathy checked her watch. It was twenty past eight. She had twenty five minutes to dry her hair and throw some clothes on.

"No, no, thank *you*. Oh, and Kathy, not a word to anyone about this."

"Of course not. Top secret."

"Great. Okay. See you soon."

*****

It was going dark as Kathy was picked up beside St Peter's Square Metrolink stop by a mini-cab driver, at exactly 8.45pm. He was nice enough, he didn't say much. They were the best kind of drivers as far as Kathy was concerned. She hated making small talk about how busy it had been, or how sunny or rainy or hot or cold it had been. Silence was always her preference.

Kathy didn't get to see the outskirts of Manchester very often, so she sat quietly in the back seat, taking in the views of the area as the vehicle headed out of the city.

"Where are we going?" asked Kathy after twenty minutes or so.

"We're not very far now, soon be there," said the driver as the scenery became less urban and started to become more and more rural. The last big landmark that Kathy had noticed signs for was Tameside General Hospital. This wasn't a place she remembered hearing much about, but she thought that it looked like a pleasant enough area. She was trying to think of something scandalous to say tomorrow, just to ensure she hit the local headlines, but this part of Greater Manchester was extremely pleasant, so she mused that she'd have to say something about the unfeasible amount of fat arses that there were in this part of Britain, and the catastrophic amount of methane that they probably produce.

By the time that her mini-cab was reaching its destination, it was dark. Her driver had pulled off the main road, and was travelling along a very bumpy, very dark country lane.

Suddenly, Kathy began to feel jumpy, and nervous. She felt an instant, overwhelming sense of panic and vulnerability. All of her cock-sure confidence was gone, and as the minicab continued to bump up and down this uneven country track, she was tempted to ask the driver to turn around, and head back to the main road, back to the reassurance of those orange street lamps in the distance.

A few things hadn't been adding up to Kathy Hopkirk. The need for this visit seemed a little bit suspect from the beginning, as soon as Piers mentioned it. But, she had agreed to it, and put her doubts to the back of her mind. However, as the arrangement began to become more and more peculiar, such as having to walk a hundred yards away from her hotel, to a very exact spot to meet her car, she had started becoming more and more paranoid. Now that this mini-cab was bouncing in and out of pot-holes and huge puddles along this dark, deserted country road, Kathy began to sense that all was not well. Her heart started pumping hard, she could feel her face heating up and her breath tightening.

"Bloody pot-holes! My bloody tyres are crying!"

"Yes, this is like a road from the middle ages."

"Not to worry. We are here now, madam," said the taxi driver in his very warm, very friendly Bangladeshi accent.

"Thanks." Said Kathy, her voice was cold, lacking any enthusiasm or warmth. The car began to slow and Kathy saw a huge black Range Rover parked up on the opposite side of an enormous puddle. The vehicle's lights were off, but Kathy sensed that this was Piers Marshall's vehicle.

"Okay, this is where I drop you off."

"You're waiting for me, aren't you?"

"I'm sorry?" asked the taxi driver, he sounded confused by the question.

"I'm here for a meeting. I'll be going back to

Manchester in a few minutes."

"No, nobody said this to me. I have to go, other jobs, see."

"No. Wait here. I'll pay you extra. I'll give you fifty quid. Please, I want you to take me back to The Midland. Here, take this twenty. I'll give you the rest later."

"Okay, trust me, I'll wait. I'll take you back, no problems."

"Thanks. I won't be long." Kathy got out of the minicab and walked around an enormous puddle, across the uneven, cratered surface of the country lane, taking care not to trip in one of the huge pot-holes using only the light from her phone. As she got half way across the dividing ground between her minicab and the Range Rover, Kathy heard her taxi-driver begin to reverse away.

"You fucking bastard!" she muttered quietly as she reached the Range Rover. Her heart was pounding, banging, up high in her chest. Something was wrong here. Something was definitely wrong. She was on a deserted pathway, in the pitch dark, all alone.

"Fuck." She whispered as she reached the passenger door. Something was definitely wrong. Everything pointed to this unavoidable conclusion. Kathy wanted to run, more than anything, she wanted to dart away, as fast as she could. But it was no use, she wouldn't get anywhere on this dark, deserted, treacherous lane. She'd fall and break her ankle, or she'd be followed by this big car and run over. Kathy felt the danger so strongly, she could smell it, she could taste it in the air.

"Hi," she said, as she opened the car door. She was acting cool.

"Kathy, hi!" said a man in the driver's seat. It wasn't Piers. He was younger, early thirties, blond, shaved hair, lots of tattoos on his huge biceps. He had a strong cockney accent. Kathy had never met this man before, she'd never seen him before.

"Who are you?"

"I'm Ben. I'm his security consultant. I've come to take you to see Piers."

"But Piers said…"

"Yeah, no, it's cool. He's been held up. Filming. Its all cool, jump in, I'll take you to see him."

Kathy stepped away from the vehicle and tried to open the back door. It was locked.

"What's wrong Kathy? Come and sit up front."

"No, I want to sit in the back. I always sit in the back."

"Well, the… the doors are locked. Piers is getting it fixed in the garage next week some time. Common fault with this model apparently."

"Bollocks mate, I'm not getting in, so shove it!" Kathy slammed the door and started walking quickly away from the car, back in the direction that her minicab had travelled. She didn't have a plan, she had no idea what she was doing, but she certainly wasn't getting in that car, that much was for certain. If she could just get back to that main road with the street-lights, or to one of those farm-houses further down the lane, she'd be fine. Kathy was planning her exit from this very fucking dodgy set-up.

And then the street lights in the distance suddenly went out. She felt a thud, right at the back of her skull, and she heard her body hit the damp, muddy floor. Nothing else.

*****

Kathy woke up with the worst head-ache she'd ever known. She was covered in mud.

"Aargh, shit, my head!"

"Aw God, Kathy, are you alright?" It was Piers Marshall. He was sat beside her, on the back-seat of the Range Rover. That guy, Ben, he was driving, pretty fast as well from what she could gather. Her window was wide open. It was the cold draft that had woken her. It was still dark outside, still night-time, they were still on a deserted country lane with no street-lights. They were still on that bumpy, dark lane. They'd put a seat-belt on around her though. That was reassuring.

"What the fuck..." Kathy placed her hand behind her head, directly at the place where she felt the most pain. There was a lump the size of a two pound coin sticking out of her skull, sticking right out, a good inch at least.

"What the..." she repeated as she touched the head-wound again, feeling for blood.

"Kathy, here, have a drink." Piers handed Kathy a cup, it was an old, manky mug with a chip on the lip. Kathy took it, and put it to her lips, but there was no liquid in it. The dirty old cup was empty.

"Aw shit, sorry, where's the water gone?" Piers took the cup back, and put it in a bag by his feet.

"What the hell..." She felt in her pocket. Her phone was missing.

"Where's my phone?" she asked.

"Kathy, listen to me, you've had a fall, it's okay though, we're taking you down to the hospital. It's not far."

"Bullshit. You're a lying bastard. You've hit me round the head when I tried to get away. What, I, you were hiding behind the car weren't you?"

"Kathy, calm down. You're confused. You've got a head injury. Just settle down now, everything's going to be alright."

"Bollocks Piers, don't talk shit to me. You're up to something. Something dodgy."

"Honestly Kathy, just stop talking, keep your strength."

"Why are you wearing those gloves then?" Kathy pointed at Piers' hands, and the tan leather gloves that were covering his fingers. "Listen to me, Piers. Three separate people know that I came up here to meet you. I've also got the tracker app on my phone. That places me right here, and I've got people watching it."

"Kathy, shush, you've had a bad knock to your head. You're not making sense." Piers was rubbing Kathy's shoulder, trying to calm her.

"And that phone you gave me, the number has been logged and it can be traced easily."

Suddenly, Piers looked troubled. "No it can't."

"It can, I rang nine-nine-nine from it the other day, because it only makes emergency calls. I asked the operator for the phone number. I told her that I was worried that it might be a stolen phone. She gave it me, read it down the line to me!"

Piers' charming side seemed to have vanished, in the blink of an eye. His voice had a nasty edge to it, it seemed as though Kathy had touched a nerve.

"That's not possible." He said, trying to assert some authority over Kathy.

"Yes it is. It's being monitored now. God, what a stupid fucking imbecile!"

Piers lashed out, striking Kathy Hopkirk around the face, his back-handed punch connected cleanly with her jaw line and she saw stars and dots, and a sudden heat began to fill her cheek.

"No more back-chat please Kathy. I hate people back chatting me. It's extremely bad mannered."

"Fuck off, you pretentious twat."

Once again, Kathy felt a searing pain down the side of her face, and those spinning, revolving, dazzling white stars were dancing around in her eyes again.

"If I were you Kathy, I'd keep that big mouth of yours tightly shut. Now, grab hold of this for me." Piers held out a door handle. It was so random that Kathy wondered if the knocks to the head were making her hallucinate. But no, it *was* a door handle from an internal house door. It was an old, dirty looking thing, it had brown paint all around its edges. Piers was holding it, gripping the flat part which is usually screwed to the door in his expensive looking glove, leaving the handle part free for Kathy to grab a hold of.

Kathy clenched her fists and refused to touch it. "What the hell…"

Bang. Piers had clobbered her again, this time it felt like a clenched fist had struck her on the side of her head. She lost consciousness for a few seconds, at least, it felt like she did. The vehicle was still driving fast, and it was still bouncing around, throwing her and Piers around on the back-seat. The light was on in the back, but despite the dazzling white light from overhead, Kathy could tell that they were still on that scary country lane. How long has this been going on for? Wondered Kathy, as her hands remained tightly rolled up in balls.

"Just grab this door handle Kathy. Grab it, and then I'll let you go. I'll be happy to let you live the rest of your life. But if you don't…"

"If I don't what?"

"If you don't Kathy, you'll end up in the same trouble as your little friend."

"What little friend?" Suddenly, it was Kathy who sounded as though her confidence had taken a knock.

Piers placed the door handle on his lap and took his phone out of his pocket and began looking through the various apps. Eventually, he selected a photograph, and showed it to Kathy.

"This is what happens when you go too far." Piers spoke slowly, coldly as Kathy tried to take in the image that was being held in front of her. The photo showed Janet Croft, sat on some scruffy old chair, her eyes were popping out of her head, it looked as though she was desperately trying to inhale oxygen. Somebody was standing behind her, holding a ligature which was very clearly, and very graphically killing the woman.

"Oh… you…"

"Oh, look Ben, its Kathy Hopkirk, lost for words! I never thought we'd see the day!" Piers started laughing manically, as his driver joined in too. Piers continued to hold the horrific picture up in front of Kathy's face as he laughed. "You didn't really think that some smelly little alky like Janet Croft was going to bring down the Light Entertainment King of Britain, did you Kathy? My God, how naïve are you?"

"That is pretty dumb!" said Ben from the front. "Did you know they are taking the word gullible out of the dictionary Kathy?"

"I can't…" Kathy stopped looking at the picture. It was the cruellest thing she'd ever seen. A brutal, nasty, vicious end to such a tragic life. It broke Kathy's heart to think of Janet Croft's wretched life, and her final, gruesome, terrifying moments. Murdered, no, slaughtered because she had an inconvenient truth to share about Bob Francis. Janet Croft had been strangled to death, to stop her from talking about the abuse she'd received.

Janet Croft was dead, and it was Kathy's fault.

The gravity of the situation was too much and Kathy felt a wave of nausea washing over her. That photo, that sick photo was a record of the most frightening, painful way to die, and it was Kathy's fault. She shoved her head out of the window and vomited, the contents of her stomach were thrown up the side of the speeding car.

Piers continued waffling on to his driver, making inappropriate comments and telling sick jokes about the dead woman, and how she was burgled once, and the burglars put in an official complaint because there wasn't anything worth stealing.

Kathy pulled her head back into the vehicle and was weeping silently, looking down at her hands, which were still balled up in fists on her lap. She couldn't hear what Piers and Ben were saying, and she wasn't really interested anyway, they were a pair of sick, twisted bastards. Kathy sat still and stayed as quiet as she could, thinking about her situation, trying to think of ways to get out of this now.

"Put my window up, please." Kathy could smell the puke that was all over the side of the vehicle, and it was making her want to go again. Ben pressed a button and the window started closing.

"Your wish is my command."

"I hope you die a slow, agonising death in a skip fire you cunt."

"Oh, now, now!" said Ben as Piers laughed manically at his hostage's remark.

Kathy sat quietly. She was going over it all in her mind. Their plan was to kill her now. Or was it? What was all that about with the empty cup? DNA. The cup was from Janet's flat. Yes, touch the door handle. Oh my days, I'm being framed for Janet's murder. Holy shit, how dumb are these clowns. These guys are stupid.

Kathy's mind was racing. She'd already guessed that Piers had under-estimated her, and that was going to be a bit of fun to focus on, a bit of a light at the end-of-the-tunnel. Now she just needed to get through this. She decided to be as bombastic and obnoxious as possible, but allow them to think she was scared. It was crucial to make Piers feel as though he was in control here, so she would make out that she was terrified. Then, when his confidence was peaking, she'd pull him apart and let him see that he'd messed with the wrong bird.

The car turned onto a main road. The street-lights brought a lot of reassurance to Kathy. She felt her own self-belief begin to grow.

"So, you want me to touch that door handle, Janet's door handle, and incriminate myself in her murder?"

Piers laughed loudly, and his driver, Ben did the same. Kathy grinned.

"Hey Tweedle Dee, does he pay you extra to laugh at his jokes?"

"Are you talking to me?" he asked, looking over his shoulder slightly in Kathy's direction. He didn't look pleased with Kathy's tone.

"Yes. Do you realise how pathetic you are, laughing at this arsehole's shit jokes for money?"

"Ignore her Ben. She's just annoyed because we killed her little friend, Janet the alky, and now she's going to be in prison for the rest of her life. That's a good one, isn't it Ben?"

"Ha ha ha, wow this is absolutely brilliant. I'm in a car with two of the shittest gangsters in the world. Thank you for getting me tickets to the grand final of the world moron championships?"

"Tell her to shut the fuck up Piers, she's getting on my tits, big time."

"Big time? I thought they stopped saying that when East Seventeen were in the charts? Boy-oh-boy, this is going to make my next autobiography a million-seller! Taken hostage by a half-wit gangster who says "big-time" this is priceless. Big time!"

"Errr… I don't think you're allowed to release auto-biographies from Holloway Kathy!" said Ben, his comment was greeted by a huge, loud laugh from Piers.

"God, you're really enjoying this aren't you Piers? This is fascinating to watch."

"Keep talking Kathy… while you still can!"

"Are we nearly at the hospital yet?"

The two men burst into laughter once again.

Kathy had seen some creepy behaviour between blokes in the past but never under these circumstances. She found Piers and Ben's general behaviour very strange, especially as an innocent, vulnerable woman had been murdered by them. She wondered if they were on something, and almost as soon as she'd considered it, Piers did a huge sniff. Yes, that was it, they are both wired on coke, they'd needed the drug to give them the balls for this. They were on a drugs-fuelled rampage, and Kathy was next. She wondered if it was possible to reason with people who were taking mind-altering substances. She'd certainly never tried before, as far as she could recall.

"Kathy, seriously. Does it not kill you that everybody hates you?"

"Why would it?"

"I mean, everybody hates you. That must hang around your neck?"

"Piers, love, can you just shut up? I'm trying to figure out what the hell you think you're doing, I've not got time to answer your boring little questions."

"Well, good luck trying to figure it out, eh Ben?" The two men laughed loudly again, as the car travelled through a small town. There was a Co-Op which was still open and a few betting shops had the lights on. A group of people were stood outside a restaurant, smoking. It was called Ferratis. Kathy was trying to see a name on a shop or sign that would give her a hint where she was. A couple of minutes later, the car passed a familiar red and white British Rail sign. Kathy clasped both hands against the glass to shield out the reflection of the internal light. The railway sign said MOSSLEY. Kathy had never heard of the place before, but it was now definitely a place she'd remember.

Piers and Ben were continuing to laugh and joke. Kathy just ignored them. Once they'd settled down again, Kathy spoke.

"Good luck trying to get away with this, you thick pair of dickheads."

This comment seemed to antagonise Piers. The smirk disappeared from his face. "You should watch your mouth Kathy. I've told you once."

"I'm just wondering why you thought that I wouldn't tell anybody where I was going. This was your downfall."

"Why, who have you told?"

"Reception staff at The Midland."

This comment changed Piers' general mood. He couldn't hide his discontent. All of a sudden, the laughter, the cocky grin, the arrogance was gone. He looked stunned.

Kathy continued talking. "I told them that I've gone for a meeting with Piers Marshall, the MD of London TV. I said that it's a very dodgy set up, and if I'm not back by eleven pm, I need them to alert three people. I wrote down the three names and numbers, along with your name and job title, along with your mobile number, to eliminate any confusion whatsoever."

Piers didn't speak. Neither did Ben. There was a long, tense silence. The car was travelling faster than the speed limit, and Kathy was hoping that a police car would pull them over and this whole thing would end very unspectacularly indeed for Piers and his side-kick.

"Have you ever heard of Saddleworth Moor Kathy?" Piers was talking in his cold, wannabe hard-man voice again.

"Yes Piers, of course I have."

"Go on then, enlighten me."

"Moors Murders. It's the famous Pennine Moor that divides Yorkshire and Lancashire. The police have dug it over several times in the eighties, looking for the bodies of Brady and Hindley's victims. Keith Bennett and Lesley Ann Downey."

"Correct. It is supposed to be one of the scariest places in the country you know. There are hundreds of children buried up there, little kiddies from the Victorian times, the poor couldn't afford funerals, so they held their own, secret ones up on the moors when a child died. The mill owners would hide children's bodies up there too, when they'd been killed in an accident in the mill."

"That's horrific," said Kathy, waiting for Piers' punch-line, or conclusion, or whatever the hell it was he was leading up to.

"They say that on a windy day, you can hear all

the children screaming up there, and it's the most terrifying sound on earth."

"Is that where we're going?" Kathy saw that the road was heading to a darker, more rural area than the small town of Mossley which they were now leaving behind.

"Well, I'll be honest with you Kathy, you've thrown us a bit of a curve-ball. I mean, we've dug a grave for you. We'd just finished it when I phoned you. Its bloody exhausting work, you know! The plan was to get you to touch all Janet's stuff, so that you'll be the prime suspect in her murder, before killing you and burying you on the moors. Then, Ben and I were going to return the items to her flat, along with a few strands of your hair."

"We were going to take them after you were dead, though," said Ben, before laughing menacingly. But it sounded fake, the laugh was hollow and Ben sounded more worried than amused.

"This was going to be the greatest mystery of our time. Killer Kathy disappears after murdering a mentally ill alcoholic woman in her own home. They'd still be talking about this in a hundred years!"

"But obviously, I'm not as thick as you anticipated, am I? So you need a plan B now, don't you Piers?" Kathy was grinning, she knew that she was holding all the cards now. The banter between Piers and Ben was over, and Kathy was the only one who knew that it was a great big fib about the staff at The Midland being told about her meeting with Piers.

"I wouldn't get too cheeky, if I were you Kathy."

"Or else what Piers? Are you going to throw one of your girly punches at me again? For God's sake grow up. You've fucked right up here, and when that cocaine hit wears off and your head starts straightening up, you'll be shitting your pants."

"You'd better tell her to shut up Piers, or I'm going to kill her with my bare hands."

"Ooh, I say, how butch!" said Kathy, before adding her trademark irritating laugh on the end for good measure.

Ben slammed on the brake, and the Range Rover came to a screeching, violent halt. He unclipped his seat belt and made to get out of the vehicle, but Piers warned him, in a very cold voice.

"Fuck off Ben! Get this car moving now you fucking moron."

"Yes! Ben! You fucking moron!" Kathy cackled again. She was scared, and felt incredibly vulnerable, and in a great deal of danger. But the two occupants of the Range Rover would never have guessed. As far as they were concerned, this woman was mad, she was mental, and she'd somehow run rings around them both. It was humiliating, to say the least. The car started moving again.

"The thing is guys, I really think that you should forget the moors idea."

"Really?" asked Ben in a sulky, sarcastic tone.

"Yes. Really. Your safest bet now is to strike up a deal with me. It's your only way out of this. Well, I don't know how far Ben has got himself involved, but as far as you're concerned Piers, you're fucked. At five past eleven, the three people I have asked The Midland staff to contact will have been informed that I've gone to meet you, and I haven't made it back. At that precise moment, all three of them will carry out the instructions I've left with them."

Piers was shaking, and starting to look ill. That flamboyant, self assured charisma was all gone, as was the grin and the flushed, healthy glow in his cheeks. Now, he looked scared, and he looked like that cocaine was wearing off too.

"What instructions did you leave them?"

"Darling, seriously. That's for me to know, and for you to worry about." Kathy scoffed again.

"So… the deal, what deal?" he asked, looking out of the window.

"Piers, will you tell your knucklehead underling to turn this car round and head back towards Manchester, or we're going to miss the eleven pm deadline. Come on guys, I know you must be shocked, and probably pretty embarrassed by how badly you've fucked this up, but snap out of it. You're heading the wrong way. Turn the car around, and we can talk about how the hell you two shite hawks are going to get away with murdering Janet Croft."

"Come on, Ben, there's no point going that way. Turn her round, let's get Kathy back. She's won."

"She's won? Are you losing your mind Piers?" Ben looked hard at Piers in the rear-view mirror. Piers stared back.

"Well what else can we do? She's got us pinned to the floor by our balls."

"Boom! I think the penny is starting to drop." Kathy was muttering to her self, as she stared out of the window. Ben began indicating to turn left and slowed the Range Rover down, before pulling into a three-point-turn. Seconds later, the car was travelling back in the direction that it had just come.

"Was that mini-cab driver involved in this?"

"What of it?"

"Oh, I'm just curious. He seemed a nice bloke. I just can't imagine that he'd knowingly take somebody to a place where they would come to harm."

"He's just a taxi driver Kathy. The only people who know about this are me, you and Ben."

"As far as you know."

"No. It's not as far as I know Kathy."

"What are you talking about Piers? Are you talking about Bob Francis or about Janet Croft ?"

"Janet. Obviously."

"But who knows about Bob?"

"I don't know. It won't be many people. Me, you, Ben, Sally, you've probably told your husband as well. Is that it?"

Kathy laughed out loud, a big, unmistakable laugh of genuine hilarity which came right from the pit of her stomach. It was ridiculous, finding such humour under such tense, scary and tragic circumstances. But none-the-less, Kathy was genuinely tickled by the bungling capers of Piers Marshall and his idiotic side-kick.

Piers looked as though he was struggling not to hit her again.

"You really are a moron, aren't you Piers? I truly can't remember dealing with such a dum-dum, never in all of my life, and I've dealt with a lot of thickos! You two remind me of those builders who spent all day building that big wall, and then realised that they had trapped their van inside it, and had to take it down again so they could go home." Kathy laughed again.

"Okay, you've had your fun. What is the deal?"

"The deal will be discussed on the luxuriously comfy sofas in the reception area of The Midland. So come on Ben, get your foot-to-the-floor!"

"We can't discuss this in a public place Kathy. Are you mad?"

"We can, and we will. So get me there, as soon as you can or the genie is going to get out of the bottle."

Ben started to indicate, and the car started slowing down.

"What are you doing Ben?" asked Piers.

"Yes Ben, what are you doing?" asked Kathy, in a sarcastic impression of Piers. Ben pulled the car onto a pub car park. The sign said "Roaches Lock" but the place was deserted. The pub backed onto the canal.

Ben leapt out of the car and threw open Kathy's door. Without warning, he grabbed two handfuls of Kathy's hair and started dragging her out of the vehicle. Kathy screamed in pain, and terror. Ben was pulling at her hair so hard, but Kathy wasn't moving, she was trapped by the seatbelt.

"Ben, for fuck's sake!" snapped Piers, he was

panicking, desperately trying to undo Kathy's seatbelt clip, as Ben was dragging at his two fists full of hair. It looked, and sounded like Kathy's hair was about to be ripped from her scalp. Piers released the clip and Kathy helped herself on her way out of the car, throwing herself out in a bid to relieve the pressure of her hair being ripped out. As she launched herself out of the car, Ben threw her onto the stoney, gravelled car park, and began kicking Kathy. Over and over again, in the head, in the body, she made no noise, she was too busy trying to curl herself up in a ball, desperately trying to protect herself from this agonising onslaught of depraved violence.

It was no good though, Ben kicked Kathy's head so hard, she flopped out on the floor. She looked dead.

"You fucking idiot!" said Piers, as quietly as he could. He looked around, there were lights of houses just across the road. A bedroom light was shining just twenty-five metres away from where Kathy was lay in a heap. "You fucking idiot. Get her in the car. Now!" Piers started lifting Kathy's shoulders. Ben just stood there, his fists clenched by his sides. He was rocking, he had tears in his eyes. Tears of pure rage.

"Ben! Come on!" Piers grabbed Kathy's shoulders and nodded to his side-kick to grab her legs. "Come on, get her back in the car. Hurry the fuck up."

A few seconds later, Piers and Ben had bundled Kathy into the back of the Range Rover. She was breathing, which was a relief to Piers. She was half lay down, half kneeling on the floor as Piers slammed the rear door shut.

"Get in, I'll drive," whispered Piers.

Ben did as he was told. He really wasn't bothered if Kathy was alive or dead, she'd pushed him too far with that fucking irritating mouth of hers. He couldn't care less, he could see that he and Piers were going to jail for killing Janet Croft, so what the hell did it matter if Kathy Hopkirk, the most hated bitch in Britain was also dead?

They'd driven here to kill her anyway. She'd just outwitted them, and now they had to face the consequences.

This had been a cock-up from start to end, and his gut feeling had told him to steer clear of this, right from the moment Piers mentioned this spot-of-trouble. But, the money that Piers had offered had been the deciding factor. And now, in the past eight or nine hours, Ben's life had gone from pretty rubbish, to completely hopeless, and all for a lump sum of twenty-five grand. A lump sum that he already owed out for debts that he'd accrued in his business. Ben had had a disastrous day, it was so bad in fact that he realised that he was in shock, as he sat in the passenger seat, lost in his own world.

"You mad fucking bastard!" said Piers as the car approached Mossley, the town they had left ten minutes earlier, when they were headed towards the moors, planning to batter Kathy to death with the spades in the boot, and bury her body in a grave close to Dovestones country park.

"Piers, seriously, shut the fuck up." Ben's voice was cold, and very threatening.

"What are we supposed to do now?"

"Piers, if you had a brain, you'd be sat in the back, wiping Kathy's fingerprints all over that stuff in the bag. The mug, the glass, the cutlery, the door handles, that poxy microwave meal packaging. You'd be wiping the rope all over her skin to get her DNA samples on the murder weapon. Everything that we planned. But you've lost the plot."

"Wait, woah, how the fuck is this my fault Ben? Come on, get a grip here. It's out of my control if Kathy has alerted people that she was meeting me. How the hell are you laying that on me?"

"It might be bullshit."

"What might?"

"Kathy telling The Midland staff about the

meeting with you. It could be a nothing more than a lie. How can we know if it *is* a lie or if it's true?"

There was a silence whilst the two men contemplated the idea in their own minds. It was a good point. Kathy could have just made it up about The Midland. It would be a pretty bizarre thing to say to hotel staff, especially for somebody as famous, and ridiculed as Kathy Hopkirk. It was quite plausible that hotel reception staff would be straight onto the newspapers about this, it was a story in itself. "Britain's most hated woman fears for her life so much, that she leaves notes at hotel reception desks to tell police where she went, just in case she doesn't make it back."

The more that Piers thought about it, the more that he mulled it over, the more he doubted that she did inform the hotel staff. Ben was probably right, it was just a bluff. A bluff to buy her time. By the time that Piers had driven to Ashton, the next town along from Mossley, and had reached the M60 motorway junction, he had decided that he was going home, back to London. He'd decide what to do with Kathy on the journey. He'd find out if The Midland story was true or false, shortly after eleven pm.

Ben was sat next to Piers, in total silence. He wasn't thinking about Kathy, or Janet, or even Piers and this latest shit, idiotic situation that he'd managed to get himself caught up in. Ben was thinking about his other problems, his drug habit, and his debts, his failing security business and the fact that he never saw his kids, and when he did, they couldn't be arsed with him. He started thinking about his ex, and how happy she was now with her new boyfriend. It hurt him, even though he'd wrecked the relationship with his violence, his reckless behaviour and one-night-stands. It hurt him to see the mother of his kids happy, because that was supposed to have been his job, and he'd failed at it. Ben was thinking about all the girls he'd managed to get with, and how they'd hated him after a few dates. Ben knew this familiar feeling, this heavy, dark come-down from his beloved cocaine. He knew it all too well. He knew that he needed to take more, or face this revolving cycle of misery and self-hate for the next few days at least.

Piers was thinking about ways around this, if Kathy had been lying about The Midland, then it left him with various options. He didn't definitely have to go to prison, they weren't that far down the road yet. Piers looked at the time, it was half past ten. He knew that he'd hear, soon after eleven pm if Kathy *had* told the reception desk that she was meeting him. One of the three names that Kathy had been talking about was bound to have been Sally King, Kathy's manager. Piers started nibbling at his nail, feeling a flip in his stomach as the thought of having another half an hour of this nerve-jangling uncertainty playing on his mind.

The car had been on the M60 motorway for ten minutes when Piers came off and joined the M56, the motorway which would take him down past the airport, and towards the M6, which would eventually get him home, in roughly four hours time. Piers had not been on the M56 long when he picked up his speed to 80mph and got settled in the middle lane. The motorway was pretty quiet, just a few wagons were meandering along on the inside lane.

Suddenly, Ben turned to Piers and said, "fuck this shit." As he said it, he unclipped his seatbelt, opened his door, barging it with his shoulder, and rolled out of the speeding car. The door slammed shut, the force of the oncoming wind saw to that.

"Whoah!" said Piers, looking in his rear-view mirror, trying to take in what had just happened. It was too dark to see anything, there were no lights along this stretch of motorway, and there was no traffic trailing behind. He couldn't see anything. Nothing at all.

"Fuck!" Piers looked down at his speedo, he was still going 80mph. He couldn't take this in. He couldn't believe that ten seconds ago, Ben had been sat there, and now, he had leapt out of the car.

"It was a trick? No, it's not a trick. That was not a trick. How the fuck could it be a trick?" Piers was mumbling to himself.

The thing that made it so surreal was the silence. Ben had just gone. The only noise was the door opening, and slamming shut and in between, the blast of air hitting the inside of the vehicle. Other than that two-second blast of noise, there'd been nothing.

"FUCK!" shouted Piers, banging his hand on the steering wheel, and pressing his foot even harder against the accelerator. "FUCK!"

"What's... where am I?" Kathy Hopkirk began stirring on the back seat. She was whimpering in pain. Piers had almost forgotten about her, chucked in the back about half an hour earlier, after taking a severe battering at the hands of Ben.

"It's alright Kathy, I'm taking you to a place of safety. You're going to be alright."

"I... need a... my head... I need a drink."

Piers handed back Ben's bottle of water from the drinks holder. "Here. Are you okay?"

Kathy turned around, she'd been knelt, her knees had been on the car's floor, her body had been sprawled on the back-seat. She'd not moved an inch since Ben had chucked her in that way. Kathy had been knocked out. For the second time in her life, Kathy was coming round from being unconscious. The only time that it had ever happened before was an hour earlier, on that dark, scary country lane where the mini-cab had dropped her off.

"Kathy, are you okay?" Piers asked again. Kathy was confused, she was in pain, as well as discomfort from how her legs had been twisted in the foot-well. She was in bad shape, but she was alert enough to remember that she was in grave danger. She drank the water, realising as she held the bottle to her mouth that her lip was severely swollen and her jaw was feeling tender too. As she opened her mouth to take some of the water, a pain shot down her jaw, and into her chin.

"Ah, shit. I'm in trouble," she said, pouring the water into a gap at the side of her face. "My mouth." She managed to say.

Piers was concentrating on the road ahead, which was in complete darkness, as well as trying assess how badly Ben had hurt Kathy. His eyes kept flicking up at the rear view mirror, looking at Kathy, and looking through the back window, convinced that blue flashing lights were going to be chasing behind him at any moment.

"I need to see someone Piers. I'm in pain." Each word that Kathy said was slow, laboured, and there was a strange sound accompanying each word. A kind of slur, as though she'd had a bit too much to drink.

"Yes, yes, don't worry, I'm on it."

"I don't trust you. You said all this. Before. Where is your psycho friend, anyway?" Asked Kathy, her speech was becoming a little more clearer as she adapted to the wounds around her mouth and face.

Kathy's question inspired Piers. It brought a much craved for moment of clarity in what had been a mixed-up, highly chaotic few hours. Suddenly, the question about Ben's whereabouts gave him a cover story. A cover story that might, just might be enough to dig himself right out of this absolute fucking disaster.

"He's. I've killed him Kathy. It was you or him. One of you had to die. I didn't want it to be you. I saved your life Kathy." Piers started crying, openly sobbing at the wheel as his Range Rover switched lanes, and merged onto the M6 motorway. Tears were streaming down his face and the bright lights of the motorway illuminated them well.

Kathy saw the tears reflecting, she heard the snot and the sniffing and wiping.

But these weren't tears of sadness. Piers was

crying because he had found a way out of this nightmare situation. These were tears of relief.

Kathy may have been accused of a lot of things through the years, but stupidity was never one of the accusations levelled at her. To Kathy, these tears looked about as sincere as Piers himself. Never-the-less, she was intrigued to know what this latest development was all about.

"Thank you." Said Kathy, before clutching the side of her face and making a sharp intake of breath as the pain from her swollen, bruised skull shot another searing, stabbing pain through her jaw.

"Come on, let's get you checked over. Try and get some sleep, we're going to be alright Kathy. Everything's going to be alright."

PART FIVE

Chapter 49

Rudovsky and Kenyon had to look away from the person standing before them at Piers Marshall's door. They trained their gazes at each other, before double-taking back at the individual stood before them. Their mouths were both wide-open, and they looked as though they wondered if this was a prank.

They could not believe what they were seeing. Kathy Hopkirk had answered Piers Marshall's front door. She looked like she'd just woken up. She looked scared, and ashamed, as though she'd just been caught stealing from an elderly neighbour. She looked beaten-up too, there were dark yellow remains of bruises all around her face, and one side of her mouth looked swollen. There was an injury above her left eye too.

"Kathy?" said Rudovsky, quietly. She didn't know what else to say.

"Come in," she said, shrugging. She had the beginnings of tears in her eyes.

"Wow, shit, wait a minute, just stay there." Rudovsky phoned Miller. He answered on the first ring.

"Yeah?"

"Back-up required urgently. Over."

The Manchester CID car was parked just around the corner, no more than twenty-five yards away. Miller, Grant and Saunders scrambled out of the car and sprinted the short distance to Piers Marshall's front door. One or two neighbours were beginning to appear at doors and windows up and down the posh street, desperate to know what all the drama was about.

"Fucking hell," said Miller, as he caught sight of the missing woman. Rudovsky and Kenyon had had a few extra seconds to get their head around this surprise, and seemed quite accustomed to the extraordinary outcome.

"Where's Piers?" barked Saunders, as he saw the state that Kathy Hopkirk was in. Kathy waved the detective into the house.

"Ah, hello, are you police officers?" asked a man, walking down the stylish staircase.

"Piers Marshall?" asked DC Rudovsky.

"The very same, and you are?" He had a very charming, very confident way about him. All five of the detectives took an instant dislike to his sleazy, insincere manner. None of the detectives spoke until Piers was standing at the door, next to Kathy Hopkirk. She was shaking, trembling, and her teeth were chattering as though it was a freezing cold morning. It wasn't cold at all.

"Piers Marshall, I am arresting you on suspicion of holding a person against their will, and on suspicion of causing actual bodily harm to that individual, you do not have to..." Rudovsky made the arrest. Piers was very submissive, he tried the usual feigning of surprise, as did most people who were being arrested, but he soon held his wrists out for Rudovsky's cuffs.

"DC Grant, can you organise a meat van please?" asked Miller. "DI Saunders, we're going to need a CSI urgent job here, and send some uniforms."

"Is there anybody else in the house Mr Marshall?"

"No... I, er... no, nobody else is here."

"Are you okay Kathy?" asked Miller. She didn't look okay. She looked ill, and scared, and battered. Miller's kind, gentle question, and the look of concern on his face made Kathy break-down in tears. She fell forwards, stumbling to her knees on the spot and began crying openly. "Thank you... thank you..." she said, though it wasn't easy to understand her through the sobs and gasps for breath.

"Kathy, don't forget, what we've been through, together..." said Piers, it was hard for the detectives to ascertain if the sentence contained a threatening tone of malevolence. They didn't know his voice, so couldn't be sure – but Miller thought he heard it, and that was enough for him.

"Right, Rudovsky, Kenyon, get this guy in another room until the meat van lands up. Kathy, come on love, let's sit you down and let you catch your breath back."

Chapter 50

"Good morning, and welcome to Sky News Sunrise, it has just turned eight o' clock and we have some very sad news to share with you this Saturday morning. The King of Light Entertainment, has died. Bob Francis, who celebrated his ninetieth birthday only months ago, died suddenly at his Hertfordshire home earlier this morning." Eamonn Ahearn, the Sky breakfast show host looked close to tears as he shared this devastating news, concerning one of the best-loved stars of British broadcasting.

"And there is another major story unfolding this morning. Kathy Hopkirk, who has been missing for the past eight days, has this morning been found, apparently safe-and-well in London, by Manchester police officers who were investigating the disappearance. Sky sources have obtained exclusive mobile-phone footage of the incredible moment that police found Kathy, as she answered the door of an address in Belsize Park, in north-west London. But first, we return to our main story this morning, which is the tragic news that Bob Francis, the undisputed British superstar of television and radio for over seventy years, has died. This news was announced just after seven am by the East of England Ambulance Service."

The screen changed from the head and shoulder shot of the news-reader, to a familiar publicity photo of Bob Francis, smiling. Beside it was a message which read, quite simply, "Entertainment will never be the same without you. RIP Bob Francis." Thirty seconds or so of complete silence passed by, before Eamonn Ahearn spoke again. The emotion was clear in his voice.

"We're joined by our media correspondent James Jeffries who is outside Bob Francis' home. A sad day, to say the least, James?"

"Oh, for sure Eamonn, not least because Bob

Francis was in remarkably good health for his age. Only weeks ago, at his ninetieth birthday celebrations, Bob joked that he felt great, and confessed that he was still partying like a seventy-seven year old."

"God bless him," said Eamonn as he laughed sombrely and affectionately at the typical sounding gag.

"There's a very strange mood about here this morning. Obviously, Bob Francis had reached a great age at ninety years, but despite that, there's still a real sense of shock here, a feeling that it's just not true, that it's not really happening. I must admit that I too feel that way, almost as though I can't quite believe that he's gone."

"The world is a poorer place without him, and many staff here at Sky Television have very openly shed tears this morning. He had a very rare gift, a talent that almost every television presenter would love to have, and the only way I can describe this talent is to say that when Bob Francis was on the television, you felt that he was right there in the room with you."

"Yes, and as this news spreads around the country, I think we'll be hearing many more thoughts about a great, great man."

"Do we have any idea why Bob Francis died, James? Any news on the cause of death yet?"

"That's a very interesting question Eamonn, and there are lots of differing viewpoints and opinions flying around on this subject. One thing that is becoming clearer, is the fact that Metropolitan police officers were in attendance at this address when Bob Francis tragically passed away. We've heard that detectives from Scotland Yard battled for almost half an hour to revive Bob Francis, but when the ambulance crew arrived from Watford General Hospital, they found that there was nothing they could do to save him, and pronounced Bob Francis extinct of life just before six o'clock this morning."

*****

Miller, Saunders and Grant were sitting in the A&E department at the Royal Free Hospital in Hampstead, watching the Sky News reports on the TV in the main waiting room. Miller had a cheeky smile on his face as he watched the news report surrounding Bob Francis.

"It's a hell of a bad karma come-back for DCI Paxman. This one will go down as the worst attempted stitch-up of all time!" Miller was speaking quietly, sat with his arms folded across his chest. Grant wasn't exactly sure what Miller was talking about, so Miller explained the way that Paxman and his team had behaved with the Kathy case since the very beginning. Paxman had back-heeled the case to Manchester as quickly as he possibly could. He now had the rest of his career to blush and cringe about that decision.

"In short, they thought they'd drop it on us, because they knew it was going to be a nightmare. Well, they were right… it *was* a nightmare, but not for us! We've come down and sorted it all out in their own back-yard, while they've caused the death of Britain's biggest A lister!"

Grant and Saunders laughed. It was a peculiar outcome for Paxman and his team, who would now have the IPCC enquiry, as well as the media scrutinising their activities. It was going to be hell for them, there was absolutely no way out of it.

"Too bad DCI Paxman," said Saunders quietly.

"Gutted!" said Grant, without any hint of sincerity in her voice.

"Hey, watch, we're on now!" Miller sat up and leaned in closer to the TV. The sound was down, but it was still very obvious what was happening on the news channel, as amateurish camera footage was broadcast. It showed Rudovsky and Kenyon banging on the front door of a big, posh house. The footage was shaky and quite blurry, it looked like it was taken by a nosey neighbour on a mobile phone, but it was good enough to see Rudovsky's and Kenyon's stupefied reaction when Kathy Hopkirk opened the door.

"Ha ha ha, aw God love them! What would you do though? That just wasn't expected, was it?"

"That is classic! We need to get hold of that footage and torture them with it!" said Saunders, laughing manically at the double, open-mouth, head-wobble that Kenyon and Rudovsky gave to one another. The TV company also seemed to enjoy this moment of bewilderment, as they showed the moment of surprise once again, forcing another huge laugh from the three detectives in the waiting area.

"Aw, we've got to learn how to do that face, and then when Rudovsky is being a dick, we can just go like that in her face!" Miller had tears of amusement running down his cheeks as he thought of the terror that this footage would unleash on his most boisterous member of staff. "Aw Jesus, I'm over tired. I always feel dead giddy when I'm too tired. Forgive me DC Grant, I'm not really insane."

"Haha, no, carry on, it's funny! It's passing the time nicely for me to be honest." Grant looked like she was having fun.

"Yeah, good point." Saunders looked at his watch. "How much longer are we going to be waiting Sir?" The DI was beginning to get a bit restless now. There was still so much to do, so many questions to find answers to. This was quite literally a waste of time for the three officers sat staring at the TV screen. The mood started to drop a little as the TV news returned to its main story, and showing photographs of Tweets that celebrities had posted after hearing of Bob Francis' unexpected death.

The waiting room was full, people of all ages, ethnicities, religions and genders were waiting for a nurse or doctor to see to their ailments. This hospital, along with the rest of the country's A&E departments was struggling to cope with demand. The government's cuts to social care and mental health services were having a negative, knock-on effect which was forcing additional care onto emergency NHS departments. This deliberate, planned chaos was designed to undermine the service to such a degree that it would seem that there was no other option available, but to privatise it. Accident and Emergency wards were the public's first point of contact, and as a result, most hospitals in the UK were habitually receiving their worst performance ratings since records began.

But, despite the six, seven, even eight-hour waiting times to see a healthcare professional, the people just sat patiently. Some were weeping with pain, others were rocking back-and-forth, trying to ease their discomfort. One or two of the patients exhaled huge gusts of frustrated air every couple of minutes. All around, the NHS staff were working tirelessly, trying their best to keep on top of things.

None of the public in the waiting room had any idea that Kathy Hopkirk was being treated here, just a few feet away from this stuffy, overcrowded, uncomfortable waiting room.

Rudovsky and Kenyon had sneaked Kathy into the A&E department with a blanket over her head almost two hours earlier. They wanted to get Kathy checked over, as she hadn't looked like she was in very good condition at Piers Marshall's house. But, as Miller text Rudovsky to ask how long they were likely to be, the DCI was surprised to learn that Kathy hadn't been seen yet.

"Fuck's sake," said Miller, as he showed Rudovsky's text to Saunders.

"Sorry Sir, we're just sat in a side room, nobody has been in to see us yet. Kathy's nodded off."

The message seriously annoyed Saunders. "Oh that's a piss take!" he said in a loud whisper.

"Well, it's not life-or-death, is it? I'll bet they are

dealing with much more serious matters than checking over a celebrity. I'll bet she'll still be here this afternoon to be honest." Miller looked disappointed, but not surprised. Kathy had a few facial wounds that needed a quick once over, and she looked a bit skinny, and pale. She didn't really look any different to an average alcoholic who'd gone on a mad one for a few days.

"Permission to go and start the interview with Marshall, Sir?" Saunders was leaning forward, the news that Kathy was still waiting to be seen had fired the DI up. He needed to be doing something worthwhile, and this was far from it.

"Not yet. I want Kath..." Miller stopped himself before he revealed the whole of Kathy's name to the bored, demoralised patients sat all around him, a few of whom were trying to figure out what all his waffle was about. "I want to hear her version first. I need to know what Marshall was on about when he was reminding her, what was it he said before we split them up?"

"Remember what we've been through," said Grant.

"That was it. We need to know what that was about, and we need to hear her version of events before we even look at Marshall. The longer we are, the longer he's stewing over anyway, so it's all good."

"Right then, I'm just going to go and lie down somewhere Sir, while I can."

"Okay. Yes, that's a good idea." Saunders' suggestion made a sudden, intense tiredness wash over Miller. "Go and do that, tell you what DC Grant, why don't you go with him, and get a few hours in yourself?"

Grant wasn't sure what to say. She wanted to say yes, thanks, seeya, more than anything. She was so tired that her eyes were watering constantly. But she was a probationer, she was working with the SCIU on a trial basis. As such, she wasn't sure what the protocol should be in these circumstances. Her mind was suddenly fizzing with conflicting thoughts.

Miller saw straight through her expression. "Go on, you look like shit DC Grant."

"Well, I'll probably be a bit more use after a recharge. Thanks."

"Yeah, no worries, and remember, one of you will be driving us back up that road, so get a good rest. There's no rush. We've got at least twenty four hours with Marshall before we need to make a decision about him."

"Alright. Nice one Sir, cheers."

"Thanks Sir."

Grant and Saunders left the waiting room and Miller focused his attentions back on the TV. A few seconds passed by before he felt a tap on his shoulder. He turned around and saw an old lady staring at him.

"You alright?" he asked.

"Yes, I was just wondering if you're one of those coppers who are on the telly. You are ain't ya?"

Miller looked up at the screen and saw himself, standing outside the address. He looked almost as gobsmacked as his colleagues had done when he saw who had opened the door. It made him smile. "No, that's nowt to do with me." Miller was polite enough, but the elderly lady didn't seem convinced.

"I've been listening to you talk all this police business for the last ten minutes. She's here, ain't she?"

"Who?" asked Miller, turning around once again.

"Kathy Hopkirk. She's here ain't she? That's why you're here, ain't it?"

All of a sudden, the sound of excitable chitter-chatter in the waiting room became unbearable. Miller tried to rubbish the old lady's suggestion, but it was too late. She'd let the cat out of the bag. Miller got to his feet and headed out of the waiting room, heading towards the exit. He was phoning Rudovsky as he walked away from the giddy patients, many of whom were already phoning and texting friends about the shocking turn-up.

"Well, here I am still waiting in A&E at the Royal Free after ten hours and a certain Kathy Hopkirk has just jumped the queue! #FML!" was one typical Facebook status update.

Within no time, the message was spreading onto the internet, and Miller knew that it was a nightmare. It was only going to be a few minutes before the press got wind-of-it and came and turned this place into a media-frenzy.

"Jo, yeah, what's happening?"

"Hi boss. Nowt, we've still not been seen. I've quizzed the staff, but they've got bigger priorities. The corridors are filled with trolleys, there are some really ill looking people everywhere Sir, its like a third-world country in here. I don't think she's going to be seen anytime soon." Rudovsky sounded as though she was half-asleep.

"How is she?"

"She's okay, she's still asleep."

"Right, well, we've got a problem."

"Oh?"

"Yeah, we've been sussed out, the press will be here any minute. We need to get out of here right now, or its going to turn into a circus."

"Oh, right. What's the plan?"

"We'll just get in the car, and go. Meet us at the door."

"Right. How long?"

"Now. And put that blanket over her head again, I don't want anyone trying to get a selfie. Hurry up, I'll be right outside the main door, in the ambulance bay."

Miller was standing outside the CID car when the call ended. It was parked in one of the reserved police bays beside the ambulance unloading bays. Within a couple of seconds, he'd reversed the vehicle into an ambulance's parking space and was watching his rear-view mirror, waiting for sight of Rudovsky, Kenyon and the under-cover celebrity they were escorting.

"Come on, come on," said Miller under his breath, tapping his hand against the steering-wheel as he noticed a couple of people coming from the waiting room, and starting to gather around the entrance doors. A few were mumbling to one-another excitedly, whilst a few others held up their phones in the expectation that they would get some pretty cool content for Facebook or Twitter if Kathy Hopkirk really was in there, and about to get in that copper's car.

"Fuck's sake Rudovsky!" said Miller as he saw the interest beginning to grow. More and more people were gathering inside, and outside the A&E entrance doors. He could see that it was going to be hard-work getting out of there, there were at least twenty gormless looking people hanging about around the doors, and another ten or so standing outside, smoking and taking photos of the DCI sitting in his car with the engine running.

"Move!"

"Get out of the way!"

Miller recognised those voices. It was Rudovsky and Kenyon, they were coming through. They were struggling, with mobile phones being held up in front of their faces, but they were making progress. The crowd starting cheering and shouting random remarks and questions.

"Kathy!"

"Ha ha is it really you!"

"Can I have a photo for my profile pic bruv?"

Miller stepped out of the car, opened the rear passenger door on his side, and then went around the car to open the other. The public were absolutely loving this unexpected excitement after spending so many boring, never-ending hours sitting in that stuffy waiting room. The excitement got too much however, and somebody at the back of the jeering scrum pulled Kathy's blanket off her head.

Suddenly, the excitement levels raised up to another level. There she was, Kathy Hopkirk, looking pale, bruised and vulnerable. Scared and confused. From what had seemed like a bit of a far-fetched suggestion from an old woman in the waiting room a few minutes earlier, to actually seeing the UK's most famous missing-person being bundled out of the hospital like this was absolutely thrilling, and the mobile phones that were being held up above all of this drama and chaos were capturing this bizarre moment for posterity.

"Get in, get in," Miller was pushing against the mob, holding them back. Kathy really did look scared, and Miller felt exceptionally sorry for her. He felt like he had stepped back into the Victorian ages, and was accompanying a criminal past a baying mob to the town stocks. Kathy sat in the car first, and Rudovsky wriggled onto the back seat beside her. She managed to close the door and lock it before any of the morons outside grabbed hold of the door-handle.

"Fuck's sake!" said Rudovsky. "I felt like I was in Shaun of the Dead then!" as she clipped her seatbelt and handed Kathy hers. Kenyon finally managed to get past the A&E patients, and jumped into the front passenger seat beside Miller.

Just as Miller was about to lift his clutch and set off, a few of the mob started to move in front of the car. Miller had to make a split-second decision, and released the clutch and started pulling away slowly, forcing the idiots who'd raced in front of the vehicle, to step away again, just as quickly. All around the car, people were banging their hands on the roof and windows, still shouting weird comments. The excitement had got too much for them, and Miller decided to increase his speed a little. Within seconds, he'd managed to pull away from the frolicsome crowd of walking wounded.

"Okay. What just happened?" asked Kenyon.

"Are you alright Kathy?" asked Miller.

"Yes, I'm okay, thank you." Kathy looked humiliated, and extremely sad.

"Sorry about that. When you guys knocked on Piers Marshall's front door, some neighbour was filming it, and now it's on all of the news channels. Then the bit came on when I joined you and some old biddy in the waiting room recognised me, put two and two together, and then all that weird shit happened!" Miller sounded shocked by his own story.

"Where we going?"

"Police station. We'll get the duty quack to check Kathy over."

"I'm fine, honestly." Kathy looked exhausted. Three minutes earlier, she'd been fast-asleep, so it was quite understandable that she looked quite washed out. Those facial wounds looked around about a week old, the last, jaundiced yellow of the bruises was fading. Miller had wanted an A&E assessment doing, as in his experience, it would be faster than waiting for a duty doctor, who could come at any time and disrupt a very important part of an interview. The idea was that they'd be in and out in half-an-hour, with an injury report that could be used as evidence. But it hadn't worked out that way, and Miller was the most surprised.

"It's like a different country, down here." He said, to nobody in particular.

Forty minutes later, Miller and his colleagues arrived at Shepherd's Bush police station with their star guest. They were led into the station through the back doors, where the police vans unloaded their prisoners.

"Sorry to bring you in this way, Kathy," said Miller. "It's to avoid the press."

"It's okay, its fine. Thanks."

"Alright, well, let's get inside, fix you up with a cup of tea or summat. Do you want a butty?"

"No, I'm not hungry. Cup of tea would be nice though, thank you very much."

"Right, the plan is to do an interview with you, just to find out what's been going on. It shouldn't take too long." Miller was being really, really nice, and Rudovsky was making mental notes to take the piss out of him for it later on. She had no idea at this point that Miller was quietly waiting for an opportunity to take the piss out of her, and the pantomime face she'd pulled at Piers Marshall's house.

"Okay, let's get in there then."

Chapter 51

"We have two major stories running concurrently this morning, and we are just going to break from the very sad news about Bob Francis' death, to focus on the latest news regarding Kathy Hopkins. The controversial celebrity, who had been missing since last Thursday, was found this morning, by police at the home of television executive Piers Marshall. Details are still very sketchy about the circumstances of this case, but we have some exclusive footage just reaching us. This video was sent in by one of our viewers. It shows Kathy leaving London's Royal Free hospital in the past few minutes, and as you can see, this footage clearly shows that Kathy has some injuries to her face and neck, and she looks extremely confused, distressed and upset. Here, we can now see the detectives putting Kathy into their unmarked police car, taking her away, we assume to speak to her about what has happened to her over these past eight days, and how or why, she was at Piers Marshall's house this morning. This is still a very confusing picture, but one thing which is starting to become clearer is that Kathy Hopkirk doesn't look like the usually confident person that we are used to seeing on our television screens."

The news channel started showing the A&E footage again, from the start. It showed Kathy and the detectives jostling through the small crowd at the hospital's entrance doors. After a few seconds, the blanket that was being used to conceal Kathy's face was ripped from her head, and the person filming got a very clear shot of a very scared, startled looking woman with several facial injuries.

"So, just to re-cap, Kathy Hopkirk has been released from hospital in the past few moments, following medical checks, and it is believed that she is now with police officers, who will no doubt be trying to build a picture of where Kathy has spent the past week or so, and under what circumstances. We'll bring you more on this breaking news story as we get it, but now, let's cross back to the BBC's showbiz reporter, who is outside Bob Francis' house, where a growing number of people are gathering to pay their final respects this morning."

*****

"Oh my God! Why the hell am I here? Get me out of this stinking cell RIGHT NOW!" Piers Marshall wasn't happy. He was standing in a police cell, his finger was pushed firmly against the intercom button. He was making his feelings quite clear to the police officers on the other end-of-the-line.

"Sir, as we have explained, somebody will be along to speak to you in due course." The officer sounded as though he was a train station announcer, casually explaining that the next train is delayed, and that he really couldn't give a toss to be perfectly honest.

"I want my solicitor!"

"Sir, I have already told you that there are procedures that we have to adhere to. Would you like a book to help you pass the time?"

"No I would fucking not like a book! FUCK YOU! Let me out of here now, do you hear?"

"Okay, please stop pressing the intercom Sir, as other guests may need to contact me."

"Guests? Are you... is this a... do you get some kind of enjoyment from this, you stupid little bastard."

"I know I am but what does that make you?"

"What, are you taking the piss? You think it's funny to take the piss. Do you know who I am? I am a very big deal! Do you hear that?"

Miller was eaves-dropping on Piers Marshall's increasingly erratic abuse on the custody desk intercom. He was happy to see that Piers was getting so wound up and stressed. He was going to be extremely easy to mess with in the interview while he was feeling so volatile.

"Okay, listen, just keep doing his head in when he presses it. It would be ideal if he's in this frame of mind in the interview."

"No problem, Sir."

"It's going to be a couple of hours away, at least, we're still gathering evidence and interviewing other witnesses at this moment in time. But if he asks when he'll be getting interviewed, just use vague words like soon, imminently and the best of all, my favourite one... presently."

"Understood Sir. And thanks for the opportunity. It would be great if we could interact with all of our guests like this!"

"Good stuff, keep going."

*****

On the opposite side of the police station, Kathy Hopkirk was in the medical room, being examined by the duty doctor. Kathy looked a lot brighter than she had done first thing, but despite the improved mood, she still appeared quite embarrassed and humiliated. She was struggling to maintain eye contact with the doctor.

"Yes, I think you're all in one piece Kathy," said the female GP, in a very gentle voice, once she had given the celebrity a thorough looking at. "She's fine to speak to, just don't keep her too long as she needs a good rest."

"Thanks Doctor," said Rudovsky, glad to hear that Kathy wouldn't need to go anywhere else. She'd had a dreaded feeling that the GP would request that Kathy be sent off for tests or x-rays or something. Something that would prolong the Manchester detectives stay in London.

"I'd just advise you to keep a close eye on that swelling around your mouth Kathy. Other than that, I think you've been really lucky."

"Thank you." Kathy was looking down at the

floor.

"That bruise above her eye looks nasty Doc. Sure she won't need any further treatment for that?"

Rudovsky's question prompted the GP to reach out and feel the wound gently with her fingers.

"Aah!" Said Kathy, through clenched teeth.

"No, I think she's fine. I just hope you catch the bastard that did this." The doctor smiled warmly at Kathy, then turned to pack her items into her briefcase. "Okay, well, see you Kathy," she said as she headed for the door. Rudovsky followed her.

"Thanks, bye." Said Kathy quietly. It was almost as if she'd become shy. Her demeanour in this medical examination room certainly wasn't what the GP had been expecting once she'd learnt who she was here to see.

As Rudovsky and the GP left the room, the door was closed firmly. "What did you mean by that, Doc? About catching the bastard?"

"Well, her head has been kicked, punched and stamped-on, judging by those injuries. They are well on the way to healing now, they're several days old, possibly a week. But whoever did that could very easily have killed her. She's lucky to be alive detective."

"Are you absolutely sure?" Rudovsky was speaking just a tiny bit louder than a whisper. "We need to interview her. It would be nice to know what we are talking about."

"Well, I've seen these injuries many times, it looks to me like a typical battered wife scenario. She's been kicked, punched, possibly stamped on. Her scalp is quite swollen as well, around the parietal ridges. I'd guess that her attacker pulled her hair, two fistfuls for a prolonged period. It's quite possible that others were involved. In any case, the injuries that she has sustained came from a very vicious beating."

"Thanks, that's really helpful."

"That's okay, and it will all be logged on my

report, along with my photos of the injuries."

"Brilliant. Nice one. Cheers." Rudovsky opened the door and went back inside the medical room. "Alright?" she asked. Kathy just nodded. She looked close to tears, and she was shaking quite noticeably too.

"I'm fine. So what happens now?"

"We need to talk to you, as soon as possible really, on tape."

"Then what?"

"I don't know Kathy."

"I just want to get out of here. I want to be alone."

"Shall we get started now, then?"

"Yes. Thank you."

*****

"The time is eleven thirty-two. My name is Detective Constable Jo Rudovsky. I am joined by my colleague Detective Chief Inspector Andrew Miller, and we are Manchester City Police officers, conducting this witness statement at Shepherd's Bush police station, in the city of London. We are conducting this witness statement in the form of an investigative interview with our witness Kathy Hopkirk. The purpose is to find out if any crimes have been committed against Kathy Hopkirk, and also to find out where Kathy has been over the past seven days, while our officers have been searching for her. Kathy, you are not under arrest, and you are free to leave at any time. Do you understand what I've just said?"

"Yes." She was staring down at the floor.

"Okay Kathy, we'll start with the basics if that's okay. Where have you been for the past week?"

"I've been at Piers Marshall's house, in Belsize Park."

"Was that for the whole time?"

"Yes, since Thursday night." Still no eye contact.

"And can you tell us, Kathy, why you were at

Piers Marshall's house?"

"I can. Piers and I are lovers. I was planning to move in with him, and we were going to start a new life together."

Rudovsky turned to face Miller who was sitting by her side. He read the look that she gave him perfectly well. It meant "oh-for-fuck's-sake, we're-not-getting-back-home-today, Sir. Bollocks."

Miller asked the next question. "Were you aware of the impact that your disappearance was having in the news?"

"Yes, and I got very scared that I was going to be in trouble for wasting police time, so I panicked and just ignored the issue."

"Could Piers not have phoned us, and informed us of the circumstances? To let us know that you were okay?"

"I wanted to phone my husband, Jack, and tell him first, but I was too scared."

"Kathy, could you tell us how you came by the injuries that you've sustained?"

"I tripped up and fell down some stairs."

"Can you talk us through what happened?"

"Well, I was coming down the stairs,"

"Where was this?"

"At Piers' house. I tripped, and fell, and banged my head a few times. It looks worse than it was."

"Was it the staircase that we saw earlier, when we came to Piers' house?"

"Yes."

"Can you explain how your hair has almost been ripped out of your scalp on both sides of your head, just above your ears?"

"No. It must have happened when I fell down the stairs."

"Were you at Piers Marshall's house for the entirety of the week?"

"Yes."

"And how did you travel to Piers' house?"

"He picked me up in his car."

"From Manchester?"

"Yes."

"Whereabouts?"

"The Midland, where I was staying."

"And you went straight down to London, and stayed in his house for the week?"

"That's right. So, sorry about all the fuss, but can I go now, please?"

"Where to?"

"I just want to… I just want to go."

"Where to Kathy?"

"Anywhere."

"What about Piers' house?"

"Yes, fine."

"Do you not want to go home and speak to Jack? He's been very worried."

"No. It's fine. Jack and I are finished."

"Kathy, we're nearly done, thank you for your patience, we really do appreciate your co-operation."

"It's fine."

Suddenly, Kathy seemed to have gained a bit of confidence. This was going well for her, and it seemed to the detectives that she felt that she had the upper-hand. Miller looked at Rudovsky, then at Kathy, and back at his DC, requesting permission to speak. He wanted to cause a bit of an earth-quake in here. Rudovsky nodded, offering him free reign.

"Can you tell me what you know about Janet Croft?"

"Who?" There was a slight jolt. Kathy's new found confidence had stalled.

"Janet Croft." Miller was smiling, ever the charmer.

"That name doesn't ring any bells with me. Do I

know her?" Kathy's face seemed to be heating up a little now, her cheeks were reddening, quite quickly. Her ears looked as though they were heating up too.

"Are you too hot?" asked Miller.

"No, I'm fine..."

"You've gone bright red. You look like a traffic light." Rudovsky was grinning, trying to force a smile from Kathy.

There was no smile. "I'm fine. Now, what were you asking me..."

"We were asking you about Janet." Miller was still smiling, this was all very light-hearted. At least that's how Miller and Rudovsky had been trying to present it.

"Janet? No, I don't think..." Kathy was struggling to make this look convincing. The two detectives were used to seeing this kind of expression. The "act-surprised-and-pretend-you-don't-know" face. Every suspect did it, and they all did it in exactly the same way too. It was very easy to spot.

"So you don't know anybody by the name of Janet Croft." Miller's voice suddenly sounded a little bit colder.

"No, I don't have any idea who that is."

Miller turned to his DC and started talking quietly. He knew that Kathy could hear him, but he tried to make out as if she couldn't.

"Jo, can I take five please? I'm really tired, and I need some rest. I'm just going to get a can of pop from the machine. While I'm gone, can you please tell Kathy everything we know about Piers, about Janet, about Bob Francis, and mention that her husband Jack and manager Sally have both voluntarily enrolled themselves on the Witness Protection programme. Don't forget to mention that Janet has been murdered, and that if Kathy doesn't start remembering things by the time I get back, we'll have to assume that she was the one who helped Piers Marshall kill Janet Croft, and we'll start building our case to that effect, we've already got enough to charge her anyway."

"Is that everything?" said Rudovsky quietly, whilst making notes.

"No. Inform her that Bob Francis has died this morning, around about the time you knocked her and her lover Piers out of bed." With that, Miller stood to leave. Kathy slumped in the chair. Her plan A was snookered and everybody in the room knew it. "Back in a bit," said Miller as he closed the interview room door behind him, winking at Rudovsky.

"Well," said Rudovsky, blowing out a huge gust of air. "I'd advise you to ditch this stupid story, and start telling us the truth Kathy, or he'll have you banged up on remand in Wormwood Scrubs by tea-time chucky-egg."

Chapter 52

Saunders was sat on the balcony of the Travelodge, he was talking on his phone, attempting to be as quiet as possible. He had the double-glazed door firmly closed, but the rumbling of his voice still managed to wake Grant up.

"Hi," she said, as she slid the door open and looked out at the view, which wasn't very much, just the back of another concrete and glass hotel.

"Oh, alright?" said Saunders, with the phone still at his ear. He looked surprised to see Grant awake. She yawned and did a big massive stretch, and as she did so, her t-shirt lifted up and she revealed a bit of her tummy. It made Saunders' heart skip a beat. He began to blush.

"Time is it?" asked Grant, but Saunders started talking on the phone again.

"Yeah, I'm still here Bill, right, nice one. Are you sure? Aw mate, that is absolutely top banana. I owe you a pint, and I'll even kiss your fod when I give it to you. No, no, steady on now Bill."

Grant started grinning and turned, heading back into the hotel room. Saunders couldn't take his eyes off her pyjama bottoms as she casually strutted away. She caught him looking at her bum as she turned around to offer him a brew, using the shaky hand gesture. He blushed again and replied using the thumb.

"No, seriously Bill, that's all we need. If you can e-mail all that across to me in the next five minutes, that will be the icing on the cake. Cheers mate, I really appreciate it."

Saunders did an air-grab as he stood up from the chair. He wandered into the hotel room, where Grant was checking her phone. "No way is it one' o'clock? I feel like I've slept longer than that, what... four hours?"

"Three."

"How long have you had?" asked Grant as she

waited by the kettle. "Why are they always dead slow, these hotel kettles?"

"I don't know. Google it."

"I might actually. Go on then, tell me, how long did you sleep for?"

"Oh, I had about an hour. I don't sleep much when I'm in the middle of a big case like this. I've got this weird thing where I can get by on hardly any sleep for ages, and then bang, I just snore my head off for about eighteen hours solid once the case is closed!"

"I wish I could do that. I get really emotional when I'm over-tired. So if I ask for a hug later, you know why…"

Saunders blushed again. "Hey, listen, I hope we can…"

"What?" Grant turned away and started putting the tea bags in the cups.

"Last night, the 'date-night' that was so rudely interrupted. I hope we can try again?"

"Why what was wrong with the one we had?"

"Well, nowt, but it *was* cut a bit short, having to race to HQ and jump on the helicopter."

"Well, as first dates go DI Saunders, you've a lot to live up to!"

"Oh. Why?" Saunders looked crest-fallen. He had a lot of self-doubt, particularly where his love-life was concerned.

"Because that was, without shadow of a doubt, the most exciting date I've ever been on!"

*****

"I am really not joking now, there is going to be a fucking thunder-storm of shit when I get out of this cess-pit, and there are going to be a lot of coppers losing their jobs. Starting with the inbred piece-of-shit who is operating this intercom! You'll be the first to pick up your cards Sir!"

"Are you done?"

"No, I am not done, captain fuck-wit."

"I find that insult very upsetting."

"Oh, go and stick your dick in a mincer."

"Is that all?"

"Seriously. GET ME OUT OF HERE!"

"You're not a celebrity."

"Oh, you're enjoying this."

"I don't know how to respond to that."

"Can you tell me, when I will be allowed out of this fucking prison cell?"

"No. I can't. But if you give me your star-sign I'll read you your horoscope?"

*****

"Right, thanks for the break, I'm jiggered. Ready for a good sleep. I'm getting too old for all these all-nighters now you know Jo. I'm telling you, once you pass your fortieth birthday, you're goosed." Miller was deliberately talking shit. It was intended to send a subtle message to Kathy Hopkirk, who was sitting opposite him across the interview room table, as he returned to his seat. The message was that this was just another day at work, and that Kathy Hopkirk might be a big celebrity out there, but in here, she was just another insignificant person that the police had no alternative but to tolerate for a small while.

"I must admit, I feel like shit."

"You look like shit Jo. Honestly, you look like you've been in a plane-crash."

"Charming!"

"Seriously. You don't want to go home looking like that, Abby will ring a priest."

"Right, shush now Sir. Can we get on with this so I can go and get my head down in the car for half-an-hour?"

"Yes, yes, sorry. Right, where were we? Oh yes! I remember, Kathy was talking a right load of old bollocks, the kind of crap that would see her in prison for perverting the course of justice at the very least, and then I went for a can of pop and a bathroom break."

"I've spoken to Kathy, Sir. She's fully aware of all the developments." Rudovsky had a sympathetic expression on her face, and Kathy seemed to have warmed to the DC.

"Yes, I'm sorry about earlier," said Kathy, without making eye contact with anybody, which made the apology seem hollow and insincere.

"Okay, let's start again then," said Miller, seemingly upbeat and cheerful. "Do you know Janet Croft?"

"Yes."

"How well did you know her?"

"I knew her very well. I mean, I haven't known her for a very long time, less than a month. But in that time, I've learnt a lot about her."

"Would you like to share that information with us please?"

Kathy told Miller and Rudovsky the whole story, from the TALK AM Facebook message, right through to the revelation about who had been responsible for the abuse. Forty years of Janet's life story was covered in just under fifteen minutes.

"That's such a heart-breaking story," said Rudovsky, sincerely moved by Janet Croft's awful story, despite having heard the most-part already from Jack Greenwood. Today's rendition, from Kathy, was made all the more tragic, as it concluded when Janet had finally found some happiness, and peace with herself.

Rudovsky had seen the poor soul involved, after the ghastly, brutal end of her dismal, pitiful life. It genuinely did upset the DC, and reminded her that sex crimes always lead onto bigger, darker, more upsetting problems further down the road. It is not a crime that just lasts the few minutes while the abuser takes their pathetic gratification.

"Are you alright mate?" asked Miller, putting his arm around Rudovsky's shoulder.

"Yeah, its fine, carry on."

"We can take five minutes if you want? Go and have a breather."

"No, it's alright, honestly, let's just crack on."

Miller looked across at Kathy. "My colleague found Janet Croft's body last night, that's why she is so upset by what you've just told us."

"You knew she was dead, didn't you?" Rudovsky had an angry tone in her voice. She hadn't meant to sound so enraged.

"Yes."

"How did you know?"

"I was shown a photograph of her, I think she was still alive on it, she was being strangled. It was the most disturbing thing I've ever seen."

"Who showed you that picture Kathy?"

"Piers. On the night I disappeared. I went to meet him, a place in the countryside near Manchester, the taxi driver took me to meet Piers there. It was somewhere near Tameside Hospital, that was the last sign I saw in the taxi. Piers showed me the picture not long after I'd been in his car, but just before he did, he'd made me drink from a mug, and handle some other items, I'm guessing they came from Janet's house. He was trying to get my DNA on it. He tried to make me touch a door handle, as well."

"A door handle?"

"Yes, from an inside door, I assume it was from Janet's flat. It was an old, scruffy thing. He wanted my finger-prints on it. He wanted to set me up for the murder, in order to blackmail me."

"Blackmail you?"

- 385 -

"Yes. It was insurance, to keep quiet about Bob Francis."

"And did you touch the items?"

"No. That's why I have these injuries."

"Good, good, this is better Kathy, this is far more helpful. Nice one." Rudovsky's tone had calmed down a little now, and the kind, caring inflection that Kathy had warmed to was back in her voice.

"Kathy, do you have any idea why Piers Marshall was so concerned about protecting Bob Francis? It doesn't add up to me." Miller couldn't make the connection. Sure, he understood that Bob Francis was a big star on Piers' TV channel back in the day. But it wasn't Piers' TV station at that time, Piers would have only been in his twenties in the seventies, so it wasn't really anything to do with him. Miller was desperate to know why this man had made himself so involved.

"I have had all week to come up with a theory about that."

"I'd like to hear it, please."

"Janet didn't name him, but the way that he's been acting, I think that he must have been one of the abusers. He worked at London TV then, while Janet was being abused. He's worked there since leaving University. His family own the business. His dad was the previous MD, so he could be trying to protect himself, or possibly his dad."

"Well the thing is Kathy, he's not protecting anybody anymore. The whole sordid thing is going to be splashed all over the news within the next few hours. Journalists are already trying to find out why we were at Bob Francis' house at five o'clock on a Saturday morning. Piers Marshall's time is well and truly up. No mistake about it."

"Why were you trying to protect Piers, Kathy?" asked Rudovsky.

"Oh, come on! For fuck's sake. Why do you think?"

"I'm asking *you* the question Kathy. I want to hear your reason."

"Because I've got no alternative have I? I'm going to have to volunteer myself onto the Witness Protection thing, like Jack and Sally."

"Why, though?"

"What do you mean, why?" Kathy looked confused. "I'm a dead-woman walking. You've seen what happened to Janet. I'm next."

"Okay, that's a reasonable point-of-view, and we both respect that. But, bearing in mind that Piers is in our custody, and Bob Francis is dead… I'm not sure who your enemy is now, Kathy. It's over. You've survived it." Rudovsky was ace at these jobs, and Miller was glad to be sat there, watching her as she skilfully controlled the witness's confidence and mood.

"It's not just Piers. There's somebody else. But I can't say anymore about it."

"What do you mean?"

"I mean, I'm not prepared to say anymore. My life is at risk. The only reason that I'm not dead is because I managed to convince Piers that he wouldn't get away with it. They were taking me to a grave they'd dug for me on Saddleworth Moors. I managed to spook him, I said that I'd told various people that I was meeting him. Since then, he made me promise to the story that we are a couple. He said that if I went along with it, you guys wouldn't have any proof that it wasn't true, and that it will all blow over in a few days."

"Kathy, if that's what Piers Marshall thinks, then he must be a very deluded person. This is not going to blow over, it's a murder enquiry, a sex abuse enquiry and a missing persons investigation all rolled into one. These kinds of jobs don't just blow over. It's not a stolen car we're investigating."

"I'm not about to defend his opinion, DCI Miller. I'm merely repeating what he told me."

"Has he confessed to you, that he killed Janet?"

"Not in as many words."

"Meaning?"

"He has never openly announced that he killed her, but he has certainly alluded to it, he has certainly made dark threats about what could happen to me."

"Is he working with somebody else?"

"I'm not prepared to be drawn into that."

"In the picture he showed you, of Janet being strangled, what could you see?"

"It was a rope or something, might have been a tie-back for a curtain, it was that kind of thing. It was being squeezed around her neck. Janet was…." Kathy began to break down as the awful image came to the front of her mind.

"It's alright Kathy, take your time." Rudovsky had found her most reassuring and sympathetic voice.

"…there were two hands, pulling at either end of the rope. The knuckles were white, like piano keys, he was pulling so hard."

"So somebody else took the photo, which suggests that at least two people were there when Janet was killed."

Kathy didn't say anything, she just wiped away the tears that were flooding out of her eyes.

Rudovsky handed her a few tissues. "Kathy, I'm sorry, I get it that you are scared, but you have nothing to fear, if we can take this other person off the streets. We have no idea who it is, and we need to go and interview Piers Marshall soon. If you want us to have a concrete case against him, you have to help us. There is no other way." Rudovsky was pleading with Kathy, but her head was still facing the floor, and she was still visibly trembling. Kathy Hopkirk was a very scared lady, it was plain to see.

Miller decided to try. "Please Kathy, we need something hard to hit Piers with from the start. As things stand, it's going to be his word against yours that you two are lovers. We need to divert him and his legal team away from that kind of bullshit right from the very start."

"I know what you want, I'm not a moron. But I'm sorry, I'm not prepared to run the risk."

A cold, prickly silence filled the air. This was a difficult situation, and Miller and Rudovsky knew that Kathy had clearly been through a lot, and was terrified of this other person. None the less, it was bloody frustrating. Miller's phone shattered the silence as it pinged with a text message. It was from Saunders. It read.

"I'm outside your interview room. Need to talk urgently."

Chapter 53

DCI Miller excused himself from the interview room, and met DI Saunders in the corridor. He didn't speak until the door was firmly closed behind him.

"Alright Keith, how did you sleep?"

"Not much. Something's been bugging me."

"Go on..."

"Cast your mind back to Monday morning. Dixon came in while me and you were having a briefing. He was grinning like a Cheshire cat."

"Yeah, I remember, had his end away the night before, was my assessment. Go on."

"Well he passed this Kathy file to us, which I was buzzing about. But he was trying to off-load another case onto us as well if you remember?"

"Yes, I do. What was it now, a suicide on the motorway wasn't it?"

"Bingo. Well, that was the assumption. Dixon suggested that the stiff had jumped off a bridge."

"That's right. What about it?"

"Well, it's been playing on my mind. The dead man was called Ben Thompson, he was from London, a bit of a low-league gangster. I just thought it was a bit strange that this had happened on the same night Kathy had disappeared."

"Oh, right yeah. I hadn't made that link. Mind you, I haven't given it another thought since Dixon left the office with the file. Where's this going Keith because Jo's getting really tetchy now, she needs a break."

"Sure, sorry, I'll get to the point, I've done a bit of digging. The dead man has worked as a bodyguard for London TV for the past fifteen years."

"Shut the fuck up!" Miller's eyes were popping out of his head as Saunders' revelation hit the back of the net.

"Seriously Sir, I've had a good scrape around.

He's Piers Marshall's hired muscle. Sorry, he *was*. He worked on an ad-hoc, casual basis, in amongst running his security firm, which has the door contract for a number of night-clubs in London."

"This is interesting stuff Keith, keep going…"

"Something very iffy was going on between Piers Marshall and him. He has invoiced the TV channel every month for the past five years for exactly the same amount. It's never gone up, never gone down."

"How much?"

"Twelve grand. Never more, never less.."

"Bloody hell. Twelve grand a month, that's, well it's a hundred and thirty odd grand a year. So…"

"So, yes. Exactly. The plot thickens."

"And the theory you have is that the squished up man on that motorway was part of the abduction plan?"

"I'm guessing so. But I feel amazingly confident Sir, it can't be a coincidence, can it?"

"Well, it could be. You've been doing this long enough to know that." Miller started stroking his chin, and realised how badly he needed a shave. His stubble was at the scratchy length that his twins found hilarious to touch.

"It couldn't Sir. It's linked, no two ways about it. The body was reported at around eleven pm, but the attending officers thought it had been in the carriageway for a while, judging by the state it was in. It just looked like an old curtain off the back of a wagon, one of the witnesses said. There were no lights on the motorway, that section is marked by cat's eyes only."

"Jesus." Miller exhaled quickly, as though the thought of the body on the motorway had given him a fright.

"So, I want to be in the interview with Marshall, Sir."

"Yes, of course."

"Here, I've brought you a picture of Ben Thompson. Why not put it in front of Kathy, see if it sparks a reaction?" Saunders handed his boss the photo. It was a police mug-shot, and the man looked cocky, arrogant. He just had that same toe-rag expression on his grinning face that Miller had seen on a thousand similar police pictures.

"You are an absolute, top drawer legend Keith Saunders. Top man. Cheers."

"Where are you up to with Kathy?"

"Come in, join in, you can put that picture in front of her yourself."

"Oh right, cheers."

Miller opened the door and gestured Saunders through.

"Kathy, I don't know if you remember my colleague from this morning?"

Kathy looked up and smiled at Saunders. "Vaguely."

"I've asked DI Saunders to come in and talk to you about something that has come to light."

"Do you mind if I sit here, next to you Kathy?" asked Saunders.

"No, no, it's fine."

"Cheers. Right, you okay Jo?" Saunders noticed that Rudovsky looked uncharacteristically miserable.

"Yes, I'm fine Sir, just want to get a nap, I've reached the drunken stage of sleep deprivation now."

"Right, soz, well, where are we up to?"

"Kathy has been extremely helpful, she's helping us with everything we ask her about. The only issue is the fact that she refuses to discuss Piers' accomplice." Miller smiled kindly at Kathy, who was still shaking quite dramatically.

"Why not Kathy?" asked Saunders, calling on his most charming and comforting bed-side manner. "We need to know who it is so we can put an end to this, once and for all."

"I'm next," said Kathy, her lips were trembling.

She was as white as a sheet, and she looked terrified. Saunders decided to get stuck in. He pulled the photograph of Ben Thompson out of his file, and placed it on the table facing Kathy, and himself.

"Do you recognise this man, Kathy?"

A noise escaped Kathy as she made eye-contact with the grinning man in the picture. The sound was like a gasp, but in reverse as all the oxygen left Kathy's chest. It was the sound of shock. All three of the detectives looked at one another. There was no disputing that Kathy had a very personal connection to the man in the picture. Kathy's shaking got worse, and now she was crying.

"Kathy, do you recognise this person?" repeated Saunders, very gently. Kathy didn't reply vocally, but her body-language told all three of them everything they needed to know. Miller nodded at Saunders. It was a gentle nod, but it was full of respect. The younger detective had done it again, and Miller was visibly proud of his DI.

"Well, I can see that this picture has upset you Kathy, so to make things a little easier for you, I should tell you that this man is no longer with us."

Kathy looked up, and across at Saunders. Rudovsky suddenly looked much more alert, too. This bombshell had really livened up the worn-out DC.

"His body was found on the motorway, just near the border of Manchester and Cheshire, last Thursday evening, a few hours after you'd left The Midland."

Kathy made another noise, this time it was a gasp that was made up completely from relief. A few seconds passed, while she composed herself. Once she was ready, she started talking, and the trembling had subsided quite considerably.

"He attacked me, really badly. He was the driver, they were taking me to the moors to kill me and bury me, they told me about it. They said they'd already dug a grave. I was terrified, but… well, I couldn't let them see it.

I started answering back, telling them that I was being followed. The driver hated me, but I kept trying to piss him off. In the end, he snapped, he pulled the car over at some pub car park and started attacking me. He was trying to kill me, aw God, it was awful, he was ripping the hair out of my head. He knocked me unconscious, kicking me, jumping on me. He's a fucking monster. When I woke up, he wasn't there. It was just me trapped in the back of the car, Piers was driving. He told me that he'd killed him, Ben, the psycho driver. I didn't believe him, of course. But, it seems that he was telling the truth!" Kathy did a weird, almost sarcastic smile. It was clear to Miller, Rudovsky and Saunders that Kathy was starting to feel the comfort of this news. She was still wearing the bruises that this man had given her, but he couldn't harm her anymore. Saunders' announcement had come as a huge relief.

"Tell us about the cover-story, the relationship with Piers. What are the details that you have revised?" Rudovsky asked the question.

"Its quite simple, Piers said we had to keep it as simple as possible, or else we would start forgetting bits. It all boils down to this. We met at Sally's office, we went for a couple of secret dates and we have been in a relationship for over a year. We are planning to get married in 2020, and honeymoon at the Olympics in Tokyo. Piers said that this would be enough to make it all sound legit."

"Okay, listen, Kathy, we're going to let you get some proper rest now. You've been through such an awful ordeal, I think you need a good break from it all. We will need to talk to you again, at length no doubt. But that can wait for now." Miller was playing a blinder at the compassionate approach, a characteristic usually delivered better by Saunders or Rudovsky.

"Thank you, I really appreciate that."

"But before we let you get on your way, can I ask you one last thing?"

"Go ahead." Said Kathy, looking as though the

weight of the world had been lifted from her shoulders.

"Do you have any idea where Piers has put the belongings that he asked you to handle?"

"I don't know about that." Kathy started thinking. The detectives could see very clearly that she was giving it a lot of thought. "It was all in a bag, a black bin-bag in the back of the car."

"And has Piers had an opportunity to remove this bag? I mean, has he been out of your sight since he took you to his house?"

"No, not really. I think he's drugged me a few times, because I've fallen into some really heavy sleeps, but then again, that might be from my head injuries. But while I've been awake, no, he's been breathing down my neck the whole time, he's even stood outside the door when I've used the bathroom."

"Okay, that's great. We know we're looking for a black bin bag. If we can find that, we can throw the key away as far as Piers Marshall is concerned, he'll never get out of jail."

Kathy was thinking hard. "You know, I'm sure it was still on the floor in the back of the car. I don't know where the car is, or anything, but the last time I saw it, that's where it was."

"Okay, thanks a lot Kathy. I seriously doubt that it will still be there, but that's really useful intelligence, thank you."

"Yeah, nice one Kathy, much appreciated," said Rudovsky, and she patted Kathy's hand gently across the table-top, in an attempt to demonstrate her sincerity.

"Right, lets go and speak to the Chief Inspector here, and see what arrangements we can make to get you out of here, and to a safer, more relaxing place."

"And to get me in a bed." Said Rudovsky, who looked completely shattered.

Chapter 54

"Okay, so we know what we're doing."

"Sir."

"Sir!"

Miller was talking to DC Grant and DI Saunders in a small meeting room on the second floor of Shepherd's Bush police station. Rudovsky and Kenyon had left an hour earlier, after being handed the keys to the Travelodge hotel room, the same one that Grant and Saunders had booked into that morning. They'd both looked glad of the opportunity to crash out, even if it was only likely to be for a few hours.

It was almost 6pm, and DCI Miller was now the last surviving SCIU team member who'd not had the chance of a rest. This shift was getting into its thirty-second hour, and Miller looked like he'd been on a bender for a few days. He really was getting too long in the tooth for this kind of craziness.

It had been a rewarding shift, though. The afternoon's developments had been very positive, particularly the SOCO reports from Piers Marshall's car, which had been discovered in the car park at London TV, seven miles away from Marshall's home in Belsize Park. Forensics had uncovered some great evidence, despite the fact that the vehicle had encountered a rather shambolic attempt at a valet. Things were looking good, and the finishing line was coming into view.

Miller handed the photo-copied planning notes to his colleagues. "Piers has had half an hour with his legal team. He's now been in police custody for thirteen hours. We need to get cracking, we only have him for another eleven, before the twenty-four hours are up. Remember what we've discussed, we need to lead him down his own little path, and then, just when he, and his brief think that he's home and dry, that's when you bamboozle him."

"Can't wait."

"Yes, absolutely itching to get in and get on with it, Sir." Grant looked full of enthusiasm for the job in hand, and that raw eagerness reminded him of Saunders' gusto for the job. DC Helen Grant was going to fit in well, thought Miller as he smiled warmly at the two detectives who were desperate to get into the interview room, and put this case to bed. He suspected that they wanted to take each other to bed, shortly afterwards.

"Just want to say, Grant, your probationary period ends in four weeks, doesn't it?"

Suddenly a new expression eclipsed Grant's face. The enthusiasm and passion in her eyes changed to a fear, an anxiety.

"Yes, Sir?"

"Well, I tell you what, if you carry on the way you've started, you'll definitely be a full-time team member. I've been really impressed, and I know DI Saunders has, too."

Grant blushed, and looked down at her lap shyly. "Thank you Sir."

"You're welcome. Credit where it's due and all that. Now, I'm going to try and have a siesta somewhere, because I feel like the next time I blink, my eyes will stay shut. So off you go, good luck, and I'll look forward to watching the video footage of you dismantling Piers Marshall's story a little bit later on."

"Thanks Sir."

"Cheers."

*****

A couple of minutes after Piers Marshall, his solicitor, and the two Manchester detectives entered the interview room, all of the formalities were done. Piers had been read his rights, and the interview commenced. Part one was going to be a doddle. At least, that was the plan.

Saunders kicked things off. "Okay Mr Marshall,

apologies for the delay in getting to speak to you."

"Its fine, we're here now. My complaints will be made to the appropriate body, at the appropriate time." Piers Marshall had a very indignant attitude. He was arrogant and huffy, and he spoke down to the police as though they were of a lower-class to him. He spoke as if they were a couple of builders who were interrupting his afternoon tea on the terrace. Piers Marshall was the archetypal upper-class, spoilt boy. His world had taught him that the family money he'd been born into made his blood warmer, his arms stronger, his family greater human beings than those with less money. He was the ultimate stereotype, clichéd English toff, and he really didn't care what anybody else thought of that, either, as a matter-of-fact.

Piers Marshall looked extremely pleased with himself, and his arrogance was truly mesmerising. If he was remotely worried or concerned about this police matter, nobody would ever have guessed. He was treating this as though he was merely here to report his car stolen. Both Saunders and Grant found a new layer of dislike for the man.

"Mr Marshall, as you will understand, we have taken a great deal of time speaking to Kathy about the activities of the past seven days."

"Yes, I'm sure you have, which begs the question, what the hell am I still doing here?" Piers folded his arms and placed his foot down on the floor very heavily.

"Kathy has surprised us with a few things today. The main one, was that she told us that she stayed with you for the past week."

"Well it's hardly a crime is it? Have you people not got any real work to be getting on with? This is absurd."

"I'm sorry, I understand that you are frustrated, and we shouldn't keep you too long now. We just want to clarify a few matters which have arisen."

"Well, lets get on with it then old boy, for heaven's sake." Piers exhaled loudly, and looked up at the ceiling.

"Okay, well, I'd just like to know if you were aware of the media appeals regarding Kathy's disappearance?"

"Yes of course I was aware. I've not been in Timbuktu for the past week. Of course I saw the media. I *own* London TV. Please don't try to be a smart Alex with me, detective." Piers had the kind of face that you'd never tire of whacking with a cricket bat.

"With that in mind Mr Marshall, did you not think that it would be a good idea to inform the police, to let us know that Kathy was safe and well?"

"Yes, well, the thought had crossed my mind, actually. But the bottom line is this, it was Kathy's call to make. It was all rather, shall we say, emotional. If I know anything about survival in this world, one thing I know is that you don't interfere with emotional women's matters."

Grant decided to rephrase, and ask Saunders' question once again, dissatisfied by the wishy-washy, nonsensical reply. "What, even when the national media are running it as the top story? Did you not think that you had a civil duty to inform us that Kathy was okay?"

"A civil duty? You're having a giggle, right? I respected a friend's wish for privacy at a difficult, emotional time. I have nothing more to add. Please feel free to charge me with failing my civil duty, or whichever ludicrous crime you believe I have committed. Ha ha, honestly! This really is quite incongruous!"

"But from what Kathy has told us Mr Marshall, you and her are more than just friends. Aren't you?"

"That's a private matter. It has no bearing on this conversation, none whatsoever. Next."

"Mr Marshall, Kathy has informed us that you and her are engaged in quite an advanced personal relationship. Can you confirm, or deny this, please?"

"Do I really have to answer such dishonourable

questioning?" asked Piers of his legal representative. The man whispered his response. Saunders thought he'd heard, "It would probably hurry things along."

After a long, rather dramatic pause, Piers nodded. "Yes, okay, Kathy and I *are* a couple. But this goes no further than these four-walls. Do you understand?"

"I understand perfectly well Mr Marshall. Thank you. But this leads us back to your civil, no, I guess moral duty to let Kathy's husband know what was going on, surely?"

Piers guffawed, a big, exaggerated wheeze of a laugh. Eventually, he stopped. "Oh, I apologise. I'm just so amused by your line of questioning, it really is a waste of my time. Look, once and for all, Kathy is safe and well, and we just want to start a new life together. The sooner you let me out of here, the sooner I can contact Jack, and tell him the news. I'll tell him that you told me to call." Piers laughed again, and it was just as insincere, and artificial as his first attempt at trivialising the situation.

Saunders and Grant looked a little awkward as Piers continued to indulge himself in his fake amusement. His legal representative didn't look as though he was particularly impressed, though.

"Okay Mr Marshall, we're nearly done here. But we just wanted to ask you about Kathy's injuries?"

"What about them?" asked Piers, his grin still covering his face. That loaded question didn't seem to phase him.

"Can you tell us how she came to receive those injuries?"

"I'm not too sure. I think she said she'd fallen down some stairs."

"Any idea which stairs?"

"Well, I can only assume that they were the stairs in my town-house, as that's where we have been staying."

"Mr Marshall, can you be a little more specific about this matter please?"

"I've just told you all I know."

"So your lover is very seriously injured at your home, and you don't even know what happened?"

"But I've just told you what happened."

"Hmmm, you seemed a little uncertain. It's making alarm bells ring. It's making me think that things are maybe not as straight-forward as we had first anticipated."

"What in the name of hell-fire are you alluding to?"

"Mr Marshall, I am alluding to the fact that your lover has suffered a number of serious injuries at your home, at a time when she is registered, very publicly as a missing person, and you don't seem certain how she sustained the injuries, or why you should have informed police that she was with you. It doesn't quite ring true."

As intended, this remark angered Piers. "Look, you bloody spiv. Kathy was a bit drunk, and she fell down some stairs. Now, please accept my apologies if I don't have Rain Man's memory, but I didn't see it happen, and I don't really entertain drunk people's hard-luck stories. Once again, if you can charge me with this crime, go ahead. I'm super-rich, I'll win the court-case. Believe it." Piers smirked, and it caused a renewed sense of loathing on the opposite side of the table.

"Mr Marshall, I cannot understand why you seem so aloof about Kathy's injuries. You should have called an ambulance, or taken her to the hospital." Grant was keeping the tempo.

"Seriously, my patience is wearing dangerously thin. You don't lecture *me*. Next question."

Unwittingly, Piers had set Saunders up beautifully for the first stomach-punch of the interview. His arrogant, "next question," remark was the perfect springboard for Saunders to explode his first bomb. This was going to make wonderful viewing for DCI Miller later, thought Saunders, as he set about wiping the smirk off Piers

Marshall's pompous face.

"Okay, my next question relates to the sad news regarding Bob Francis' death this morning."

Piers Marshall changed colour before Saunders' and Grant's eyes. His puffed-up blotchy-red complexion turned sheet-white, almost blue.

"Bob... I'm sorry, Bob Francis?" Piers was in shock. Saunders' announcement had hit him like a lightning bolt. One-nil.

"Yes, Mr Marshall, Bob Francis. He sadly died this morning when our officers went to speak to him regarding Kathy's disappearance."

"Kathy's disappearance?"

"Yes Mr Marshall, we had reason to believe that he was involved." Two-nil.

"No, what... Bob? No..."

"Oh yes, and we also have very strong evidence that suggests he was involved with the murder of Janet Croft."

"Jan... wait, Kathy, Janet..." Piers Marshall's face was a picture. He knew that he looked like a rabbit in the headlights, a rabbit that was desperate to dart away, back into the shadows, but was too startled. Piers' brain couldn't work quickly enough. He was very visibly trying to think of a way out of this, desperate to pull something out of the bag, but Saunders' barrage of damning points just kept coming, each one rendering him more and more powerless. It was like a conveyor belt of devastatingly bad news.

"And the unexplained death of Ben Thompson." Four-nil.

"Wha... Ben wasn't... you mean... I'm?" There was a greasy, shiny film covering Piers Marshall's deathly-white forehead. He was a jibbering wreck, he couldn't articulate his thoughts, he couldn't string a sentence together. The look of sheer exasperation, the reluctant acceptance that he wouldn't be blagging his way out of this very easily, was a total joy for Grant and Saunders to witness. They didn't care that they were grinning at the man in the seat opposite them.

This slimy, cocky, piece of murdering scum was beginning to realise that his rather idiotic notion of walking out of this place in a few minutes time was actually nothing more than an absurd fantasy.

"Can you tell us where you were last Thursday, between the hours of twelve noon, and midnight, please Mr Marshall?" asked Grant. Her stunning smile made Saunders' stomach flip over again.

"I'm requesting a break, please, if that's okay?" asked Piers Marshall's solicitor.

"By all means, take as long as you need." Said Saunders, who had deliberately adopted the smug and arrogant persona that Piers Marshall had left well behind, as he sat trembling, looking down at the floor, realising that he was snookered.

"Before we break off though, I must inform you that when you come back in here, we will be asking you a number of questions, including why this was found in the foot-well, under the passenger seat of your car," Grant produced a transparent plastic evidence bag which contained a dirty, old door handle. "And we'll also be asking you why the back-seat has produced hundreds of traces of Kathy Hopkirk's and Ben Thompson's blood."

Piers was silently sobbing, shaking so much that it looked as though he was rocking in his chair.

"And, I'll show you these photos before we break off. This shows Piers Marshall's Range Rover, on the M56 motorway, last Thursday evening. If you look closely, you will make out that Piers Marshall is driving the vehicle. In the passenger seat is a man, and we believe this man to be Ben Thompson. This next photo was taken six minutes later, on the same stretch of motorway, and Ben Thompson is no longer in the passenger seat. And we all know why, don't we Mr Marshall? Anyway, I'll leave you with that. See you in a bit."

Chapter Fifty Five

"Good morning, and welcome to Sky Weekend News. Our top story on this Saturday morning. The owner of one of Europe's best known television channels has served the first night of three concurrent life-sentences for the murder of Janet Croft, and the attempted murder of Kathy Hopkirk. In a sensational court-case which lasted six weeks, the Judge said that Piers Marshall will die in prison for the callous, wicked and depraved crimes that he and his accomplice Ben Thompson carried out last summer. During the course of the trial, the court heard that the TV celebrity Kathy Hopkirk was trying to get justice for historical sex crimes against Janet Croft, when London TV's owner Piers Marshall attempted to stop revelations…" Miller turned the TV remote off, and threw the remote control on the couch.

"Right, come on, who fancies a day at the seaside?"

"Yeaaahhhh!!!" shrieked the twins.

"Noooo!!!" wailed Clare.

"Yeeeaaaaahhhhh!!! Shouted the twins, joined by their dad this time.

EPILOGUE

Kathy Hopkirk managed to turn her image around, thanks to Janet Croft. Once the court case was heard, and the national media reported the facts of what had gone on during that terrifying week, the British people found a real affection for Kathy Hopkirk's courage and tenacity. But Kathy doesn't really like being popular, and as such, she does very few media or Twitter appearances nowadays. She has become the patron of several charities, particularly those that try to deal with the psychological scars that sexual crimes always leave behind. Kathy has set up a charity, which raises funds to send addicts to rehab. Her charity is called The Janet Croft Foundation.

Her updated auto-biography, "Lucky To Be Alive" has been a number one bestseller across Europe, Australia and in several US states too. All profits are being used to support sexual abuse survivors, shared between the various charities that Kathy has become heavily involved with.

The sickening revelations about Bob Francis came as a great shock to the British public, for a day or so. But the public quickly resigned themselves to the fact that this was yet another reprehensible episode of a sexual-deviant managing to operate above the law, as a result of their fame, success and power. This type of crime has been witnessed so many times over recent years, it has completely lost its "wow" factor. People have become cynical about the celebrity world, and most are desperate to learn that this shameful period is over, and that no more horror stories are going to come out about the telly and music stars that they have loved and respected through the years.

Several women came forward to name Piers

Marshall as the man who physically and sexually abused them, during their apprenticeship at London TV. Piers' father, Timothy Marshall was also mentioned, as was Bob Francis. The fact that Piers and his father were both involved in the abuse, often at the same time added an extra layer of repugnance to the shocking and disturbing crimes that took place inside one of the nation's most revered broadcasting houses.

The trial for Piers' sex crimes is due to take place at a later date.

Sally King was very quickly relieved of her Witness Protection status, once it became clear that the people who posed the threat were out of circulation. She still runs her management agency. Kathy is no longer on her books.

Jack Greenwood's decision to volunteer himself onto Witness Protection saved him from facing any charges in relation to posting the spoof video on Youtube. He said that he had posted it, to save himself from becoming the next victim. If anything, the ageing DJ did rather well from his exposure in the media. His appearances on the news inadvertently created a nostalgic reminiscence amongst older members of the public. This rediscovered interest in Jack Greenwood led to a regular show on Radio 2. Memories of his old shows sparked a nostalgic yearning for happier, more enchanted time in many older people's lives. A time when there were only three telly channels, you could leave your front door wide-open and best of all, two of you could have a night out, watch a film, get a KFC bucket meal, and the bus home for two pound fifty, and still have enough for a Marathon bar with the change. And nobody had been sick at the bus-stop.

DC Helen Grant got the job in the SCIU. Her and Saunders celebrated by taking a week's holiday to Portugal. They seem to be getting on pretty well. There were a few minor spats when Grant moved into Saunders' apartment, but over-all, they keep their work and private lives separate.

Nobody else within the SCIU has been told about Grant claiming back the £3,000 donation money. Not yet anyway. Saunders refuses to rule out the possibility that it *will* come up, especially if Grant ever reveals anything embarrassing about *his* private matters.

DCI Paxman still doesn't know who tipped off the press. The London CID officers don't take the piss out of northerners anymore, and they prefer not to talk about the time that Kathy Hopkirk disappeared.

THE END

Printed in Great Britain
by Amazon